You are my Renaissance

VOL.01

ROSÉ AND RENAISSANCE

STARRING XIA XIQING	STARRING ZHOU ZIHENG	AUTHOR ZHI CHU	

Only roses match you.

The moment I met you was the Big Bang. Every particle left me and flew toward you.
After that smallest instant, the universe was truly born.

Rose and Renaissance

An imprint of Via Lactea Ltd.

Author: Zhi Chu
Translator: MS; XiA; Meiling
Editor: Michaela M

CONTACT:
Customer Support: info@vialactea.ca
Wholesale & Distribution: market@vialactea.ca
Other Cooperation: https://vialactea.ca/pages/cooperation
Discord Channel: https://discord.gg/vialactea

Follow us on Twitter/Instagram/Facebook: @ViaLactea_Ltd
Official Website: www.vialactea.ca

ISBN: 978-1-77408-358-1(pbk)
Printed in Canada

LOCATION:
Shops At Waterloo Town Square
#27, 75 King Street South, Waterloo, ON
Canada
N2J 1P2

ROSÉ
AND
RENAISSANCE

It takes both courage and patience to hug a rose.
I know that the thorns will get stuck in my skin, that
they'll insert themselves into my veins, but it's okay. Just
give me a minute. I'll pull them back out. These pains are
only temporary.
But I still want to hug that rose.

Only roses match you.

ROSE AND
RENAISSANCE

CONTENT

THE MOVIE STARTS ◎ ◎ ◎

C.01

:

Born to Be Rebellious

Hangovers are the most tormenting experience in the world.

If booze didn't result in such annoying side effects within just a few hours, he would enjoy drinking a lot more; at least, that's what Xia Xiqing tells himself as he wakes sprawled on the carpet with a headache. He leans against the sofa and barely manages to pull himself up. The headache is intense, so he finds a tablet of Ibuprofen in a drawer of the coffee table and swallows it before pulling out his phone to look at the time.

13:24

His mind numbed by alcohol, his memory begins to slowly return to him, and he suddenly remembers: there's a press conference scheduled tonight at six for the release of Zhou Ziheng's movie. He even managed to get a VIP pass for it—of course he has to go.

Zhou Ziheng began as a child star, having first appeared

on-screen at the age of six. Currently only twenty years old, he's been active in the entertainment industry for fourteen years. The television series he filmed in his first year just so happened get top ratings, which allowed him to become the most popular child star of the era—but because of that, he remained stuck with the label of "child star" even after he'd performed in countless other films and television series.

He stopped filming for a few years in order to prepare for the National College Entrance Examinations and disappeared from the public's notice. He didn't even take the special version of the NCEEs for students of the fine arts; instead, he took the standard ones like any other normal high school senior. With an astonishingly high score under his belt, he was admitted to the physics department of Peking University—one of the best universities in the country. For the entire duration of his mandatory military training, he remained a trending topic in Weibo.

Despite that, he seemed to want to remain low-profile. After he started university, he started filming less and less. Everyone assumed he wanted to quit acting altogether to focus on his studies, but he was shoved back onto the trending list when a series of candid photographs of him at school were leaked.

The photos show him in the middle of a basketball match, participating in some kind of tournament. The smooth yet solid lines of muscle flowing under his red jersey, the sharp contours of his eyes beneath his short hair, the droplets of sweat rolling down his jawline, and his faintly frowning eyebrows as he lines up a shot... The details of those candid shots, so removed from flashy professional photography, left an impression of perfect aggression.

Thanks to the twist of fate that allowed those photos to

leak, a new moniker was bestowed upon the former child star: "Walking Hormones." It accidentally changed his public persona to the ever-popular "alpha male" stereotype, and Zhou Ziheng gained a whole slew of schoolgirls as new members to his fanbase. That much of course would be typical, but even women a few years older than him wound up falling into his hormone trap.

He'd almost stopped taking roles in television altogether after he came of age, and not once did he ever take on a romance film. Unlike other young actors, the style of films he appears in are fairly consistent—all are realistic, and all are focused on minority groups. Even though there'll finally be a female lead in this most recent movie, she'll be the older sister to Zhou Ziheng's role as her younger brother. This leads to a significant amount of complaining on the internet about his looks being squandered—the most squandered, even, among all male actors. Even so, his fans and other netizens can always dig up content to squeal over from the variety shows he occasionally appears on.

Xia Xiqing only became his fan after the persona shift. He had been studying abroad at the time, and when he stumbled upon Zhou Ziheng's infamous basketball photos, he'd been struck by the desire to draw him—after all, his body's proportions and muscle structure was absolutely perfect. As such, he did a quick watercolor and posted it to Weibo...but little did he know that the piece would be discovered by Zhou Ziheng's fans and fanatically shared within the fandom, eventually going viral.

And he, in turn, also rose to the position of "Big Name Fanartist" within the fan community.

Facing the mirror, Xia Xiqing realizes that his hair really has gotten a bit too long. He was overdue for a haircut.

Rummaging around his desk, he finds a rubber band amidst a bunch of paintbrushes. He sets the brushes down on his desk with a clatter and casually ties up his hair, then he finds a collared white shirt from his closet and throws it on. Topping it all off with a black face mask, he steps out the door.

When he arrives at the conference location, the movie cast has yet to arrive. He posts a photo of it on Weibo and quickly gets some responses from fans.

@MisterHeng: aaah, is summer-*taitai*[1] also there?!!!

@No1AlphaInTheUniverse: Whoa, it's summer-taitai! Wasn't summer-taitai overseas? Aaah I'm so excited!

@IAmMrsZhou: omg I want to meet Summer-taitai in person so bad~

@NoPassingByHeng: Oh I'm also here! Summer-taitai is so close to the stage, are you VIP??

@CoolestHeng: OMG VIP?! Even the owner of the Forever-Heng fansite isn't so close.

To prevent any more speculation, Xia Xiqing picks a random comment and answers it.

@Tsing_Summer:
A friend gave me the ticket.

And speak of the devil, he then gets a text from said friend—Xu Qichen.

> Xiqing, I already told the event manager but I've got something going on tonight and I can't make it, sorry.

> It's alright, I'm already here.

He sends off the message, then spins his cellphone around in his hand.

---

1 On the internet, "taitai" is an honorific title or suffix given to artists and writers who operate primarily online. Literally, it means "grand-grand."

Xu Qichen is a young writer; the movie that Zhou Ziheng recently starred in is based on his novel. It's actually quite serendipitous, for Xia Xiqing and Xu Qichen met back in high school and have stayed good friends ever since. The VIP ticket came from him, but the author himself is now unable to attend.

Growing bored after half an hour of waiting, Xia Xiqing wanders out of the conference hall, through a long corridor, then into a smaller room. Looking at the Goya painting on the wall, he judges the hotel to have decent taste—the counterfeit is of pretty good quality.

As he admires the painting, he is suddenly plowed into from behind. He almost falls over, and his phone does fall from his grasp. Turning around, Xia Xiqing sees a few body-guards in black uniforms surrounding an even taller man in sunglasses. Almost immediately, Xia Xiqing recognizes him as Zhou Ziheng.

Similarly, Zhou Ziheng also immediately notices his bodyguards' rude behavior. His originally hurried stride stops, and in a series of fluid movements, he dexterously picks up the phone from the floor and hands it back to its owner through the crowd.

"Sorry."

Zhou Ziheng's voice is calm in a way that doesn't seem to fit a twenty-year-old kid like him. It has a strange sort of charisma that straddles the line between youth and masculine maturity. The many fans surrounding them begin to squeal, raising their phones to capture the moment. Such a heartwarming scene, if posted to Weibo, would surely be widely shared around—it might even make it outside the fandom.

The sudden encounter surprises Xia Xiqing a little, for

this is his first time being so close to Zhou Ziheng. But he remains calm, effortlessly molding his expression into a warm and polite smile.

"No worries. Thank you."

When Xia Xiqing reaches out and receives his phone from Zhou Ziheng's hand, the cold tip of his finger brushes against Zhou Ziheng's in a seemingly unintentional manner.

It lasts about half a second.

Zhou Ziheng's facial expression undergoes very little change—no reaction. Xia Xiqing sees this very clearly, but he continues to smile all the way until Zhou Ziheng leaves. Then, he also heads back to the conference hall.

Sure enough, he's utterly and completely straight.

When he next enters the conference hall, Zhou Ziheng's fans are giving out promotional merchandise. A girl in her late teens waves him down.

"Hello! Whose fan are you? Do you want support swag?"

As he's wearing a mask, Xia Xiqing smiles with his eyes, curving them into crescents. With a gentle voice, he says, "Sure."

The girl excitedly opens her bag, revealing headbands, badges, bracelets, and glow sticks. "Which one?"

Xia Xiqing chooses a badge and gently thanks her. He pins the badge at his breast and returns to his seat.

The press conference begins mostly on time. After the moderator welcomes the audience and introduces the event, the producers and the cast walk onstage one by one. The movie is based on Xu Qichen's novel, *Seagull*. It stars a young man named Gull—after being introduced to a job by an acquaintance, he finds himself sold to Thailand. The story details how he became a wageless provider of slave labor on an unlicensed shrimp boat and how he escaped that terrible life.

Zhou Ziheng plays Gull in the movie, and, in order to make himself more physically compatible with the role, he lost over twenty pounds in pursuit of that malnourished, skin-and-bones type of aesthetic. The first time he was in full costume, he wore a ragged tank top and a pair of shorts so dirty you couldn't determine the original color. His face leathery and mottled from past sunburns, his shoulders and back deeply tanned and red—he was almost unrecognizable. Even the director couldn't stop nodding, praising that he was Gull come to life.

Half a year has gone by since filming wrapped, and Zhou Ziheng's skin has lightened quite a bit since then. His physique, too, had returned to the well-muscled state it'd been in before shooting—all thanks to an insane fitness routine. Xia Xiqing can't help but sigh in awe; being an actor really isn't something just anyone could do—they have to be balloons, gaining and losing weight as the job requires.

The buzz cut that Zhou Ziheng had gotten for the movie has also grown out, but it's still pretty short, making his features look keen yet profound. Unlike many celebrities his age, with their pretty faces and mild attitudes, Zhou Ziheng gives off a masculine, testosterone-filled vibe. There was a natural sort of aggression to the irrepressible sharpness of his bone structure.

Ever since the shift in Zhou Ziheng's public persona, Xia Xiqing has praised his costuming team more than once to his friends, and he's not disappointed this time either: Zhou Ziheng is wearing a grayish-blue shirt tucked into dark gray dress slacks to the conference. The outfit wraps neatly around his solid muscles, and he cuts an excellent silhouette with his wide shoulders and thin waist—his torso was an almost perfect golden ratio. Standing at six foot four inches, his stature is both steady and distinguished.

Although his overall style today is sophisticated and simple, he's wearing a pair of gold-rimmed glasses. A fine gold chain runs behind his ear, glimmering under the light and adding a sense of self-restraint to his natural sharpness.

A carefully made-up woman wearing luxury brands walks up to Xia Xiqing. As she sits down, her hand brushes him—seemingly an accident, but potentially not.

"Sorry."

Xia Xiqing looks at her and nods slightly to show friendliness.

Taking this opportunity, she smiles and extends her hand. "Hello. I'm Jiang Yin, the producer of this film."

After glancing at her delicately manicured nails, Xia Xiqing politely removes his mask and shakes her hand. "Hello. Nice to meet you."

The moment he removes the mask, Jiang Yin's gaze brightens. She's seen many attractive people after working in the entertainment industry for so long, but what she sees now is quite rare—the young man in front of her could almost be described as pretty. His features are slightly feminine, but his charisma is very masculine. His hair is slightly longer than typical, enough for half of it to be tied up, revealing charming eyes with dark irises and a subtly upturned shape.

And with that tiny mole at the tip of his nose, it made for an easy face to remember.

To put it more bluntly, the man has a face that people would forgive no matter what he does; one with absolutely no aggression. It would draw out protective feelings in any onlooker. This type of face was the easiest to make popular with any audience, and upon seeing it, Jiang Yin cannot help but enter into work mode.

"I don't recognize you; I must not have met you before now." Letting go of his hand, she smiles and asks, "You're not in the industry, are you?"

Xia Xiqing also smiles slightly. "The original author of *Seagull* is a friend of mine. It's all thanks to him that I can see my idol up close."

"Oh?" Jiang Yin grins and casts a look at the female lead actress, who is currently speaking on stage. "She's the type of girl you like, then?"

Xia Xiqing chuckles and shakes his head, looking lazily to the one standing next to the actress—Zhou Ziheng.

"He's the type of boy I like."

Jiang Yin shows no sign of embarrassment. Instead, she makes an expression of realization and smiles calmly. "My intuition has always been quite bad."

Just then, the female lead on stage finishes speaking and passes the microphone to Zhou Ziheng.

The moderator asks him a few questions about the movie. "We've just seen the scenes from the early-release trailer, and Ziheng, you've had such a breakthrough in this film! I didn't even recognize you at the beginning. I bet we're all pretty curious: do you have any particularly memorable experiences or sentiments?"

Zhou Ziheng grips the mic and thinks for a moment before saying, "In terms of sentiment, it'll probably be half a year before I want to eat any seafood again."

Offstage, his fans all laugh. The dry manner in which he delivers this type of dark comedy is very fitting.

"As for memorable experiences... Actually, the entire experience has been pretty memorable for me. Honestly, it was my first time attempting this topic and Director Wang is a bit of a perfectionist. Eighty percent of the scenes were done on an actual boat, without any green screens. I was seriously seasick at first, and it took me a while to get my act together. The whole crew was always very tired, and I was a little moody too. Every time I thought about how there are real people who, like Gull, have been deprived of human rights and made into slaves, I felt very..." Zhou Ziheng contemplates his wording before continuing, "...devastated. Yeah, that's probably the feeling that encouraged me to push through and finish filming. I think the crew and my fellow castmates must feel similarly."

Head tilted, Xia Xiqing watches him and listens very carefully. To be honest, he's always thought that Zhou Ziheng was a very bad fit for the entertainment industry—the product of a sterile environment, with a heart that longs to be the savior in any and all dangerous and complicated situations he happens upon in the outside world.

In other words, a delusional idealist.

After finally getting this close to Zhou Ziheng, Xia Xiqing finally understands why fangirls are so eager to see their idols live. Pretty celebrities look even more attractive in person.

He studies Zhou Ziheng onstage, contemplating his perfection from every angle. He would be an excellent replacement for all those texture-less plaster sculptures he uses for sketch references. As a side effect of his profession, he subconsciously scans and analyzes every inch of Zhou Ziheng's body as if he weren't wearing any clothes. Of all the bodies that Xia Xiqing has seen, Zhou Ziheng's is the finest.

Xia Xiqing sighs internally, thinking about how much he

wants to make a statue of him.

"Now it's time for us to open the floor to questions from the audience," the moderator says, passing the mic to Zhou Ziheng. "Ziheng, you can go first."

The fans all begin to shriek as if their lives depended on it, and the atmosphere becomes quite excited. Zhou Ziheng squints a little as he gazes into the audience, and Xia Xiqing finds the face he makes extremely adorable.

One onstage and one offstage, two pairs of eyes meet. Xia Xiqing lifts the corners of his mouth just a little bit, making sure that his slight smile reaches his eyes, habitually trying to make his gaze seem especially meaningful.

"You."

He's pointing in Xia Xiqing's direction.

"The girl in the floral print dress," Zhou Ziheng quickly adds.

It's the girl behind him. Xia Xiqing laughs to himself. *Boring straight man.*

Whatever meaning he managed to squeeze into his gaze has been utterly blocked by a wall of heterosexuality, but Xia Xiqing isn't discouraged by this small setback. Instead, a fire ignites in his gut. Perhaps it's the same logic as hunting for deer—the more evasive the prey, the better the gun feels in the hunter's hand.

Paying little attention to the question and answer exchange, Xia Xiqing sets all his attention on examining the contours of Zhou Ziheng's muscles as if he were in an art museum admiring a flawlessly sculpted masterpiece—his gaze full of yearning, full of imagination.

The conference lasts two hours. Afterward, Xia Xiqing goes looking for the restroom. The press conference was held at a high-end hotel, so the floor plan is very convoluted. After several wrong turns, he encounters a hotel employee.

With a polite smile, he asks, "Excuse me, do you know where I can find the restroom?"

The employee is a young woman, and she seems a little flustered when faced with Xia Xiqing. "Turn right—oh sorry, umm...turn left and at the end of the hallway there's a VIP restroom..."

"Thank you." Xia Xiqing smiles, sticks his hands in his pockets, and begins walking in the direction she pointed.

His phone rings the instant he walks into the restroom. Seeing the caller ID, Xia Xiqing's good mood completely vanishes.

That guy's been calling all night—doesn't he find it exhausting?

"If I remember correctly, we never started anything, no?" Xia Xiqing clamps the phone to his ear with his shoulder as he washes his hands. "I don't think that I had any problems whatsoever." There's a brief pause. "Really? You want a relationship?"

Chuckling, he shakes the loose drops of water from his hands before taking a couple strips of paper towel from the box beside him and beginning to wipe his fingers dry carefully.

"When we first met, I distinctly remember saying that I don't do relationships. You've just got a face palatable enough to go out for drinks with—whenever I'm bored enough for that kind of thing. I mean, in those places, who isn't there for that? They just refuse to say it out loud, and I'm upfront about it. But then I heard you talking, and I realized that you're..."

His last syllable stretches out as if he's hesitant about the end of the sentence.

He hesitates too long, and his tone cools completely down. Slowly, syllable by syllable, he says, "Utterly useless."

The caller continues to speak—ceaselessly so, and Xia Xiqing tires of it. "Seriously? Come on. I dread hearing that from people; it's all bullshit. Who do you think you are? The lady lead of some tragic romantic drama?"

Unbelievable. After blatantly flirting with another guy at the bar yesterday, being so shameless that the two of them almost got down to business right then and there... And the most humiliating part was that initially, people assumed Xia Xiqing was being cheated on. *And now you're trying to confess your feelings?*

"We're both adults. If we deal with this in a civilized manner, maybe next time we see each other we can still have a friendly drink together. With the time you've wasted on me so far, I'm sure you could've found someone else. Besides, didn't you have fun with that other guy yesterday? Wow, are you really so indiscriminate?" He shakes his hand. The volume of the call suddenly increases, the caller yelling loudly enough that it begins to hurts his eardrums. He frowns, then grabs his phone out from between his ear and shoulder.

The tone of his voice changes completely.

"I'm warning you. Stay away."

He balls up the paper towel and throws it into the garbage bin.

"If you keep prattling on about this, I'll find someone to get rid of that thing you've got between your legs. You'll be the one lying down getting fucked either way, so it's not like you need it."

The voice on the other end of the line becomes silent.

Xia Xiqing laughs. Then, looking at his reflection in the

mirror, he adjusts his expression and smiles softly.

"Relax, I'm joking. How could I bear the guilt?" His voice has become soft and warm, and he leans against the wall of the restroom like he's comforting his most intimate lover. "So how about you behave and disappear from my sight, hmm?"

He hangs up the phone and turns toward the stalls—and just then, a man walks out of one of them.

Grayish-blue shirt. Tall. It's the shining star who was onstage just a few minutes ago—Zhou Ziheng.

Fuck. Well, that backfired.

His actions unflustered by the reveal of his true colors, Xia Xiqing gracefully directs a soft smile at Zhou Ziheng.

"Hey, what are the chances?"

Zhou Ziheng frowns faintly at Xia Xiqing, unable to hide the disgust in his expression. No, not unable to—hiding emotions is what actors do best.

He's simply too lazy to hide it.

Zhou Ziheng's gaze drifts down, seeing the silver badge pinned at Xia Xiqing's breast—the one that represents his own fans. Xia Xiqing notices the look and also glances down, then raises his hand to touch the badge.

With a smile, he says, "Mmm hmm, that's right; I'm your fan."

Impassively, Zhou Ziheng walks around him and stops at the sinks, turning on a faucet.

Xia Xiqing shrugs, walks into a stall, and hooks the door shut with his foot.

He's antagonized his idol. What a misstep.

Normally, he would never give the game away on a first meeting. His typical façade of friendly warmth is as easy as breathing for him. His angelic persona comes so naturally to him only because everyone else is so eager to give their trust away to someone who looks as kind as he does. This seriously is some terrible luck. Disgusted, Xia Xiqing moves that clingy bastard from earlier into his blacklist.

Forget it. It's not as if he was ever a true fan; to him, Zhou Ziheng is more of a sexual fantasy.

Hmm, does being disliked by one's idol count as a type of special regard? Xia Xiqing thinks this over with a sense of self-deprecation. The door shuts with a bang and he walks to the enormous mirror to look at himself. The kind and gentle person reflected there is nothing like his real self. He exits the restroom, then leaves the venue.

After staying at the bar till 3:30 AM, Xia Xiqing gets a call from Xu Qichen.

"Xiqing, you're trending."

The music at the bar is so loud that Xia Xiqing has a hard time hearing him. He walks outside, frowning, then dizzily squats down at the side of the road. He'd drunk so much that his tongue has gone numb.

"What did you say?"

"You're trending on Weibo. It seems as if someone posted a video from the press conference, and you were in it."

Xu Qichen speaks calmly, but Xia Xiqing knows that he's simply a naturally calm person. They have a brief conversation, after which Xia Xiqing sits down on the curb. He finally sobers up a bit as he feels the cold breeze of the pre-dawn hours blowing in his face. Frowning, he opens Weibo and flips to the trending page.

The topmost trending topic glares at him imposingly.

white shirt man from the seagull release press conference

White shirt? With some effort, he tries to remember last night's outfit. Seems it was a white shirt... He clicks into the topic. The most shared video is Zhou Ziheng's Q&A session with his fans. In it, the camera pans from Zhou Ziheng onstage to his lucky fan offstage—the girl who'd been sitting behind Xia Xiqing. As the camera moves, Xia Xiqing's face appears in frame for a few seconds—and these few seconds alone have been enough to make him trend on Weibo.

He suddenly remembers that he never put his mask back on after he'd removed it. How careless.

There are almost ten thousand comments under the video.

@WatermelonNotWintermelon: I need every piece of info about this man within the next 10 minutes.

@VikiViki: mom i think i just saw an angel [tears.jpg]

@LooksAreEverything: OMG with a face like that why didn't he become an actor??? He's too attractive, even his long hair looks so good, like he's some sort of divine spirit.

@33IsMyWife: just passing by, and i'm astonished. his smile is like an angel's. he's better looking even than most male idols.

@ForeverTopHeng: Yeah his appearance is definitely god-tier. But if my eyes don't deceive me, isn't it our Heng's fanclub support badge that he's wearing on his chest? [screenshot attachment]

@FirstMadamZhou: it is it is! omg i can't believe he's our heng's fan. i'm so sorry i've brought down the average appearance rating of our fan community [kneeling down]

@MostAlphaZhouZiheng: Oh my, it's as they say: the fans take after the idol. This level of good looks could probably bankrupt so many of the current idols. I've brought shame to our Heng's fan community [bawling]

@GossipyMing: Nowadays, you can't even chase idols without being attractive enough.

Xia Xiqing is still scrolling through the comments when

someone stops in front of him, casting him in shadow. He looks up lazily and sees a decently attractive man.

The man lights a cigarette, smiling. "No company?"

Xia Xiqing blinks at him, slowly. It's strange, he currently feels absolutely no interest whatsoever. He raises an eyebrow, then asks coldly, "Do I look like someone without company?"

With that, he stands up, preparing to leave.

The other man is a little surprised that a man with such delicate features would be so tall, but he still reaches out and tugs at Xia Xiqing, smiling and saying, "Hey, don't be in such a hurry. At this hour, not having any company is nothing to be embarrassed about; let me buy you a drink. Since I'm also alone right now, we can have some fun together."

This man has the look of an experienced player. The hand he set on Xia Xiqing's arm has already migrated to his wrist—evidently, he was unwilling to give up without at least having a taste. Xia Xiqing's eyes shift a little, and he grins, shifting his demeanor to one of flirtation.

With one finger resting on the man's shoulder, he says, "Drinking is so boring... You see, handsome, I go for twenty grand an hour. How about this—since you're a new client, I'll give you a discount. What do you say about sixteen grand?"

The man's expression quickly shifts, his eyebrows knitting together. "You're sick."

"But I'm healthy." Xia Xiqing's expression is guileless. "I'm completely clean. You want to see a report?"

"Twenty grand? What a price tag." The man gives him a once-over. "You got gold plating in your ass or what?"

Seeing the man assess him, Xia Xiqing's gaze immediately cools down. In a mild, low voice, he spits out a sentence that is quite contrary to his sweet appearance.

"I've got diamonds in my dick."

He lights a cigarette for himself, his previously flirtatious expression replaced instantaneously by one of delinquency. He glances at the man through a cloud of grayish-white smoke.

"No money? Why are you even talking to me if you've got no money? With your looks, I'd still have to think about it for a while even if you sprawled out naked on bed and paid me to fuck you."

"You..." The man seems displeased, his gaze scanning Xia Xiqing's face over and over, trying to get a read off him. "What the fuck are you saying? Someone like you..."

The man doesn't finish before he scoffs—clearly, this is simply a bottom pretending to be a top.

"Do you think we're not compatible? Don't worry, my technique is excellent. You'll see."

Xia Xiqing's eyebrows furrow in a display of clear irritation.

"Do you not fucking understand human speech?" He lowers his head to take a drag, then puffs out a smoke ring. "I don't bottom. And even besides that..." he trails off, then gives the man a careful once-over before smiling scornfully. "I don't deal with inferior goods."

The man is rendered temporarily speechless. Xia Xiqing ignores him, straightening out his suit before walking away without a backward glance.

Arrogant guys like him never give up unless you completely destroy their bubble of hollow confidence. Xia Xiqing walks down the block before hailing a cab and climbing in.

On his way home, Xia Xiqing continues to browse Weibo. The video indeed came from the official channel for the movie, and the online discussion seemed spontaneous and genuine...but if this remains such a hot topic, there'll eventually be investors coming in and trying to hype this up to make money.

His mood sours at the thought. Upon reaching the apartment he's been temporarily renting since his return from overseas, he takes a hot shower and goes to sleep.

Unsurprisingly, when Xia Xiqing wakes up next afternoon, he finds that his muted cellphone has logged over forty missed calls. He scrolls through the notifications—even his parents have phoned him, and usually they don't even call during the holidays.

He begins to enjoy this moment a bit. Though he's suddenly gone viral, he's also been forced into everyone's awareness—and that includes the father who ignores him and the stepmother who hates him. It brings him no small sense of achievement to make them so agitated without even seeing them in person.

After washing up quickly, Xia Xiqing ties his hair into a careless little ponytail at the top of his head, changes into work-wear that's not exactly clean, and sits in front of his canvas. Beside him is a painter's palette, on which red and blue paint have mottled together into a dirty gray-purple. He closes his eyes and the scornful look on Zhou Ziheng's face from last night comes into view.

Like wisps of clouds, the scene gradually floats from his memories into the forefront of his mind, becoming clearer and clearer. Xia Xiqing captures it in lines, imprisons it on canvas.

His prominent bone structure, his sharp features, and the subtle beginnings of a sneer on his quirked lips—all of it is laid down in thick layers of oil paint on the canvas' placid surface, forever trapped there.

Hand still holding the paintbrush, Xia Xiqing leans against the back of his chair, one bent leg resting on the edge of his worktop. He examines this somewhat casual sketch carefully, and feels a vague sense of dissatisfaction. The subject's real-life charisma surpasses the expression captured in paint by a thousand-fold or more. Even the extent of his disgust is impossible to replicate.

His phone rings again. Xia Xiqing stretches out across the worktop to grab it, and sees that it's an unknown number.

Habitually, he injects his tone with false friendliness. "Hello. May I know who I'm speaking to?"

"We've met before. Perhaps you still remember me?"

The voice is indeed familiar; it only takes a few seconds for him to put a name to it.

"Ah, this must be Ms. Jiang."

"Yes, the very same. You have an excellent memory." Jiang Yin laughs. "Have you been flooded with calls? You've gone viral."

Xia Xiqing lets out a laugh and stretches his spine a little. "It hasn't been that bad; I slept through it all. You're the first call I've actually picked up."

Jiang Yin is a little taken aback. This young man is truly calm and collected—after all, he hasn't even asked her how she got his contact information.

By the time they meet up at their rendezvous point, it's already nearing sunset and there are few others in the coffee shop. The amber sunlight shines through the clear glass of the window wall and melts into the heavy fragrance of coffee, encasing Xia Xiqing within it.

Jiang Yin stirs the foam in her mug around and around with a spoon, dispersing the design it had arrived with.

Meanwhile, she studies the young man sitting across from her.

His dark hair is tinted with warmth from the setting sun and outlined with a halo of light. His delicate features have a faint smile to them, and the small beauty mark at the tip of his nose is gentle and enchanting. She didn't notice previously, but he has a long, thin scar on his chin that runs almost exactly along his jawline so as to be barely noticeable. Xia Xiqing is dressed more casually than she thought he'd be, wearing simple, oversized worn coveralls that are speckled with paint stains both new and old. And yet she recognizes the brand almost instantly—it's a luxury label, popular with celebrities for airport fashion. Furthermore, the exact piece he's wearing seems co-branded; a limited-edition version. He clearly is not frugal about clothing whatsoever.

"Were you painting?"

"Yeah." He looks down and sees a large patch of blue paint stuck to the outer edge of his palm. Even after he rubs at it with a finger, the paint doesn't budge. Without looking back up, he asks, "If I may ask, what's the purpose of this meeting?"

Seeing how forthright he is, Jiang Yin doesn't waste any time with small talk and asks directly, "Have you ever thought about making a debut?"

As if in contemplation, Xia Xiqing taps his finger against the side of his coffee mug as he watches the passersby outside. "Making a debut?"

"You have very good qualifications. The audience loves you, as evidenced by your most recent visit to the trending list." Jiang Yin has subconsciously begun to speak with the confidence of an accomplished agent. "To those of us in the business, there are different levels of talent. The lowest level is home to those who can never make the headlines no matter how hard they try—and that's most actors in the industry. With enough time to improve their skills, those with slightly higher talent levels are able to eventually encounter an opportunity and achieve their fifteen minutes of fame. And the highest level is home to those who were simply fated to be renowned. They achieve more attention than anyone could ever dream of as soon as they show up on screen—without even speaking a single word."

She leans in slightly.

"You're that last type."

Outside, a child walks by with a helium balloon. With an accidental slip of his grip, it floats off into the sky. The child watches blankly as the balloon flies away before he suddenly bursts into tears. Seeing this, Xia Xiqing can't help but laugh.

Feeling ignored, Jiang Yin coughs, and Xia Xiqing turns his head back to her lazily.

"Ms. Jiang, I can tell that you're an expert in this industry, but even the highest authority can make mistakes sometimes."

"What do you mean?"

"I am your mistake." Xia Xiqing leans back on the sofa, too lazy to keep up pretense. "I'm not that last type you just described. Let me be blunt: I'm big trouble." His smile reaches his eyes, and his eyes fill with the same warm light as the setting sun outside. "If you pull me into the entertainment industry, you'll regret it eventually. I'll be a constant source of trouble for you."

Jiang Yin stares at him for a while. Finally, she opens her mouth to say, "I can understand that you don't want to debut as an actor. I still have a plan B."

Xia Xiqing quirked an eyebrow; he was bored anyway, so he might as well hear her out. "I'm all ears."

"There's a reality show coming up. I need a few laymen for it—people unknown in the entertainment industry." Jiang Yin takes a proposal from her bag and hands it to Xia Xiqing. "I'm part of the management team, and I would like to invite you on the show."

"Invite me?" Xia Xiqing opens the proposal and takes a quick glimpse through it, immediately understanding the situation. "Ah, so you've been planning this for Zhou Ziheng all along. This was actually your plan A, no?"

"You really are the smartest person I've ever met." Jiang Yin makes no attempt whatsoever to her true motives. "I guessed that you wouldn't agree to debut and that I'd be rejected if I suggested it, but I still wanted to try. You probably know this already, but I'm a shareholder in Zhou Ziheng's agency—of course I'm also more than just that, though that's not something I can explain to you right now. Zhou Ziheng is an actor our agency is currently working very hard to promote. He has excellent acting skills and qualifications, but you must know that actors who debuted as child stars often have a certain problem—they have very few die-hard fans. Zhou Ziheng currently has a nationwide fanbase; almost everyone knows of him, and almost everyone likes him. But that type of fame isn't where money comes from these days. He needs people who will pay attention to his sponsorships and spend money accordingly: die-hard fans and idol-chasers."

"You need commercial influence." Xia Xiqing pokes at the milk foam in his latte with his spoon, ruining it.

"Exactly." She taps the surface of the table, then adds,

"With his acting skills and his looks, commercial influence is what will allow him to become an absolute phenomenon. That's what I want for him."

Though Xia Xiqing now understands her goal, he still finds it a bit curious. "And you think he can increase his influence through me?"

"Why else would I be here? Influence comes from trending topics. That's to say, the quickest way toward more influence is to bait a pairing."

"That's true, but I just find it strange—there are already plenty of pairings involving him, all young and successful stars. Why would you want me, someone completely unknown to the industry?"

Though Xia Xiqing asks this, he already has an idea of her reasons: if two celebrities bait a pairing and the resulting profit or attention is distributed unevenly, it'd only create even bigger problems for their management teams. Someone like Xia Xiqing—without an agency, without a fanbase—would be a much more stable when put into a pairing's supporting role.

"You're a hot topic right now; you currently attract the greatest amount of public interest out of the entire audience of non-actors and non-performers. The Weibo trends from the past couple days alone speak to the potential in that face of yours." Jiang Yin is an old hand at flattery. "The initial plan for this reality show was to do an escape room, but I vetoed that; it wouldn't create enough interest. Similar programs in the past all failed. Sometimes, the audience just wants to see something that's actually interesting."

"Like what?" Xia Xiqing cups his chin in the palm of his hand, expression unchanged.

"Like a celebrity getting trapped in a room alongside his

fan, and them trying to escape together." Leaning her own chin in her palm, Jiang Yin smiles at Xia Xiqing. "And if the fan in question is also a handsome young man, I think fangirls would be more interested."

That explains it.

"You paid for me to trend on Weibo yesterday, didn't you?" Xia Xiqing lets go of his coffee spoon, propping it against the side of his coffee mug with a clink before retracting his hand.

Jiang Yin doesn't seem to mind her scheme being exposed, and explains calmly, "I was merely adding fuel to an already burning fire. But allow me to clarify that the video being posted in the first place was an accident. When we first met, I did think that you'd get noticed, but I didn't think it'd be this dramatic."

So you straight up took advantage of it? Xia Xiqing thought. *What a frightening professional habit.*

He wonders how the beneficiary to this scheme might feel after learning about this. But now that his mind has turned to the topic of Zhou Ziheng...that look of abject disgust on his face floats before his mind's eye.

Xia Xiqing straightens up, suddenly extremely interested. He smiles, once again cupping his chin in his palm. "Your suggestion is definitely quite interesting. But you probably don't know that my idol hates me right now. *Very much.*"

The last two words are purposefully dragged out. He smiles proudly, his eyes becoming two happy crescents.

Jiang Yin is bemused. "You've met before in private? Why would he dislike you? He's usually very nice to his fans."

"Hmm... I did meet him in private, once, and uh..." It was such an awkward situation that he can't quite find a proper way to explain it, so he gives up. "Well, in any case, it didn't go well. I bet that he'll refuse to be on the program if he knows it'll be alongside me."

Jiang Yin remains silent for a moment before she asks, "What if I manage to persuade him? Will you come then?"

Xia Xiqing looks up from examining a speck of paint on his fingertip, his gaze filled with pleasure. "Sure."

His tone is light, and Jiang Yin finds it a bit suspect; this is too easy.

"Really?" Eyeing him dubiously, she says, "Just like that, you'd agree? I can't help but find it somewhat strange."

Xia Xiqing nods again. "I mean it; I agree."

He feels excited at the thought of Zhou Ziheng being in the same room as him despite disliking him so much.

Excitement is the source of creation.

"Oh right. Are you sure you want to invite me onto an intelligence-based reality show?" He laughs. "What if I can't do anything useful at all? What if all I do is hold him back?"

This concern does have some basis in reality. After all, Xia Xiqing is a fan; he understands Zhou Ziheng's background. When Zhou Ziheng took his National College Entrance Examinations, he'd forgone art school and ended up in Peking University in the physics department. Even Xia Xiqing had been surprised at this turn of events; he hadn't expected for the little child star to be such a smarty-pants STEM nerd. He half-expected Zhou Ziheng to quit acting entirely and instead embrace a socialist love for academic research, but the kid ended up back in acting all the same.

Even without acting school, his dramatic skills are top tier. When God decides to open a door for someone, chances are that the windows will be opened too. Everything remains closed otherwise, as dark as a solitary confinement cell.

This is simply cruel reality.

"Originally, I thought that Zhou Ziheng would be smart enough on his own, that it was better for you to serve as a foil to him." She smiles, incredibly honest about her original plot. "But I looked you up—professional habit, you know— and you amazed me. A graduate of the Accademia di Belle Arti di Firenze[2]? Oh, and I accidentally came across your record in the High School Mathematical Contest in Modeling too."

Accidentally?

This woman is scary. Though Xia Xiqing doesn't show it on his face, he's secretly in awe of her investigation skills. The HiMCM had happened so long ago, and she still somehow managed to find it. This is no small feat, especially considering his family background.

"You definitely won't be the weakest link." Jiang Yin's smile doesn't reach her eyes.

Xia Xiqing responds with the same superficial smile. "I'll do my best."

After saying goodbye to Jiang Yin, Xia Xiqing decides to go visit Xu Qichen. On his way there, he discovers a newly opened bakery, so he pops in and picks out some of their newly released flavors with a speed that even surpasses his rapidity when browsing the dating market.

"So you're really going to be on TV?" Xu Qichen asks. His mouth is still full of cake, making his slightly surprised question come out muffled.

Xia Xiqing is sitting on the floor, and he nods, extending his legs and crossing his ankles. He can't help but roast Xu Qichen, and says, "On TV? No, grandpa, I'm going on a reality show."

---

2 Also known as the Florence Academy of Fine Arts.

"Same thing."

Xu Qichen ate his cake too quickly and it's now a little stuck in his throat, so he jumps off the sofa and rushes to the fridge to find something with which to wash it down.

Watching from behind him, Xia Xiqing clicks his tongue. "You're not wearing socks. If Xia Zhixu finds out he'll scold you again." He catches sight of the milk packaging and can't resist asking, "Do you have anything alcoholic?"

"You shouldn't drink so much. It's either cigarettes or alcohol with you Xias, isn't it? Bad habits must run in the family."

Xu Qichen pushes a single-serve milk box into his hand. Xia Xiqing is slightly reluctant, but he takes it anyway, flashing a wicked grin at Xu Qichen.

"You're one to talk. That kid's biggest unhealthy habit is you."

"No, you," Xu Qichen retorts out of habit. "Don't laugh. It'll be you next, sooner or later."

Xia Xiqing shrugs. "Then we'll see which unfortunate bastard ends up with me as their bad habit."

Xu Qichen suddenly remembers the reality show. "Why did that producer invite you? That type of reality show is pretty rare, and it must be difficult to get guests for it."

"That woman somehow found the records of that contest I did with Xia Zhixu way back when, and then there's also the Weibo trending thing." Feeling a headache coming on, Xia Xiqing squeezes the milk box. "This is why I say I hate the internet."

"But then again..." Xu Qichen leans on a sofa cushion, wearing a smirk that clearly hopes for escalation of the dramatic spectacle he's watching. "If you go on the show, you'll get to be up close to your idol."

"Not my idol. He's my sexual fantasy." Xia Xiqing is more enthusiastic about this topic. "But see, that's the thing. If she'd asked me before all of this, I probably would've refused. Having my every move be recorded? How disgusting! But now that Zhou Ziheng seems to dislike me so much, the idea has suddenly become more interesting"

Xu Qichen is a bit bemused at this. He doesn't know what the VIP pass he gave to Xia Xiqing has brought about, nor does he understand Xia Xiqing's thought process.

Being hated by someone you like—how could that be something to be excited about?

"Aren't you a sadist? Why are you starting to seem more like a masochist?"

Xia Xiqing laughs, reaching out to pinch Xu Qichen's cheeks lightly. "Chen-Chen[3], you're so naïve. Watching someone who hates you work with you while the cameras roll, having to force down his unkind sentiments toward you—don't you think that sounds very... fun?"

He'd hesitated on the wording near the end; he'd originally wanted to say "sexy." In his mind, the idea of Zhou Ziheng trying to be nice and friendly to him while keeping his true feelings buried is truly very sexy.

It makes him want to do everything he can to provoke Zhou Ziheng and discover his hidden limits.

It's late by the time Xia Xiqing gets home, and yet another unknown number calls him. It's well-timed, so Xia Xiqing picks up—only to be confronted with his stepmother.

Xia Xiqing can't think of a single reasonable excuse to call him at this hour.

---

3 In Chinese, this method of reduplicating characters is often affectionately used to make diminutive nicknames.

"Xia Xiqing, why didn't you let us know you were back from abroad?"

That disingenuous tone of hers hasn't changed. Xia Xiqing puts her on speaker and sets his phone aside.

"If we'd known you were coming back from Florence, your father and I would have sent someone to pick you up. And now the only way we can find out that you're back is from television? Such a hassle!" Her voice is as slick as an eel, and smells just as fishy. "You're a member of the Xia family, after all. It's not good for the family's image for you to always be abroad, and now you're on TV? Your father—"

Xia Xiqing scoffs and walks to the kitchen to fetch an iced bottle of water from the fridge. Unscrewing the cap, he takes a few gulps, feeling the cold water trickle into his heart. His insides are frozen.

"Are you done? Missus Xia the *second*?"

She pauses, obviously taken aback. When she speaks again, her voice has lost some of its previous strength: "Why must you be so hostile? I'm just trying to be considerate of your best interests—"

"Hostile?" He slams the fridge door shut with a thud. "You've tried so hard to pretend to be kind. Let me think; what could your motive possibly be today? Hmm, could it be that you want me to move some of my mom's assets? Or is it that Xia Yunkai is sorting out his affairs?"

"You!"

Sounds like he was right.

Laughing, Xia Xiqing continues, "You don't have to try so hard with me. You'd be better off begging your husband to take fewer mistresses and sire fewer bastards to compete against your son when it comes to the inheritance. How's that? Is that the type of advice you're looking for?"

"You..." Having been seen through so completely, her shame shifts to anger and the false kindness from earlier disappears completely. "You shameless little slut, you're just like your father! You—all either of you know is how to screw around!"

"If he didn't screw around, how could you have ever joined the Xia family?" Xia Xiqing's voice becomes gentler as he says, "You should be grateful."

She begins cursing him out again, the same phrases repeated over and over: *you and your father are the same, you shameless perverts; both of you will get what's coming to you.* Xia Xiqing has heard it all before, ever since he was little. He's already used to it.

As he waits for her to finish bitching, Xia Xiqing puts his water bottle back on the table and turns around, leaning against the countertop. Finally, he speaks again.

"No."

The voice on the other end of the line pauses, a bit confused, then asks, "What did you say?"

Annoyingly enough, Xia Xiqing finds it a little difficult to breathe.

With one hand, Xia Xiqing unbuttons the top button of his shirt, the restates, "I said that I'm not the same as Xia Yunkai."

Now things feel better.

"He screws women. I screw men."

Habitually, Xia Xiqing checks his Weibo before going to bed. He'd originally created the account to share his art, but it ended up becoming a fan account.

How did he get so many notifications? Xia Xiqing is spooked; though he's one of the most well-known artists in the fandom and gets fellow fans seeking him out from time to time, it's never been this bad. He's gotten so many notifications that his Weibo is starting to lag.

He has to restart the app for it to fix itself.

@BunnyBunny: Tsing-*da*⁴! You're the one in the white shirt, right?

@HengMeFaceOn: Wow, really? It's Summer-da?? It can't be, can it?

He was found out? Still slightly dubious, Xia Xiqing scrolls through his notifications. As expected, the comments are all from Zhou Ziheng fangirls, and there are countless private messages too. All of them are about the press conference.

So he *did* get found out. It seems that it really is impossible to be completely invisible on the internet.

He should just come clean and save all the fangirls the trouble of guessing.

With the attitude of it-can't-get-worse, Xia Xiqing switches to the camera and takes a selfie. The shot is taken a bit too closely, his damp hair still messy from his shower, and he's also taken the photo from below, creating a weird angle. He dithers for a moment, but then decides that it looks enough like himself, and so he uploads it to Weibo in a slapdash way.

@Tsing_Summer:
[image attachment]

From the moment he posts, his phone starts to vibrate ceaselessly, notifications coming in like waves. He can almost feel the excitement of the fans coming out of the screen.

@No1AInTheUniverse: Aaaaaah! It really is you!! So hot!

4 On the internet, "dada" is an honorific title or suffix given to artists and writers who operate primarily online. Literally, it means "big-big." As a suffix, it can be abbreviated (as it has been in this case) to "-da."

Our fandom's average appearance rating must be unreal!

@WatermelonNotWintermelon: OMG too cute! The mole on your nose is everything!

@BunnyBunny: Skin, check. Nose, check. Eyelashes, check. How have you managed to pull off such a terrible angle? Evidently a godtier fan [kneeling]

@FirstMadamZhou: I've always thought that Summer-da-da's art was godtier, but now I understand that you are yourself a deity, thank you for visiting us mere mortals [crying]

@HengsOnlyMomFan: Oh wow, why rely on your talent when you have this face?

...

Xia Xiqing's Weibo ID quickly enters the top trending list and he becomes a new social media celebrity. He gets a bunch of business inquiries in his private messages, including even some sponsorship offers.

In this new era of extreme shallowness, a pretty face is the most direct and the most tasteless shortcut toward success.

His phone vibrates again: it's a message from Xia Yunkai.

Why didn't you come to the office to find me when you came back from abroad. Come home this weekend, I have something to tell you. —Dad

The darkness of his bedroom is like a cold, wet blanket, wrapping around him, suffocating him.

I don't have time to go to your place. If you have anything to say, say it over the phone.

After sending the text, Xia Xiqing walks onto the balcony and lights a cigarette. Grayish-white smoke blends with the soft yet cold light of the moon, creeping into his head, filling up the cracks within, and blurring away his consciousness.

Like most citizens of the internet, Zhou Ziheng is also

browsing through Weibo while getting his makeup done in preparation for a magazine cover shoot.

The day Xia Xiqing had first gone viral, Zhou Ziheng had been almost certain he'd only pretended to be his fan to make himself stand out more—maybe bought a few fan accounts to get himself trending and waited for everyone else to follow, thereby making himself go viral. After all, he really does have a nice face; nice enough that he could easily become famous off of it. But then Zhou Ziheng learned from Jiang Yin that he'd refused to sign with her and debut as an actor, and he began to doubt himself. Could he really be a fan?

So here he is, shirking his responsibilities in his busy schedule by logging on to his personal Weibo account. He clicks into the trending list and easily finds Xia Xiqing's fandom Weibo.

Turns out he really is a fan. And an artist at that.

But it seems Xia Xiqing almost never posts on Weibo, nor does he share any of Zhou Ziheng's live performance feeds like his other fans. Xia Xiqing seems to just quietly post his art, the style of which is very unique. With a few simple lines, he can depict a human body's structure in a way that unleashes a flood of hormones even through the screen.

Scrolling down the Weibo blog, Zhou Ziheng also skims through the comments. Besides praising the divinity of Xia Xiqing's art, they're all along the lines of "Zhou Ziheng is so alpha! He's so alpha I can't close my legs! I'm begging you please fuck me!"

Uh... Why are teenage girls nowadays all so...

Unconsciously, he scrolls faster and faster down the blog until, suddenly, an image flashes past his eyes. He pauses, then scrolls back up.

This image had trended once. It's a side portrait of him doing a layup. The shadows interspersed with sunlight that fell on his body, the long fingers tightly grasping the basketball, the red jersey soaked in sweat, and the solid lines of his muscles from top to bottom.

He closes Weibo, opens his personal photo gallery, and finds that same painting in an album called "fan-art." He'd never noticed it before, but there's a handwritten signature in the lower right corner—*Tsing*.

It seems that he's previously seen Xia Xiqing's art. He even downloaded it to show off to his friends.

After logging off, Zhou Ziheng hesitates the entire night, but eventually decides against deleting the image from his phone.

And yet something still feels off.

Perhaps to take advantage of Xia Xiqing's recent fame, the reality show Jiang Yin mentioned hurriedly wraps the planning stage they had previously been stalling on. The guest list is finalized, and the shooting is set to start on Saturday. On Friday, by request of the production team, Xia Xiqing obediently moves into the hotel room that they've prepared for him. That night, Jiang Yin even finds the time to come to the hotel to check on him.

"Are you so afraid that I'll run off?" Xia Xiqing sits crosslegged on the bed wearing only his cotton pajama pants, drying off his dripping hair.

She looks him over. His abs are distinct, clearly the product of long-term exercise. His muscles aren't exactly robust, but they're certainly lean. It seems somewhat at odds with that beautiful face of his, and she's a little surprised by it. She put a thin stack of documents on his table.

"Of course. This is some information about our show; you can take a look in your spare time."

"Have you got a script?" Xia Xiqing stretches his neck a bit, then puts on a loose T-shirt. It makes him look like a high school student. "First things first: I won't follow a script, so give up any hopes you might have about that."

Jiang Yin's expression is a little helpless, seeming to have already realized the futility of such an endeavor. "I knew you'd be like this. In truth, we do have a script, but it doesn't concern you. The production team hired someone to write a plot for the escape room itself." Upon saying that, she makes a quick segue: "Though you don't need to worry about a script, we did assign you a persona, and I'll need you to conform to it. Besides, aren't you pretty good at wearing a mask?"

Once again, Jiang Yin has spoken a bit more directly than politeness would typically demand, but Xia Xiqing is starting to get used to it.

"If that's the case..." He straightens his legs, throws the towel onto a chair, then leans against the wall with his hands folded behind his head. He speaks with an unconcerned tone: "Tell me, what's my character design?"

Sitting by the table, Jiang Yin calmly replies, "Well, think about it. Ever since Zhou Ziheng's persona shift, his popularity has increased exponentially, so our agency of course wants him to continue with this more aggressive character design. And since we want to encourage shipping, what type of person do you think we should pair him with in order to make the ship truly popular?"

Still reclined on the bed, Xia Xiqing watches her, blinking slowly in a way that makes his eyes seem as if they were the zoomed-in focus of a slow-motion camera. A pristine and harmless smile begins to appear on his face, tinged with a sense of innocence by the tiny mole at the tip of his nose.

"An angelic persona. Someone lovable and pure."

Jiang Yin shrugs. "Clever."

He scoffs, completely abandoning his earlier façade of gentleness.

"Seems like all of you have already decided on the sexual dynamics of our hypothetical relationship." Xia Xiqing retracts one of his legs, propping his chin in his palm and his elbow against his knee. He watches Jiang Yin with an unreadable expression.

"No, it's just that... I mean, Zhou Ziheng's persona is... But of course, in the end it'll still be determined by the audience and what they say online."

Jiang Yin was puzzled at first; she hadn't expected that kind of comment. After speaking, she suddenly realizes that Xia Xiqing gives off a fairly domineering vibe despite how pretty he looks.

For all that Xia Xiqing isn't concealing his personality around Jiang Yin anymore, she still has no idea about his spirited history of past conquests, nor does she know that he's always been a top. And so, she rationalizes his comment about sexual dynamics by attributing it to a masculine obsession with dominance.

"Oh, so that's how it is. Don't worry about it, then." The corners of Xia Xiqing's lips curl up, and his eyes regain their previous warmth. "I'm quite the easygoing guy."

Seeing how many times Xia Xiqing's expression has shifted within just a few minutes, Jiang Yin finds herself impressed—though she also laments to herself that his natural talent for acting has been squandered for so long. Though she held witness to how skilled he is at pretense, she still doesn't understand why he accepted her invitation.

"You agreed to participate, but you haven't even asked how much we'll pay you."

"Doesn't matter." Xia Xiqing leans back again, falling supine on the bed. "Don't worry. Though I can't guarantee much else, I can definitely ensure that people will have plenty to talk about." Seeming to have suddenly remembered something, he flips onto his side to face Jiang Yin. "But Zhou Ziheng probably won't believe the persona you've given me."

"That's alright; I'll talk to him. I'm sure he'll know how to play his part after so many years of being an actor."

Xia Xiqing merely raises his eyebrows. Things might not be as simple as Jiang Yin seems to think.

The next day, Xia Xiqing arrives early to the set. He's taken to the makeup room for a simple clean-up. The makeup artist is a young woman, who, despite already being accustomed to pretty celebrities, is still a little stunned by Xia Xiqing. As she does his makeup, she keeps asking him about his skincare secrets. A young assistant they call *Xiao-Jie*[5] walks into the makeup room, and Xia Xiqing smiles at the reflection of the young man in the mirror, making Xiao-Jie feel a little shy.

"Mr.—Mr. Xia, Jiang Yin-*jie*[6] has assigned me to be your assistant. Please let me know if you need anything during the shoot."

5 "Xiao-" is a prefix used for making diminutive nicknames, often used affectionately for children or for someone who's younger than whoever is speaking. Literally, it means "little" or "young."
6 "Jie(jie)" is an honorific title or suffix that is used any girl or woman of the same nominal generation as the speaker, occasionally even for those who are slightly younger than the speaker, especially if they have some other form of seniority over the speaker. Literally, it means "older sister," but it is used regardless of familial relation and also sometimes regardless of relative age.

"I feel like 'Mister' is something that's only used for older men." Xia Xiqing dons his expert expression of gentleness. "I thought I still looked fairly young."

"Ah? No, no..."

"No?" Xia Xiqing widens his eyes, deliberately teasing the poor kid.

"Ah, I meant... Sorry. You look like a college student. I—I'm new and I'm just a little nervous..." Xiao-Jie waves his hands frantically. "And..."

"Just call me Xiqing."

The makeup artist only does the basics, evening out Xia Xiqing's skin tone and doing his eyebrows, so it's over sooner than expected. Xia Xiqing stands and turns toward Xiao-Jie, extending his hand.

"I'm twenty-five, so I should be slightly older than you, but I'll be in your care for the next couple days."

"Then I'll call you Xiqing-ge[7]." Xiao-Jie shakes Xia Xiqing's slender hand. "I've still got a lot to learn, so please bear with me if I make any mistakes."

The kid's so honest! Xia Xiqing is internally surprised, but also thankful; he'd expected Jiang Yin to assign someone more resourceful to keep him in check, but it seems he'd been a bit paranoid. The shooting is scheduled for the evening, so Xiao-Jie leads Xia Xiqing to a studio where he'll be doing a promotional photo shoot for the morning hours. Inside, Xia Xiqing sees two of the other guests that are here for the show. Though Xia Xiqing has been abroad until quite recently, he's still fairly familiar with the mainland

---

7 "Ge(ge)" is an honorific title or suffix that is used any boy or man of the same nominal generation as the speaker, occasionally even for those who are slightly younger than the speaker, especially if they have some other form of seniority over the speaker. Literally, it means "older brother," but it is used regardless of familial relation and also sometimes regardless of relative age.

entertainment industry and recognizes them both. One of them is Cen-Cen, a female singer. She's a solo artist whose popularity has recently skyrocketed. The other one is Shang Sirui, a member of HighFive, a male idol group that's also been quite popular of late.

Xia Xiqing turns to Xiao-Jie. "Am I the only layman here?"

Xiao-Jie nods, then shakes his head. "No, there's another one, a girl. She's apparently a member of Mensa."

Xia Xiqing nods. Soon after, it's time for him to be photographed. Unlike typical non-performers, Xia Xiqing is not afraid of the camera. The photographer tries out a few shots, then flips through the preview to find that they're not bad.

Pleasantly surprised, he asks, "You have modeling experience?"

"Sort of."

Xia Xiqing recalls the time at the Accademia when he'd helped out a friend majoring in fashion design by modeling some outfits in a short fashion video. It had been a strange experience.

"But it wasn't at all professional."

"Still pretty good. Your limbs are slender, good for the camera."

The photographer tries another few shots before finally beginning to do the promotional photos. During the last set, Xia Xiqing catches sight of a tall man walking into the studio.

"Ziheng is here."

Xia Xiqing detects him instantly. He needs no time at all to distinguish Zhou Ziheng from the crowd; it's rare for anyone to be as tall as him, let alone have as nice of a face.

Long time no see. Xia Xiqing looks back at the camera, revealing a smile.

Zhou Ziheng seems to have come from another event, and rushes in with a gray-green windbreaker. Upon entering, he greets the workers around him.

"Sorry I'm late."

The wide hood of his jacket covers half his face, leaving only the deep contours of his eyes exposed.

"Oh, it's Ziheng!"

He's quite popular; he'd been on shows for this television station often in the past, and the regular employees seem to like him. Zhou Ziheng is a mere twenty years old, so most folks in the business treat him like a little brother. His characteristic commanding demeanor and general aura of aggressiveness often make people forget about his age.

The makeup artist pulls him aside to have his hair and makeup done. Zhou Ziheng is quite sleep-deprived, as he was up late for the magazine cover shoot last night and attended a promotional event for the movie all morning. As the hairstylist blows his hair into shape, he closes his eyes in hopes of catching a wink or two of sleep."

The makeup artist smiles. "The outfit Xiao-Heng is wearing today looks very good!"

His sleep-deprived brain reacting half a beat slower than usual, Zhou Ziheng opens his eyes and replies truthfully, "I've been sponsored by the outfit's label."

"Pfft." The makeup artist laughs. She sprays him with setting spray, saying, "I see you're as honest as ever."

Seeing Zhou Ziheng's state of exhaustion, his personal assistant Xiao-Luo had gone out to quickly buy him an iced coffee, and returns just as Zhou Ziheng's hair and makeup are complete. Zhou Ziheng takes the coffee with a thanks, then walks out of the makeup room.

Walking around the studio section, he heads into the

semi-open-concept space that serves as the lounge area. He takes a couple sips of coffee, then sets it aside as he sits on the sofa. He glances around, looking at his surroundings— that is, taking in everything except for Xia Xiqing, who was at the center of the spotlight.

"Okay, Xiqing's all done!"

Xia Xiqing thanks the photographer before his gaze drifts to Zhou Ziheng, who's sunk into the sofa. The collar of his jacket is upright, covering half of his face and revealing only his attractive eyes and tightly-knit eyebrows. The word "unhappy" seems to be written all over him.

How is he so cute? It's as if he's been physically dragged here. Xia Xiqing walks over and finds the line between Zhou Ziheng's eyebrows deepening the moment he approaches.

Don't want me to sit here? Xia Xiqing quirks an eyebrow, then plops down right next to Zhou Ziheng. Turning, he smiles at him, then greets him with the same words as last time.

"Hey, what are the chances?" Xia Xiqing smiles, making sure it reaches his eyes. Though the man before him is well aware of his true colors, he still wants to present a façade of harmless innocence. "You're on the show too?"

Zhou Ziheng looks skyward wordlessly, then scooches a bit to the side, thinking, *Why must you continue this charade?*

Though Zhou Ziheng understands what's going on, he remains silent, turning his head to the side coolly as if Xia Xiqing wasn't even there.

Even though Xia Xiqing's friendliness has been met with such a cold shoulder, he doesn't feel embarrassed at all; instead, he finds this version of Zhou Ziheng to be even more fun. He smiles, leaning into the sofa and stretching out his legs, which were clad in slacks.

Not only does Zhou Ziheng not want to see Xia Xiqing, he doesn't want to hear him either. And so, he pulls out his phone and a pair of earbuds, and starts to put the latter into his ears. But then he hears Xia Xiqing say:

"So this is how you treat your fans. Maybe I'll expose how I've been treated and resign from your fanclub."

The hand Zhou Ziheng was using to put in his earbuds freezes as Xia Xiqing's sentence comes to an end. He seems to hesitate for a moment, but then turns toward him.

Seeing how useful the word "fan" seems to be when it comes to Zhou Ziheng, Xia Xiqing snickers internally.

After an awkward moment of silently staring at each other, Zhou Ziheng finally begins to speak. Probably to be polite, he even unzips the collar of his jacket.

"I don't have anything against you personally," he says soberly. "It's just that I tend not to like people who aren't serious about relationships."

Xia Xiqing is momentarily dazed by the response.

This... Where did this little angel come from? How is someone with such a scummy alpha sort of face so honorable?

Xia Xiqing smiles, lips curling up like a sly cat's. "How do you know I'm not serious about relationships?"

Zhou Ziheng's frown deepens, remembering back to the scene in the restroom when he first met Xia Xiqing; how this person—who looked so completely unaggressive—had spouted such vicious words.

Watching the complex emotions playing across Zhou Ziheng's face, Xia Xiqing sobers, eyes glowing with integrity. "Really, I'm not who you seem to think I am," he defends himself earnestly. "It's all just a misunderstanding. It's a long story, but that guy wasn't my boyfriend. He kept harassing me, and it also turned out that he'd been seeing other people at the same time. I really couldn't stand it anymore, so that's why I said all of that—it was to scare him away. I look like such a pushover; if I don't talk mean, people will take advantage of me." He purses his lips, donning a gloomy sort of you've-wronged-me expression. "I've really been feeling awful since that day. I was the one being harassed, but now my idol evidently thinks I'm some sort of scumbag."

The word "idol" is effective, and Zhou Ziheng's expression visibly softens quite a bit. Xia Xiqing sighs, eyes innocent and forlorn.

"I swear: I'm not the kind of person you described."

Just the type of person who wants to flee the moment he feels like the other person might have caught actual feelings. Just someone who likes the feeling of the chase, who likes a good challenge just a little too much to be healthy. The moment of success is like cold water poured over the fire of his passion, leaving him immaculately extinguished.

With a mask of honesty so perfect that even a professional actor would have difficulty seeing through it, he meets Zhou Ziheng's eyes, unafraid of any scrutiny whatsoever.

"I really, truly like you a lot. I did a lot of art of you."

Seeing the suspicion in Zhou Ziheng's eyes ease a little, Xia Xiqing extends his hand. "I'm so sorry that we met in such awkward circumstances, and that such a misunderstanding happened. Let's start again with a clean slate."

Zhou Ziheng's arms cross in front of his chest, not completely willing to shake Xia Xiqing's hand. His eyes roam over Xia Xiqing, hesitating awhile, but he eventually gives in once he remembers that painting of Xia Xiqing's.

The temperatures of their hands meet and merge, resulting in a remarkable sensation.

"My name is Xia Xiqing."

Zhou Ziheng nods, his perfect jawline leading the movement of the muscles at the sides of his neck. For all that the fan in front of him surely knows his name, out of politeness alone, he still gives his full name: "Zhou Ziheng." Upon saying that, he begins to pull back his hand, but then he feels Xia Xiqing holding on to it, so he looks at him uncertainly.

Xia Xiqing smiles. "Hey, don't you want to know the characters used in my name?"

Such a strange person.

Zhou Ziheng lifts his chin a little, a thread of irritation showing in his eyes. This expression somehow adds to his innate charisma. Fighting his impatience, he asks, "What are the characters?"

"'Xi' is the same character as the one in 'study[8].' As for 'qing'..."

Before the sentence ends, the slim, pale hand holding onto Zhou Ziheng's suddenly exerts force, pulling him toward Xia Xiqing. The carefully guarded distance between them shrinks rapidly. Zhou Ziheng's dark pupils dilate minutely as he almost crashes into that seemingly innocent face, the space between the tips of their nose becoming so small it's nearly invisible.

The smell of Xia Xiqing's cologne becomes the most cunning assailant; invading, suffusing, taking advantage.

The brief moment of intimacy seems slowed down by a factor of infinity, playing out frame by frame. Too close. Their proximity has warmed even the air of their exhaled breaths. The sharp spiciness of peppercorns, the rich fragrance of tobacco, and the mellow scent of musk have

8 The most common word for "study" is *xuexi*, which shares the *xi* character with Xia Xiqing's name.

all entwined together, and Zhou Ziheng frowns under their assault. Just as he reaches the limits of his acceptance, he senses a thread of profound sweetness piercing into his breath unerringly, seeping into his core.

A similarly enigmatic voice emerges from within the complexities of this fragrance, creeping from the corners of smiling lips.

"It's the same as the one in 'unclear[9].'"

Xia Xiqing lets go of his hand. The left corner of his lips curls higher, and he looks the very image of mischief.

One moment he's trying to defend his good name, and now exposing his true wicked colors.

He really must never, ever trust this face again.

Xia Xiqing originally thought this supposed escape room reality show would be just a bunch of video jockeys following guests around in a semi-open studio as everyone follows the script and acts out an "escape."

The real thing turns out to be completely different from his expectations. Without being told of even the escape room's theme, he gets blindfolded and led away. Before he leaves, the director even emphasizes to everyone, "Please don't speak before the game starts."

After a long walk guided by two workers, he's pressed into a chair. And after that, he gets tied up quite snugly with a long length of rope. Now immobile, he hears the clink of metal and a coldness settles around his wrists.

He's been handcuffed, arms bent awkwardly at his front.

---

9 The term originally used was *buqingbubai*, which literally means "neither clear nor white." While this term most commonly means "unclear" or "ambiguous," it can also carry a derogatory implication and mean instead "unclean" or "impure." Individually, the *qing* character in it that is shared by Xia Xiqing's name means "clear."

If he wasn't so sure that he's here to film a show, he would really be wondering if he's being kidnapped.

At least he now understands why the director kept saying, "This show is trying to be as realistic as possible. As members of the crew, we won't be intervening at all, so even we can't be sure how things will go."

Zhou Ziheng hears the vague sound of footsteps, more than one set of them. His hands lay over his knees, which have been tied with rope. His ankles, too, are tightly bound. Just as he was beginning to have doubts, his blindfold is removed by a member of the crew.

He squints slightly, unused to the sudden clarity of vision he's been allowed. He's in a sealed room, the atmosphere of which differs from most horror-themed escape rooms— the lighting in here is quite decent, with dim yellow light shining overhead. Everything other than the two rows of bookshelves against the wall looks a little odd; there's also some furniture covered in white cloth.

But that's not what surprises him, because what's in front of him is far more surprising than the escape room itself.

Xia Xiqing, who'd been messing with him just two hours ago, is currently tied to another chair. The two of them are just over a foot apart.

Perhaps in accordance with the viral video, the production team has put Xia Xiqing in a collared white button-up and black dress pants. A length of black cloth wraps around his eyes, and a lock of hair at his temple has escaped from his ponytail, hanging down the side of his face to brush against his sharply delicate jawline.

With his bright eyes hidden behind the blindfold, the small beauty mark at the tip of his nose seems to stand out

all the more, making him seem both helpless and docile.

Even though Zhou Ziheng knows without a doubt that he is neither of those things.

The handcuffs at his wrists glint coldly under the dim light. The bones of his wrists protrude slightly, looking so sharp that it feels like they would clink against the metal that surrounds them. The rope winds around his torso like a thin snake, so tight that the contours of his muscles are almost visible through the fabric.

The black fabric of the blindfold veils that pair of flirtatious eyes from Zhou Ziheng's sight, and this seems to be his first chance to examine this man unabashedly—this man who he's certain is so duplicitous and sly.

Viscerally, Zhou Ziheng realizes how pitiful Xia Xiqing looks right now—or, in other words, he realizes that he has developed a deviant urge to make the man even more pitiful.

For some reason, Zhou Ziheng has gained a sudden understanding of the psychology of those people with perverse desires.

"The game has now officially begun," says a voice from above Zhou Ziheng's head, digitally distorted and tinny. It interrupts him from the inappropriate thoughts that are growing like rampant weeds in his mind.

"Welcome, everyone, to *Survive and Escape*. Now, please forget about who you previously were. In this game, you are all players trapped in an escape room. Please note: there is more than one room in this scenario, and they're all connected to each other. Which means that when you open the room you're currently in, you will enter another one, in which there might be another person who is also trapped. The person who escapes from all of the locked rooms and leaves this house in the shortest amount of time will be the winner, and will obtain the highest score. Everyone else's scores will be calculated based on their escape time; one point will be deducted for every ten minutes after the winner's escape."

This game sure seems to take itself seriously, Xia Xiqing thinks as he smiles to himself, but the voice continues:

"There is another rule. *Survive and Escape* is most unique in that it is not simply an escape room reality show. Among all you players, there is a Killer. Unlike normal players, the Killer must hide their identity, and they will have the ability to "kill" a player. The player who is "killed" will receive zero points in a given round, and a Killer can "kill" only one player per round. Of course, all the normal players can also try to deduce who the Killer is, and when everyone gathers in one place, players can vote to "kill" the potential Killer. If the Killer becomes the winner of a given round, their points will be doubled, and every normal player in that round will be considered dead and receive zero points.

"Throughout the game, players will need to think carefully and use every bit of cleverness and deductive reasoning that they possess. If there is truly a problem you cannot solve, you can use your game time to buy hints, and your final score will decrease accordingly. The winner of this season will be the player with the highest total score combined from each round, and they will also receive a mystery grand prize.

"Currently, none of you carry any special equipment that might help you solve puzzles—except for a modified cellphone. This phone has only four features: one, an interface that will display messages from the production team. Two, an interface where you can buy hints. Three, a timer that will begin after the first player gets out. Four, an interface to vote for the Killer anonymously. Please note that players cannot send messages to each other using this cellphone. If you want to speak to each other, you can only do it face-to-face. This concludes the introduction of the rules."

The voice paused as a ticking countdown sounded three times.

Three.

Two.

One.

"Now, the game begins."

At this, Xia Xiqing lets out a sigh, slouching into his chair and tilting his head back. Zhou Ziheng watches his movements, secure in the knowledge that his presence is unknown to Xia Xiqing—and thus blatantly playing the voyeur.

Even though this kind of peeking was not something to be encouraged per Zhou Ziheng's personal moral standpoint, Xia Xiqing has made himself an exception. He's never met anyone like him, with such treacherous guile and such a boundless lack of shame. When facing him, Zhou Ziheng's normally upright behavior always seems to slip helplessly and malfunction.

Xia Xiqing tries to reach for his blindfold, but he can barely lift his arms; they've been almost entirely bound. He strains to lift them several times before finally giving up. He sighs in exasperation and begins to mutter quietly to himself.

"I can't even see. What am I supposed to do, wait around the entire game?"

Zhou Ziheng wants to laugh. For some reason, watching Xia Xiqing seems to have lessened the urgency of escaping this room.

Unable to see and unable to move, Xia Xiqing just taps his heels, head tilted back and body slouched lazily against the chair. He doesn't speak, and the room remains eerily silent. Zhou Ziheng also keeps deliberately silent despite understanding that, being similarly trapped, the best tactic should be to help each other. Moreover, they're filming; it's not as if they should continue to suffer through this in silence. It's just that all Zhou Ziheng wants to do right now is have a good laugh at Xia Xiqing.

Perhaps it's because he really is a terrible person, so he deserves a little grief in Zhou Ziheng's opinion.

It gives him the illusion of being an agent of karma.

But then, quite unexpectedly, the man who just moments ago seemed to have completely given up the will to fight suddenly sits upright, facing Zhou Ziheng with perfect posture. It was as if that hidden pair of eyes could see through the black cloth of the blindfold, and were looking unerringly at him.

Yes, he is "looking" at him.

Certain that he hasn't made a single sound, Zhou Ziheng frowns.

Suddenly, Xia Xiqing tilts his head, his lips forming a gentle curve.

"How about you help me take off this blindfold?"

Impossible. He obviously can't see.

C.02

:

Survive and Escape

Zhou Ziheng is taken aback by Xia Xiqing speaking to him. Though he remains silent, his quickened heart rate betrays his surprise.

Zhou Ziheng squints, but Xia Xiqing just continues to look at him. The stalemate lasts for a short while before Xia Xiqing opens his mouth again.

"Did they gag you? It's alright, I just need you to help me take off this blindfold."

The firmness of Xia Xiqing's tone makes him difficult to refuse. Zhou Ziheng flexes his neck, silently considering.

To be honest, he really doesn't want anything to do with this guy. But...if they keep up this stalemate, neither of them will be able to leave. Not to mention that they're on a reality show, and he doesn't want to make things difficult for the production team.

After much deliberation, Zhou Ziheng surrenders; he has no choice but to give up spectating Xia Xiqing's struggles.

He shifts his weight forward onto his feet, forcing the rotating office chair he's sitting in to spin so that he's facing a long desk. Very close to him, there sits a white porcelain vase full of white chrysanthemums. Struggling to stretch out his bound hands, Zhou Ziheng reaches for the vase. Finally, he wraps his fingers around the neck of the vase and resolutely dashes it against the edge of the desk with a resounding crash.

Zhou Ziheng raises his legs, sets the soles of his boots against the edge of the desk, and kicks off. The motion sends him and his chair over to Xia Xiqing.

"I can take off your blindfold, but in exchange, you have to help me untie these ropes."

After spending two solid years genuinely fanboying over him, Xia Xiqing recognizes Zhou Ziheng's voice instantly, and he finds the current situation well within his expectations. He smiles, then says, "Deal."

The moment Xia Xiqing agrees, Zhou Ziheng reaches behind Xia Xiqing's head with his bound hands and removes the blindfold, throwing it aside.

His obscured vision quickly clears, and Xia Xiqing turns to the side and abruptly realizes how close the two of them are to each other. He can almost smell the refreshing scent of Zhou Ziheng's aftershave.

Xia Xiqing squints slightly against the light, and the confusion on his face morphs fluidly and flawlessly into surprise.

"Ziheng? So we've been trapped here together." Xia Xiqing's smile is very sweet, and the mole at the tip of his nose makes him look incredibly pure. "It feels like I'm in a dream. I still feel a bit dizzy."

That act of his is too good. As a professional himself,

Zhou Ziheng can't help but be impressed. He just doesn't get it—how is it that Xia Xiqing can wear that kind of smile without any sense of incongruity? Without seeing his true colors, almost no one would be the wiser.

The escape room is full of cameras; not an inch of it escapes their gaze. Not wanting to be accused of being frigid toward his fans, Zhou Ziheng can only smile warmly in return. Forcing his voice gentler, he says, "I was blindfolded too, and I was also pretty surprised when they took it off."

Even though Zhou Ziheng really doesn't like guys like Xia Xiqing, his pride as an actor and Jiang Yin's reminders have forced him to patiently endure this. He holds out the sharp piece of porcelain to Xia Xiqing.

"If you don't mind."

"Of course not. I'm a longtime fan; I've seen all your films."

Xia Xiqing awkwardly accepts the shard of porcelain with his handcuffed hands and bends forward to help Zhou Ziheng sever the rope.

Zhou Ziheng smiles without feeling. "Thank you."

The two of them, both accustomed to playacting, have turned pretense into a contest.

The rope is tough. As Xia Xiqing works on it, he says in a relaxed tone, "Ah, did they only explain the rules once? I'm still a little confused."

Coming out of his reverie, Zhou Ziheng doesn't hear Xia Xiqing's question. To avoid embarrassment, he changes the topic.

"Oh, right... I wanted to ask you—how did you know there'd be someone to help you take off your blindfold?"

Xia Xiqing knew he would ask this question. There's only the two of them here, and Zhou Ziheng is fully aware of why he'd been invited onto the program—and also why he agreed to come. If he's not a bit more candid, he'll lose even more trust, and that will make the rest of the game more difficult to handle.

It's better to be straightforward here.

The pair of artist hands forcefully guide the broken shard back and forth across the rope. Xia Xiqing stares at the rope as it slowly begins to separate, explaining in a soft voice, "Though this is the first time I've appeared on a program, I used to go to escape rooms a lot with friends, so I've got some experience.

"In this type of situation, you never want to be completely immersed. You have to always be aware of how the designer of the game would approach things."

He cuts through the rope and starts to pull it out from between Zhou Ziheng's hands.

"The reason they locked us in here is to see us escape, not to watch us stay stuck for the entire game. If I was really alone in this room, hands and feet both tied, unable even to see, the chances of me escaping on my own would be close to zero. So, there are only two possibilities. One, I'm waiting for someone else to escape their room and come find me here, where they can either help me or kill me. Two, there's someone else in here and we need to work together to escape. And if you think about it from the perspective of watchability..."

At this, Xia Xiqing raises his head slightly, meeting Zhou Ziheng's gaze. He doesn't finish the sentence, just silently stares at him for three seconds.

Then, abruptly, he smiles.

At once, Zhou Ziheng gets a strange impression of being able to hear the words that Xia Xiqing didn't quite say out loud.

It's strange. They only met each other a few days ago—they're not close, so the phenomenon of unspoken agreement should be impossible for them; but Zhou Ziheng is able to completely understand what he's implying from Xia Xiqing's gaze alone.

And if you think about it from the perspective of watchability, the best way to generate online interest is if you and I are together.

"I was just trying out the second possibility. I didn't think I'd be lucky enough to hit the nail on the head."

Another lie.

And then Zhou Ziheng realizes that Xia Xiqing already finished untying his hands at some point.

"All good."

"Thank you."

Zhou Ziheng is still a little dazed. He feels like he's a pretty smart guy, but the awful first impression has clouded his judgment of this man. If he wants to win this game, he has to get over his prejudice.

Once he pulls himself together, Zhou Ziheng finds that Xia Xiqing has bent down and is using his handcuffed hands to try to untie Zhou Ziheng's bound feet.

His hands are free now, so he's able to untie this knot completely on his own. He has no need for other people to help him violently saw through it with a piece of broken vase.

"I can—"

Before Zhou Ziheng finishes his sentence, Xia Xiqing raises his head with a questioning gaze. His lips are slightly flushed, and he's holding the shard of porcelain in his mouth. The collar of his white shirt, a few buttons undone, reveals his prominent collar bones.

His eyes, now unveiled from the blindfold. His tied-up, grown-out hair. The angle at which he's bending, his posture bringing him so close to Zhou Ziheng's knees. The handcuffs, the beauty mark at the tip of his nose, the sharp piece of broken vase, the pretty but capricious curve of his lips, the tips of his teeth holding onto the porcelain.

The weird atmosphere of this moment has sketched these broken elements into a strange piece of art. It was very foreign and, at the same time, brushed with a pigment that suffused it with an enigmatic sort of chemistry.

Zhou Ziheng doesn't know why he suddenly feels so embarrassed; he's never felt like this before. He bends forward, reaching for the ropes at his feet.

People will always subconsciously become afraid in the face of the unknown.

Xia Xiqing doesn't seem to care about getting rebuffed. He removes the piece of porcelain from his teeth and hands it to Zhou Ziheng. "The knot seems pretty impossible. Try using this?"

Zhou Ziheng shakes his head, and unties it with slight difficulty.

His offer of help rejected, Xia Xiqing straightens. Then, as if throwing a dart, he nimbly tosses the shard of vase into some corner of the room.

Finally untied, Zhou Ziheng has recovered his basic freedom of movement, able to at least leave that accursed chair. The earlier scene has left him somewhat creeped out even now, so he puts it off as merely the aftereffects of being tied up. Trying to relax, he turns his head to stretch out his neck, then cracks his knuckles. Meanwhile, Xia Xiqing is still handcuffed, unable to untie the restraints on his legs by himself.

It's a shame that he only asked for his blindfold to be removed. Their deal is done now, and Zhou Ziheng is completely free to leave him here as a sacrifice in the game—especially since he dislikes Xia Xiqing so much.

Xia Xiqing considers his options. They're on a show right now, and abandoning a teammate is typically considered too cutthroat a move; celebrities usually wouldn't go for it. But this show is special in that it also presents a more psychological challenge: the hidden Killer will naturally make players doubt each other, so neither Xia Xiqing nor Zhou Ziheng can really regard the other as a teammate.

It would be completely logical if Zhou Ziheng chose to leave him here.

Meanwhile, Zhou Ziheng is also considering the situation. The truth is, his morality doesn't allow him to simply abandon someone like this, even if it's just a gamified survival simulation. It's just that he really doesn't like Xia Xiqing—he's trouble through and through, a time bomb waiting to go off. If he saves him now, he might just get betrayed at some point later in the game.

Wearing the smile of an angel even as he pushes him into the abyss—that's exactly what Xia Xiqing would do.

For a brief moment, they both struggle and deliberate.

"Even though you're my fan, I can't be sure that the production team wouldn't use that to lower my guard in a game like this."

Just as Xia Xiqing reasoned, Zhou Ziheng gives an argument that can best defend against future audience criticism. But then again, he doesn't care even if the audience really does get upset, because he really doesn't want to get stuck with Xia Xiqing.

"I mean, if you're the Killer, I'd become your unwitting

accomplice."

And what if you're the Killer? Xia Xiqing wants to ask, but he refrains. The question is too blunt and contradicts the harmless persona that he's been assigned.

He is truly at a loss.

Having fully mentally prepared himself, Zhou Ziheng turns around without reservation. But the moment he takes a stride away, he feels a foot hooking his shin.

"Don't go."

Zhou Ziheng turns back to see Xia Xiqing gazing at him from the chair. It's so strange—those eyes are on such a deceitful body, but they're somehow always able to give such unbearably innocent looks.

"How about we form an alliance, Ziheng? I'll help you win this game; no conditions."

Xia Xiqing smiles, but his expression is not at all that of someone asking for help—rather, it's that of someone who holds all the leverage.

"Really? But in this game..." Zhou Ziheng quirks an eyebrow. "...The way to win is to not trust anyone."

Pretty smart. Xia Xiqing chuckles.

"I'm not asking you to trust me." His eyes, dark as the abyss, exude sweet temptation. "I'm asking you to use me."

As he kneels down moments later to help Xia Xiqing untie the ropes around his legs, even Zhou Ziheng doesn't know how he was bewitched into softening his resolve and acquiescing to this man's request.

It's all highly illogical.

Trying to find an excuse for himself, he puts it off to the fact that they're filming a program—Xia Xiqing made a request, so it'd make him look bad to not accept.

"Thanks."

Xia Xiqing's tone is light and cheerful even though he remains handcuffed. He stands up from his seat, rotating his ankle in a quick stretch as he looks around to observe the room. Meanwhile, Zhou Ziheng goes to remove the white cloths covering the furniture and piles them all in a corner.

The room's not too big, but its furnishings seem to be those of a stylish study. The most important feature is a touchscreen password lock on the door, which will open if they input the correct four-digit pin.

The walls are accented with subtly patterned light brown wallpaper, as well as a couple of paintings and a wood-framed oval mirror. To the right of the mirror, leaning against the wall, is a freestanding redwood cabinet—and on it, there sits a record player with a record ready to play.

But Xia Xiqing doesn't focus on these things. Instead, he carefully looks for signs of camera placement. After all, the puzzles have already been planned out, and this is a reality show, meaning that there will be cameras ready for close-ups of the puzzle-solving process.

After doing a rough count of the cameras, Xia Xiqing feels a lot more clear-headed. Professional curiosity makes him look to the paintings hanging on the wall. Zhou Ziheng approaches as well, but his intention is to look at the backs of the paintings for clues.

"What do you think of this one?"

Hearing this, Zhou Ziheng's hand pauses on the frame of the painting. Art is not his specialty; for all that he's been acting since a very young age, there is still a huge difference between the visual and performing arts.

"I don't really understand this stuff," Zhou Ziheng says with honesty.

Xia Xiqing smiles. "This is Goya's *The Clothed Maja*. It's got a very interesting story behind it."

Zhou Ziheng puts the painting back and glances at Xia Xiqing. He's actually not at all interested in Xia Xiqing's story, but, considering they're on a show, it seems a bit rude to say nothing.

Somewhat reluctantly, he says, "What story?"

"In the eighteenth century, due to various historical reasons, Spain was shrouded in asceticism—nudity was completely banned in all artwork across the country. The only exception was *Venus at Her Mirror*, which only survived due to the King's protection."

Xia Xiqing stretches out his still-handcuffed hands and strokes along the edge of the frame. A bit confused, Zhou Ziheng looks at the lady in the painting. She reclines upon a divan upholstered in green velvet, wearing a gauzy gown of white chiffon. A wide sash the color of roses defines the soft curves of her waist.

"But she's wearing..."

Xia Xiqing's hand pauses and he glances at Zhou Ziheng, raising an eyebrow.

"She wore nothing at first. Some say that she was the mistress of a Spanish noble, and that she had commissioned a full-length portrait from Goya." Xia Xiqing suddenly chuckles. "Who knew he'd be so bewitched by her beauty that he'd paint her in the nude? After it was discovered, the nobleman was very angry. To appease him, Goya painted another one, exactly the same, entitled *The Clothed Maja*. And in the end, both paintings were taken away."

Zhou Ziheng looks wordlessly at the lady in the painting, his forehead slightly furrowed. Xia Xiqing drops his cuffed hands and turns to Zhou Ziheng.

"Are you thinking about the other painting?"

At this, his frown deepens and he stares at Xia Xiqing like a little puffed-up tiger with raised hackles. "I am not."

Xia Xiqing nods, smiling, and gently says, "I was just kidding."

He hadn't been kidding.

Seeing the fake smile on his face, Zhou Ziheng grows more annoyed.

This guy... he really has no shame at all.

He walks resolutely away, headed straight for the desk to examine it for clues. Xia Xiqing continues to look at the painting; staring at it.

Why would they put this here?

After a few minutes, Xia Xiqing turns around to see Zhou Ziheng standing beside the desk, looking at something on top of it. He walks over and sees that it's a large book and the torn remains of a sticky note.

"It's completely shredded. The crew was so diligent," Xia Xiqing says wryly, seeing the snowflake-like scraps of paper.

As Zhou Ziheng silently flips through the book, a bookmark falls out. A line of text is written upon it:

Whatever I touch crumbles to pieces.

— Kafka

Xia Xiqing leans in. "It's from *The Blue Octavo Notebooks*."

Feeling Xia Xiqing's proximity, Zhou Ziheng becomes a little ill at ease. He puts the book aside and picks up a piece of shredded paper, looking at both its sides. He frowns in thought, then, without another word, begins to piece the note together. Xia Xiqing doesn't like tedious tasks like this, so he walks over to the record player. He glances his fingers lightly along the tonearm and carefully guides the stylus needle onto the record.

There's a strange sense of inspiration that is unique to

vinyl records like these, and, with a few fast-paced notes, the feeling quickly washes over the dull atmosphere of the enclosed space. Xia Xiqing leans against the cabinet, watching the young man who seems as dull as the room.

"Have you ever heard this before?"

Eyes fixed on the desk before him, Zhou Ziheng does not raise his head. "I'm not very well-versed in music."

He has little interest in the arts, nor does he have any goodwill for some idle artist who's never done a day of honest work in his life.

Xia Xiqing smiles. His hands are still cuffed, but he still looks like a professional music connoisseur, standing in front of that redwood cabinet and silently appreciating the music. It's a while before he speaks again.

"It's the first movement of *Miroirs*, by Maurice Ravel. It was inspired by the concept of moths flying at flames in the dark." He turns to look at the spinning record and chuckles. "Though music critics usually say that the scattered semitones are like the flutters of a butterfly's wings, I feel like they sound more like a mirror shattering across the floor."

He starts to regret his words the moment they leave his mouth, feeling like he shouldn't really be saying so much on a show. But Zhou Ziheng suddenly raises his head from his heretofore unbroken concentration on those shreds of paper and glances over at Xia Xiqing.

Perhaps it's because he likes Xia Xiqing's metaphor, but Zhou Ziheng, previously focused, also begins to listen to the incessant music as he works, trying to appreciate it. It is only when the torn sticky note is returned to faultless completion that he finally straightens.

"It's done? How impressive."

Xia Xiqing is a little surprised. All that's on the paper is a bunch of broken letters, and it'd been shredded into so many tiny pieces. Xia Xiqing isn't a particularly patient person, and just looking at it had made his head hurt. He walks over to the table where Zhou Ziheng is in the middle of using a roll of transparent tape to secure the shreds of paper into a complete note.

Xia Xiqing takes a look. The letters are legible now, but they're random.

PGOEUDEAENHNRD

It's obviously a code. Xia Xiqing frowns, curious as to how Zhou Ziheng had managed to piece it together so quickly.

"You did it so quickly; how did you do it?"

Zhou Ziheng flips the note over to show the back, which has a line of beautifully handwritten words:

Tonight at 10, see you at Sophia (the restaurant).

"It was much easier to piece together using the information on the back."

Xia Xiqing nods. Even after realizing that the back had a complete sentence, it would still take some time to distinguish it from the front.

Wait—front and back.

Xia Xiqing picks up the sticky note. As he suspected, it's specialty paper; though its two sides don't look all that different, the contrast can be felt. The front is very smooth, and the back is much rougher.

"You really are very attentive." Xia Xiqing puts the note back down on the table, smiling at Zhou Ziheng. "As expected from Ziheng."

Even though the words are so clearly complimentary, Zhou Ziheng doesn't believe in their sincerity. He answers somewhat stiffly, "This kind of paper is common in escape rooms. If you weren't distracted by music, you'd have noticed too."

"What can I do? Art is life."

Xia Xiqing's hands are a little sore. He shrugs and looks down at the note. For some reason, the previously seamless music starts to lag; strange stutters beginning to emerge. The sound could make one displeased.

"Your 'art' seems to be getting on in years." Zhou Ziheng's voice carries a rare hint of sardonic mockery. The stuttering music makes him unable to concentrate, so he prepares to go over and turn it off.

However, Xia Xiqing simply stands still, staring blankly into space. He seems almost dazed.

"Wait." Just as Zhou Ziheng touches the tonearm, Xia Xiqing stops him. "Don't turn it off."

"What is it?" Zhou Ziheng looks at Xia Xiqing, a little irked, only to find that he'd gotten a pen from the desk and is now noting something down on the paper from before.

Did he find something? Zhou Ziheng slowly retracts his hand, starting to properly listen to the strange, choppy music.

The stutters in the music seem random—sometimes it'd lag for a brief moment, sometimes it'd be longer. But upon paying closer attention, he finds that the lagging stops for a few seconds every two measures before reemerging. The lagging between the music notes seems without order; some long, some short. Even the length of the pause seems consistent.

Like some sort of cycle...

Zhou Ziheng quickly realizes that every cycle is another repetition of the code.

Long—Short—Short—Short—Music
Short—Long—Short—Music

Short—Music

Short—Long—Music

Long—Short—Long—Music

...

Morse code.

He stands before the record player, listening for a few measures. Meanwhile, Xia Xiqing straightens from the desk, checks over the notes he just took, then walks over to Zhou Ziheng.

"You solved it?"

Zhou Ziheng is somewhat astonished. As far as he's aware, Xia Xiqing majored in fine arts. How could he solve Morse code so quickly?

Xia Xiqing nods, a small frown creasing his forehead. He walks over to the mirror and stares at it carefully for a while, then tells Zhou Ziheng, "Stand back a little."

Zhou Ziheng doesn't understand, but he backs up a little anyway. He watches Xia Xiqing remove the tonearm, abruptly pausing the music. He's about to ask what the code was trying to say, but he's too late. Xia Xiqing steps back with his right foot, raises his handcuffed hands in front of his chest, then, using a practiced stance and movement, performs a side-kick.

The oval mirror shatters with a crash. He pulls his foot back, and the reflective shards fall to the cabinet and floor in a rush of crystalline clinks. As the glass falls away, the true form of the florally-carved frame finally emerges.

The wooden frame has a gray backing, to which a silver key is glued.

"If you don't mind." Turning around to glance at Zhou Ziheng, Xia Xiqing shows him his bound hands.

The extent of Xia Xiqing's cleverness has honestly surpassed Zhou Ziheng's expectations.

For but a second, he considers taking advantage of Xia Xiqing's lowered guard and grabbing the key for himself to use as leverage later on. After all, Xia Xiqing is such a cunning man, and he's also very likely to be the Killer.

But he ends up deciding against it. Seeing that pair of wrists, red from friction with the handcuffs, Zhou Ziheng feels his earlier thoughts were truly somewhat contemptible.

If he gets stabbed in the back later in the game, well, it would certainly be unfortunate, but it is what it is. Zhou Ziheng steps up to take the key from the frame. Whoever was in charge of the prop was truly diligent—the key has been secured very well, and it takes him no small amount of effort to detach it.

Xia Xiqing obediently extends his arms, presenting his wrists to Zhou Ziheng. The scene of him bending over his hands to unclasp them is an extremely enjoyable sight to Xia Xiqing.

This angle highlights the jut of Zhou Ziheng's nose and the exquisite shape of his eyes. It's a testosterone-fueled type of carved exquisiteness. The beautiful curve formed by the join of his brow ridge to the bridge of his nose looks like it came from a windswept mountain range. The shape of his lowered head and the focus in his staring eyes remind Xia Xiqing of Paolo from Rodin's sculpture, *The Kiss*.

If they weren't on a reality show, Xia Xiqing would definitely lean in and whisper into his ear:

You have a very kissable face.

"Done."

Handcuffs successfully unlocked, Zhou Ziheng raises his head, unexpectedly meeting Xia Xiqing's direct gaze. He frowns subconsciously before glancing sideways and clearing his throat. He flicks his wrist to remove the loosened hand-cuffs, grasping them in a single hand before setting them down on top of the cabinet with a click.

Xia Xiqing smiles, saying a soft "Thanks," as he touches his wrists. Remembering back to when he'd been finishing up with the code and Zhou Ziheng's expression as he listened to the music, Xia Xiqing asks, "You also figured out it was Morse code, right?"

Zhou Ziheng nods, reaching into his pocket to check the time. "But I never memorized the exact Morse code correlations to letters, so I found it a bit difficult to solve."

Xia Xiqing resumes the paused music and explains, "At first there's a long lag, then three short ones before the music resumes. Long-short-short-short corresponds to B. After that is a sequence of short-long-short, which is R." The coded music continues to play. "The sequence of short on its own is E. Short-long is A. Long-short-long is K."

B-R-E-A-K—Break

Before Xia Xiqing explains the remaining two words, Zhou Ziheng says in English, "*Break the mirror.*"

"Exactly." Xia Xiqing laughs.

This laugh seems different from before, more candid. Zhou Ziheng figures that he's probably just imagining it.

"Why are you so familiar with Morse code?" Zhou Ziheng walks over to stop the music, then picks up the vinyl record he hadn't paid much attention to earlier and observes it, squinting.

"My Math Olympiads teacher from middle school mentioned it, and I found it very interesting. I even used it to send answers during exams. I haven't used it since I joined the liberal arts stream in high school, so it took me a little while to remember it just now." Xia Xiqing toes the ground with his dress shoes. "But the way the production designed this, isn't it a little too hard? If a contestant didn't just happen to know this stuff, it'd probably be impossible to solve, no?"

"They actually thought it through quite well." Zhou Ziheng passes the vinyl record to Xia Xiqing, on which is written the English word, *Mirror*. "You put this on when I was piecing together the sticky note. If a contestant is familiar with classical music like you, they might recognize it as *Miroirs* on their own, and thus associate it with the mirror beside the record player. But if they didn't know, they could find it on the vinyl record itself, so it's inevitable that they'd think about the mirror."

"And to connect it with breaking the mirror..." Xia Xiqing thinks back to the bookmark they found in the book. "*Whatever I touch crumbles to pieces.*"

Zhou Ziheng nods. "I think that the torn-up note is also a hint. The production team prepared quite a few ways to solve the puzzle. You just chose the most direct path."

"Yet it also required the greatest amount of brainpower." Xia Xiqing shrugs a little. "But compared to the efficiency in making all these connections, math is much quicker and much more precise."

Zhou Ziheng wonders how someone who studied art could be so good at math. Meanwhile, Xia Xiqing has already shifted his focus to the note that Zhou Ziheng put together.

"The scrambled letters should be another code, but probably with a different key." He walks over and picks it up. "Maybe this will lead to the code we need to open the door."

This coincides with Zhou Ziheng's thoughts, but he can't help feeling that the room contains more information beyond that sticky note. It's just that he's yet to find a good way to differentiate useful information from trivial.

The two of them return to the once-shredded sticky note that was pieced back together. Xia Xiqing flips the note over to the side with words, carefully examining it. Then, he takes the bookmark out of the book and proceeds to say something that currently seems somewhat useless.

"Don't you think the handwriting is different on these two things?"

Zhou Ziheng had noticed it as well. The handwriting on the bookmark is less reserved, seemingly belonging to a man, whereas the sticky note was written in a more delicate script. The difference isn't that glaring, but judging from the force with which the strokes begin and release, it does seem like two different people wrote those two sentences.

He points at the bookmark. "I think this one was written by the owner of this study."

Xia Xiqing actually agrees with him, but for the sake of the show and the audience's understanding, he kindly asks, "But what if the owner of the study borrowed this book? The bookmark could very well belong to someone else."

Zhou Ziheng shakes his head and raises his hand, pointing at the bookshelf. "On the third row, counting from the left, the first six books belong to the same series as this novel, and this one is the finale. Other than this series, there are a bunch of other series on the shelf too. I don't think a person who likes to collect entire series of books would borrow a book for reading, especially a series finale."

Xia Xiqing puts on the reverential expression that fans so often use. "Wow, it's such a waste of talent that our Heng-Heng hasn't been cast as a detective yet."

Our Heng-Heng?!

For all that Zhou Ziheng has already gotten used to seeing

this term of address in his fan community, upon hearing it come out of this guy's mouth, Zhou Ziheng feels his typically excellent control over his expressions starting to slip.

Seeing such seemingly genuine worship in Xia Xiqing's eyes, Zhou Ziheng can't help but mentally retort:

It's also such a waste of talent that you're not an actor.

Remembering again that they're on camera and that he shouldn't act too aloof toward such an enthusiastic "fan," Zhou Ziheng clears his throat, then mutters, "It's not certain that I won't be."

For some strange reason, Xia Xiqing finds Zhou Ziheng just the slightest bit adorable right now. He shakes himself mentally—he must be addled to think that.

When Zhou Ziheng sees Xia Xiqing about to step on a piece of the vase that he smashed at the beginning, he feels compelled to warn him, reaching out and dragging at his arm.

"Careful."

Xia Xiqing heeds his words and looks down. "Oh, it's the vase that got smashed at the beginning—I almost forgot about it. Perhaps the theme for this room of ours is 'fragments.'"

His words were casually intended, but as Xia Xiqing thinks it over, something feels off. Zhou Ziheng had that theory of association about how contestants could have connected "break" to "mirror" by looking at the bookmark and the vinyl record—so shouldn't the equally fragile vase also reveal clues upon being broken?

It seems that Zhou Ziheng might have picked something up from Xia Xiqing's words as, in tacit agreement, the two of them squat almost simultaneously to examine the shattered remains of the porcelain vase and the scattered bouquet of white chrysanthemums on the floor.

Using the stem of a flower, Xia Xiqing turns over the mess of broken shards. Sure enough, he finds a thin roll of paper. "Found it."

The guy who wrote the script for this room really was thorough; there are so many clues stuffed into every little nook and cranny. If they hadn't thought of the overall theme, fragments, then they probably wouldn't have smashed the vase.

No, that's not it. He very quickly backpedals.

Zhou Ziheng suddenly says: "So the crew tied us up, but didn't give us anything to cut our way out—except there was a decorative vase within my reach. That was probably just so we'd smash it."

Their thoughts have aligned. Xia Xiqing is a little surprised, but he quickly replies with a hum of affirmation. "It should be just like you said. But we shifted focus early on, so we didn't find the clue in the vase at first."

Like when you play *Pac-Man* or *Snake*: no matter where you start or where you go, you have to eat all the dots that the game gives you—otherwise, it's game over.

He suddenly begins to appreciate the script writer a bit. Whoever wrote this escape room is smart—the clues don't come in chains, where you always need the previous clue in order to find the subsequent one. It's much more playable to design the room so that the order in which a player finds the clues doesn't matter; even creating multiple potential ways to solve a single puzzle. Also, the writer added a villainous role, the Killer, and with that simple change turned a pure puzzle game into complete psychological warfare.

Interesting.

They open up the scroll, revealing a short poem.

We are two pieces of what once was a whole.

Destiny took you out of my body, from my bones, my flesh, my heart, bluntly piecing these meaningless organs together.

With you, who were also taken apart and reconstructed, one after the other, I was buried.

Buried under this fence covered with roses in full bloom.

Only disassembly anew,

Will return you to me, will return me to you.

From above to below, connected to each other.

Only then will everything have meaning anew.

It seems to be a somewhat gothic poem, but Xia Xiqing keeps feeling there's something off about it. He turns the scroll and finds words written on the back in English:

2 you.

"There must be a reason for using the Arabic numeral '2' instead of the English word 'to.'"

Xia Xiqing can't be sure of much else, but he's certain about this. So far in this game, the only regularity has been that they can't let go of anything out of the ordinary.

Zhou Ziheng keeps staring, brow furrowed, as if very carefully considering this poem.

Suddenly, their cell phones ring. Thoughts interrupted, they take out their phones. Displayed on the screen is a new notification:

Please be warned that the first player has escaped their original room and has gone into the room of another player.

"Wow, that was fast." Xia Xiqing looks around. Smiling, he puts his phone away, his expression both innocent and relieved. "But they haven't come to our room. If that person is the Killer, able to go into any random room... This is a scary game."

Zhou Ziheng asks in response, "But what if they're a regular player and they walk into the Killer's room?"

Xia Xiqing turns to him, choosing an angle that avoids all close-up cameras. Then he reaches up as if to adjust his collar, but instead he covers the mic that's on him. Fully exhibiting his terrible personality, he smirks lazily and mouths in a mocking manner, "A lamb entering the den of a tiger—isn't that more exciting?"

Zhou Ziheng distinctly feels the change that has overcome Xia Xiqing. Just moments ago, he'd been somewhat distant and half-hearted, but now, upon finding out that someone else has broken out of their room, Xia Xiqing has completely gotten his head in the game.

But he also knows that Xia Xiqing isn't particularly competitive; it's just that he wants to get out to find the excitement and watch all the fun.

Unfortunately, finding a messy situation and making it more chaotic is probably his real intention.

"Don't you think the poem is very strange?"

With a pen that he got from who-knows-where, Xia Xiqing underlines a few lines at the end:

Only disassembly anew,
Will return you to me, will return me to you.
From above to below, connected to each other.
Only then will everything have meaning anew.

He then takes out the sticky note that Zhou Ziheng had pieced pack together, the front of which shows a line of scrambled letters.

"I think this poem is telling us how to decode this message."

Zhou Ziheng nods in agreement. He silently reads the poem, this time more carefully:

We are two pieces of what once was a whole.

Destiny took you out of my body, from my bones, my flesh, my heart, bluntly piecing these meaningless organs together.

With you, who were also taken apart and reconstructed, one after the other, I was buried.

Buried under this fence covered with roses in full bloom.

Only disassembly anew,

Will return you to me, will return me to you.

From above to below, connected to each other.

Only then will everything have meaning anew.

Pieces of a whole, taken out, pieced together, buried one after the other...

Without quite meaning to, he reads aloud: "Buried under this fence covered with roses in full bloom..."

Fence, fence...

Fence.

Suddenly, the light of realization flashes through him.

"Rail Fence Cipher."

One in English, and the other in Chinese, the two of them speak simultaneously. Then, they look at each other with surprise.

Xia Xiqing laughs. "They say that fans take after their idols. It must be true; we seem pretty in sync."

Zhou Ziheng sneers internally. Sorry, but he does not at all want to be idolized by this type of person. However, he has to admit that Xia Xiqing's reaction speed surprised him.

"How do you know about the Rail Fence Cipher?" Zhou Ziheng asks.

Xia Xiqing responds casually, "My nephew is in IT. He and I researched a little cryptography at some point."

Your nephew? Zhou Ziheng frowns at Xia Xiqing. *How old are you?*

He doesn't ask it out loud, and neither does he believe Xia Xiqing's words. He picks up the pen Xia Xiqing found earlier, ready to decode the message.

Xia Xiqing flips the poem over, revealing the "*2 you*" message on the back. Laughing, he says, "The production team was actually pretty obvious with this clue. This '2' here isn't the English word '*to*'—it's hinting at how the message is a two-rail fence, right?"

Zhou Ziheng hums in agreement and starts to count the letters in the message. Finding the center, he draws a line down the middle to separate them into two groups. Though he knows Xia Xiqing should be familiar with the deciphering process for this code, Zhou Ziheng still explains it aloud for the sake of the audience.

"The first half of the poem describes the encryption process, and starting from '*Only disassembly anew*,' hints at the decryption process. Based on the '2' written on the back, we can divide the letters into two groups, each containing seven letters."

PGOEUDE | AENHNRD

"'*Will return you to me, will return me to you*,' should suggest that we rearrange the positions of these two groups." Zhou Ziheng rewrites the two groups in two rows, lining up the letters:

PGOEUDE

AENHNRD

Bent over the code, Zhou Ziheng recites the second-to-last line of the poem, "'*From above to below, connected to each other.'"*

With his pen, Zhou Ziheng draws a line, starting at the P, then going down to the A right below it, then going back up to the G, and so on and so forth across the entire code, drawing the line through every letter until he arrives at the last one, D.

"Then if I write it down in sequence..." Zhou Ziheng carefully writes down the final solution:

PAGEONEHUNDRED

Page one hundred.

"Page one hundred."

Xia Xiqing picks up that incredibly thick book beside him, turning to the one hundredth page. The entire page is covered in characters tiny as ants, but the forty-second line contains four Arabic numerals:

I live only for my desires, for this cliff of fiery passion.

If I could, the moment before my desire burns to ash, I want to be the 1414th rose in the sea of flowers within your heart.

No more, no less, I want to be that exact one.

"1414."

Xia Xiqing puts down the book, walks to the front of the study, and puts these four numbers into the password lock. The lock emits blue light in response, flashing thrice. Then, a green message appears on the screen:

PASSWORD CORRECT!

Xia Xiqing gently tries the door, pushing until he hears a creak. The door is indeed unlocked. Xia Xiqing is about to leave on his own when he notices the close-up camera on the door lock, so he turns back to smile at Zhou Ziheng.

"We can leave now. Shall we?"

Leaning against the desk, Zhou Ziheng takes a long

look at him before finally stuffing his hands into his jacket pockets and walking over.

There's the sound of a new notification.

Please be warned that two players have just escaped their original room and have gone into the room of another player.

"Our alliance is still on?" Zhou Ziheng suddenly asks.

Xia Xiqing smiles and pushes the door fully open. "Of course, if you haven't yet squeezed me dry of all utility."

The words "squeezed" and "dry" are subtle—subtle enough that Zhou Ziheng doesn't even realize that he's being teased as he innocently follows behind Xia Xiqing out of their original room.

The house has a strange layout; there's no hallway between one room and the next, so they open their door and walk right into a new room. The guy in the room is hunched over something when he hears the wall—at least, what he'd thought was a wall—suddenly open behind him. He startles with a shudder.

Dedicated to his character design, Xia Xiqing smiles in greeting at the room's original occupant. "Hi. We're the players who just escaped our first room. You should've gotten the production team's message by now."

The man before them is wearing an oversized hoodie in pastel yellow. His hair looks quite fluffy, and it's been bleached brown. Having turned around toward the sound, he sees Zhou Ziheng and a relieved expression appears on his attractive face.

"Oh, it's Ziheng! I'm so glad it's you." Then he smiles at Xia Xiqing. "Hello, hello... Oh, aren't you the one who recently—a couple days ago on Weibo..." He trails off in an inquisitive tone.

Xia Xiqing considerately introduces himself, "Xia Xiqing." Then, as the guy is about to introduce himself, Xia Xiqing immediately adds, "Shang Sirui, right? I really like your group's songs."

Shang Sirui is the central member of a male idol group called HighFive. He and Zhou Ziheng once worked together on a movie, though Shang Sirui had taken on more of a cameo role. Xia Xiqing doesn't actually like the type of music that idol groups usually make—saying that he does was pure politeness on his part. However, this idol group is pretty well-known by their generation; especially Shang Sirui, who, with his pretty face and somewhat absentminded personality, has become the most popular member.

"Really?" Shang Sirui laughs. "Oh, you escaped so quickly. You must both be amazing at this game. I feel like I've been flailing around blindly this whole time; I still haven't gotten much of anything in terms of useful clues. It's just so weird— what possessed my manager to pick such a hard show for me?"

Xia Xiqing almost laughs out loud. This idol talks like he's doing stand-up comedy. No wonder the internet likes to make fun of the things he says.

"Two is better than one." Zhou Ziheng walks over to Shang Sirui to look over his progress.

Xia Xiqing hadn't realized it when Zhou Ziheng and Shang Sirui stood apart, but now that they're next to each other, Xia Xiqing notices how tall Zhou Ziheng is; how his shoulders are wider. Even Shang Sirui, whose physique is pretty ideal for a member of a male idol group, begins to seem delicate when standing next to Zhou Ziheng. If Xia Xiqing remembers correctly, there's even a shipping fandom for the pairing between these two.

Zhou Ziheng's mega-alpha persona really does fit him well.

Even though both Shang Sirui and Zhou Ziheng have countless fans who follow them only for their looks, the ways in which they're attractive are completely different. Shang Sirui's features are more subtle, giving him a youthful vibe and making him seem young enough to still be in high school. Meanwhile, Zhou Ziheng's features are sharper; there even used to be people who mistook him for being mixed-race.

It is of course the latter aesthetic that's more attractive to Xia Xiqing.

After this round of admiration, Xia Xiqing looks around the room. This space is very different from where he and Zhou Ziheng had come; it's a simply furnished bedroom with a wardrobe made of dark wood, a round table on a wool rug, and a mid-size bed.

Shang Sirui's strategy seems a bit different from theirs—it looks like he gathered up everything that looked like a clue to him and put them on the round table to analyze one by one.

"Ziheng, can you help me see if this stuff is useful in the slightest?"

Zhou Ziheng makes a noise of affirmation and walks over to help him look over the clues.

Xia Xiqing doesn't approach them, instead walking around the modest space. Unlike the study, not much decorates the walls of this room. He feels along the finely textured wallpaper and finds a tiny camera on the wall facing the bed. But it's strange—the camera's scope is limited to a stretch of almost completely bare wall.

Suddenly, he notices two tiny nails on that wall. They

blend in completely with the texture of the wallpaper, and thus would be very difficult to detect. Xia Xiqing reaches out to touch them, sensing something off about it all.

Was there maybe a painting that once hung here?

"Xiqing? You should also come and take a look at these clues. I can't make head or tails of them," Shang Sirui says, waving at Xia Xiqing.

Pulled from his thoughts, Xia Xiqing turns back to see Shang Sirui and Zhou Ziheng crowding around the round table. He hums obediently and walks over to them.

There aren't many clues on the table: a slip of paper, an organizer, and a laptop. As Shang Sirui explains to Zhou Ziheng where he found these clues, Xia Xiqing moves the laptop's cursor. In response, the monitor lights up, showing the interface of an internet browser. The window has three tabs open, and Xia Xiqing clicks through them. The first one contains information about an art exhibition, and the second one is in the middle of pre-ordering a book. Once he clicks to the third one, he comes to a sudden realization.

"Sirui, have you done anything on this laptop?"

His conversation with Zhou Ziheng interrupted, Shang Sirui turns to Xia Xiqing. "Huh? No, I haven't. This laptop has no internet access. Those three webpages were already open when I got here."

Zhou Ziheng glances over. Lit by the light of the laptop monitor, Xia Xiqing blinks slowly, as if very deep in thought.

"What did you find?"

Hearing Zhou Ziheng's voice, Xia Xiqing turns to him. "Do you remember the sticky note in our room? It had something written on the back."

Xia Xiqing is about to continue, but Zhou Ziheng takes the note out of his pocket. Xia Xiqing is surprised; though he's already witnessed how detail-oriented Zhou Ziheng can be, he didn't think it could be to this extent.

"I can't believe you brought it here."

"Who said taking clues was against the rules?" Zhou Ziheng quirks an eyebrow and puts the note down on the table. He pulls a chair over from beside him and sits down, reading the message out loud: "Tonight at 10, see you at Sophia (the restaurant)."

"Sophia?" Shang Sirui asks, frowning.

"Yes." Xia Xiqing moves the laptop so Zhou Ziheng and Shang Sirui can see better. "The last tab is the official webpage of the restaurant 'Sophia.'"

Shang Sirui squints at the screen, then sheepishly scratches his head. "Oh, it's all in English..."

Internally, Xia Xiqing can only shake his head in exasperation. *Can't you have some self-awareness? You're a celebrity!* If this had been a live-stream and didn't have a production team to cut that line in post, Shang Sirui's anti-fans would have a field day—they might even start saying that he's illiterate. His competitors would of course pay to publicize this, and then he'd really never hear the end of it.

"'Rose Day'?" Zhou Ziheng seems to have found something interesting on the webpage.

Shang Sirui looks confused, so Xia Xiqing explains, "It seems to be a couples' event. It says here that on the day of the event, the restaurant will be decorated with thousands of roses, and they'll even have a special menu with food and drinks that contain roses as an ingredient."

"Does this have anything to do with us getting out of the room?" Shang Sirui, bending over at the waist, looks up at Xia Xiqing.

Even though he's kind of at the end of his rope with this

guy, Xia Xiqing smiles gently at him in response. "I don't know either."

At that, Shang Sirui turns his questioning face to Zhou Ziheng, who props his chin on his left hand and pokes at the note with his right index finger. "Two clues have pointed to this restaurant. It can't be meaningless."

He's right. If there had only been one, then it could be just filler detail. But two? It has to have been intentional.

Seeing how confused Shang Sirui seems, Xia Xiqing, who is burdened with an angelic character design, fears he might become embarrassed. Xia Xiqing also fears that the show might be impacted overall, so he tries to shift the focus off this incomplete chain of clues about the restaurant.

"Did you guys find anything from the other clues?"

Xia Xiqing picks up the slip of paper from the table. The front shows a line of characters written in a script that has yet to lose its childishness. The writer must not be too much older than ten.

Dad, the teacher gave me a question today, but I can't solve it. Can you please help me?

Xia Xiqing flips to the back, where a four-digit number is written alongside two empty brackets.

1634 ( ) ( )

Is it a sequence?

But there's so little information given.

Based on their experience from the first room, it doesn't seem like the production team would make things so difficult for their guests. Meaning that, if this was supposed to be some sort of sequence, there should at least be three numbers in the pattern already. But there's only one number here, and it's got four digits. What a headache.

Xia Xiqing looks to Shang Sirui. "Sirui, where did you

find this piece of paper?"

Shang Sirui points at the nightstand. "Over there, but it was the only thing on there."

Xia Xiqing nods. Even though he believes him, he still feels like this kid isn't very careful about things, so he walks over for a closer inspection. Indeed, there's nothing else atop the nightstand, but he still feels like something is off; the crew must have hidden something else. As he walks around the nightstand, searching, he finds a small, easily overlooked wastebasket in the crack between the nightstand and the bed. He takes it out and pours everything in it on the floor.

"Oh wow, I didn't even see that."

Seeing Xia Xiqing's discovery, Shang Sirui immediately stands up and approaches, crouching before Xia Xiqing and mirroring what he's doing. One by one, he unfolds the balls of crumpled paper, spreading each page all out on the floor.

"What's inside all these?"

"I'm not sure either, but the production team deliberately created so much trash—there must have been a reason for it," Xia Xiqing replies, all the while continuing to sort. Finally, he opens up a piece of crumpled paper and sees a couple of equations written on it. He examines it more closely and realizes that it's a half-finished calculation.

"Got it."

Paper in hand, Xia Xiqing stands up and walks over to the round table, where Zhou Ziheng is still looking at the Rose Day advertisement on the restaurant's website. His face wears an unreadable look that, as soon as he sees Shang Sirui and Xia Xiqing, is quickly replaced by his normal expression.

"What did you find?"

"Calculations. Here, don't you think this handwriting looks familiar?"

Xia Xiqing passes the scrap paper to Zhou Ziheng, who takes it and looks it over before setting it on the table, the corners of his lips curving very slightly.

It's such an attractive smirk. Xia Xiqing is momentarily stunned.

Zhou Ziheng really is his exact type.

Wait, he's getting distracted. He's getting distracted by a pretty face.

"The calculations here and the bookmark in the study were written by the same hand. We must be correct in thinking that the sticky note was written by a woman." Zhou Ziheng puts the piece of crumpled paper back on the table. "At this point, we can probably confirm that our protagonist is a married man who's already a father."

"And also possibly having an affair." Xia Xiqing sneers.

Shang Sirui is completely lost. Bewildered, he asks, "How did you two figure that out?"

Xia Xiqing blinks. "Just a random guess."

"Oh," Shang Sirui says, then begins to laugh in an adorably air-headed way. "I feel like I'm not even in the same dimension as you two. You're so in sync with each other! It's like you both instantly understand what the other is saying."

It's not that we're in sync; it's just that we've both got a functional brain, Xia Xiqing thinks.

He picks up a pen and bends down to underline the calculations on that scrap paper. "Anyway, let's look at this first."

The question only gave 1634, and this piece of paper only contains one line of calculations.

$$1 \times 1 \times 1 \times 1 + 6 \times 6 \times 6 \times 6 + 3 \times 3 \times 3 \times 3 + 4 \times 4 \times 4 \times 4 = ?$$

Xia Xiqing quickly works through the equation. He immediately understands, but before he voices his discovery, Zhou Ziheng, still looking at that webpage, beats him to it.

"It's a narcissistic number, isn't it? The four-digit ones are called four-leaf rose numbers."

Xia Xiqing crosses out the question mark in the calculations and writes a number behind the equal sign: 1634.

But wait, how did he know?

"Exactly." Xia Xiqing raises an eyebrow and levels a questioning look at Zhou Ziheng. "How did you know it's a narcissistic number without even working through the calculations?"

Isn't he majoring in physics? How can he be so good at mental arithmetic?

Zhou Ziheng points at the laptop. "Look: the roses on this webpage."

Shang Sirui, who's never been good at arithmetic, had been looking at the webpage alongside Zhou Ziheng and also figured out the secret. "Oh! The roses on here are all the same image, just copy-pasted everywhere. They all look the same and they all have exactly four leaves. And I was wondering why they all felt so off." Quickly, a confused look resurfaces on his pretty face. "But...what's a four-leaf rose number?"

Xia Xiqing points at the equation. "This is the definition itself. See, 1634 is the sum of the fourth powers of its digits. It is a four-digit narcissistic number."

Shang Sirui nods, looking like he only has a hazy notion. Seeing as the two of them knew about this sort of number, he gladly says, "Ah ha! So the rest of the two numbers are also four-leaf rose numbers? We know the answers now?"

This kid is too optimistic. Xia Xiqing feels a headache coming on. He subconsciously twirls the pen in his hand and bluntly answers in the negative, "I don't know the answers." Eyeing Zhou Ziheng, he asks, "Do you know what the other four-leaf rose numbers are?"

Zhou Ziheng shakes his head. "I just know that there are three of them."

Well, he is a physics major, not a mathematics major. Probably the only people with the leisure time to study this stuff would be mathematicians.

Who'd be so bored as to memorize this? Xia Xiqing sighs. He gets a headache every time he encounters anything that requires patience. He pokes at the paper with the tip of his pen.

"So, what do we do? Trial and error?"

"'Til this season ends?" Zhou Ziheng asks self-deprecatingly. "Brute force calculations might not be too useful in situations like these."

"Trial and error? Brute force calculations?" Shang Sirui rubs his face furiously, seeming hopelessly confused. "Are you guys speaking Chinese?"

Xia Xiqing laughs, tucking his too-long hair behind his ear. "Well, the point is that we can't do it by hand, so it's perfectly fine if you didn't understand."

"If only I'd known this show required brains. I'd have gotten my manager to turn it down..."

Shang Sirui is naturally friendly. Hand resting on Xia Xiqing's shoulder, he grins so widely that his eyes become slits, completely abandoning any composure that would befit an idol.

"There's a reason my character design is 'airhead,' after all."

This kid is too fun. In terms of flirting, Xia Xiqing is used to attacking with gentleness. Having done it so much, it's mere habit that makes him turn to Shang Sirui and smile.

"A small correction: even if you are an airhead, you're still a pretty airhead."

"Oh?" Shang Sirui drapes his arm around Xia Xiqing's neck, pulling him very close. "But I feel like you're prettier than I am..." Shang Sirui dissolves into laughter.

Seeing them stand so close to each other, acting all touchy-feely, Zhou Ziheng is so viscerally discomfited that it almost becomes a physical sensation. On one hand, he feels his antipathy for Xia Xiqing deepening, but on the other, he's a little worried about Shang Sirui—the kid's a bit clueless.

The way Xia Xiqing was speaking just now, the tone he used—Zhou Ziheng is certain that it had been flirting. As a person, Xia Xiqing is practically poisonous. No matter who he's talking to, he always smiles so sweetly, as if there's syrup coming out of his eyes.

But is it possible...could he be into Shang Sirui? The idea scares him. Zhou Ziheng frowns and clears his throat, catching the other two's attention.

"I think we must have missed some key clue. The production team wouldn't make it so hard for us guests, and it's practically impossible to solve this by hand."

Xia Xiqing nods in agreement. They wouldn't make it so hard for their guests; especially not the original occupant of this room, Shang Sirui. This room seems easier than their previous room, so there must be some important detail that they missed—otherwise, the chain of clues wouldn't have ended so abruptly here.

It's just that he really doesn't like anything that requires trial and error to complete. Going through each number and checking to see if it works, repeating the calculations thousands of times—this type of tedious work shouldn't be done by humans. At this thought, he chuckles a little.

"Ah, if only my nephew were here. Stuff like narcissistic numbers—that's what they get as practice questions when they first start learning to code. He must've done so many of those questions by now that he might've even memorized the answers."

"Whoa, your nephew? How old is he? Did he start coding in elementary school or something? What sort of family is this? Are you all gods?" Shang Sirui's arm is still draped around Xia Xiqing, and they're so close that almost half his weight is leaning on him.

Xia Xiqing suddenly realizes what he just said. He looks at Zhou Ziheng, and finds Zhou Ziheng looking back at him knowingly. Their weird chemistry resumes.

Zhou Ziheng takes control of the mouse, moving the cursor up to minimize the initial web browser. Then he searches through the desktop and various folders.

Xia Xiqing mutters, "No, you won't find anything like that. There has to be a directory address." He walks back to the garbage bin.

"Hey, what are you doing?"

"There might be a clue. I hope."

He collects all the papers and checks each of them carefully. Some say irrelevant things, some are children's drawings. He stops when he finds one with a single line of text on it—a directory address, just as he expected.

"Under the D: drive." Xia Xiqing passes the paper to Zhou Ziheng, who inputs the address accordingly and finds a file named Rose.exe. After clicking on it, a line is printed.

1634 8208 9474

"Science and technology are the primary productive

force." Xia Xiqing lets out a relieved sigh and copies the numbers down.

Zhou Ziheng leans against the chair, spreading his legs shoulder width apart and shoving his hands inside his pockets. He focuses on sorting out the clues they currently have.

"If this room is like the last one, then the two missing numbers that we've just found should be the password for something in this room. Right now, we don't have anything that requires a password, which means we've missed a clue."

Zhou Ziheng's voice is deep. It reminds Xia Xiqing of the bell ringing on Giotto's Bell Tower, and the sunset at Florence Cathedral. Whenever he walked by, carrying his palette on his back, the deep sound of the tolling bell vibrated through his soul like electricity coursing through his body.

"Umm?"

Xia Xiqing leaves his thoughts behind upon hearing Zhou Ziheng's question.

"What do you think?" Zhou Ziheng looks at him, confused.

Xia Xiqing nods. Even though he missed some context, he can guess that Zhou Ziheng was talking about the missing clue.

"Yes, our goal right now is to find the clue missing from our chain."

He looks at the only clue on the table that they haven't yet solved, the organizer. The thing is the size of his hand, and he begins to flip through it.

Shang Sirui spent most of his time looking around the room, and says as he looks at the organizer, "I found that beside the pillow; I went through it but didn't find anything useful. Most of the things in there are like meeting notes, reminders to pick up the kid, and stuff like that. Oh, and the kid also writes in it; all sorts of random stuff."

A kid?

Xia Xiqing is alarmed. He quickly checks the organizer again, and indeed, there are some notes written in the same childish handwriting that wrote the four-leaf rose number. The notes consist of wishes that his dad would take him out to play, or participate in the parent-teacher meet, and so on.

He goes through it again, but still doesn't find anything worth thinking about.

So why does he feel something isn't right?

Xia Xiqing puts the organizer down and cups his chin, thinking. Zhou Ziheng takes the organizer and plays with it for a while, then suddenly says, "There's a page missing here?"

"Really?" Xia Xiqing raises his head. He didn't notice it before, but there does seem to be a page missing.

"So, in the garbage bin..."

Xia Xiqing suddenly remembers that there was a piece of crumpled paper about the right size for the organizer. It had the same ten-year-old or so kid's handwriting on it. He walks over, kneels, and eventually locates that piece of paper. Shang Sirui goes to him and reads the message that's on it aloud.

"Dad, the pen you gave me fell under the bed and I can't reach it. Can you help me find it?"

Pen?

Zhou Ziheng walks to them and kneels in front of the bed to check its underside. However, the bed goes all the way to the floor with no spare space under it, and seems solid.

Xia Xiqing knocks on the surface of the wood.

Hollow.

The moment he stands up, he spots a camera on a leg of the bed, which only confirms his theory. "We need to move the bed."

"What? Really?" Shang Sirui is doubtful. "I mean, uh, are we sure we're looking in the right place? A pen could mean nothing, and besides, there's so much information in that organizer..."

Zhou Ziheng shakes his head and asks, "Is this paper in the organizer?"

"Of course not, it's ripped out." Shang Sirui doesn't get the point.

Zhou Ziheng nods. "So, if you're the owner of the organizer, why would you rip out one page?"

Shang Sirui stands there, thinking, arms crossed in front of his chest. "Ripped out... I think there are many possibilities. For example, it could be useless? Ah, but I think the whole organizer is kind of pointless. Or it could mean that he doesn't want anyone else to see it?" Shang Sirui suddenly understands the point Zhou Ziheng was trying to make. "He doesn't want people to see it!"

Zhou Ziheng smiles with a rather gratified look.

Xia Xiqing is on one side of the bed, trying to lift it up. Just as he is about to ask for help, he finds that the bed is extremely light and he can do it all on his own.

It sure is a prop...

They easily move the bed away. There's not much under the bed, just a box—or strictly speaking, a safe that requires two lines of passcodes, each with four digits.

There's also a rose on the safe, the stem of which has retained four tiny leaves.

"Wow, I really feel like I got carried by two Masters." Shang Sirui happily picks up the safe and inputs the two passcodes, and after two clicking sounds, the safe opens.

Xia Xiqing smiles in resignation. More like a noob player accidentally stepping into a pro-level game. Zhou Ziheng sees his warm smile and wonders—is Xia Xiqing really into Shang Sirui?

A complete and utter misunderstanding.

"A key!" Shang Sirui takes a key out of the safe eagerly, disregarding everything else. "We can finally leave!"

Xia Xiqing, however, sees that there's something else in the safe—a folder. He opens it and finds a copy of an asset transfer agreement inside. His expression suddenly darkens and he puts the document aside.

Leaning against the wall, Zhou Ziheng quietly observes Xia Xiqing; it's one of his hobbies as an actor. It's strange— did this guy just forget to mask his emotions? He's normally more careful about his facial expressions.

"Is there anything else in there?" he asks.

There is indeed something else inside the safe, and it seems to be an empty medical record folder.

"It's stuck in there." Xia Xiqing tries and fails to remove it from the safe. "Just an empty medical record folder. No name or age or anything on it."

Shang Sirui is not interested in the newly discovered clue. Getting out of the room seems to be the most important goal for him, so he puts the key into the lock on the door. "Hey guys, the key works."

"Careful—you don't know who's outside the door." Zhou Ziheng warns him.

Xia Xiqing laughs and lazily eyes Zhou Ziheng. Their eyes meet again.

You don't know who's inside the door, let alone outside.

Startled, Shang Sirui pulls his hand back. "Wait, so, do we still open it?"

Xia Xiqing walks over to him with a smile and takes the key from him. "Of course we do. We put so much time into finding this key."

He then opens the door with Shang Sirui standing behind him.

Their phones ring again. At the same time, they hear the same ring coming from the new room.

It's an alert for someone getting out of their room.

"Wow..." Shang Sirui turns his head and looks past Xia Xiqing. "This room is big..."

He then sees two girls standing in front of another door in this room. He recognizes one of them from her side profile.

"Hey, it's Cen-Cen-jie..."

The girl whose name he called is in a white dress with a rose-colored belt, and her black hair is long enough to reach her waist. Her makeup is light except for her deep red lipstick. Her aesthetic, though not gorgeous, has a naturally distant vibe to it. She waves at Shang Sirui with a light smile.

"Hi, Sirui."

Xia Xiqing is not into pop songs, but he knows Cen-Cen. She was the lead singer of a band for a while, but she eventually left due to health conditions. She became a solo singer when she recovered, and is known for her influence among female fans.

"Cen-Cen-jie." Seeing a familiar face, Shang Sirui walks over fearlessly. "Are you from this room?"

Cen-Cen shakes her head. "I just came out of mine."

Xia Xiqing checks his phone. Ah, it seems that the two messages announcing the newest escapes had happened at around the same time. They currently stand in a much larger room that seems to serve as a living space.

The structure of this place finally seems clearer to him. This must be a five-room suite, with four outer rooms and a living space in the middle. Their starting room and Shang Sirui's starting room are on the same row, while the starting rooms of these two girls lie on the opposite row. However, only Shang Sirui and Cen-Cen's rooms are connected to this living space, and the rest of them—him, Zhou Ziheng, and the other girl—have to go through someone else's room before they can get to the living space.

Why this setup? Xia Xiqing ponders it over.

He finally notices the girl beside Cen-Cen, who stands there in a black ensemble with a knit top and skirt. She has medium-length hair, delicate makeup, and naturally beautiful eyes.

Xia Xiqing suddenly remembers that the other layman on this show is a girl who's a member of Mensa. That should be her. So she was the first one to escape?

Xia Xiqing realizes that the production team must have assigned them their rooms based on the difficulty level and the guests' personal skills. They wanted to make sure that all of the players could meet in the living space around the same time. After all, they can't make a show out of someone escaping before he or she even sees any other players.

But why would they put Zhou Ziheng and him together in one room? Is it only to increase watchability? That was what Xia Xiqing thought initially, but now he's not so sure. After escaping from two rooms, his impression of the production team, or more precisely, the script writer, has changed. There seems to be a purpose to every single one of his arrangements.

So, why exactly this setup?

Zhou Ziheng is quiet around Cen-Cen. They're both the quiet type, and since they come from two fairly different circles within the greater entertainment industry, they don't have much to talk about.

"Hello everyone. My name is Ruan Xiao," the other girl greets them.

Her aesthetic, contrary to Cen-Cen's, is on the sweeter side of pretty. Xia Xiqing feels that she looks a bit familiar to him, but he's not too certain, so he simply smiles when their eyes meet.

They quickly introduce themselves, then begin to inspect the spacious living area. The area is large, including a semi-open dining room with a big round dining table. There's also a sofa arrangement. On first glance, nothing seems out of place. None of them has much luck with clues.

There's an electronic lock at the entrance, and it's different this time—the touch screen requires two passcodes to open. The first code takes four digits, and there's a number pad with nine numbers to choose from. The second code takes three digits. Xia Xiqing touches the input space for the second code, and the screen instantly displays a keyboard containing twenty-six letters.

So, it needs a word?

"We could try and see?" Shang Sirui suggests.

Ruan Xiao rejects the idea. "Each digit of the code has twenty-six different letters as possibilities. That means twenty-six cubed, or seventeen thousand five hundred and seventy-six possibilities in total."

Shang Sirui laughs awkwardly. "Ah, never mind."

As expected of a member of Mensa—she is astonishingly fast at mental calculations. Xia Xiqing is duly impressed. And she's right—in this game, brute force is the least likely way to solve anything. There should be clues for the codes.

He walks around and sees a circle on the floor beside the sofa. The circle is just big enough for one person to stand in it.

Shang Sirui has followed Xia Xiqing around, and he's paused to read aloud the words written beside the circle: "Elimination seat?"

Xia Xiqing hums in agreement. "Probably where we vote out the Killer."

Shang Sirui lifts a foot as if to step inside the circle. Xia Xiqing stops him, adding, "The method of elimination is probably to drop the supposed Killer down a hole..."

"Ah?" Shang Sirui retracts his foot and laughs nervously. "Are you trying to scare me?"

"Just a guess." Xia Xiqing smiles and turns around. Head up, he meets Zhou Ziheng's gaze, but the kid turns away after seeing Xia Xiqing.

Am I that scary? Xia Xiqing smiles helplessly.

He walks to the door that leads to the other set of rooms and directs his next question at the girls who are in the middle of investigating the fridge: "You two weren't from the same room, right?"

Ruan Xiao shakes her head. "We were in separate rooms." Then she walks over and leads everyone through the door.

"Cen-Cen-jie's room is this one, behind the door." She pushes the door open, and Xia Xiqing smells the scent of roses. He frowns at the overwhelming odor.

The layout of this room is very different from other two.

There are lots of paintings hanging on the walls, and there's an easel by the bed, on which is a blank piece of paper. The layout of the room is that of an art studio, and Xia Xiqing is very familiar with those.

Ruan Xiao takes them to an enormous wardrobe in the left corner. After she opens it, she pushes all the clothes to the side to reveal a door.

"This is the room I started in."

One by one, they go through the door in the wardrobe. Xia Xiqing is six feet tall, and he finds the door a bit cumbersome to go through. He remembers that Zhou Ziheng is taller than him, so he turns around only to find that Zhou Ziheng hasn't been following the rest of them. Hmm. He stands on the other side for a while to wait for him, and eventually, he sees him trying to contort his way through the door. He can't help but laugh at the sight.

"Eh? What's so funny?" Shang Sirui gives Xia Xiqing a confused look.

Xia Xiqing shakes his head, wiping the smile from his lips. "Nothing."

"Let's go then." Shang Sirui tries to drag on Xia Xiqing's sleeve, but finds that he's out of reach, having stayed back to hold the door open for Zhou Ziheng.

Stepping out of the wardrobe, the first thing Zhou Ziheng sees is Xia Xiqing's pretty face. For some strange reason, the way Xia Xiqing smiles makes him feel mocked, and he finds his mood souring. But they're currently on camera, so he can only smile, hide his grumpiness, and thank Xia Xiqing.

"You're welcome."

Is this how a flirtatious guy speaks? Everything that comes out of his mouth seems coquettish.

Ruan Xiao, Cen-Cen, and Shang Sirui walk in front while

Xia Xiqing and Zhou Ziheng walk behind them. This new room seems to be a woman's bedroom—there is a very exquisite vanity table stocked all sorts of cosmetics and perfume. The wardrobe is also filled with lots of expensive outfits and formal ensembles. The white European-style bed has a carved headboard made of solid wood, and above it is the painted portrait of a beautiful woman dressed in black.

"Is this painting famous too?" Surprisingly, Zhou Ziheng is the first to speak.

Xia Xiqing smiles and nods. "Kramskoi's *The Unknown Woman*. It's a very famous portrait."

Shang Sirui turns around, looking impressed. "Wow, I feel like Xiqing is like a walking, talking art encyclopedia."

If you want to know about physics equations and theorems, I can start spouting off facts too. I can also give an introductory summary of world-famous physicists, Zhou Ziheng silently retorts.

In the next instant, he's taken aback by how his childish his thoughts were just now.

Maybe it's because he dislikes Xia Xiqing too much on a personal level—he finds himself uncomfortable even with other people praising such a two-faced guy.

After exchanging a bit of small talk with Xia Xiqing, Shang Sirui shifts his attention to Ruan Xiao. "So, you had to get out of this room before you entered Cen-Cen-jie's room, right? And all by yourself? Wow!"

Ruan Xiao waves her hand, smiling. "Maybe my room is relatively simple." Her smile is sweet, but somehow also formidable.

"What was your puzzle?" Zhou Ziheng asks.

"Hmm, a sliding block puzzle." She walks to the drawer

beside the bed and opens it. In it is the sliding block puzzle she mentioned. "I found this drawer locked, so I was convinced a clue was in it. Then, I went to look for a key. After I solved the sliding block puzzle, a red laser beam appeared."

She presses some buttons inside the puzzle box, and a red laser beam points to the corner of the room. "My door is unusual, with no passcodes or key holes. I didn't know how I could open the door until I found out I could move things around and get the laser beam to reflect onto the metal door handle. Then it just automatically opened."

"Oh wow... I couldn't have gotten out of this room if my life depended on it." Shang Sirui is utterly impressed.

"But you did still manage to escape from your own room, didn't you?" Cen-Cen says, smiling.

"Yeah, with the help of these two masters." Shang Sirui laughs, moving closer to Xia Xiqing.

Xia Xiqing doesn't back away. Instead, having suddenly remembered those seemingly irrelevant clues in his and Shang Sirui's rooms, he turns to Ruan Xiao. "Did you find other information in your room? I mean...any clues you couldn't quite use."

Ruan Xiao's eyebrow twitches slightly, but only for a split second. She smiles. "Hmm, not really. There isn't much in my room."

She's lying.

Xia Xiqing doesn't actually find this response that unreasonable. Ruan Xiao is a smart girl, and acting on the defensive, especially against other smart people, is very normal. Right now, with every player in the room, there's no way she'll give away her clues.

He'll just need to find them on his own, then.

In curiosity and awe alike, Shang Sirui asks Ruan Xiao

about how she unlocked the door of this room. As she solved her own room with Ruan Xiao's help, Cen-Cen simply hangs around. Eventually, the three of them walk together out of the room and into the next, then finally out into the central living space.

Xia Xiqing stays in the room. He follows the specialty camera lenses step by step until he stops in front of the wardrobe. For some reason, his attention is drawn to a small trash can. Taking advantage of the other three having left, he quietly walks over, but discovers that Zhou Ziheng has also approached. It seems that they have once again found themselves thinking in sync.

Zhou Ziheng has also arrived by following the cameras, only he came from the other direction.

"Suspicious?" Xia Xiqing asks. He leans over and empties the trash can onto the floor. Bits and pieces of paper scatter at his feet.

Zhou Ziheng nods. "This game has taught me two things. One, all pieces are valuable pieces."

"And?"

Zhou Ziheng picks up a piece of trash and looks at Xia Xiqing. "Multitasking requires prioritization."

While everyone's focusing on solving puzzles and escaping the room, they've neglected a very important aspect of the game.

"We can solve all the puzzles and escape all the rooms, but if we can't find the Killer, the game is over for us."

He's got a point. The goal of the game is to capture the Killer. Escaping is useless if the Killer manages to get away. If that happens, all their efforts would be wasted.

Xia Xiqing turns it over in his head. If he were the Killer, what would he do?

First, he'd do all he could to hide his identity, as well as any evidence that could reveal his identity. However, it's inevitable for his identity to be revealed eventually, since someone has to die in this game. Secondly—

Zhou Ziheng interrupts, "Everyone is here, so we'll probably start voting for elimination soon."

Very little time is left for the Killer. Xia Xiqing scratches his head and looks at Zhou Ziheng. "If you were the Killer, what would you do right before voting begins?"

They exchange a look, both cognizant of their current danger.

"Kill the one most likely to guess the Killer."

Xia Xiqing smirks and licks his lips. "Exciting!"

Xia Xiqing knows that he himself can't be the Killer, and seeing how much effort Zhou Ziheng is putting into trying to find the Killer, he isn't either—unless he's a good enough of an actor to flawlessly pull off pretending to be an ordinary player.

Xia Xiqing chooses to believe that, despite being one of the most talented actors of his age, Zhou Ziheng is not the Killer. After all, if he were, he probably would've already killed Xia Xiqing.

Regardless, Xia Xiqing is well aware that he himself is currently the most favorable victim. He's a normal player, and he's been responsible for solving way too many clues. Also, the only person that could be considered his ally right now kind of hates him.

"I know you don't believe me, but out of curiosity, how much do you believe of what Ruan Xiao said earlier?" Xia Xiqing asks.

Zhou Ziheng doesn't look up. Instead, he just quietly responds, "She was truthful about how she solved her room, but it's false that her room has no clues."

Saying that, he points at the torn-up pieces of paper on the floor.

Right on.

It seems that he's the only one against whom Zhou Ziheng is prejudiced. Xia Xiqing finds himself strangely pleased at that thought.

The paper shreds are clearly the remnants of what was once a complete document. The two of them work together to piece everything back together. Zhou Ziheng doesn't speak; he's trying to recall the fragmented clues from earlier. He is both afraid that he's missing something, and also afraid that his judgment is clouded in regards to Xia Xiqing due to his first impression of the guy.

Suddenly, Xia Xiqing asks, "Do you believe me when I say I'm not the Killer?"

Zhou Ziheng stares at him, but Xia Xiqing seems unbothered by his penetrating stare. Xia Xiqing wants to know what Zhou Ziheng is trying to find in his eyes. If only he knew what Zhou Ziheng is looking for, then he could give it to him.

A few eternal seconds later, Zhou Ziheng finally admits defeat to the staring contest and continues to piece together the paper shreds, completely ignoring Xia Xiqing's question.

Knowing he won't get a direct answer, Xia Xiqing smiles. "Anyone else you suspect?" he asks, then amends, "I mean, other than me?"

Without raising his head or even any consideration at all, Zhou Ziheng gives in to his desire for a quick retort to Xia Xiqing's question and blurts, "You'll always be my suspect."

In the face of such a double entendre, even an experienced player of the dating game like Xia Xiqing has to pause for a moment.

About three seconds later, Zhou Ziheng finally realizes that he seems to have misspoken. He suddenly looks up, eyes wide with alarm. The thought process of a STEM major had rendered him for a very brief moment unable to tell the difference between "You'll always be a suspect to me," and "You'll always be my suspect." How awkward...

The two sentences have the same subject, the same predicate, and the same object, but a small difference in the bits and pieces that connect those three main elements have caused so much ambiguity. Why must language be so vague and tricky?

"In which case..." Xia Xiqing's voice softens. "I must say I'm honored."

What had been meant as a comeback has been rendered flirtatious. Zhou Ziheng has no one to blame but himself. Speechless, Zhou Ziheng returns to the work at hand.

But Xia Xiqing notices: Zhou Ziheng's ears have turned red.

He was clearly the one who initiated the flirting, so why does he also get to play the blushing maiden?

Negligent arson is still arson!

Under Zhou Ziheng's hands, the pieces of paper begin to slowly come together and turn into a single legible document.

"Divorce... settlement?" He reads it out in a low voice, then recalls the document from Shang Sirui's room.

"The document in the safe earlier—was it an asset transfer agreement?" Zhou Ziheng asks. When he receives no answer, he looks up to see Xia Xiqing staring blankly at the words on the document.

Xia Xiqing doesn't return to himself until Zhou Ziheng

nudges him. With a strange look on his face, he responds hastily, "Oh yes. I think it was."

Despite not knowing Xia Xiqing for long, Zhou Ziheng has seen him wearing many different personalities. However, whatever that was just now was especially odd.

Realizing that his emotions have gotten away from him, Xia Xiqing quickly schools his features. Feeling that he's been staring a bit too much at Xia Xiqing's face, Zhou Ziheng also decides to retreat from this awkward moment. He begins to examine the document in front of them. Strangely enough, the divorce settlement agreement is actually pretty thorough, detailing matters like asset division and the custody of the couple's fourteen-year-old child with very convincing jargon. The production team is really very meticulous.

"Are you finished? I have to tell you something." Xia Xiqing gathers the torn-up pieces of paper and returns them to the trash.

"Come with me." Then he stands up and pulls Zhou Ziheng toward the wardrobe.

Seeing them emerge from the wardrobe, Shang Sirui tries to wave them down.

Zhou Ziheng quickly answers, "We're going search the room for more clues." As he speaks, the hand that was gripping his sleeve shifts to his wrist. "Hey!"

Xia Xiqing pulls Zhou Ziheng further into the room, then shuts the doors.

"What did you want to say?" Zhou Ziheng stares at Xia Xiqing.

Xia Xiqing walks over to the bed and sits down. With the doors closed, the smell of roses in this room is suffocating. "We've met everyone by now, which means that we've already met the Killer."

Zhou Ziheng crosses his arms and nods in agreement.

"Have you noticed that every room has two sets of puzzles? One set is for leaving the room, and the other set seems completely unrelated." Xia Xiqing is in full work mode now, listing off his every deduction. "Things like the note about Sophia, the laptop webpage about the same restaurant, the asset transfer agreement, and the empty medical record, even the divorce settlement agreement in the woman's bedroom. There must be a similar set of clues in this room, too."

Xia Xiqing pauses, looking around.

"What do you think these clues lead?" Zhou Ziheng questions.

Xia Xiqing lies back on the bed. The clues are so scattered that it's giving him a headache. He removes the rubber band tying his hair and scratches his head. As he turns his neck, Xia Xiqing suddenly notices a painting on the wall.

"Well?" Zhou Ziheng asks, "Anything else you want to share?"

Xia Xiqing sits up and approaches the painting. His hair loosely scatters around his ears, making him look all the more gentle. He walks over to the painting and carefully examines it. Then, very firmly, he says, "The owner of this house is having an affair." He looks at Zhou Ziheng. "And his lover is the owner of this room."

"Because the room smells like roses?" Zhou Ziheng actually has his own suspicions, but he did not jump to conclusions given the lack of more convincing evidence.

Xia Xiqing shakes his head. "Not completely." Then he points to the painting. A man in a white shirt has his arms slung around a woman's waist. "This is Fragonard's *The Lock*, a famous painting about the passion of an affair."

Zhou Ziheng walks over to take a closer look at the

painting. As he has no prior knowledge of art, he can only ask, "How can you tell?"

Xia Xiqing enjoys being questioned by Zhou Ziheng; more than that, he also enjoys answering Zhou Ziheng's questions. He smiles and begins to explain, "See the flowers in the bottom right corner? Those are for his lover. But when he enters the room and sees her, the flowers are thrown aside as he embraces her with one arm and reaches out with the other to lock the door. Can you imagine the scene?"

Startled, Zhou Ziheng really does find an image recreating itself in his mind. This guy's really too perverted to always be asking him such things so bluntly. He probably won't be able to look at the word "imagine" the same way again.

To cover up his embarrassment, he frowns and changes the topic. "So what does the painting have to do with the room?"

"It's not just this one. It's all the paintings in this room. They're either themed around love, or they're portraits of men. Look at the easel and the clothes in the wardrobe. All signs point to a female artist." Xia Xiqing walks toward the easel. "I believe the unused clues around this house tell a story, and what an interesting plot it must have."

Like most escape rooms, there's a theme, and that theme will be used to help solve certain riddles. This show, however, doesn't tell you the story before you start the game. Every room seems to be isolated, yet there's a chain of clues—independent of unlocking the room doors—that relies on you to piece it together to unravel the plot as you play. As far as the details of the story, Xia Xiqing has yet to uncover them, finding the existing clues too confusing to put together.

There must be one very important piece of the puzzle that remains hidden.

Examining Xia Xiqing's side profile, Zhou Ziheng notices a long scar along Xia Xiqing's chin. It seems to have endured stitches once upon a time. In truth, Xia Xiqing suits his palate a lot more when he's concentrating. And with that pretty, harmless face of his, he can deceive everyone.

Time is ticking, and Zhou Ziheng is struggling. He's never faced such a hard choice before. It has been a few hours, and the first round of voting is about to start. He doesn't know if anyone will be killed during voting.

Fine...

Resigned, he reaches into his pocket and pulls out a small brown vial, placing it in front of Xia Xiqing.

Surprised, Xia Xiqing casts a glance at Zhou Ziheng as he takes the vial. Zhou Ziheng has an odd look on his face; reluctant and awkward.

Xia Xiqing can't help but laugh. "What's this, hmm?"

That frivolous lilt again. Zhou Ziheng feels vexed in spite of himself; he's even starting to regret sharing his secret clue. He looks at Xia Xiqing's long, slender fingers wrapped around the mouth of the brown vial, almost wanting to take the item back.

Better yet, snatch it back. Now.

Xia Xiqing looks into his eyes with raised eyebrows. "You have anything to say?"

This time, he draws out the end of his sentence even more.

Zhou Ziheng coughs. *Forget it, it's already done.*

"I found this in the living space. It had fallen to a corner of the dining table."

Xia Xiqing examines the bottle, finding it labeled with chemical symbols. As the STEM major, Zhou Ziheng makes himself useful by directly giving the answer to Xia Xiqing.

"It's cyanide. Extremely toxic."

Hearing this, Xia Xiqing freezes. Everything had come together in his mind.

No wonder...

No wonder there was a vase full of white chrysanthemums in the study. No wonder the furniture had been covered in white cloth.

"The owner of this home was murdered." Xia Xiqing looks at Zhou Ziheng, who meets his gaze and gives a light nod of his head.

"Doesn't the story make sense now?" Zhou Ziheng asks.

Yes indeed. Xia Xiqing begins to string it all together. "The owner takes the female artist as a mistress, then attempts to transfer his assets and divorce his wife. Now he's dead..."

"The typical suspect would be the wife," Zhou Ziheng says, then continues, "Upon seeing the divorce settlement, the wife tears it apart and, in a fit of passion, murders her husband."

Xia Xiqing frowns. "The artist very obviously invited the husband to the restaurant. But what if the husband didn't end up going through with the divorce and instead chose to stay with his wife? That way, the lover is equally likely to have committed the murder."

Zhou Ziheng stares at *The Lock*. "That could make sense. Too many hidden messages have come from the paintings."

Without a connoisseur of art like Xia Xiqing, these clues would certainly seem quite vague, but could it be that he's over-analyzing things?

But he could also be right.

"Yeah, the paintings hold a lot of information." At Zhou Ziheng's reminder, Xia Xiqing attempts to sort out the paintings. "Most of these paintings signify affairs. *The Unknown Woman* in the wife's room, and the..."

The Clothed Maja.

Xia Xiqing suddenly remembers what the Maja was wearing in that painting. He gapes for a brief moment before asking, "Have you noticed? The Maja's clothes..."

"Yeah, it's the same outfit Cen-Cen is wearing," Zhou Ziheng agrees.

The players of this game have actually been cast as the various characters of the story.

Xia Xiqing rakes his hand through his hair in disbelief. Then he notices that all the men in the paintings are wearing a collared white button-up shirt. Just like his own.

"So... I've been cast as the husband?"

Not even the players know who they're supposed to be in the story until they solve the puzzle.

Who could have written such an unnerving script?

C.03

Roleplay

Zhou Ziheng frowns. "By that logic, whoever is assigned to a room automatically assumes the role of the character associated with that room. For example, you were dressed by the production team specifically to match your character. But to induce immersion in the game, that information was kept from you."

"All that to set up the moment of realization we just experienced."

Xia Xiqing leans against the back of a chair and puts a foot up on the frame of the easel board. He feels a bit miffed at having been so successfully played by the production team, but then he notices a missing link.

"But you and I both started in the first room, and only the owner should be in that study. If I'm supposed to be the dead husband, then who are you?"

Zhou Ziheng frowns, equally perplexed by this problem. He glances over Xia Xiqing's white shirt, then recalls the outfits of the other players. Finally, he looks down at his own windbreaker.

"The production team didn't arrange my outfit. I came as-is, in my own clothes..." Zhou Ziheng begins to deduce from what he knows. "You're the dead husband, so you were blindfolded and tied up—it's because you're already 'dead.' My role must be to aid you in seeking the truth."

"In that case, you're probably some sort of detective. And if that's true, you'd be on the other side of the fourth wall. The rest of us are characters in a game that you are playing," Xia Xiqing concludes.

Xia Xiqing thinks it over. He's the husband, Ruan Xiao is the wife, Cen-Cen is the lover, Shang Sirui is the child, and, finally, Zhou Ziheng is the detective player who's trying to solve this murder mystery. The Killer of the game is the actual murderer within the plot. This person needs to be found by Zhou Ziheng.

It's like a jigsaw puzzle—they need every single piece, and they also need to put them together correctly before they can see the whole picture.

Xia Xiqing looks at the "vial of poison" in his hand and hands it back to Zhou Ziheng. Then he scratches his head, revealing the slight widow's peak on his forehead. With his peach blossom eyes shining, he says, "Since you told me such a big secret, I'll offer one in return."

I don't want to know your secret, Zhou Ziheng thinks.

Seeing Xia Xiqing's "ask me" face and reminding himself that he is on camera, Zhou Ziheng reluctantly asks, "What's the secret?"

"I'm afraid of the dark."

I knew it. There's not a word of truth in this man's mouth.

Zhou Ziheng quirks his lips a bit. "Oh, really?"

"Yes. Seriously." The smile on Xia Xiqing's face grows a lot more restrained as he turns to look at the easel. "So... If there are any upcoming dark rooms, you should just leave me behind. Wouldn't want me to weigh you down, no?"

As if I'm so eager to keep you around, Zhou Ziheng silently retorts. The atmosphere suddenly turns strange and unfamiliar, putting him at a bit of a loss. This guy is such a practiced liar that Zhou Ziheng can't not be suspicious, but the tone that Xia Xiqing is using seems somehow different his time.

Xia Xiqing very quickly changes his expression and stretches out his legs, one of his extended legs almost but not quite brushing against Zhou Ziheng's shoe. "Now do you believe me when I say I'm not the Killer? You know, given that I'm already dead and all."

Having fallen for this trap before, Zhou Ziheng elects to remain silent. He looks down at Xia Xiqing's dress shoes, his dress pants, and the strip of his ankle showing in between.

How can a man be so fair?

"And, either way, I'm also no longer a suspect," Zhou Ziheng says while avoiding Xia Xiqing's question.

"The remaining three..." Xia Xiqing explains, thinking that most of the clues are pointing toward the female artist, including the painting in the first room. "What do you think of *The Clothed Maja*? Do you think it's hinting at anything? I feel like the other woman might be the prime suspect."

The other woman...

What a harsh way to phrase it.

Looking at his expression, Zhou Ziheng can tell that Xia Xiqing is currently pretty immersed in the game, but he seems to have ignored his own advice from when they were in the first room together.

You never want to be completely immersed in the experience.

Zhou Ziheng tries to pull Xia Xiqing out of it. "The paintings do seem to be giving us a lot of pointers, but think about it. There are so many paintings—almost every room has one. The first one was *The Clothed Maja*, which hints at Cen-Cen's role. The paintings in this room all point toward your role, and most of them also help establish the storyline about the affair. Then there's *The Unknown Woman* in the wife's room—the woman in the portrait is also dressed all in black, so it probably points to Ruan Xiao. The kid's room, however..."

Xia Xiqing, who was half listening and half fiddling with the sheet of paper that's clipped to the easel board, notices something off about it. After a closer inspection, he confirms his suspicions.

It is not a regular sheet of white paper.

Xia Xiqing looks around and finds a paint station on top of the wooden cabinet on the other side of the easel board, so he picks up a wide paintbrush, wets it in the water, then uses it to dilute some watercolor pigments into a more workable paint.

"What are you doing?"

Xia Xiqing grins. "Obviously, I'm painting."

Saying that, he begins to brush down the page with broad strokes of watercolor paint. At first Zhou Ziheng thinks he's just being a weirdo again, but then he notices that there are certain patches of the canvas that seem to repel the paint, slowly revealing a line of white characters as the watercolor sinks into the paper around it.

Xia Xiqing unclips it to show to Zhou Ziheng. "Aha! You see—"

"What are you guys up to?" Shang Sirui voice interrupts.

Xia Xiqing immediately returns the sheet of paper to the

Without looking up, Xia Xiqing puts the finishing touches on his rose. More out of habit than anything else, he puts his signature at the corner—*Tsing*.

Shang Sirui sighs in satisfaction. "It feels so good to have talented friends!"

Xia Xiqing puts down his paintbrush, then turns around and laughs. "You're exaggerating."

Only, the first person he sees when he turns around isn't Shang Sirui—instead, it's Zhou Ziheng.

Has he been standing behind him this whole time? And what's that look on face supposed to mean? He seems slightly upset and also a bit surprised at the same time.

Strange.

Suppressing his urge to laugh, Xia Xiqing stands up and takes down the two sheets of paper clipped to the easel board. As he approaches Zhou Ziheng, he gives them a couple of haphazard folds and stuffs both the rose and the clue into Zhou Ziheng's pocket.

"A present!" Xia Xiqing gives the pocket a pat and gives Zhou Ziheng a smile that looks sweet enough. "Hope you don't mind how messy it is."

They exchange a brief meaningful look before Xia Xiqing walks over to Shang Sirui and wraps an arm around the latter's shoulder. "By the way, there were some divorce documents in Ruan Xiao's room. Did you see them? I think they may have something to do with that thing..."

Xia Xiqing diverts the topic with Shang Sirui, and Zhou Ziheng reaches into his pocket. There's a pleasant warmth to the papers Xia Xiqing gave him.

"Thanks," Zhou Ziheng says to Xia Xiqing's back, half a beat too late.

You should *thank me*, Xia Xiqing thinks, but he simply

gives Zhou Ziheng a wave of acknowledgment over his shoulder, not even bothering to turn around.

The piece of paper had four very simple words written on it in white—*sofa, flashlight, office, darken.*

Not long after his conversation with Shang Sirui, the PA system starts up with an announcement from the production team: "Attention, everyone. There are thirty minutes left until the elimination vote. A timer will start on your phone accordingly. Please consider who you think is the Killer and proceed to the dining table when the time comes to take part in the vote."

So soon? Xia Xiqing feels a bit of anxiety come over him.

It's a little bit like playing Mafia or Werewolf of Miller's Hollow. Everyone is a suspect, and no one knows who's voting for whom. If they're not careful about how they vote, it'll be very easy to condemn an innocent player to exile and thus make the game more difficult afterward.

Then again, it's a reality show, and it's just a game. But Xia Xiqing hates nothing more than getting that GAME OVER that comes from failure. He's the type of person that lives for victory.

He must not make any decisions without solid proof or logic.

Having come to the wife's bedroom together, Xia Xiqing and Shang Sirui find Cen-Cen and Ruan Xiao, who are Xia Xiqing's prime suspects. However, he still has no proof, nor enough clues to make a logical deduction.

As for trying to sound them out in direct conversation... It'd be too obvious.

"Xiqing," Ruan Xiao starts, "I'd like to ask you some questions about art. I'm not very well-versed in that kind of stuff."

"Of course." Xia Xiqing smiles gentlemanly.

Shang Sirui begins chuckling. "For some reason, seeing the two of you together makes me want to imagine a romantic story about a young noblewoman and an artist, hehehe..."

Shang Sirui's comment eases the tension that came from the earlier announcement, but this much-needed comic relief is interrupted by Cen-Cen. Her indifferent face, which has always been expressionless, is now dubious, and the contrast of the deep red lipstick makes her expression look even colder.

"You're an artist? But I don't understand, how did you figure out all those problems so quickly if art was what you studied? Did your artistic abilities help so much?"

While it's a valid question coming from anyone unfamiliar with his background, Xia Xiqing can't help but sense a bit of hostility from Cen-Cen. It makes him feel a little ill at ease— or more accurately, displeased—but Xia Xiqing still replies with a smile.

"I am indeed an artist, but I like math, too—a hobbyist mathematician, if you will. Van Gogh once said in a letter to his brother that his paintings are the results of complicated calculations. You'll find that many great artists have excellent foundations in mathematics."

Shang Sirui chuckles again. "Xiqing is a very good artist, but his math skills really are impressive. Back in the other room, he solved a lot of the puzzles, including the math-heavy ones. He's really god-tier."

Xia Xiqing frowns. There's something strange going on, but Xia Xiqing isn't sure if it's something someone said or just the general atmosphere.

"Is that so?" Cen-Cen smiles. "I was thinking that we don't know how much information would have been given to the

Killer. After all, it's a bit unfair to play without teammates against the rest of us—the Killer may very well be given some extra clues, or even solutions. So...what if you're not just a regular player?"

The way she's asking... Is she trying to sound him out? Or is she trying to divert suspicion from herself? Either way, Xia Xiqing realizes that he's in a dangerous position.

Everyone watches Xia Xiqing for his reaction. When he smiles, it's steady and untroubled by the accusation, warm and friendly in a way that does not at all suit his response:

"If I were the Killer, the first thing I'd do is to kill Zhou Ziheng."

Cen-Cen is surprised by this response. The way she sees it, those two should be allies. "But you've stuck together since you got out of the initial rooms. Aren't you two—"

"What about now? Am I with him right now?" Xia Xiqing crosses his arms and leans against a wall. "Where is Zhou Ziheng now?"

Xia Xiqing sweeps his eyes across the players. Ruan Xiao still lacks any expression, and Cen-Cen has gone silent. Shang Sirui, on the other hand, lets out a few dry laughs.

"No way. It can't be Zhou Ziheng. He's constantly been helping with puzzles."

"So have I." Xia Xiqing blinks. "Haven't I?

"Lemme give you a piece of important information," he continues. "It was much harder for me to escape than it was for Zhou Ziheng. I was blindfolded and tied to a chair, unable to move without his help. Think about it. Why would the game be designed to make it so difficult for the Killer right off the bat? Meanwhile, Zhou Ziheng was given an easy escape. He's been clear-headed from the very beginning. Doesn't that make you suspect that he might have been given the script?"

Cen-Cen stares at Xia Xiqing with a conflicted expression. Xia Xiqing, who has been spouting bullshit with a straight face, looks back at her dauntlessly.

As she makes to leave the room, however, Xia Xiqing stops her. "I would advise against that. If I'm right and you approach him now, then you're walking into your own death."

Cen-Cen freezes. She seems quite reluctant, but Xia Xiqing's reasoning must have convinced her.

Observing the expression on her face, Xia Xiqing smirks internally. For all that mathematics is a favorite hobby, his true calling is in the art of manipulation.

He can't just let himself get voted out like this. Ruan Xiao is the type of person that he wouldn't be able to influence, but Cen-Cen is different. If she originally planned to vote out Xia Xiqing, her plans are certainly disrupted now, which means that he'll have a chance at survival. As for Zhou Ziheng, an extra vote won't hurt an upstanding guy like him.

But who will Shang Sirui vote for? Xia Xiqing turns to him, but the kid is sitting in the corner and staring off into the distance, seemingly preoccupied with something.

"Ignoring the potential suspects for now," Ruan Xiao breaks in, "you still haven't explained these paintings."

Xia Xiqing straightens and nods. He walks over to *The Unknown Woman* and points to it. "Is this what you want to ask about?"

Ruan Xiao looks up at the painting and nods, then adds, "But not just this one—all of them. Every room in this house has a painting and I feel they're all suspicious. They can't have been placed randomly."

Despite knowing less than Xia Xiqing and Zhou Ziheng,

Ruan Xiao still has very sharp and very accurate instincts. Xia Xiqing understands what she's trying to get at.

"You're not wrong, but it's not quite true that *every* room has a painting. Other than the living space..." He glances toward Shang Sirui. "Your room didn't have a painting, no?"

Shang Sirui freezes, then looks thoughtful. "You're right. No painting in my room, and none in the central room either."

Wait, why did he hesitate?

"Your room never had a painting in it? From the start?" Xia Xiqing tries to confirm.

Without hesitation this time, Shang Sirui replies, "No, never."

Xia Xiqing nods, turning away. Cen-Cen takes this chance to suggest that she return to her room to check it over again for any missed clues. She catches Shang Sirui as she's leaving, and asks, "Sirui, can you come help me move the bed? I want to see if there are any clues under it."

Shang Sirui agrees and follows Cen-Cen off to her room.

After so long, Zhou Ziheng should've had enough time to figure out the clue...right? But Xia Xiqing is still a little worried that Cen-Cen and Shang Sirui might disrupt Zhou Ziheng's sleuthing.

The most crucial clue is in Zhou Ziheng's hands right now.

The moment the wardrobe door shuts, Ruan Xiao takes a piece of paper out from her handbag and wordlessly gives it to Xia Xiqing.

This move comes out of the blue, but it is well within reason. As he expects, Ruan Xiao is a smart person. In making such a decision, the odds are that she has ruled him out as a suspect.

Xia Xiqing looks the paper over.

It's a page from a medical record. One particular line catches Xia Xiqing's eye:

Patient (14M) Diagnosis: Bipolar Disorder

Bipolar Disorder...which causes both depressive and manic episodes, either of which might result in unexpected and extreme behavior.

"Where did you find this?" Xia Xiqing asks in shock, thinking back to the empty medical record folder in Shang Sirui's room.

"In Shang Sirui's room, well-hidden in a jacket in the wardrobe," Ruan Xiao replies softly. "Very well-hidden, as if whoever did so didn't want it to be found. I don't think the production team was behind it."

Wrong.

He's been wrong since the start.

Xia Xiqing leans against the wall, trying to quickly collect his thoughts and remember their initial encounter. It seems that every action, every word, has been a part of a carefully crafted play—only it's Xia Xiqing being played.

In programs like this one, it's inevitable for someone to be designated the "Muggle" of the game—the one player almost completely oblivious to the more intricate goings-on. Xia Xiqing had pinned this character design on Shang Sirui, and he couldn't have been more wrong. The one who actually got assigned as "Muggle" by the production team must be Cen-Cen. Moreover, Xia Xiqing's existing prejudices against adulterers had clouded his judgment.

He quickly tries to figure out what strategy the Killer might have. If he manages to take full advantage of this voting phase, then he might be able to take out two regular players—one with the built-in power he has by virtue of being the Killer, and another via voting.

As for who the Killer would want to eliminate—it is unquestionably Zhou Ziheng and Xia Xiqing.

Upon this realization, Xia Xiqing turns to Ruan Xiao. "You're going to help me make a play."

Ruan Xiao frowns. At this point in the game, with the votes happening so soon, they should by all rights be trying to win the trust of the remaining regular players in order to ensure survival. Xia Xiqing clearly knows who the Killer is already, so what type of play is he trying to make? "What are you trying to do?"

Xia Xiqing rakes his hand through his hair. He licks his slightly chapped lips, then says, "Kamikaze."

Cen-Cen looks anxiously at the empty space beneath the bed. "Still nothing?" She turns to Shang Sirui. "What do we do now?"

Shang Sirui sighs, then replies, "I guess we wait for the voting phase." He takes out his phone to look at the countdown. "Thirteen minutes."

"Who do we vote for then? Still the one we previously agreed on?"

Shang Sirui puffs his cheeks out a little, frowning like a child who was denied sweets. "Cen-Cen-jie, are you really so convinced by Xia Xiqing? Do you really think Zhou Ziheng is the Killer? It's just—I don't think so. He just doesn't act the way a bad guy would act, you know? And we already know that he's super smart, so it makes sense that he'd be good at these puzzles. It doesn't necessarily mean that he has outside information. I feel like what we should be doing right now is voting off the most suspicious person as soon as possible."

Cen-Cen pauses, then uncertainly asks, "Should we...try

to convince Zhou Ziheng to side with us?"

Shang Sirui shakes his head. "It's probably a lost cause. He's been allied with Xia Xiqing since the start. I doubt he'd suddenly turn on him. And Ruan Xiao has already agreed to vote with us, so if we all vote together..." He trails off, having suddenly heard something.

He quietly opens the wardrobe door, letting in the sound of Ruan Xiao's voice: "Okay, you've convinced me. We can vote for Zhou Ziheng together."

Then comes the sound of Xia Xiqing's voice: "Trust me, it has to be him."

Hearing their footsteps approach, Shang Sirui quickly backs up. Xia Xiqing and Ruan Xiao exit the wardrobe to see Shang Sirui and Cen-Cen standing between the bed and the empty space it once occupied.

"Did you find anything?" Xia Xiqing asks.

Shang Sirui heaves a sigh. "Nope. I feel like we've already found everything there is to be found."

Xia Xiqing raises his eyebrow, then gives Ruan Xiao a meaningful look. "I think I'll go find Ziheng now. You guys wanna come with?"

Ruan Xiao and Cen-Cen meet each other's eyes. Cen-Cen seems to be optically signaling something to Ruan Xiao, who hesitates, then says, "I... umm... I think I'll stay here for now."

Shang Sirui seems pretty relieved by this.

Seeing that these three seem intent on staying together, Xia Xiqing is also quite relieved. Being careful not to show it on his face, he walks out of the room, thoughtfully shutting the door behind him.

If he's not mistaken, Cen-Cen and Shang Sirui will do their best to convince Ruan Xiao to add her vote to theirs and vote Xia Xiqing out. This way, Ruan Xiao should be able to keep them occupied and therefore buy invaluable time for Xia Xiqing and Zhou Ziheng to find more evidence.

Shang Sirui isn't stupid. Once he realizes that things aren't quite going to plan, he'll naturally try to kill Xia Xiqing out of desperation—and that's exactly what Xia Xiqing needs. As long as Shang Sirui uses his automatic kill on Xia Xiqing, then Zhou Ziheng will be protected from harm.

But before that happens, Xia Xiqing has to find enough evidence to convince Zhou Ziheng that Shang Sirui is the Killer. Otherwise, given Zhou Ziheng's sub-par predisposition toward Xia Xiqing, he might not take him at face value.

The living area is empty. Xia Xiqing doesn't know where Zhou Ziheng is, and he's running out of time.

He takes out his phone and glances at the timer—eight minutes.

Briskly striding into Shang Sirui's room, Xia Xiqing rolls up his sleeves and heads directly for that empty stretch of wall that's monitored by a camera. It's just as he remembered—there are in fact two nails here.

There *has* to have been a painting here.

Xia Xiqing grabs all the clothing from the wardrobe and lays it out on the floor. Staring at the empty wardrobe, Xia Xiqing tries to put himself in Shang Sirui's shoes.

Judging from the other paintings, this one would have been in a frame too, unless he removed it—*no*, too troublesome, and there aren't any tools with which to disassemble it. It has to still be intact. Also, Shang Sirui couldn't even remove the contents of the medical record from the room, let alone a sizable painting.

Xia Xiqing takes a glance around. It's got to be in this room *somewhere*.

But where?

Time is tight. Xia Xiqing's palms start to sweat.

He breathes deeply in, trying to calm himself down as he scans the area. The room isn't very big. There aren't many places that can hide a painting.

The rug? No way; they've been walking all over it. Xia Xiqing lifts up a corner and finds nothing. The table? Probably not, but he still bends down to make sure. As expected—nothing.

It can't be anywhere obvious.

He goes to the storage tower by the bed and opens all its drawers. Nothing. A painting wouldn't even fit in here, anyway.

Then, his gaze pauses on the bed.

Suddenly, Xia Xiqing remembers that when they found the clue in the organizer about the pen being under the bed, Shang Sirui had been somewhat reluctant to move it.

Considering how he'd looked when it'd been first suggested... No, he's certain now, there has to be something up with the bed. He immediately strips it, layer by layer, until even the mattress is on the floor, leaving only the empty board beneath.

Nothing. Still nothing.

Impossible.

Once again, Xia Xiqing tries to see things from Shang Sirui's perspective. Remembering his words, his expressions, he tries to think.

His memory isn't perfect, but he is certain of one thing— Shang Sirui did not want to move the bed, so moving the bed must risk discovery in some way.

Suddenly, Xia Xiqing thinks of something that's almost impossible.

He starts to move the bed. More precisely, he starts to

lift the bed, tilting it up until it's standing on its side and propped up against the wall. This way, its entire underside is revealed.

And voila! There's a painting haphazardly taped to the very bottom.

The subject of the painting is a handsome young man with brown hair. Wrapped around him is a feminine creature with a beastly body but a beautiful face. Her claws have a tight hold on his chest, and her gaze is full of temptation.

Xia Xiqing recognizes this painting. It's *Oedipus and the Sphinx* by Gustav Morrow.

Oedipus is probably the most tragic and the most infamous figure of Greek mythology. He was an intelligent king, a paragon of mortal virtue, yet he was ultimately unable to escape the prophecy of patricide that haunted him.

"Oedipus... Patricide... He killed his father!" Xia Xiqing furrows his brow. Of course. He's been deceived since the start.

This painting is the biggest clue regarding the Killer. The adulterous father; the parents too preoccupied with their own worsening relationship to spare any love or attention for their child.

A son who can only communicate with his father through paper notes—that'd be when he's in a depressive episode. And when he's in a manic episode, the overwhelming sense that his father betrayed him, betrayed his entire family, causes him to commit the unthinkable.

The plot is so realistically chilling. But right now, time's too tight for him to dwell on any visceral reactions to this realization. He kneels and starts to rip off the tape. But it's stuck on too well—he can't get the painting loose.

"Xiqing? Xiqing, where did you go?"

It's Shang Sirui calling for him.

Xia Xiqing's heart starts to pound. He weighs the urgency of the matter as quickly as he can and decides to abandon his quest to take the painting.

But something like this can't be known by him alone. He has to tell the others. He originally intended to take this painting to Zhou Ziheng, or that kid would never believe him otherwise. But it's too late now; he'll have to just explain it to him.

He's running out of time. Shang Sirui won't wait much longer.

Before he's killed, Xia Xiqing will give Zhou Ziheng the best possible chance at victory.

Xia Xiqing heads over to the door between the current room and his original room. With luck, he'll find Zhou Ziheng in the study. If not, well, he's kind of screwed, as Shang Sirui is approaching from the other side and blocking their way to the voting area.

Beyond the door that leads to the study is a sea of pitch-black.

In an instant, he feels short of breath, even light-headed.

He hesitates, his feet disobeying him by pausing in face of the shadowy depths ahead. The blackness of the room slowly consumes him, like a black hole that stretches into infinity and beyond. Tar-like, it encroaches past the boundary between light and darkness and latches on to him, sucking in his toes, his feet, his calves...forcibly dragging him deeper and deeper.

He can't stand it.

He gropes for the light switch, but before he can find it, someone else's hand grabs his wrist and pulls him further inside. He really can't stand it. Just as he's about to let fly the expletives at the tip of his tongue, that unreasonable hand on his wrist shifts and pins him against the wall, covering even his mouth.

"Shh... I found the clue. We can escape now..."

It's Zhou Ziheng.

With every inch of his being in the midst of a fight-or-flight response, Xia Xiqing doesn't even ask Zhou Ziheng how he knew it was him coming into the study. He clearly could not have seen a thing.

On the other side of the door, Shang Sirui's voice is getting louder and closer.

Unable to speak around the hand over his mouth and unable also to wrestle his way free of Zhou Ziheng's strength, Xia Xiqing bites down on Zhou Ziheng's palm.

"Ow—what are you doing!?" Zhou Ziheng lets go.

"I can't escape anymore," Xia Xiqing replies. He's leaning against the wall and panting, his voice slightly hoarse. He gropes in the darkness for Zhou Ziheng's hand and grasps it. Low and urgent, he says, "Shang Sirui is the Killer. Please believe me. I swear I'm not lying to you this time."

The way he says it is so urgent and panicky. Zhou Ziheng's heart pounds against his ribcage—strange, he doesn't know why his heart rate is picking up. Maybe because Xia Xiqing's behavior in the darkness of the study is simply too foreign.

Before anything else can be said, that tinny voice descends from the ceiling:

"Player Xia Xiqing has been killed. Player Xia Xiqing is now dead."

The death announcement repeats over the PA system, flooding the pitch-black room.

For all that he can see nothing beyond the darkness that surrounds them, Zhou Ziheng can still feel the loosening of the pair of cold hands gripping him, fingers slowly leaving the rapid fluttering of the pulse points at his wrists.

"Starting now, player Xia Xiqing has lost the right to speak. Please proceed to the elimination zone in the living space."

Zhou Ziheng reaches for the light switch and turns on the lights. Xia Xiqing is standing against the wall. Fine beads of perspiration have condensed on his brow, and he's looking down, his head half-drooped and his lips paper-pale. His chest rises and falls shallowly.

For some reason, Zhou Ziheng can't help but associate the Xia Xiqing of this moment with that rose he painted earlier.

Xia Xiqing's words suddenly return to him, resurfacing in his thoughts.

I'm afraid of the dark.

Yes. Seriously. If there are any upcoming dark rooms, you should just leave me behind. Wouldn't want me to weigh you down, no?

He was actually telling the truth.

He really is afraid of the dark.

From their very first meeting, Zhou Ziheng has had the impression that Xia Xiqing is villainous but strong—too crafty, too confident, too clever. This type of person would never have any major weaknesses. Yet right now, Xia Xiqing's weakness has been laid bare before him.

The complexities of Zhou Ziheng's current feelings are indescribable. There's a sense of gratification, like he's on the receiving end of some sort of special privilege. At the same time, there's also an aberrant surge of protectiveness.

But no. It can't be. How can "protectiveness" be applied to someone like Xia Xiqing?

It must be that the perverseness of this reality show has

finally driven him insane.

Xia Xiqing leans motionlessly against the wall, seemingly still in the midst of recovery.

The clever and crafty villain is the first to die. Zhou Ziheng has strangely complicated feelings about this.

Of course, clever people tend to be made a target in this type of game. But Zhou Ziheng doesn't get it—why didn't Xia Xiqing play dumb?

Zhou Ziheng can't have known that Xia Xiqing has been purposefully drawing attention to himself for the past half an hour—ever since the timer started. If the Killer's attention is fully occupied by Xia Xiqing, then Zhou Ziheng might be able to safely escape.

To Xia Xiqing, as long as the Killer doesn't win, his own sacrifice won't count as a loss.

Xia Xiqing places a hand on the wall. Then, slowly, he straightens himself up and walks wordlessly out the door.

"Hey..."

Xia Xiqing turns around, but he doesn't meet Zhou Ziheng's eyes. Silently, he places his index finger to his lips in a shushing gesture. His bangs are mussed, falling messily over his face and covering the beauty mark on the tip of his nose.

He's already lost the right to speak.

Zhou Ziheng doesn't try to speak again. They silently exit the study and continue into the central living area.

Cen-Cen, Ruan Xiao, and Shang Sirui are all standing there already. Ruan Xiao wears a serious expression, as if she already knew this would happen. Cen-Cen also looks quite uneasy. Her attention flits between them, looking first at Xia Xiqing, then to Zhou Ziheng following behind.

Xia Xiqing feels somewhat recovered. He doesn't particularly want other people to see his weak side—even if the other person in question is Zhou Ziheng. Especially if it's Zhou Ziheng.

Xia Xiqing smirks as he walks toward the exit. This habitual smirk of his does not at all belong on the face of someone who's just lost. He looks to Shang Sirui, his "murderer." The kid has really exceeded the limits of the dramatic training expected of an idol like him.

For all that he seems a little stunned at first, he quickly recovers his composure and turns it into bewilderment. "Xiqing, you..."

Impressive. Honestly, Xia Xiqing can only blame himself. He's always been the type of clever that only ever treated other clever people as being worthy of interest and vigilance alike. Those relegated to the category of not-smart-enough have always been, to Xia Xiqing, no better than pets—cute and silly, but also daft and helpless.

Bad habits are the breeding grounds for failure.

But Xia Xiqing doesn't feel like he's failed. As long as Zhou Ziheng succeeds, he still wins.

He doesn't respond to Shang Sirui's trailed-off question. He merely raises his hand, pinches together his thumb and index finger, then draws them horizontally across his lips, zipping them shut. Then, he slowly walks toward that small marked circle in the corner of the room and steps inside it meekly.

Zhou Ziheng doesn't want to look at him. He looks everywhere except at Xia Xiqing—the dining table, the sofa, the carpet. Only once his other options are exhausted does he finally set his gaze on Xia Xiqing.

Having gone a full circle, it's as if he didn't set out with the intention of looking at him.

Xia Xiqing meets Zhou Ziheng's gaze. He tilts his head slightly, then grins, all white teeth and brilliance. It stabs, needle-like, into Zhou Ziheng. Even after looking away, he can't stop mentally replaying that adorable grin.

When he tilts his head, his overgrown bangs brush across the tip of his nose, strand by strand by strand.

Unbelievable. He's clearly about to be kicked from the game. Yet he's still smiling...

"Player Xia Xiqing will be eliminated in three, two, one."

Suddenly, the circle of floor beneath Xia Xiqing disappears. Xia Xiqing, too, disappears, falling through the hole and getting killed out of the game.

Zhou Ziheng stares at that trap door, feeling strangely ill at ease.

Cen-Cen breaks the silence first. "So Xia Xiqing was right? Ziheng, you really are the Killer?"

Ruan Xiao wants to defend Zhou Ziheng, but then she remembers what Xia Xiqing advised her to do before he got killed and swallows it back.

Zhou Ziheng turns around. Hands tucked in his pockets, he calmly says, "If I were the Killer, I would indeed prioritize killing him." He grins. "He's too smart to let live. It really is a pity."

"A pity?" Cen-Cen asks. "A pity that he was killed?"

"A pity that I'm not the Killer, that I couldn't kill him myself." Zhou Ziheng calmly says these somewhat chilling words before he walks over to the dining table and sits down. "Less than a minute left, let's all gather up and vote."

Cen-Cen sits down beside Zhou Ziheng. "How can you prove that you're not?"

Zhou Ziheng rubs his chin and raises his eyebrows. "If I were, I wouldn't have helped him out of his handcuffs at the beginning of the game."

Cen-Cen doesn't seem to be finished with this line of questioning, but she's interrupted by the PA.

"Time's up! The first round of voting has begun."

Cen-Cen doesn't seem to buy his explanation. After all, she did watch him and the freshly-killed Xia Xiqing walk out of the same room. That fact alone seems like a pretty convincing argument to her.

"Whether you admit it or not, I guess we'll find out after we vote."

"No, we won't." Zhou Ziheng chuckles. "Even if you vote me out, you won't know who the Killer is, and you won't find until the game ends and you lose utterly and completely."

Cen-Cen has no retort for that. Shang Sirui and Ruan Xiao also approach and sit down. Cen-Cen gives Ruan Xiao a meaningful glance, and Ruan Xiao nods, still saying nothing.

For all that Zhou Ziheng appears calm on the outside, he is nevertheless still a little nervous. Cen-Cen seems convinced that he's the Killer, so her vote will likely reflect that. And if Xia Xiqing is right about Shang Sirui being the killer, then Shang Sirui's vote would also be one to vote him out. As for Ruan Xiao...

Zhou Ziheng hasn't interacted much with Ruan Xiao, but it seems that she's formed a bit of an alliance with Cen-Cen.

He'd be lying if he said he was calm. His palms are getting clammy.

"Attention, all remaining players. Please submit your votes on your phones. You have only one vote, so please be sure before submitting it. You have ten seconds, starting now.

"Ten... Nine...."

It's strange.

At this moment, what flashes to mind for Zhou Ziheng is the smile Xia Xiqing had right before he was ejected from the room, and also what he'd so confidently said back when they were in the dark.

"Eight... Seven..."

Shang Sirui is the Killer. Please believe me.

It was as if Xia Xiqing already knew how the game would end.

"Six... Five... Four..."

As much as he hates to admit it, the only true ally he has in this game is Xia Xiqing. If he gets eliminated because he trusts Xia Xiqing, then so be it. Plus, he was already suspicious of Shang Sirui. He just lacked the proof.

"Three... Two..."

Zhou Ziheng selects his vote, then hits submit without hesitating.

"One... Voting is now over. Please stand by as the votes are totaled."

The four of them sit around the dining table, staring at each other. The atmosphere is tense. Zhou Ziheng's eyes are focused on Shang Sirui like he's a cheetah preparing to pounce on his prey. Shang Sirui looks down, avoiding his gaze.

Truth be told, Shang Sirui really doesn't look like he's that good at lying, but Zhou Ziheng is still going to trust in Xia Xiqing's judgment.

"The votes have been totaled. According to the anonymous vote, the person to be eliminated this round is..."

The PA pauses. Zhou Ziheng finds his heart rate quickening.

If he dies, what will happen to the information he has?

He'd be forced to give out his clues in front of all three

of them, if he wanted to share his information. But then the Killer would be guaranteed to win, no matter which of these three is really the Killer.

At this thought, Zhou Ziheng can't help but despair.

"No one!" The PA continues. "The votes have resulted in a tie, so no player will be eliminated as a result. The game may now resume."

This result is a bit unexpected, especially to Cen-Cen, who glances first at Shang Sirui, then at Ruan Xiao. "Which of you didn't vote for him?"

Ruan Xiao puts on an innocent frown. "Well, *I* did."

Zhou Ziheng, as an outsider to this coalition, observes them closely. Throughout the exchange, Ruan Xiao kept fidgeting, tapping the table with a finger. Meanwhile, Shang Sirui seems strangely unsurprised by this result.

Knowing who he voted for, Zhou Ziheng can easily deduce the rest. Since Shang Sirui would have surely voted for him, if Cen-Cen voted for him as well, then Ruan Xiao must've caused the tie by voting for Shang Sirui.

Upon ascertaining how the players stood, it becomes even more evident that Shang Sirui must be the Killer. And for Xia Xiqing to have been killed so quickly—he must have found evidence of that.

Zhou Ziheng currently has all the clues needed for escaping the house—it's not even necessary for him to prove Shang Sirui's identity at this point. All Zhou Ziheng needs to do is escape, then it's game over.

At that thought, Zhou Ziheng stands up.

"Where are you going, Ziheng?" Cen-Cen asks.

"I want to go look for more clues," he replies. "No one was eliminated, but we can't just sit here; we still have to escape."

He heads straight for the study, but as expected, Shang

Sirui calls out, "Ziheng, I can come along."

Zhou Ziheng makes no attempt to stop him. "Sure."

And so the two of them enter the study.

The study is practically the same as it's always been. Shang Sirui gently closes the door, then asks, as if just trying to feel him out, "Hey Ziheng, who did you vote for?"

Zhou Ziheng, pretending to look carefully around the room for clues, throws the question right back at Shang Sirui. "Who did you vote for?"

"Oh, I forfeited my vote." Shang Sirui glances around the room, then casually sits down at the desk. "I didn't know anything, so I figured that it was better to not vote at all than to accidentally vote out an innocent."

Forfeited vote? Clever answer.

Zhou Ziheng looks at him, then nods. "That's fair."

He walks over to Shang Sirui. The chair he's sitting on is the same as the one Zhou Ziheng had been on at the beginning of the game. It's a well-crafted office chair with armrests at its sides.

Perhaps it's because he's nervous, but the hand Shang Sirui has on the armrest is slightly trembling. To hide that, he grips the armrest and tries to look more normal.

But Zhou Ziheng sees it. Shifting his gaze, he says, "Now that Xia Xiqing is out of the game, I feel like I need a new ally." He digs into his pocket and pulls out a piece of paper. He puts it on the desk in front of Shang Sirui. "Look, this is an important clue I found." As he speaks, he reaches into his other pocket.

"Clue?" Shang Sirui leans forward for a better look.

In the two seconds that Shang Sirui is focused on the so-called clue, Zhou Ziheng takes out the handcuffs that he picked up near the record player where Xia Xiqing had left them and swiftly chains Shang Sirui's wrist to the office chair.

And Shang Sirui finally realizes the paper in front of him is blank.

Zhou Ziheng picks up a length of rope from the floor and begins to tie Shang Sirui to the chair.

"Ziheng! Hey! What are you doing?" Shang Sirui flails but Zhou Ziheng shows no signs of stopping.

"You've got the wrong guy! Or are you the Killer?" Shang Sirui continues to struggle, and Zhou Ziheng continues tying him up.

"Shh," he says. "Drop the act. The game will be over soon."

His work done, Zhou Ziheng extends a leg and pushes firmly against the base of the office chair, sending it along with Shang Sirui all the way across the room.

"Sorry! How about you take a little break?!"

No matter how Shang Sirui squirms, he can't escape. He can only watch as Zhou Ziheng walks out of the study and shuts the door.

Little does he know, Zhou Ziheng already had all the clues needed to escape this house before he stood up from the dining table. The only reason he led Shang Sirui here at all was to trap him so Shang Sirui would not preemptively use his identity as the Killer when he finally cracks the case open.

Prior to all this, back when Xia Xiqing was keeping everyone else busy, Zhou Ziheng had opened Xia Xiqing's painting. In accordance with the clue of "*sofa, flashlight, office, darken*," he assembled a flashlight out of a bunch of parts left scattered under the sofa. After searching around, he discovered some text that's only visible by flashlight.

It's at the front door to the house. There is one sentence written beside the input pad for the three-digit password.

Who is the Killer?

But that's just one of the passcodes; there's still another one. Then he remembered the second half of the clue. He turned off the lights in the study and found glowing red writing in each corner of the room—2, 3, 7, and the English word "*prime*."

As a STEM student, Zhou Ziheng quickly realized that, between the written numbers, the only possible missing digit that's also a prime number is 5.

He strides briskly from the study straight to the living area, and Shang Sirui's yelling still is clearly audible.

"What's wrong with Sirui?" Cen-Cen heads toward the study.

But Ruan Xiao stops her. "Cen-Cen-jie, wait just for a bit."

"Wait? What for?"

Meanwhile, Zhou Ziheng is already at the front door, rapidly entering the corresponding passcodes:

2, 3, 5, 7

Then, at the second input:

SON

The Killer is the son.

The touch screen turns blue. Then, three flashes, and green text appears:

PASSWORD CORRECT

Congratulations, you have escaped!

The door opens with a muffled bang.

Zhou Ziheng looks straight ahead as he walks out. He had a very clear idea of what would likely be outside—cameras, or maybe members of the crew. He's even thought ahead about what to say.

But he never expected that the first thing he sees after such a tense and sweat-inducing moment of escape would be Xia Xiqing standing on the other side of the door.

Xia Xiqing is still in his white dress shirt. The crew is behind him, and the spotlight highlights the contour of his shoulders, shining past it to land at Zhou Ziheng's left breast. Xia Xiqing's face is shadowed, his features indistinct save for the curve of his smile.

"Excellent."

As soon as it's said, Xia Xiqing steps forward and pulls him into a tight embrace, the kind that men tend to use when celebrating victory.

Zhou Ziheng is a bit stunned, so he allows this hug to be stolen from him by this sly man without offering even a token resistance.

It's strange. Xia Xiqing smells different. The smell of tobacco has faded, and the scent of musk has been buried. Instead, Zhou Ziheng has been softly enveloped in a woodsy fragrance. The scent, the warmth, the touch of a palm against his spine, and a tone of voice that always makes this man seem like he's being insincere.

"I just knew that we'd win!"

The game took about five hours to film, having gone from seven in the evening to midnight, so the crew has been here for quite some time. When Zhou Ziheng emerges from the door, almost everyone backstage starts to cheer.

Ruan Xiao and Cen-Cen follow Zhou Ziheng out of the house and are immediately greeted by the film crew with party crackers and confetti.

Cen-Cen is still confused. "Did we win or lose?"

Ruan Xiao laughs. "We're the second ones out! And we scored pretty well, too."

Cen-Cen looks shocked. "So... Zhou Ziheng's not the Killer?"

Xia Xiqing grins jokingly and says, "No, I am!"

Cen-Cen stares at him, shocked.

Ruan Xiao gives him a playful shove. "Stop teasing her."

While the shove wasn't serious, she's still managed to knock him directly into Zhou Ziheng, who reflexively catches him by the arm to help him right himself. In the process, Xia Xiqing's hair brushes lightly across Zhou Ziheng's chin, sending a strange tickle through him.

Xia Xiqing didn't expect Ruan Xiao to throw him off-balance, and he glances back with some surprise when Zhou Ziheng reaches out to steady him. Their eyes meet. He quickly regains his composure.

"Thanks," he says softly.

The word is just like that inadvertent sweep of his hair earlier. Xia Xiqing takes the initiative to back away a little. Acting like nothing happened, he continues to joke.

"Ruan Xiao, you look so soft and cute; I didn't realize you're so freakishly strong!"

"Well, why would I go around proclaiming that I got into Mensa through brawn?" Ruan Xiao arcs her spine in a stretch. "I was so nervous in there, but now that we're out, I'm suddenly starving."

"Yeah! I'm hungry too..." Cen-Cen agrees.

Zhou Ziheng offers a rare suggestion. "Let's go out for a late-night supper, then?"

"Okay!" Ruan Xiao wraps her arm around Cen-Cen. "Let's go for hotpot!"

Hotpot discussion is already in progress when Xia Xiqing

realizes something is off. He sweeps his eyes around them, then glances into the doorway before voicing his doubt, "Hey, where's Sirui?"

"Oh, Sirui!" Ruan Xiao suddenly remembers. "I heard him yelling in the study before we left."

The sound of celebration has totally drowned out Shang Sirui's cries for help.

When everyone gets to the study, they discover Shang Sirui still tied to the office chair where he was left by Zhou Ziheng. He has already given up crying for help.

"Oh, you've finally remembered about me," says Shang Sirui. His head had been tilted back, leaning on the headrest as he stares at the ceiling, but he sat up straight the moment he heard the door.

They all bowl over with laughter. Zhou Ziheng feels like laughing too, but it seems inopportune for him to laugh now, so he could only stifle his laughter as he walks over and frees Shang Sirui from the chair.

"It's just—Ziheng, why so serious?" Shang Sirui stands up and stretches out his limbs. "Handcuffs alone weren't enough? You just had to use rope?"

"It was exactly like this when we were first put in this room."

Zhou Ziheng unties the rope and tosses it aside, then looks at the handcuffs and realizes he doesn't have the key. Just when he's about to turn around to search for it, a hand comes out of nowhere to hand it to him.

Of course, it's Xia Xiqing, smiling earnestly.

Zhou Ziheng takes the key. He has to tell himself that he can't trust this innocent face.

"He wasn't handcuffed at the start," Xia Xiqing tells Shang Sirui. "Only I was. At least you weren't also blindfolded like

I was in the beginning."

"Whoa. Sounds like you had a tough time just trying to start playing," Shang Sirui exclaims.

Shang Sirui and Xia Xiqing begin chatting while Zhou Ziheng silently uncuffs Shang Sirui. This reminds him of the time when he uncuffed Xia Xiqing earlier. Shang Sirui also has pretty hands. Only—if he's honest with himself—Xia Xiqing's hands are longer and fairer.

But why is he comparing hands? Zhou Ziheng releases the cuffs and snaps back to his senses. What's there to compare?

Shang Sirui, finally free, hops on his toes a few times. Then he slings his arms around Xia Xiqing and Zhou Ziheng's shoulders. "Finally! It ends!"

A few crew members come around to remove their microphones. Xia Xiqing feels the tension leave him and raises a hand to knead his neck. The moment he turns his head, he notices some pieces of confetti still stuck to Zhou Ziheng.

He reaches out to remove them.

"What are you doing?" Feeling a touch of cold, Zhou Ziheng turns around and sees Xia Xiqing's hand at his neck.

Like a startled little tiger kitten.

Careful not to laugh, he gives a quiet apology and plucks a strip of confetti from Zhou Ziheng. He's not sorry. He was purposefully looking for an excuse to touch him.

Long fingers pinch the confetti strip, dangling it in front of Zhou Ziheng before slowly letting it fall, feather-like, onto the floor before him. The confetti strip is conspicuously bright, just like Xia Xiqing's smile.

Zhou Ziheng feels very awkward, but he ends up grunting a thank you.

"You're welcome."

That tone of voice that Xia Xiqing keeps using—it always

sounds flirtatious; like a frivolous cloud in the wind that he can't catch.

The director of the production approaches them with a pair of cameras. "We'll film some bonus footage in a moment," he says, handing one camera to Shang Sirui and another to Cen-Cen. "Feel free to look around the house and film whatever you feel is appropriate. This house took our entire team nearly three days to put together!"

"Alrighty! Leave it to us, director. I wanted to check it out anyway." Shang Sirui is all grins as he takes the camera and aims it at Zhou Ziheng's face. "Is it already on?"

"Yup! Go for it!"

Seeing Zhou Ziheng wanting to hide, Shang Sirui grabs his arm and points the camera at himself. "Hello everyone! It's your stand-in host for tonight, Shang Sirui, from HighFive! Now, allow me to introduce you to—dun dun dun dunnn!" He points the camera to Zhou Ziheng. "Zhou Ziheng! Wow, you look so good on camera!"

Zhou Ziheng jokingly covers the lens with his palm. After a bit of struggle, Shang Sirui frees the camera and points it toward Xia Xiqing.

"And this is Xia Xiqing! Super-duper smart. He was unbelievably good at the game. If it weren't for him, I think I might have won!"

"Is that indignation I sense?" Xia Xiqing retorts. "Look, how's this, you were also unbelievably good. I was fooled until almost the end!"

"Hehe." Shang Sirui turns the camera toward the house. "Now, let's have a tour."

The Shang Sirui after the main recording has concluded is like a kid on steroids, zapping in and out of the rooms with the camera in hand. Zhou Ziheng and Xia Xiqing follow behind, speaking only when the lens is pointing at them in prompt for a response.

Shang Sirui becomes even more excited as they approach the study. "And this room...this is the room where I was held hostage. I was kidnapped and tied to that chair right there!" Then he points the camera to Zhou Ziheng. "And this handsome man here was my kidnapper!"

"Pfft!" Xia Xiqing couldn't hold back his laughter.

Zhou Ziheng, facing the camera, calmly says, "Well, that's what you get for tricking everyone."

"I was forced to! With the role I was given, I was scared to death, okay?" Shang Sirui explains. "By the way, how did you find the password to the front door? I searched for so long but never found it."

"In this room, actually." Zhou Ziheng takes out a flash-light. "I found parts to this under the sofa in the living area and put it together."

He continues to explain the "*sofa, flashlight, study, darken*" clue to Shang Sirui. Before Zhou Ziheng can finish, Shang Sirui reaches for the light switch.

"So there are clues you can only see with the lights off?"

Zhou Ziheng grabs Shang Sirui's hand. "Don't turn it off!"

Xia Xiqing is startled. He himself hadn't even processed that darkness would be imminent, but somehow Zhou Ziheng had.

"Why?" Shang Sirui asks, his face full of doubt.

Truth be told, not even Zhou Ziheng is sure why he did what he just did, or even how he did it. It just sort of happened spontaneously.

"What he means is that you're still filming—pretty sure that camera can't see in the dark." Xia Xiqing grabs Zhou Ziheng's wrist and takes his hand down. "Right?"

"Yeah," Zhou Ziheng soundlessly extracts his hand from Xia Xiqing's grip. "I'll just tell you. When the room is dark, the four corners light up with clues. Three numbers, then the English word *'prime.'* You just have to figure out the missing digit."

"Oh, so that's how you got it." Shang Sirui sighs regretfully. "Seems like I was only missing one last clue. Ugh, I was so close! How infuriating!"

After going over the last room, the group arrives at the chute built for eliminating players. A very narrow corridor beneath it leads directly backstage to the crew. Zhou Ziheng carefully squeezes himself through the narrow passage.

Thank goodness there's light.

Thank goodness? Why does he care that there's light?

Zhou Ziheng feels like he's beginning to lose track of himself. It's like a little voice now resides in his head, always saying these strange inexplicable things to him.

Shang Sirui walks at the front, excitingly filming an outro to the bonus content. Xia Xiqing follows closely behind Zhou Ziheng. The narrow corridor compresses them all tightly together. They're so close that they can feel each other's breaths, as if the air molecules between them are actually a cloud of floating microorganisms.

Zhou Ziheng suddenly feels a tug on the back of his shirt, so he turns back a little. Not expecting Zhou Ziheng's quick reaction time, Xia Xiqing finishes the step he'd been taking when he first started tugging on his shirt, wanting to say a word.

And just like that, the distance closes.

All Zhou Ziheng can see is the tip of Xia Xiqing's nose, and he watches as that little mole at its tip grows larger as it approaches and touches the corner of his lip for the briefest moment, brushing past like a shooting star before retreating again.

A microscopic particle, floating like a glowing jellyfish, very suddenly stops.

The air condenses between them.

In the dimly-lit corridor, as Shang Sirui's childish voice slowly fades into the background, another sound emerges.

Thump—

Thump-thump—

Zhou Ziheng panics and tries to retreat, forgetting that they're in a confined space that does not accommodate his six feet and four inches of height.

"Careful!" Xia Xiqing warns as Zhou Ziheng bumps his head on the ceiling. He tries to catch himself, but fails as Zhou Ziheng ducks his grasp by slipping and falling completely.

The tension that had been floating between Xia Xiqing and Zhou Ziheng like so many tiny particles now fall, landing like a rain of coarse sugar crystals clattering over Zhou Ziheng's fallen form. Zhou Ziheng shakes his head, trying to clear his head of his bizarre imagination.

This situation could not be more embarrassing.

Hearing the commotion, Shang Sirui turns and calls back to them, "Everything okay back there? What happened?"

"All good," Xia Xiqing replies. "Ziheng slipped and fell, but everything's alright. You go on ahead."

Then he extends his arm to Zhou Ziheng.

Zhou Ziheng ignores the proffered hand and instead picks himself up. He dusts off his clothes and continues to walk forward with a hand supporting himself against the wall.

"Are you okay?" Xia Xiqing asks.

"Yeah."

Xia Xiqing chuckles.

Zhou Ziheng feels uncomfortable, as if he was belittled. In an attempt to break away from this awkward atmosphere, he tries to divert the topic.

"What did you want to say earlier?" he asks with his back to Xia Xiqing.

"Oh, you still remember?" Xia Xiqing's tone regains its strange flirtatiousness. Just like a breeze that can stir up a storm in one's heart.

"Are you gonna say it or what?"

Such a fierce tone, yet the tips of his ears are red.

"I was going to ask you," Xia Xiqing says as he walks toward Zhou Ziheng, treading on the latter's shadow, "how you knew that it was me entering the study. It was completely dark. You couldn't possibly have seen my face."

Zhou Ziheng suddenly goes quiet. They approach the end of the tunnel and he ascends the steps in silence.

Xia Xiqing is experienced in flirting. He knows exactly how to handle awkward silences, how to divert it before it escalates into even more awkwardness.

"My guess... Was it my cologne?" Smiling, Xia Xiqing follows Zhou Ziheng up the stairs. "Is your sense of smell that good?"

Zhou Ziheng still says nothing.

They climb the last step, leaving behind the quiet corridor for the noisy din of the backstage. The crew is still celebrating the completion of filming for this first round of the program. Shang Sirui and Cen-Cen are still grousing to each other. Ruan Xiao is laughing sweetly. The atmosphere is filled with all kinds of happy voices and other accompanying sounds.

Through all this noise comes the deep tone of Zhou Ziheng's voice:

"It was a gut feeling," he finally replies.

It wasn't until after I approached and grabbed your wrist that I noticed your cologne, but that only served to confirm my instincts.

Xia Xiqing's last step falters midair for just a moment as he tries to comprehend what he just heard.

Gut feeling...

Then his step falls, and he looks up at Zhou Ziheng's silhouette ahead. This guy probably doesn't even understand how much insinuation that sentence carried—how impressive of a line that would be if he had been trying to flirt.

After they wrap up, Shang Sirui's assistant finds a hotpot restaurant that's open late into the night and books a private room. The five of them all head there together right after they're released from the program.

Shang Sirui orders for them all, seemingly pretty familiar with the menu. "I've been around here for filming many times before with the group, so I've tried this place before. It's really good! They've got that super authentic Szechuan style of cooking," he praises.

"You're from there?" Cen-Cen asks.

Shang Sirui smiles widely. "No, I'm from Beijing." He looks at everyone in turn. "Do any of you drink?"

Cen-Cen shakes her head. "I can't. I've got a tour soon, so I need to take care of my voice."

"I don't drink either," Zhou Ziheng says, taking off his jacket and grabbing a bottle of water for himself. "No need to order alcohol for me."

From the moment he takes off that jacket, Xia Xiqing's eyes do not leave his body. He's in a plain white T-shirt, looking light and free; the perfect embodiment of a college student.

Xia Xiqing examines the hand that grips the bottle of water—the slightly protruding tendons, the defined joints of his slender fingers. He looks at his profile—the dense curtain of long eyelashes, the jut of his brow bone. Every extracted piece of the image is perfect. His gaze follows the lines of Zhou Ziheng's neck, the way the supple lines of his muscles disappear into the wide collar of his T-shirt.

Why must this man be his exact fucking type?

"Xiqing, how about you?" Shang Sirui asks, interrupting his daydream.

"Me?" He returns to himself, and in that instant he sees that Zhou Ziheng, for all that he's still in the same position as before, had very briefly glanced over to meet Xia Xiqing's eyes. It was only a split-second, for now he's looked away again, frowning.

How fun. Xia Xiqing puts an elbow on the table, then leans his head into it as he turns to Shang Sirui. "Sure! I want wine."

"As in grape wine? With hotpot?" Shang Sirui chuckles. With friendly sarcasm, he says, "You sure know how to pair your alcohol."

"I'm not actually that hungry." Xia Xiqing continues to smile at Shang Sirui. "I just want a nice glass of wine to relax and unwind."

Sharing a meal around the same table is probably the best and quickest icebreaker for any group of strangers. And anyway, the five of them have already shared the high-tension experience of *Survive and Escape*, so it's easy for them to grow closer over dinner conversation as they unwind from their earlier stress.

In order to protect her voice for her upcoming tour, Cen-Cen is also avoiding spicy food. Seeing Zhou Ziheng also avoiding the spicy side of the hotpot, she asks, "You don't eat spicy food?"

Zhou Ziheng shakes his head. "No, I can't really tolerate it."

Shang Sirui jumps in. "Yeah, Ziheng is super healthy! I remember when I filmed with him before—he doesn't drink or smoke, and he sticks to super healthy food with lots of veggies. Also, he always carried around a thermos of goji berry tea."

What an old soul—those are the habits of three generations ago. Xia Xiqing can't help but chuckle.

No, wait, they're also the habits of a goodie-two-shoes.

As Ruan Xiao starts to cook the tripe in the hotpot, she asks a question through the rising steam of the pot, aimed at Shang Sirui: "Do you often behave so differently off-stage? I have a friend who's a fan of your group, though she stans a different member. But, well, she's seen you in person plenty of times, and she said that you generally act kind of muddled in person."

Biting the tip of his chopstick, Shang Sirui lets out a long hum as he hesitates. Then he replies, "Well, I'm usually not that oblivious. But how do I explain... It's just that we're all pretty young in HighFive, so we've got a lot of mom fans. You know, fans who treat us like we're their children. We always get comments like 'Mama loves you!' So because of that, the company wants us to play up the childishness and the innocence, which means I'm kind of stuck with a public persona of 'cute airhead' nowadays."

Shang Sirui fishes a meatball out of the pot and into his bowl. Then he says to Ruan Xiao, "Oh, uh, your tripe might be getting a bit overcooked."

"Ahh, oh no, you're right!" Ruan Xiao quickly tends to her tripe.

Cen-Cen takes this chance and asks, "But doesn't it get tiring? Always acting according to your character design? Having to always present a personality that's not your own?"

At this, Xia Xiqing feels a pair of eyes on him. He looks up, and indeed—Zhou Ziheng is staring at him.

But it's so fun! How would it ever get tiring? Xia Xiqing smiles very faintly at Zhou Ziheng, then breaks eye contact and takes a sip of his wine.

"It's not that bad. I'm kind of forgetful in real life too, so the character design isn't too hard to stick to." Shang Sirui sighs. "Ah, the *one* time I get to play a villainous role, and I got so close to winning, too. It's such a shame. My plan was seamless! But then Xiqing stirred the pot and I suddenly began panicking."

Xia Xiqing laughs. "How is that my fault? You shouldn't be so easy to stir up."

"What was your original plan?" Cen-Cen asks.

"Well, the plan was to first get you and Ruan Xiao on my side. I was pushing all suspicion onto Xiqing, and you were believing me. I had to get him voted out in the first round because he's too dangerous to let stay. After that, I could wait for Ziheng to get the clues together, use my kill card on him, and reap the rewards of his hard labor. Flawless!"

Shang Sirui explains all this to excellent dramatic effect, then leans back in his chair like a wilted eggplant. "Ah, such a pity that Xiqing saw through my plans. He found evidence that could reveal me as the Killer, and it was so close to voting time that I panicked and immediately used my kill card on him. No consideration whatsoever!"

Hearing this, Xia Xiqing smiles. "Was it instant regret?"

"Of course! So many regrets," Shang Sirui admits. "But it was too late for regret, so I figured I could still try to go against Ziheng head-on. Unfortunately, by then he'd already found all the clues for escape and he also knew I was the Killer." Shang Sirui stuffs a piece of rice cake into his mouth and turns to Zhou Ziheng. "Oh right, Ziheng. How did you find out about that? Did Xiqing tell you?"

At the mention of Zhou Ziheng, Xia Xiqing very purposefully does not turn toward him. Instead, he keeps his gaze fixed on Shang Sirui, his expression gentle to the max. Zhou Ziheng hums in affirmation.

Beside him, Cen-Cen lets out a chuckle. "And so you believed him? Just like that?"

Zhou Ziheng has no reply to that. There's no good way to answer, so he stays silent.

Ruan Xiao returns to the conversation. "Logically, the clue for the final passwords must've also been given to you by Xiqing, right?"

Shang Sirui comes to a sudden realization. "It was that painting, wasn't it?" Waving his chopsticks, he turns to Xia Xiqing. "That one with the rose? Ahh, I should have just taken it from you right then and there." He smacks himself on the forehead. "Dumb, dumb, so dumb!"

At this sight, Xia Xiqing begins to laugh. Lazily, with one hand still propped under his chin, reaches out with his other hand to hold onto Shang Sirui's wrist, preventing him from doing further damage to himself.

"Quit hitting yourself in the head, you can't spare the brain cells."

"Shit—it *was* that painting." Arm captured, Shang Sirui grabs back onto Xia Xiqing's wrist, then swings their clasped limbs back and forth beseechingly. "No. This is too upsetting. I need restitution for this emotional damage you've caused me—paint for me! I want big ones—two of them. One for my dormitory and one for my mom!"

Though Xia Xiqing isn't drunk off the wine yet, the shaking does make him a bit dizzy. He smiles in appeasement. "Alright, alright! Just two paintings, right? I'll start tomorrow."

It's a habit for Xia Xiqing, when faced with attention-hungry people, to spoil them with that which they seek—that is, before he bores of them. As such, the other party, upon being indulged so kindly, often starts to assume that they're closer to Xia Xiqing than all the rest of the rabble. They never realize that it's all just a lie.

But to Zhou Ziheng, it looks real.

He's not bothered or anything, it's just that he really doesn't get it. He can't figure out why—this guy is so clearly claiming to be his fan, and he was so earnestly confessing his admiration for him, but now, he's having dinner with his supposed idol. Shouldn't he be trying to make conversation with him?

Throughout this entire evening, Xia Xiqing has barely looked at Zhou Ziheng.

Strange and puzzling.

And he seems pretty promiscuous—so he must be into Shang Sirui now, one hundred percent. Evidently, the fanaticism of fans is never truly reliable. One day they're hardcore stanning you, but then they hop into another fandom and you'll be lucky if they don't say anything slanderous on the way out.

Chopsticks in hand, ears filled with the cheerful conversation of the pair of men across the table from him, Zhou

Ziheng finds that he's unable to eat anything.

Hotpot takes hours. As they're about to wrap up, Shang Sirui suddenly thinks of something. "Hey! Let's make a WeChat group!" He pulls out his phone. "This way we'll be able to chat when we're not filming together."

Zhou Ziheng does not at all want to join, but it's too late—Shang Sirui already has him added on WeChat, so he's already been pulled into the group chat. Immediately, his phone starts buzzing with endless notifications. He pulls it out and sees that they're all from a group called "guess who's the Killer today."

"Everyone please give yourself a nickname in the group chat," Ruan Xiao reminds.

Thus, Zhou Ziheng changes his alias from his normal WeChat username to something more easily understood, then opens the members page for a skim. Immediately he sees Xia Xiqing, but not because of his name—he hasn't yet changed his alias. No, Zhou Ziheng simply recognizes his profile image.

It's that painting he once did of Zhou Ziheng in that red basketball jersey.

Strangely enough, Zhou Ziheng feels more at ease after this. He just frowns, squinting at that tiny little icon—not even opening it for the full image in case someone looks over his shoulder to see what he's staring at. It's a long moment before he finally looks up from his phone to glance at Xia Xiqing, sitting across from him.

Xia Xiqing is completely slumped in his chair, head tilted so that his hair covers half his face. Zhou Ziheng can't quite tell if his eyes are open or not.

He seems pretty drunk.

Seeing Zhou Ziheng looking, Shang Sirui follows his gaze.

"Oh, Xiqing! Are you drunk? Are you alright?" Brushing his hair away, revealing Xia Xiqing's bright red face.

Xia Xiqing makes a vague noise of assent, sounding hoarse with intoxication. It's unlikely he heard what Shang Sirui said. He's so drunk... Zhou Ziheng spitefully thinks that it'll be unlikely for Xia Xiqing to get home on his own. He almost fails to hold back an eye-roll at the situation.

"Where's his hotel?" Cen-Cen asks. "I saw that he had a PA earlier, but it's so late now..."

"How about he stays with me?" Ruan Xiao offers as she pulls out her phone to call a taxi. "My place is pretty close."

"Unless you want to be in tomorrow's gossip headlines, that's probably not a good idea," Shang Sirui explains. "There might be paparazzi outside. He can stay with me; it's better since we're both guys." But then he suddenly remembers something. "Wait no! I actually have an early flight tomorrow. He'll be left all alone in the morning, so that's probably not a good idea either."

Everyone discusses Xia Xiqing's situation, but Zhou Ziheng doesn't participate. There's a strange feeling of being in class and waiting in fear as the teacher prepares to pick someone for an answer.

"Ziheng, how about you take him to your place? I remember your hotel is pretty close, and you drove here, right?"

And Murphy's law succeeds again—this is exactly what Zhou Ziheng was hoping to avoid. Through his resignation at the challenges of fate, Zhou Ziheng hums an agreement.

Shang Sirui helps Xia Xiqing into Zhou Ziheng's car. Closing the door on the passenger's side, he says, "Well, I'm off then. Early day tomorrow."

Zhou Ziheng nods.

"Don't forget his seatbelt!" Shang Sirui yells from some

distance away.

Slouching on the passenger seat like a drugged cat, Xia Xiqing is very difficult to straighten. Zhou Ziheng struggles for a while to get a seatbelt around his torso, but it's to no avail.

So troublesome.

Cunning, shameless, a compulsive liar, an outstanding sleaze. But now Xia Xiqing has become no more than a puppet sitting there. Zhou Ziheng gives him a mental label of "Trouble."

After this show, he never wants to see Xia Xiqing again. With no one to hear his complaints, Zhou Ziheng can only think these vicious thoughts at Xia Xiqing.

But then, suddenly, the troublesome drunkard makes a whimper like a baby animal and puts his arms around Zhou Ziheng, hugging him close. His head burrows into the juncture between Zhou Ziheng's chest and neck.

Zhou Ziheng feels the gentle press of a pair of lips rubbing against the side of his neck. He feels like a current is running through him, as if crackling sparks were leaping off of him. He's numb from neck to fingers, and the cavity of his chest is filled with this sourceless electricity.

His heart stops.

For the first time in two decades, Zhou Ziheng feels this strange and wondrous feeling, and in the throes of such a novel experience, he once again forgets. This drunkard who's so tightly embracing him...is very good at deception.

C.04

Habitual Deceit

The hug makes Zhou Ziheng freeze.

What's happening? Why's he hugging me?

"Hey! Wake up!" Zhou Ziheng strains to free his hand before giving Xia Xiqing a push in an attempt to wake him up.

The movement seems to make it worse. Not only does it not wake him up, it makes Xia Xiqing collapse even more onto Zhou Ziheng; his face is now right up against his neck. The scent of red wine on his breath spreads from Zhou Ziheng's neck up to his ears like a burning flame engulfing his body.

Zhou Ziheng suddenly returns to himself, strange alarms going off in his head.

"Hey!"

He quickly escapes Xia Xiqing's embrace, gives up on buckling the seatbelt, and starts the engine. He begins to drive toward the hotel.

Zhou Ziheng didn't drink tonight, but he is nevertheless tired and unable to stay focused. Memories from earlier this night cloud his mind, especially that brief near-hallucination of his in the tunnel. A strange yet powerful feeling overwhelms him.

Zhou Ziheng puts a hat on before getting out of the car. However, in his hurry, he forgets to put on his face mask as he helps the limp Xia Xiqing out of the vehicle and into the hotel.

Fortunately for Zhou Ziheng, Jiang Yin already told him where Xia Xiqing would be staying. Otherwise, Zhou Ziheng wouldn't even know where to drive. It's nearly three in the morning, so hotel staff is at minimum. One friendly steward comes to help Zhou Ziheng, supporting Xia Xiqing and helping him stay upright as he's led into the elevator. Zhou Ziheng gladly lets go of this annoying person and allows the helpful hotel staff to take over carrying him.

The elevator suddenly falls silent.

The steward keeps staring at Zhou Ziheng, who realizes that he's not wearing a mask. Has he been recognized?

The steward continues to look at Zhou Ziheng. Maybe this guy is a fan? Zhou Ziheng wonders.

"Umm..." The steward begins to speak in a nervous tone, "Sir..."

Zhou Ziheng gives a professional smile. "Sorry, but can we wait until we're upstairs before any pictures or autographs?"

"No, sir, it's just..." Awkward, the steward coughs as he supports Xia Xiqing, who is about to slide down. With an apologetic look, he explains, "This elevator needs a key card to work. It won't go up otherwise."

He points to the scanning device. Zhou Ziheng wishes very hard for this elevator to explode.

It's awkward enough to mistake someone for a fan, but it's even more embarrassing to have completely misunderstood why they'd been waiting in silence.

Zhou Ziheng checks all of Xia Xiqing's pockets, but doesn't find a key card.

"Umm... doesn't seem like my friend brought his key card." Zhou Ziheng's scalp is going numb from embarrassment, although he still maintains the façade of composure expected of a renowned actor. "How about I book a new room for him?"

For two decades, Zhou Ziheng's life has gone quite smoothly. Until now. Until he met Xia Xiqing. Everything that can go wrong is starting to go wrong. The amount of awkwardness and embarrassment is record-breaking.

The girl working reception was a lot more energetic and friendly than the steward. With eyes glued to Zhou Ziheng, she smiles and asks, "Hello sir, how can I help you?"

"Any vacancies?" Zhou Ziheng replies. He sees a different staff member in the distance pulling out her phone to take a photo. Nothing much he can do to hide apart from pulling up his collar to hide half his face.

"How many rooms do you need?" The receptionist gives an even sweeter smile.

Zhou Ziheng looks behind him and finds the unconscious Xia Xiqing passed out on the couch. He thinks to himself, *I'll just get him a room here and then go back to my own hotel. It's not that far.*

Zhou Ziheng turns back and says, "Just one, please."

The girl looks down at her computer and checks the bookings. "All we have left is an executive suite. Would that be alright?"

"Yeah," Zhou Ziheng replies. Not that it matters—it'll just

be Xia Xiqing by himself in there.

The steward helps Xia Xiqing back into the elevator. This time, Zhou Ziheng scans the key card right away and looks over at the steward who's struggling to keep Xia Xiqing upright. Xia Xiqing is relatively skinny, but he's still a grown man and about six feet tall to boot. Drunk as he is, he's nothing but dead weight.

The executive suite is none too shabby. Everything is spacious and the bed is a king size. Looking at the decorations in this room, Zhou Ziheng can't help but inwardly roll his eyes. Even so, he still turns to the steward and thanks him for all the effort with a smile.

"Thank you very much! I'm sorry for all the trouble."

"No worries!" the steward replies. Maybe it's because he's tired, but his face is pretty flushed right now. "It wasn't any trouble at all!"

Zhou Ziheng smiles at him. There's a moment of silence as he waits for the steward to excuse himself, but nothing happens.

"Umm..." he starts.

The steward finally speaks: "I, um, I'm actually a big fan of yours. I've watched a bunch of your shows and movies. Could I please get an autograph?" With this, he pulls out a marker out of nowhere and presents it to Zhou Ziheng. Then, he undoes his uniform jacket, revealing the white T-shirt underneath. "On the back of my shirt, maybe?"

The T-shirt is even the same sponsored brand that Zhou Ziheng wore today. He feels truly embarrassed now. If this person wasn't a fan, the earlier incident would probably be forgotten sooner or later. But since he is...

How embarrassing. Right in front of his own fan.

Zhou Ziheng takes the marker and signs the shirt with a

very professional fake smile plastered on his face. "Thank you for your support!"

Very pleased, the steward smiles at Zhou Ziheng. "Go get 'em, Ziheng! You'll always have my support." He walks toward the exit. "And please take care of yourself, it'll be flu season pretty soon."

Zhou Ziheng sees him to the door, wanting to close the door for this fan who is reluctant to leave. He even makes a special point of reminding him with a smile, "Remember not to post about this on Weibo!"

"Uh-huh, of course! Bye!"

The world finally returns to peace and quiet.

Zhou Ziheng almost forgot about the troublesome drunkard sleeping on the bed. He wonders if he should find some fortune teller to check feng shui or fate these days, feeling that everything is going especially badly. He looks at Xia Xiqing, unsure what to do next. He wonders if he should help wipe down his face or put him in a more comfortable position. The only problem is that he doesn't really know how to take care of anyone; after all, he's never had to do this before.

Still hesitating, he begins to play with his jacket zipper.

Well...he's already come this far...

Zhou Ziheng walks to the bathroom for a towel, then dampens it with warm water. He uses it to wipe down Xia Xiqing's drunk red face.

This guy has very good skin; better than most of the female stars he's worked with. So good that Zhou Ziheng decides to wipe more gently.

He takes the towel and runs it over Xia Xiqing's face, across his nose bridge, across that sesame-like mole. He looks so well-behaved in his sleep.

Well-behaved? Forget it...

Zhou Ziheng puts the towel back in the bathroom. After looking around to make sure that nothing is out of place, he decides to head out.

Just as he's about to walk away, something wraps around his wrist. He turns and finds Xia Xiqing's hand grasping his wrist. The guy is still half-conscious, muttering something indiscernible.

Seems like he doesn't want Zhou Ziheng to leave.

Why is his hand so warm? Zhou Ziheng grasps Xia Xiqing's palm with his fingers. It really is scalding hot. Xia Xiqing has been wearing a flimsy white shirt the entire day, and then he drank wine and was exposed to the wind. He must have caught a cold.

Honestly speaking, if it were anyone other than Xia Xiqing on the bed right now, Zhou Ziheng would probably stay behind to help out and make sure they're okay.

But it is Xia Xiqing, and Zhou Ziheng, for all his strong moral sense, hesitates.

Xia Xiqing grunts, frowns a little, and curls up, still not letting go of Zhou Ziheng's wrist.

Zhou Ziheng feels his resolve weakening. But no, he can't! It's just one night. And the fever doesn't seem that severe. He's a healthy young man. He'll be fine. Zhou Ziheng has already done his part.

Excuse thus prepared, Zhou Ziheng heartlessly escapes from Xia Xiqing's grasp and walks briskly out of the hotel room.

Meanwhile, Xia Xiqing almost dies from anger.

I gave him plenty of hints, didn't I? Xia Xiqing thinks to himself. *Apart from using the alcohol as an excuse to land a kiss on him, I did everything. Is he really so straight that it didn't work?*

Xia Xiqing opens his eyes and glares at the ceiling. He was clearly willing to escort him upstairs, and he even wiped his face and put a comforter over him. But then...then he just leaves?

Is this really the behavior of a healthy young adult?

As he continues to internally curse out Zhou Ziheng, Xia Xiqing hears the door open again. He quickly closes his eyes and pretends to sleep.

He's back again? What's up with this kid? He needs to make up his mind.

But it's not that Zhou Ziheng has changed his mind—as soon as he left Xia Xiqing's room, he realized he couldn't find his own hotel key card. He's returned because he thinks that maybe he left it here.

"Where is it? Did I forget to bring it?" Zhou Ziheng mutters softly to himself.

Xia Xiqing is pleased beyond measure. Excellent! Even the heavens are helping him seduce men.

Zhou Ziheng searches the room with no luck. He reckons that he probably did not bring it at all, and sits down on the couch and cards a hand through his hair in frustration as he looks at the motionless Xia Xiqing on the bed. After struggling with himself for a long time, he gives up his plan of going back to his hotel. He pats the sofa and finds it nice and soft.

Maybe he'll just get by on the sofa. Just one night. He's been through worse. This is nothing. Plus, Xia Xiqing has a fever—if anything happens to him, who's going to be responsible?

All sorts of odd thoughts run through Zhou Ziheng's mind. He sighs and walks to the bathroom for a quick wash.

When he's done, he walks over to stand over Xia Xiqing, who's wrapped in the comforter with his face covered by his hair. Looking weak and vulnerable.

He reaches out, wanting to check Xia Xiqing's forehead for his temperature, but then he decides against it, and his hand pauses in mid-air.

The shadow of his hand slowly recedes from Xia Xiqing. He'll be fine. Just let him sleep.

Zhou Ziheng walks away from the bed. He was about to shut off the lights when he suddenly remembers the panic attack Xia Xiqing had earlier in the escape room. Instead, he leaves a lamp on.

He looks at Xia Xiqing one last time and treads softly to the couch. After an entire night of filming, he's exhausted, and he falls asleep almost immediately.

Xia Xiqing doesn't know how long he's been here. But he hasn't closed his eyes since Zhou Ziheng went to sleep, his expression as calm as the surface of the sea under the moonlit night.

And then there's the lamp that Zhou Ziheng left on. The yellow light engulfs the room, seeming to penetrate through the comforter to fall across his shoulder blades.

A plan is always just a plan...

His original plan had been to hook up with Zhou Ziheng tonight. Obviously they wouldn't be going all the way tonight, but he still felt like he should do something. He really doesn't believe that Zhou Ziheng could really truly remain so frigid toward him. The kid's in his early twenties—that's the age at which no man can resist seduction.

At least, that was his original plan.

When Zhou Ziheng left that lamp on for him, all of these notions evaporated from him, disappeared like the burst of smoke from a detonated smoke bomb. In their place is a strange, inexplicable feeling, knotted up right at the center of his chest.

It's very uncomfortable.

Xia Xiqing hates these feelings. He hates all feelings that make him feel vulnerable.

Xia Xiqing tosses and turns repeatedly. After a while, he finally decides to flip back his comforter and get off the bed. He slowly walks toward the sofa to find the tall Zhou Ziheng scrunched up in an uncomfortable looking position. He doesn't even have any covers.

He looks like an abandoned puppy.

Xia Xiqing stares at Zhou Ziheng lazily, painting him a perfect portrait in his mind.

Zhou Ziheng is deep asleep. Xia Xiqing sticks out his index finger and places it less than an inch from Zhou Ziheng's face. He runs it down, tracing the contours of his exquisite facial features from his forehead to his three-dimensional brow and the high bridge of his nose.

Xia Xiqing stops at his exquisite lips.

His fingers curl. He begins to pull himself closer to Zhou Ziheng.

Closer...closer again...

It's like an intimate scene in a romantic movie.

Part of Zhou Ziheng's face is now covered by Xia Xiqing's shadow. The distance between their lips narrows to a fraction of an inch. Xia Xiqing can feel Zhou Ziheng's breaths on his face. His face is split by dark and light; the darkness of the night, and the warm yellow light of the lamp.

Right before their lips touch, Xia Xiqing pulls back. He runs his fingers through his hair in frustration.

What am I doing?

Only a girl would do this. Like a fool.

He grabs the comforter and casually places it over Zhou Ziheng after removing the jacket that the kid was trying to use as a makeshift blanket.

Xia Xiqing sits back on another couch and tries to relax and sober up. He lights a cigarette and tilts his head back. When he finishes the cigarette, he feels more awake. He grabs Zhou Ziheng's jacket and walks out of the room.

Upon arriving in the lobby, he sees at the front desk the steward that helped him up to the room. The guy watches him step out of the elevator doors with a puzzled look. Xia Xiqing takes off his hat and walks over. His peach blossom eyes curve into crescents.

"Thank you, by the way."

"You..." The steward snaps back to his senses and hurriedly corrects himself. "I mean, sir, weren't you the one who was, uh, drunk? So, then... he..."

"Oh yeah. I just woke up. I feel fine now." Xia Xiqing taps his fingers on the marble counter. "When Ziheng wakes up tomorrow, can you tell him I took his jacket?"

With that, he shoves his hands into the jacket pockets, tucks his head into the collar, and says, casually, "So cold today..."

Like this, he boldly walks out of the hotel.

Back at his apartment, Xia Xiqing stays in for the entirety of the day. Recording the show has completely sapped him of energy, and it takes him a few days to get back on his feet. Once he's fully energized, he takes out his brushes and canvas to catch some valuable painting time outside. Just when he's about to leave his apartment, he gets a call from Chen Fang.

Chen Fang is a childhood friend of his. Straight as a ruler.

Xia Xiqing always jokes around with him, but they have a good relationship.

"Hey, Xiqing?"

"Oh hey. I see you still remember me."

Xia Xiqing locks the door with great effort. This place was built a century ago. He chose it for its uniqueness and its artistic feel—rent isn't cheap here. The only issue is that the building is pretty old, so the amenities are dated and not everything works as well as more modern installments. Previously, he hadn't been home much, so that hadn't been a problem for him. But now, since he's already declined offers from abroad, he's ready to find a proper place to fully settle in.

And how lucky that Chen Fang has called him. "Oh right, aren't you in real estate right now? Have you heard of any good apartments recently?"

"No, you're in real estate," Chen Fang replies. "You entire family is in real estate."

"Excuse you, we actually do development. We don't get to live in them." Xia Xiqing smiles. "No, but for real. I'll buy an apartment from you guys. Keep an eye out for me."

Chen Fang lets out a long sigh, but then he plays along. "Of course, sir. What type of apartment is the Young Master Xia looking for, if I may ask?"

"Good view, quiet, not too far out of the way—I don't want to see a sea of darkness when it starts to get dark, you know? Price is not an issue."

The last few words stab, knife-like, into Chen Fang. Rich kids will be rich kids... Out loud, Chen Fang says, "These requirements are really something. Quiet places with good views are usually standalone houses in more suburban residence zones, which aren't exactly city-center... Begging your pardon, sir."

"Oh, cut the crap. You got something or not?" Xia Xiqing takes the elevator downstairs. It's a nice day out, warm and sunny. "If you don't want to do business, I can always go find someone else."

"I'm not done yet. Though these requirements are a bit particular—certainly not something that just anyone could fulfill, but I, Chen Fang, am not just anyone. I recently got a listing for a two-story loft apartment, one of the penthouse units of a luxury apartment building. Over four thousand square feet both floors combined, and all window walls. And the neighborhood is excellent—all rich people, so it's very private. Want to go take a look with me later?"

This Chen Fang really doesn't drop the ball when he's needed.

"Sure. I'll go find you at your office in the afternoon."

"Please, I'm begging you, don't drive too nice of a car."

Chen Fang remembers back to when he just started his job. He'd managed to get an in with the cute intern and they were about to go downstairs for noodles, but then Xia Xiqing came to deliver watermelons and showed up in a Maserati. With just a few words, the girl was completely bewitched by him.

Xia Xiqing snickers. "Don't worry, I'll take a cab."

It's been a while since Xia Xiqing has had a suitable place to sketch. He used to live by the Yangtze River, and he'd go to the riverside all the time to sketch. The soft yellow branches of willows in spring, the blooming sunflowers in summer, the swathes of tall, quiet reeds swaying to the autumn wind, the snowy winter days.

Standing in front of an artificial lake in a park, Xia Xiqing feels as if he could hear the howls of the wind from the river.

His heart feels empty.

He's struggling. There's no scenery here. Nothing worthy. Boring. Xia Xiqing casually ties up his hair behind him and stands before the easel, with his left hand in his pocket and his right holding a sketching pencil. He does a perfunctory job of sketching. A few girls walk over and pause to sneakily photograph him. He doesn't pay them any mind—they probably recognized him from Weibo.

There's a young man sitting on a bench. He's quite handsome. He spends most of his time staring at his phone, but he occasionally looks up in Xia Xiqing's direction.

As he begins to sketch, a young girl, about five or six, comes up to Xia Xiqing and tugs on his sleeve. "Gege, hi, can you draw me?"

Xia Xiqing looks at the girl eating a lollipop bigger than her face. Then, in a serious tone, he asks, "Why should I draw you?"

The little girl can't find an answer at first, but then she stammers, "I... I just want a drawing."

Xia Xiqing smiles. He looks around but sees no adults nearby. "Where are your parents?"

"I don't know." She licks her lollipop and replies in a childlike voice, "Mommy was right here."

Ah. So she's lost. Xia Xiqing sighs, then says, "Okay, I'll draw you, but you have to promise to not move, alright?" Xia Xiqing points toward a flowerbed. "Remember, models don't move. Sit still and behave, okay?"

"Okay!" She runs off to the flowers excitedly.

The little girl sits motionlessly by the flowers. He turns to the girls that were taking photos of him and asks, "Hey, excuse me. Do you mind doing me a favor?"

They instantly blush as if they've just met their idol. Xia

Xiqing tells them about the little girl being separated from her parents and asks them to inform nearby security guards.

Ever since Xia Xiqing called her a model, this little girl has become the best-behaved kid on the planet. She gives up licking her lollipop and sits like a statue beside the flowers. Xia Xiqing feels like laughing at the sight.

Ten minutes go by and Xia Xiqing is almost done with his drawing. A young woman approaches from the distance, calling out what's clearly a nickname.

"Gege, that's Mommy. Can I move now?"

Xia Xiqing quickly finishes up his drawing and nods. "Sure!"

"Mommy! I'm over here." The little girl hops, holding her lollipop high up in the air. The young woman rushes over and hugs her.

"Oh, there you are! I turned around and suddenly you were gone. You gave me quite the scare. Why are you here?"

The little lass points at Xia Xiqing with her lollipop. "This gege is really good at drawing. He drew a picture of me! I was being a model so I couldn't move."

Xia Xiqing takes the painting off the easel and hands it to the girl. "Here, your painting. Remember, next time you lose track of Mommy, you need to be a model and stay exactly where you are and wait for her, okay?"

She happily takes the drawing. It's of an adorable little girl with pigtails, and the lollipop in her hands is now a fairy wand. She's so delighted it's as if she has found a treasure.

"Okay! Thank you, gege!"

The young mom had been so fretful, and now she's equally thankful. She offers to invite Xia Xiqing out for a thank-you meal, but he just smiles and refuses. He pats the little girl on the head and says, "Your mom is so good to you."

He returns to his easel, ready to pack up and leave. The man that had been sitting on the bench earlier approaches Xia Xiqing. Xia Xiqing has been running in this circle for a long time, so he can tell whether a person is straight or gay at a glance.

"Are all artists so kind?" he asks.

Kind? Xia Xiqing hasn't heard that in a while. "What's this, are you interested in me?" he flirts back.

The man didn't expect him to be so straightforward, so he pauses for a beat, but then he chuckles.

"Got a cigarette?" Xia Xiqing asks with a quirk of his eyebrows as he starts packing up.

The man pulls out an expensive pack of cigarettes and hands one to Xia Xiqing. He even holds out a lighter.

Xia Xiqing allows him to light his smoke. "Thanks!"

Just as the man is about to speak, Xia Xiqing's phone chirps several times in succession. He opens the messages. It's from a WeChat friend whose alias he hasn't yet changed.

ZZH: Who said you could take my jacket?

ZZH: Please return it to me.

ZZH: You've overstepped, taking it like this.

Amused, Xia Xiqing laughs. And here he was wondering who'd be messaging him; turns out, it's Zhou Ziheng.

Tsing: Like "this"? Like what?

Tsing: Oh, btw, you didn't do anything to me that night, right? I woke up all sore.

Zhou Ziheng stops replying.

Xia Xiqing can picture Zhou Ziheng's current speechless expression even through the phone screen. The more he thinks about it the funnier it gets, to the point where he begins to neglect the man standing beside him.

Feeling as if he has been ignored, the man coughs. "Who's

that? You seem so happy."

Xia Xiqing lifts his head. "The husky I've got at home," he replies, deadpan. Then his phone chirps again.

ZZH: You are literally the worst person I have ever met.

Why do his insults sound like they belong to an elementary school playground? He's clearly a very successful movie star. At the reminder of Zhou Ziheng's face, he suddenly finds that the man in front of him has become mildly disappointing—plain, even. He gives the man a polite smile.

"Sorry, but I still have some errands to run. I have to go."

The man seems a bit surprised at this sudden turn of events. "But can't we exchange WeChat IDs?" he asks.

"I don't think that's quite necessary. Thanks for the smoke though!" Xia Xiqing waves goodbye.

"Why not?" The man grabs hold of him. "Don't you want to get to know each other?"

Xia Xiqing hates clingy people. His expression darkens as he turns to the man. Slowly, he enunciates, "Because we're sexually incompatible—unless, of course, you'd bottom for me." He sneers at the man's reaction. "Ugh, I don't get it. Why do people always want to top me?"

At that, he pats the man on the shoulder, picks up his things, and walks away. He also tosses the barely-smoked cigarette in the trash.

Once he's in a cab, he gets another message.

ZZH: Give me back my jacket.

So persistent. Do all movie stars have so much spare time? A terrific idea begins to form in Xia Xiqing's mind.

Zhou Ziheng is actually quite busy. The day after filming that episode of the escape room, he got asked to help a director he's long been familiar with. The original actor had been caught in a cheating scandal and the internet has yet to shut up about it, so his role—an important secondary character—has to be redone.

For the past three days, Zhou Ziheng has been practically living on set in order to fill the scenes that need redoing. The other actors are also working hard, to the point that one of them keeps getting stomach cramps. It's when his partner taps out on such a cramp that Zhou Ziheng finally finds some spare time.

Xia Xiqing taking his jacket really made him angry. Zhou Ziheng thought he was doing a good deed for him, but that guy...instead of being grateful, he runs off with his jacket, then he asks... How dare he suspect him of *that*?!

Zhou Ziheng sits in a chair writing a long message to Xia Xiqing in an attempt to teach him a lesson. But then, right before hitting send, he decides against it and deletes all the words.

Knowing the type of person Xia Xiqing is, Zhou Ziheng sends only the last sentence, asking for the return of his jacket. Then he puts his phone down and closes his eyes to rest.

His phone vibrates.

Zhou Ziheng picks it up and opens the message.

Xia Xiqing has sent him a picture.

It's a selfie of Xia Xiqing, chest completely bare of any inner shirts, wearing Zhou Ziheng's gray-green jacket. It hasn't been zipped up and the image doesn't actually show that much skin—just a strip of torso from his hips to his collarbones, exposing some of the faint definition of his abs, the lines extending downward until the edge of his low-waist black sweatpants. The effect, however, is all the more sensual and tantalizing.

This pervert...

"Hey Xiao-Heng! What're you looking at so intensely?"

One of Zhou Ziheng's older male colleagues walks over. Flustered, Zhou Ziheng quickly exits the chat window.

"Uhh... Not much, just scrolling through Weibo."

"Really? You've practically grown up in this industry and you still like to look at online gossip?" His colleague grins. "The director's looking for you. Can you go see what's going on?"

"Okay. On my way!"

Zhou Ziheng awkwardly slips the phone back in his pocket and goes to find the director. As he gets the debrief on the next scene, Xia Xiqing sends him no less than a dozen messages. His phone vibrates ceaselessly.

"Xiao-Heng, your phone's vibrating like an electric toothbrush." The director teases. "Why don't you check to make sure everything's okay?"

What can be so important? Zhou Ziheng shakes his head in embarrassment. "It can wait."

Xia Xiqing is dying of laughter. He hasn't met anyone so entertaining in a long while. He'd taken that picture not long after he got home with the jacket; he just never thought it'd actually come in handy.

"We're here," says the taxi driver.

Xia Xiqing phones Chen Fang as soon as he gets out of the cab. Not long after, he sees Chen Fang emerge from the office. He's wearing a well-fitted suit, and his hair is buzz cut. He waves at Xia Xiqing from afar.

"You really didn't drive." Chen Fang laughs and bumps his shoulder against Xia Xiqing's. "Hey, I heard you were filming for a show a couple days ago. You gonna enter the industry?

And he t was fretting about how to sell all your darkest secr o the press."

Xia Xiqing raises his chin and looks down his nose at Chen Fang. "Wanna try?"

"No, no, I wouldn't dare." Chen Fang laughs and pulls out a set of keys. "Let's go take a look at your new apartment, shall we?" He begins to walk but then turns around. "By the way, if you aren't doing anything later, let's grab dinner."

"I've got nothing going on." Xia Xiqing steps into Chen Fang's car and buckles his seatbelt. He suddenly remembers Zhou Ziheng and laughs a little to himself.

"Oh, to be rich enough not to work for a living..." Chen Fang sighs as he starts his car. "It must be nice to be you. I hate going to work."

Xia Xiqing buckles his seat belt and casts a glance at Chen Fang. "You want to be me?"

Chen Fang suddenly recalls Xia Xiqing's family drama. Realizing he has spoken out of turn, he quickly corrects himself.

"Umm, maybe I just want to be as hot as you are. I'd immediately enlist in the entertainment industry and start rolling in cash."

"Shut it." Xia Xiqing leans against the window and chats mindlessly with Chen Fang about idle gossip. For some reason, images of Zhou Ziheng keep popping into his head—specifically, the way he feigns composure when he's actually at a loss at Xia Xiqing's antics.

When they arrive at the apartment, Xia Xiqing notices many high-end security measures installed all around the premises. All doors require access cards and elevators are fingerprint-activated.

When the elevator opens, there are only two suites. Chen

Fang points to the one on the right and says, "Tl... one is yours."

"What about that one?" Xia Xiqing asks, pointing to a suite on the left.

"I don't know," Chen Fang replies. "The suite was sold as a floor plan before the building was even completed, but all information about residents is kept pretty secure. Eiter way, they've got to be *very* rich."

The apartment is beautiful. The floor-to-ceiling windows allow for plenty of natural light. The wide space of the central living area is minimally decorated. The most eye-catching feature is the staircase, which is in the shape of a Fibonacci spiral.

"There's room for a heated swimming pool on the second floor if you want." Chen Fang winks at Xia Xiqing. "You can party it up!"

"Alright. This one it is, then." Xia Xiqing says unflinchingly, not even blinking as he makes the payment in full.

It doesn't take more than a few minutes before he's dragging Chen Fang out for some food and drinks to catch up. They chat about the reality show and life in general. When the topic of Zhou Ziheng is brought up, Xia Xiqing's facial expression totally changes.

"Hey, isn't Zhou Ziheng that movie star you really like?" Chen Fang's eyes brighten. "So you were sleeping with your celebrity crush that night?!"

Fortunately they're in a private room, or Xia Xiqing would be seeing his own name in tomorrow's headline again with how loud Chen Fang just spoke.

"Nope. Failed." Xia Xiqing takes a sip of his wine. "He slept on the couch, and I slept on the bed. Then I left halfway through the night."

"Really? Since when could you stay in the same room with another man and not do anything?" Chen Fang bowls over with laughter.

"What are you talking about? Am I that bad?" Xia Xiqing raises an eyebrow, then he finishes the rest of his wine in one go.

Chen Fang laughs. "You tell me."

He's right. It really isn't like Xia Xiqing to have just left him alone.

Xia Xiqing checks his phone. Zhou Ziheng hasn't responded yet.

Seeing him look down, Chen Fang smirks. "Why do you keep looking at your phone? Is it whoever you're seeing right now?"

"Look, I've been keeping myself chaste these days, okay?" Xia Xiqing clicks on Zhou Ziheng's profile picture. Weird. He's a full-grown adult man, but his profile image is an origami flower.

Childish.

But then he remembers how much of a goody-two-shoes Zhou Ziheng is, and he starts wanting to laugh. He clicks on his profile and gives him an alias.

Moral Role Model

Xia Xiqing doesn't know what's wrong with him; playing such childish games with Zhou Ziheng. Maybe it's because he's a celebrity, and if he plans to sleep with someone so high-profile, he needs to plan it thoroughly.

Or maybe Zhou Ziheng is just too difficult.

But difficult ones are Xia Xiqing's favorite.

When the director finishes describing their next scene, Zhou Ziheng turns to walk away, but the director stops him.

"Wait, don't go yet, Xiao-Heng! It's been a few tough days; let's all go out for a nice meal. My treat."

Zhou Ziheng isn't really into group meals like this, but this director has known him since he was very young, so it's difficult to say no to him. He goes, and they all have a great time eating, laughing, and chatting. For almost the entire night, Zhou Ziheng forgets all about Xia Xiqing.

"Drink?" one of the other actors offers, holding up a bottle of beer.

"Xiao-Heng doesn't drink," the director replies before he can. "Oh right, Xiao-Heng, your phone kept going off earlier and you still haven't checked to see what's wrong. What if it's something important? Don't let us keep you from it."

What could be so important? Zhou Ziheng scoffs to himself. Without much expectation, he looks through the long string of messages that Xia Xiqing sent him earlier.

ZZH: Return my jacket.

Tsing: You want your jacket? Beg me.

Tsing: You really didn't do anything to me that night? I remember someone touching my face. You wouldn't take advantage of me, would you?

Tsing: But seriously, what do you think of me? Do you think anything could happen between us? I feel like we're not very compatible as friends, but surely we can be something else to each other.

Tsing: I really like you, and not just in the way that a fan likes an idol.

Tsing: I like you in the way where I could get hard just looking at your jacket.

Seeing the last message, Zhou Ziheng begins to panic. He fears that someone around him may see it, so he quickly covers it with his hand. However, he accidentally clicks into Xia Xiqing's profile instead.

He has a new icon. The selfie he sent earlier today is now his icon.

This guy has gone insane...

Zhou Ziheng glares at the picture for a long while. Then, he backs out of the image and, teeth gritted, he changes Xia Xiqing's alias to something more fitting:

Terrorist

In the ensuing days, Xia Xiqing doesn't reach out to Zhou Ziheng again. Obviously, Zhou Ziheng wouldn't reach out to Xia Xiqing either. It's not often that Xia Xiqing encounters someone as reticent as Zhou Ziheng; the last time he did, he'd resolved the issue within the week. However, it's a little different with Zhou Ziheng.

Xia Xiqing is willing to be patient this time.

Anyone and anything that can satisfy him like this, he's willing to invest time into.

When it comes time to move in to his new apartment, the plan is to invite Xu Qichen and Chen Fang and that lot over later in the day for a housewarming party. It works out, since it's also the day that the first episode of *Survive and Escape* is supposed to air.

A lot of money has been spent on marketing this show. The trailer has been shared over twenty thousand times, and the five guests of the show all seem to have exploded in popularity overnight. Even Xia Xiqing, who's emerged from obscurity as a fan himself of Zhou Ziheng, seems to have gained a hefty following.

The first trailer is pretty typical of the suspense genre, all fragmented scenes and mixed lines along with fast and heavy background music.

Compared to traditional escape rooms, this room contains an extra element—the Killer. This further enhances the suspense of the scene.

Since it's the trailer for a variety program, Xia Xiqing knows it's supposed to be extra intriguing to bait more viewers. But he hadn't expected the bait to be so well-executed.

"So...what if you're not just a regular player?" Cen-Cen's voice plays over the footage of Zhou Ziheng unlocking Xia Xiqing's handcuffs. Then, it switches to a shot of Xia Xiqing's smiling face as he leans against a wall: "If I were the Killer, the first thing I'd do is kill Zhou Ziheng."

There's a clip of Ruan Xiao digging through a jewelry box, and also one of Shang Sirui sitting down as he says, "Oh, I forfeited my vote."

Then it cuts to Xia Xiqing and Zhou Ziheng face-to-face with each other at the very beginning of the game—one blindfolded and handcuffed, the other bound in rope. Once again, Cen-Cen's voice plays over the shot: "So Xia Xiqing was right? Ziheng, you really are the Killer?"

Suddenly, it cuts to black.

No, it hasn't cut off. Xia Xiqing presses his earbud closer, listening to the sound of quiet panting. The scene has been shot in infrared: Zhou Ziheng presses Xia Xiqing against the wall, hand covering his mouth. Zhou Ziheng's voice plays over the footage. "If I were the Killer, I would indeed prioritize killing him."

There's a series of clips, each of the players in their starting rooms, then a blurred-out clip of someone leaving the final door.

Then Xia Xiqing's own voice, weak but calm.

"I can't escape."

With the sound of a slamming door, the title card *Survive and Escape* appears, and the trailer ends.

Xia Xiqing takes out his earbuds and shakes his head. He's baffled at how the production team is able to take apart the footage and piece it together in a way that creates suspense without spoiling the plot. Using conversations out of place and out of context, it creates a perfect illusion of conflict centered between him and Zhou Ziheng—perfect for distracting from Shang Sirui's identity as the real Killer.

It's very well done.

Xia Xiqing scrolls down to the almost ten thousand comments below to see what the viewers have said, and indeed they are well within his expectations.

@NotCute: Ahhhh what kind of enemies-and-lovers romance-murder type of plot is this? Fanfic writers are gonna get overindulged

@Shinyyyy: oh wow escape room mixed with werewolves of millers hollow!!! the pair who, if theyre the killer, each wants to kill the other first! its been so long since ive seen something this exciting. not a zzh fan but hes great in here!

@IFailedAllMyClasses: WOOT! Super Alpha Zhou Ziheng! The scene where Xia Xiqing was pressed against the wall... mind-blowing!

@ButterflyNotButtFly: the little gege in the white shirt is so cute! he's practically angelic when he smiles—definitely not the killer.

@33TheCutie: I gotta say pastel yellow Sirui is suuuper cute. High IQ games are not like him though.

@SiruiSweetAsCandy: Hahaha our 33[10] is so clueless to everything!!!! Hahahaha

---

10 "San-San" is a nickname for Shang Sirui, but its literal meaning is "three-three," so it is sometimes written as 33.

@LoveliestSirui: Please don't let Rui-Rui die first. I feel like he might die first...

@SisterTreasure: Does anyone else see this show as a feast for pretty faces? Look at that Mensa girl, pretty and smart! What a goddess!

@MarryMeCenGe: OMG Cen-Cen!! Hubby so rarely goes on reality shows and the one time she does she spends all her time questioning others hahahaha!

@ILOVECC: My Cen is sooo pretty! Marry me plox

@KarenLee: Not a fan but I came across this trailer. Seems like a good plot with very realistic props.

@NotARealZombie: Very few good and intense shows like this recently. I got goosebumps from just watching the trailer.

@HeeHeeHee: Something strange and dark is going on here. Can't wait to find out. Great job in choosing the cast, Zhou Ziheng and his fan make for a very good blend of shippy feels and IQ. Romance and murder, I love it!

...

Jiang Yin really deserves her good reputation. Xia Xiqing had expected a good response, but he certainly hadn't expected the shipping fans to bite so easily. Almost half the comments are about the Zhou Ziheng/Xia Xiqing ship.

Xia Xiqing is curious about how Zhou Ziheng feels about this trailer. He imagines his face, blank but with a hint of unhappiness. Wanting to tease him a little, Xia Xiqing pulls out his phone and opens Zhou Ziheng's chat window, but then he hesitates.

Looking at the last message that still hasn't received a reply, Xia Xiqing slowly closes the app and tosses his phone at the sofa off-handedly.

As soon as he does so, it begins to ring. At first Xia Xiqing is quite pleased, thinking that it might be Zhou Ziheng, but then he sees the caller ID and finds his good mood rapidly evaporating. He hesitates, but eventually answers.

After the call, he grabs a cigarette and walks around his room a bit, then gets dressed and goes outside.

Before getting into his car, Xia Xiqing sends a message to the relevant WeChat group.

Xia Xiqing: Let's postpone tonight's get together.

Chen Fang: Are you flaking?

Xia Zhixu: [CHEER.jpg]

Xu Qichen: What's wrong? I was just about to ask Zhixu to bring some groceries over so I could cook for you.

Xia Xiqing: Something came up. Tomorrow! Tomorrow I'll prepare booze and we'll have seafood.

Xia Xiqing starts his car. It's nearly rush hour and traffic is really bad. He is not in a good mood, and begins to drive as it starts to rain.

Luckily, he has an umbrella in the car. He pulls over and gets out. The gates of the school he's stopped by is flooded with the colorful umbrellas of students and parents on their way home.

He looks around but doesn't find what he's looking for. Suddenly, someone hugs him from behind.

"Ge!"

Xia Xiqing sighs and breaks free from the hug. He turns around and finds Xia Xiuze's smiling face. His hair is wet from the rain and water is dripping down his cheeks. His eyes, so similar to Xia Xiqing's own, are happy little slits.

"Why didn't you call your dad?" Xia Xiqing asks this so-called little brother of his. Then he says, "Here," and hands him the umbrella.

"He's on a business trip in the UK." Xia Xiuze takes the umbrella from Xia Xiqing. Though he's only a sophomore, Xia Xiuze is only half a head shorter than Xia Xiqing.

Why didn't you call your mom? Xia Xiqing wants to ask, but instead he says, "So what if you haven't got a parent to send? It's not like your teacher can make him come back from abroad."

"Everyone else has a parent in attendance... I, if I don't... It just doesn't feel proper."

"How's it improper? I graduated just fine," Xia Xiqing replies bluntly. Still, he starts walking toward the school.

Xia Xiuze understands this as the tacit assent it is, and happily follows along, holding up the umbrella for his older brother and using it as an opportunity to stick close to him. He's always looked up to his older brother; he thinks his brother is the best, the most impressive. Everyone likes his brother, and he's the one who likes him the most.

Unfortunately, they're not exactly full siblings. Xia Xiuze's mother invaded Xia Xiqing's family; a family that had already been falling apart. And from this invasion and subsequent eruption of the original Xia family, Xia Xiuze was born.

Growing up, Xia Xiuze had not been on the receiving end of Xia Xiqing's many charms. In fact, quite the opposite— Xia Xiqing was quite cold to his little half-brother. Being ten years younger, Xia Xiuze grew up afraid of his brother, since he had always completely ignored the very existence of him and his mother.

That is, until Xia Xiuze's sixth birthday. He'd been having a party upstairs with his friends when he looked out the window and saw his brother sitting on the front steps. That day, Xia Xiqing had gotten beat up very badly.

He looked everywhere through his things, but he could only find a very small adhesive bandage. He rushed downstairs with it and approached his brother, but was so intimidated that he didn't quite know what to say.

Finally, his older brother turned to him, smiling. The bright splotch of blood at the corner of his lips had looked like a proudly blooming rose.

"Are you happy?"

Birthdays are supposed to be happy.

Seeing me brought so low—that should bring you happiness.

Xia Xiuze didn't dare to reply. He held out the tiny adhesive bandage, then said, "Gege, I can help you stick this on. It won't hurt anymore if you have a bandage on."

That night, Xia Xiqing hugged his brother for the first time; hugged him as if they were real siblings.

Burying his head into his tiny shoulder, Xia Xiqing cried.

To most people, Xia Xiqing seems cold and hostile toward his brother. Only Xia Xiuze knows that his brother truly cares for him.

Xia Xiuze was short in junior high, so he got bullied a lot back then. The bullies would lock him in the restrooms and threaten to beat him up unless he gave them all his money. One day, he'd forgotten his wallet at home, and so they beat him up quite badly.

Coming home all bruised, his father had demanded to know if he'd been picking fights at school. For that, he almost got beat up again, but his mother had stopped his father. That night, his parents had fought the entire night away, each trying to pass the blame onto the other.

To this day, Xia Xiuze still remembers how Xia Xiqing had just stood in the corner and watched the entire thing impassively without any attempts at interference.

But the next day, when Xia Xiuze locked himself in his room and refused to go to school, Xia Xiqing had been the one to drag him out and bring him there. They found the bullies and Xia Xiqing had beat the living hell out of them.

"This kid really is both a coward and a wimp, but he's my brother and you bastards don't get to teach him any lessons for me."

Xia Xiqing shoved Xia Xiuze bit by bit until he stood in front of the bullies.

"If you lose another fight to these morons, you can stop telling people that I'm your brother."

Ever since that day, Xia Xiqing has been Xia Xiuze's hero.

"Alright." Xia Xiqing sends Xia Xiuze off at the classroom door. "You can stop following me now."

The crowd around them were all Xia Xiuze's classmates. They all stared unblinkingly at Xia Xiqing. The girls especially seemed a bit excitable, quietly whispering amongst themselves.

Xia Xiqing is attractive, so he's used to some attention, but this seems a bit out of the ordinary. Then he remembers that he's pretty much internet famous at this point, especially now that the trailer of *Survive and Escape* has been released.

"Xia Xiuze, is this your..."

"My brother!" Xia Xiuze hangs off of Xia Xiqing's arm. "Isn't he even more attractive than most celebrities?"

"Your family's got good genes..."

"Gege is really cute!"

Xia Xiqing shakes Xia Xiuze off, slightly annoyed. "You can go home now. I'll be off when the conference is done."

"I forgot the house keys, and our nanny took a week off

the day before yesterday." Xia Xiuze replies, looking rather aggrieved. "Mrs. Zhang's son got surgery, so she has to be home to take care of him. I've been eating at school."

Xia Xiqing raises an eyebrow. "What about Yu Fangyue?" Blatantly disrespectful, he uses the full name of Xia Xiuze's mother.

Xia Xiuze's expression wavers. "She went to the UK too."

Like a watchdog, the bitch is keeping close track of the man she's stolen. How interesting. Xia Xiqing hands his car keys to Xia Xiuze. "Go wait in my car."

Xia Xiqing has always been quite cold to his brother. At first, he was disgusted by him—seeing his innocent smile always reminds him of his own terrible childhood. He had always treated Xia Xiuze as a stranger rather than a family member; at least, that was until the day he saw his father take a swing at him with a golf club. In that scene, Xia Xiqing had seen a younger version of himself.

The arguments between his father and his step-mother were ceaseless, just like they had been with his own mother—over money, over responsibilities, over other women. And Xia Xiuze got stuck in between.

Slowly, Xia Xiqing began to empathize with Xia Xiuze. Perhaps it's because his own childhood had been so disgustingly terrible that he just couldn't bear to see another child grow up in the same situation.

It was like looking into a mirror. Very discomfiting.

The parent-teacher conference doesn't last too long. Xia Xiqing is very good at pretending. He fools the teacher into thinking that he's a perfect role model of elder brotherhood, a caring adult that can function as a positive influence on Xia Xiuze.

The rain has gotten heavier by the time the meeting ends. Xia Xiqing takes off his suit jacket, preparing to use it as cover for the outside, but when he gets to the lobby he finds Xia Xiuze just standing there. He's still got his huge backpack on, and the umbrella is still in his hand. His head is hanging, too, and with his dark green uniform, he looks like a wilted scallion stalk.

Hearing the sound of Xia Xiqing's footsteps, Xia Xiuze perks up and dashes, puppy-like, toward his brother. "All done? I'm hungry."

"Then go home."

"But no one is home to make me food. I want the noodles you make, ge."

Xia Xiqing rolls his eyes and agrees reluctantly. It's a miracle that someone likes his cooking. But he couldn't shake off Xia Xiuze no matter what he says; he sticks to him like glue. With no other options, he could only drive him to his new house. Plus, it would be nice to get himself some dry clothes.

Xia Xiuze beams and yakks away the entire trip back to Xia Xiqing's apartment, mostly just idle gossip.

"Wow! This place is super cool!" Xia Xiuze exclaims as they exit the elevator. Knowing this is a private elevator and there'd be no one else around, he hugs Xia Xiqing's arm the moment he steps out.

"Can I come here more often? I can do my homework here and maybe you can help me with the questions I don't know how to do."

Xia Xiqing is tired after pushing him away one time too many, so he simply lets Xia Xiuze hug all he wants. He just wants to rest. "Aren't you the third best student in the class?"

"Maybe next time I can be the best," Xia Xiuze replies with excitement. "I can come do work here. I swear I won't be trouble. You don't have a boyfriend, right? I won't be a bother? So can I come? I can, right?"

Boyfriend... When was the last time he had a proper boyfriend...?

But kids are easy to lie to. If he rejects him now, Xia Xiuze will keep pestering him given his personality. Xia Xiqing activates the lock to the room and answers him perfunctorily, "Whatever you want."

Suddenly, there are sounds coming from the suite across the hall—keys jingling and locks unlocking. Xia Xiqing has lived here for more than a week now and hasn't seen or heard anyone come out of that apartment.

"You're the best! I love you!" Xia Xiuze offers Xia Xiqing a tight hug. "Quick! Open the door, I want to see the inside."

Before Xia Xiqing can unlock his own door, the door across the hall opens.

"C'mon, let go of me, I can't unlock the door," Xia Xiqing complains.

"Nope."

This kid... Xia Xiqing tells himself silently. He was just about to lecture him, when—

WHAM—

Does his neighbor need to slam the door so loudly? Where are his manners?

Xia Xiqing turns around and freezes on the spot. *What the actual fuck...*

His expression almost cracks.

Zhou Ziheng?

His neighbor?

Zhou Ziheng is wearing a black coat. He crosses his arm and leans against the door. He stares at Xia Xiqing indifferently, then glances at Xia Xiuze.

He was on his way out for dinner when he heard Xia Xiqing's voice outside the door. He thought it he was hallucinating it; that it was just because he's been so paranoid about running into him. But it's real.

He looks at Xia Xiuze again. Must be his new hookup, he thinks.

"Let me go."

Xia Xiqing nudges Xia Xiuze while eyeing Zhou Ziheng. Seeing the seriousness in his brother's eyes, Xia Xiuze releases him quietly. He's gotten a look at Zhou Ziheng. This face has graced countless magazines and stickers of the girls in his class, and has also appeared many times in his older brother's studio. Xia Xiuze subconsciously felt that his relationship with his older brother was not that simple, so he pouts.

"Can you open the door first? I want to go in."

Xia Xiqing unlocks the door, and Xia Xiuze goes into the apartment.

"I'll just wait inside." Xia Xiuze looks at him worriedly and whispers before closing the door softly.

Wait inside? Wait inside for what? Zhou Ziheng frowns.

Xia Xiqing slouches lazily by his door and flashes a smile at Zhou Ziheng, his earlier astonishment long gone. "Hey! What are the chances?"

Still the same words, still the same smile—this guy hasn't changed a single bit.

Xia Xiqing has no bounds. He doesn't play by the rules. And no word of truth comes out of his mouth.

Inexplicably enough, Zhou Ziheng is ticked off. There's fire in his voice and anger in his eyes. "Really? Even minors? You really are a scumbag."

The strange thing is, Xia Xiqing finds it very hot to hear Zhou Ziheng say the word scumbag. "Scumbag. Yep, that's me." He steps forward with an innocent and guileless smile, his eyes brimming with tenderness that's even warmer than the sun in spring.. "You're right. Even kids."

Zhou Ziheng feels strange hearing these words. It makes him wonder if Xia Xiqing has ever truly given his heart to anyone else.

"So, why do you think I'll let you get away?" Xia Xiqing asks.

Before Zhou Ziheng can react, Xia Xiqing reaches his long arm out and places it on Zhou Ziheng's shoulder. He runs his long fingers down the center before flicking one of the buttons sewn to the front of Zhou Ziheng's long black jacket. He gazes into Zhou Ziheng's eyes.

"Hey," he starts.

He blinks slowly.

"This jacket is quite nice too."

What's this guy doing—is he actually flirting?! He's got one inside his apartment already.

Zhou Ziheng grabs Xia Xiqing's wandering hand and asks firmly, "What you trying to do?"

Xia Xiqing's eyes shift lazily toward his wrist, which is in Zhou Ziheng's tight grasp, then back into his eyes. Expressionless, he says, "Ouch."

An almost involuntary "Sorry," pops out of Zhou Ziheng's lips as he loosens his grip.

Wait. He started this. Why am I apologizing...?

Xia Xiqing really enjoys teasing Zhou Ziheng. He enjoys getting him to the point where he's angry but still restraining himself from retaliating. Just like a baby tiger, fierce but cute; a little teasing makes him angry. Catch him in a tiny, delicate, and beautiful cage, and watch him in the frenzy that he can't snap out of. There are only two possible outcomes: tame him, or be devoured by him.

Obviously, the confident and proud Xia Xiqing could only consider the former.

"Don't you think fate brought us together?" Xia Xiqing rubs his smarting wrist. "I mean, I obviously didn't know you lived here when I bought the place. Do you live alone?"

Zhou Ziheng remains silent. He moves slightly to the side, blocking the view of his apartment from Xia Xiqing's line of sight.

Xia Xiqing takes the silence as confirmation. "Me too. I live alone as well."

"So you can bring home whoever you want," Zhou Ziheng replies with disgust.

"See, why do you have to put it like that? Like I need your permission to bring people home."

Zhou Ziheng is speechless. He's also confused about why this concerns him so much. Why is he so angry? Why does Xia Xiqing's promiscuity bother him? There shouldn't be any reason why he's concerned with Xia Xiqing's private life.

Is there?

"Don't be alarmed if you hear strange sounds." Xia Xiqing follows up. "But with such an expensive building, sound insulation should be excellent."

Zhou Ziheng gives him an annoyed and impatient look. "If I hear anything, I'll move out."

"Move to where?" Xia Xiqing asks with a smile and a flirtatious tone. "Move in with me?"

Shameless...

Just as Zhou Ziheng is about to give out a disgusted look, Xia Xiqing's apartment door opens slightly. A small head pops out of the opening. Zhou Ziheng immediately puts on his hood and face mask and begins to walk away.

I'm moving, he thinks. *I'm moving tonight. Calling my moving company right after dinner.*

After only half a step, Zhou Ziheng feels a bind stopping him. He looks down and sees the strange kid with his arms wrapped around his waist.

"Uhh... What are you doing?" he asks.

Xia Xiuze lets out a wide smile. "Zhou Ziheng-*gege*! I love your films. Can I get an autograph?"

What the hell?

Zhou Ziheng isn't the only one confused—Xia Xiqing too is quite baffled.

"Wait, what?" Zhou Ziheng struggles a bit. "Let go of me first."

"Where are you going, Zhou Ziheng-*gege*?" Xia Xiuze asks without the slightest ease to his grip.

Xia Xiqing rolls his eyes at his brother's behavior and grabs him by the arm. "What's going on with you?"

Even under Xia Xiqing's tugging, Xia Xiuze refuses to let go.

"I'm eating... I'm going out to eat," Zhou Ziheng finally replies, maintaining the last of his celebrity dignity. "Can you let go of me now?"

Xia Xiuze's eyes light up. "Really? Come over to our place for dinner! My brother was about to cook."

Brother?!

Stunned, Zhou Ziheng is trying to comprehend the situation when Xia Xiqing jumped in and kicked Xia Xiuze in the foot. "Who the hell said I was going to cook?!"

"Ah!" Xia Xiuze looks aggrieved as he turns to hide behind Zhou Ziheng, his hands still wrapped around his waist. Seeing Xia Xiqing still about to strike again, he subconsciously shields Xia Xiuze.

"Don't hit him!" Zhou Ziheng calls out.

What the heck? Xia Xiqing is puzzled. "I'm educating my little brother. What business is it of yours?!"

"He's really your brother?" Zhou Ziheng asks, not really expecting an answer. Now that he looks again, they kind of do look alike.

He feels a sense of relief putting out his anger. Following that relief, he suddenly feels guilty for having accused Xia Xiqing based on nothing but prejudice. Zhou Ziheng looks at Xia Xiqing. He's frowning slightly—it looks like he's really unhappy.

"Zhou Ziheng-*gege*." Xia Xiuze seizes his chance to butt in. "Come over for dinner."

"Xia Xiuze! Are you looking for even more punishment?" Xia Xiqing interrupts.

"Hey, hey, calm down. All the same family, right?" Zhou Ziheng attempts to ease the situation.

"Same family?" Xia Xiqing looks up and raises his eyebrows. This time there's no smile on his face, fully revealing his true personality. "Who's the same family? Us?"

He stares at Zhou Ziheng. Xia Xiqing gives Xia Xiuze a mean look and turns around. He kicks open the door with force and storms into his apartment.

Seeing his brother leave, Xia Xiuze lets go of Zhou Ziheng.

"Zhou Ziheng-*gege*, you're a great actor. I really like your role of... umm... Yang Wei... and umm... Feng Ziming." Xia Xiuze says, trying to not mess up his fanboy act. He'd only just asked a few female classmates for this information earlier as he was waiting inside.

Zhou Ziheng stares down at Xia Xiuze, wondering if this kid is indeed a fan. He then remembers all the paintings Xia Xiqing painted. If the older brother is a fan, why not the whole family? Zhou Ziheng tells this to himself.

And just like that, A-list actor Zhou Ziheng is convinced by this fake fan.

Zhou Ziheng sits on a couch. He feels strange, but he can't exactly pinpoint why. Xia Xiuze is all grins as he sits beside him, asking him a whole bunch of questions like he's doing some sort of questionnaire.

"Zhou Ziheng-*gege*, do you have any siblings?"

"Zhou Ziheng-*gege*, what do your parents do?"

"Zhou Ziheng-*gege*, how often do you visit home?"

"Zhou Ziheng-*gege*, are you dating anyone?"

"Zhou Ziheng-*gege*..."

Xia Xiuze is interrupted when he is picked up by the back of his collar. He looks back—it's his older brother with an artificial smile plastered on him.

"Shut up and come here!"

"Okay." Xia Xiuze reluctantly scrambles off the couch, flashes a smile at Zhou Ziheng, and walks into the kitchen with Xia Xiqing.

"Alright," Xia Xiqing says while continuing to cook. "What are you trying to do?"

"Nothing really." Xia Xiuze walks around the kitchen and starts poking around. "It's just that, you know, you like Zhou Ziheng-*gege*, so I'm trying to talk to him for you."

Xia Xiqing grabs a spatula and taps Xia Xiuze's head with it a few times. "Who told you I like him?"

Xia Xiuze pouts while rubbing his head. "I think you do. I mean... you know... you have all those paintings of him. And you weren't mad at him when he misunderstood the situation back there."

Xia Xiqing turns around and gives Xia Xiuze a cold smile,

then returns to looking at the stove. "That's because I don't like him, so I didn't feel bothered enough to explain."

"Then why are you afraid of me talking to him?" Xia Xiuze stands closer to Xia Xiqing. "If you don't like him, then you wouldn't really care if I mess something up with him."

That makes Xia Xiqing think for a second. The kid's got a point. He throws a displeased glance at him and grabs him by the collar. "I just don't want you to interfere with my life. I promise I don't like him."

"Alright, alright." Xia Xiuze steps back with his hands up. "I won't interfere."

Xia Xiuze walks out of the kitchen, but right before his shadow disappears, he pops his head back in and says, "Don't make promises you can't keep!" He then chuckles and runs for his life before Xia Xiqing can retaliate.

This kid; he's been too nice to him recently. Give him an inch, and he takes a mile. Absolutely no respect.

Xia Xiqing curses and kicks the cabinet door.

Zhou Ziheng is still sitting on the couch, bored and awkward. He has nothing to do other than look around the room. There are only two suites on this floor, and since he owns the other one, the layout is basically the same. However, the decor is significantly different; being an artist, Xia Xiqing has fully customized his space to fit his personality.

"Zhou Ziheng-*gege*..."

Xia Xiuze's voice suddenly appears, and it startles Zhou Ziheng. He turns and sees the kid's adorable smiling head pop up from behind the couch.

He smiles just like Xia Xiqing, Zhou Ziheng admits to himself.

If Xia Xiqing also smiled like this while calling him "Zhou Ziheng-*gege*"...

"Zhou Ziheng-*gege*?"

Zhou Ziheng flinches and answers, somewhat flustered, "Yeah, what's up?"

"Oh, nothing really." Xia Xiuze maintains his smile and kneels on the carpet. "Do you know how to cook?"

Zhou Ziheng looks at Xia Xiuze and begins to walk toward the kitchen. He notices the smell of burnt food as he approaches.

Xia Xiqing had been distracted looking at his phone. Hearing Zhou Ziheng's voice, he immediately turns off the stove.

"What are you doing here?" Xia Xiqing asks.

"Are you trying to poison us?" Zhou Ziheng stares into a pan of black stuff. "What's this?"

Xia Xiqing looks at the pot and back at Zhou Ziheng. "Eggs. Can't you tell?"

Zhou Ziheng sighs loudly and grabs the pan from Xia Xiqing. He dumps the so-called eggs into the trash bin and rinses out the pot. "How about you let me do the cooking? I don't want tomorrow's news headline to be 'Zhou Ziheng Dead from Food Poisoning.'"

"More like you don't want to be found dead here at my place," Xia Xiqing says as he shrugs and leans against the kitchen counter. He removes his apron and tosses it aside, giving up on his eggs. Tapping on the marble counter with his finger, he continues, "You don't want to be seen with people like me."

The flirtatious tone of voice is back again.

"I'm sorry."

Xia Xiqing looks at Zhou Ziheng, baffled. His finger pauses mid-action. He raises his eyebrows like he misheard something.

Zhou Ziheng pours some oil into a pan. "I'm sorry for how I spoke to you earlier. I shouldn't have judged you like that. My prejudice toward you was unfair." He looks at Xia Xiqing and proceeds to crack an egg. The sound of sizzling masks the awkward silence.

Zhou Ziheng feels apprehensive, unsure if his apology was sincere. He knows even less about how Xia Xiqing feels.

"I—"

"Umm... Why... Why are you apologizing?"

Both speaks up at the same time, killing the awkwardness in the air.

"I just feel like I should," Zhou Ziheng replies while flipping the egg. "Misjudging the situation was my fault, and I should apologize for that. I shouldn't accuse you of anything without evidence."

"Evidence?" Xia Xiqing smirks. "Why are you making it sound like I was caught red-handed in bed?"

Zhou Ziheng is speechless. He feels misinterpreted once again.

"But no need to apologize to me," Xia Xiqing says before Zhou Ziheng can respond. "Because you're right. What you saw today is not the norm."

Xia Xiqing is a person who likes to formulates his words carefully. After all, lies and deceptions take time to weave. However, upon hearing Zhou Ziheng's apology, he blabbed out the first thing that came to mind.

Concern and apologies have never been a normal part of Xia Xiqing's life. In face of this, he feels at a loss; weak and vulnerable. Zhou Ziheng, on the other hand, has no lack of them. It is as if he's his natural nemesis who holds all his weaknesses in his hands.

Xia Xiqing turns around to wash his hands. "Don't think

you know and understand me. Maybe your prejudiced judgment of me is actually the correct one."

These words ring inside Zhou Ziheng's head. As he watches Xia Xiqing rinse his hands in the sink, he imagines a scene where a murderer is washing blood off his hands.

Xia Xiqing turns off the faucet and reaches for some paper towels. "I'm the type of person that likes to pursue. It gives me satisfaction to see another person offer me their whole-hearted sincerity and devotion." He dries his hands with the paper towel and tosses it away. "But once I get what I want, I'll get tired of it. I'll think of ways to leave, sans the burdensome heart they gave me. I only like the chase. Yes, I'm a scumbag like that."

Xia Xiqing closes the trash can and leans his head over Zhou Ziheng's shoulder, like a lover offering a kiss. His eyes stare directly into Zhou Ziheng's soul. "Are you afraid?"

Zhou Ziheng does not understand what Xia Xiqing is trying to do. Why would he come clean now? Given his character, the wise strategy would be to deceive as long as he could. Like a peacock spreading its tail, showing you his most gentlemanly, gentle face to attract you and seduce you so that you'd willing fall into the trap yourself. What type of deception is this? What is he trying to accomplish?

To be honest, Xia Xiqing doesn't even know himself at this moment. He feels strange and exposed. It's like he involuntarily ripped off his own mask and revealed his vulnerabilities.

Amongst all the prey Xia Xiqing has romantically pursued, Zhou Ziheng is special. He's known since the very beginning that Xia Xiqing's gentleness is an act. He's been on guard since the start. All disguises fail in front of him, and now he has even chosen to tear apart the lie of " love." It's like Xia Xiqing's showcasing the most rotten and ugly parts of himself in front of his eyes, like a strange artwork to be viewed and judged.

Perhaps for this reason, Zhou Ziheng is his most prized target.

Zhou Ziheng, who's been quietly cooking, turns around and gazes at Xia Xiqing's beautiful yet frivolous eyes. The perfectly sculpted face shows no expression, save for a cool indifference.

"What should I be afraid of?"

Just like the conversation they had in the escape room's dark study, Zhou Ziheng's voice is like the bell of the Cathedral of Santa Maria del Fiore, striking his heart, toll after toll.

"Afraid of you pursuing me? Or afraid that I'll give you my heart?"

These words make Xia Xiqing's heart pump louder and blood flow faster.

"If it's one of those two, then I'm not afraid," Zhou Ziheng replies with a quirk of his lips.

Not afraid of either? Not afraid of the former is a lack of interest. Not afraid of the latter is a lack of temptation.

At the moment, Xia Xiqing feels his blood begin to boil. His pride and confidence are challenged. He reaches out his hand and strokes Zhou Ziheng's chin. Before Zhou Ziheng can react, Xia Xiqing gives a very flirtatious smile, and looks into Zhou Ziheng's eyes with undisguised sensuality.

"You'd better not be."

C.05

The Game Is On

Zhou Ziheng arrives in the central living area with three bowls of noodles and a plate of fried eggs and bacon.

"There wasn't much in the fridge. This will have to suffice for dinner." He puts down the food on the dining table.

Xia Xiuze appears very excited. He takes off his school uniform jacket and plants himself on a chair, then grabs his chopsticks and quickly places the largest piece of bacon into his mouth.

"Thank you, Zhou Ziheng-*gege*!"

Zhou Ziheng is contemplating how to call Xia Xiqing for dinner. After all, the two rivals just had a verbal battle and Zhou Ziheng is uncertain how Xia Xiqing feels. Without saying a word, Zhou Ziheng sits down at the table with Xia Xiuze.

Xia Xiqing silently walks into the room, drenched in the deep smoky smell of cigarettes. He sits down in front of a bowl and slurps his noodles.

"It's delicious." Xia Xiqing looks up at Zhou Ziheng with a smile.

Zhou Ziheng is a bit dazed by this, having not expected this reaction from Xia Xiqing. Despite growing up famous, he was never good at handling praise. Every time someone offers him compliments, he always comes up with self-deprecating things to avoid the credit.

"Nah, too much salt, and it's missing a few items. Next time, I..."

Next time?

What next time? There won't be a next time. Zhou Ziheng is shocked by these words that rolled off his tongue. Xia Xiqing lets out a soft laugh and continues to eat his noodles in silence.

Zhou Ziheng is a smart guy. High IQ. Always an overachiever academically. But when it comes to emotions, he is extremely inexperienced—clumsy and often caught off-guard, like a thief falling off a roof and incapacitating himself before he can celebrate his loot.

Xia Xiqing can't think of any reason why he would fail in his pursuit of Zhou Ziheng. If he did, then he would have learned nothing in his past years.

They've exchanged insults, and Xia Xiqing even admitted to being a scumbag—but Zhou Ziheng seems okay with that; maybe even tempted. Xia Xiqing asked if he was afraid, and he was unmoved. For everything he says, he has a rebuttal.

So, let the game begin.

Xia Xiqing feels warm inside. He is unsure if it's due to his situation with Zhou Ziheng or the hot bowl of noodle soup in front of him.

"Hey, brother! Your show is about to start!" Xia Xiuze runs toward the television with his bowl. "How do I turn on the TV?"

Finishing up his last bite, Xia Xiqing rolls his eyes and clicks something on his phone.

"It's on!" Xia Xiuze exclaims.

Zhou Ziheng is secretly examining the brothers; they are indeed a strange pair of siblings.

Xia Xiuze runs over from the couch. "Zhou Ziheng-*gege*, let's watch it together."

"Umm, I should go home."

"Don't go back." Xia Xiuze drags Zhou Ziheng to the couch and sits him down. "Do you still have work?"

"Not today..."

"Then no excuses!" Xia Xiuze sits down next to Zhou Ziheng. "You live so close by. You can stay and watch the show with me. If there's something I don't understand, I can just ask you."

This kid is really persuasive. Having run out of ways to decline, Zhou Ziheng elects to stay.

Xia Xiuze's spell doesn't only affect Zhou Ziheng—Xia Xiqing is caught within it as well. The three of them sit on the couch to watch the first episode of *Survive and Escape*. The first episode begins with staff members taking the blindfolded guests to the room.

Not long after the show begins, Xia Xiuze moves from sitting on the couch to sitting on the floor closer to the TV.

"What are you doing?"

"I like to sit on the floor," Xia Xiuze replies around a mouthful of snacks. "Zhou Ziheng-*gege*, was there a script?"

"A script? We didn't get scripts. Only the Killer got any information."

"So, the room is fully locked down? Or you all pretend that there's no exit?"

"Yes, fully locked in."

"Did any of you try to pick the lock? I would try to..."

Xia Xiqing nudges Xia Xiuze on the back. "Shut up already."

"I was just asking..." Xia Xiuze scoots closer to Zhou Ziheng, feeling bullied by Xia Xiqing.

The first scene of the show is a shot of Zhou Ziheng tied to a chair.

"Wow, Zhou Ziheng-*gege*, you're so handsome!"

Seeing his own face on television is not a new experience for Zhou Ziheng, but at the moment, he is nervous. The camera switches to Xia Xiqing, focusing on his blindfolded face, half-tied hair, and white dress shirt.

The shot only includes Xia Xiqing's upper body. Nonetheless, Zhou Ziheng is able to recall everything that had happened at the time.

"My brother looks handsome too!"

The real Xia Xiqing and the Xia Xiqing on TV are obviously the same person. Yet, for some weird reason, Zhou Ziheng feels there is something different between them. It makes him want to stare directly at Xia Xiqing.

Xia Xiqing sits quietly on the couch watching the show. More precisely, he is watching Zhou Ziheng. No matter how good of an actor Zhou Ziheng is, he couldn't hide everything. Xia Xiqing can sense the self-preservation and hostility Zhou Ziheng has toward him. However, it has lessened since the escape room.

These thoughts urge Xia Xiqing to stare, and he cannot help but turn his head toward Zhou Ziheng. Coincidentally, Zhou Ziheng is also turning his head toward Xia Xiqing.

Their gazes collide and spark against each other, accidental and brief.

Zhou Ziheng quickly turns his eyes back to the TV, pretending to be watching the show blankly. The scene has changed to Xiao's room.

"Zhou Ziheng-*gege*, you're definitely not the Killer, right?" Xia Xiuze is deeply immersed in the show. If this was a regular suspense show, he'd start analyzing clues and begin guessing at the ending. But this time, two of the show's guests are sitting right in front of him, making him barely able to sit still.

"Zhou Ziheng-*gege*, what was that password about? I didn't get it.

"Ah! That's Morse code! I don't remember how to decode. Let me check.

"What happened to this lady? I missed it while searching for Morse code. Zhou Ziheng-*gege*, what did she find?"

...

Unable to take another moment of Xia Xiuze's chatter, Xia Xiqing grabs him and puts him into a neck-lock, then whispers into his ear. "Shang Sirui is the Killer. I was killed by him. Zhou Ziheng was the first to escape."

The mysteries of the show are shattered to pieces, as is Xia Xiuze's innocently optimistic worldview.

"Why?! How can you be so cruel? Are you a monster?" Xia Xiuze rolls over on the floor, kicking the air angrily. "I hate you!"

Seeing these two idiotic individuals, Zhou Ziheng can't help but smile. Something about this scene grabs his attention, making him want to turn his head.

His sight follows his desires and moves to Xia Xiqing, who is lying on the couch and laughing. His eyes are slitted like two half-moons. This is the first time Zhou Ziheng has seen such a childish expression on Xia Xiqing.

"I don't want to see you anymore. I want to go home. I want to watch it by myself!" Xia Xiuze continues to complain.

Xia Xiqing is nonreactive to Xia Xiuze's tantrum. He has one arm across his chest while the other one waves Xia Xiuze goodbye. Seeing his brother's lack of concern, Xia Xiuze grabs his backpack and storms toward the front door. He opens it vigorously and stands still for a moment.

"Are you going or not? If you're going, close the door on your way out."

Zhou Ziheng is unsure what to do. He wonders if he should offer to drive the kid home. Part of him is slightly worried.

Having given it some thought, Zhou Ziheng offers, "Well, I can drive him..."

"Death upon the spoiler's entire family!" Xia Xiuze suddenly shouts. He then turns around and dashes out the door, loudly slamming it behind him.

Xia Xiqing is so angry that he's amused. "What the hell? Did he just curse himself?"

Zhou Ziheng has no words to describe these two brothers. They're so hopeless that it's funny.

The show returns after a commercial break, and they're back in the room where he and Xia Xiqing cracked the Morse code. The camera was placed near the mirror; the point of view is totally not what Zhou Ziheng had in mind, having been there in person.

The camera angle and editing made Xia Xiqing's kick into the mirror a lot more dramatic than it actually was. The background music fits perfectly. But somehow, Zhou Ziheng still feels that something is missing.

While everything was suspenseful and dramatic, it's impossible to recreate the level of shock Zhou Ziheng received when Xia Xiqing kicked the mirror in the study.

Xia Xiqing's eyes are focused on the TV as the scene of him presenting his handcuffs to Zhou Ziheng plays out.

"Come to think of it," Zhou Ziheng breaks the silence. "I should have kept the keys to your handcuffs. Could have been useful later on to get some leverage against you."

Xia Xiqing stares at Zhou Ziheng with an expressionless face. His eyes curve slightly and the corner of his mouth exposes his white teeth; eliciting images of white snow on the roof of a house on Christmas Day.

"For all I knew, you were the Killer. I had to be on high alert." Zhou Ziheng turns his head back to the television as he sees himself unlocking Xia Xiqing's handcuffs, and continues in a soft voice. "But the truth is, if it wasn't for you, I wouldn't have made it out alive."

Xia Xiqing watches Zhou Ziheng on the television; bent over to uncuff his partner who was only a few inches away from him. "Do you know what I was thinking?"

Zhou Ziheng glances at Xia Xiqing's side profile. Lights from the television flash various colors onto his skin. "What?"

"I was thinking..." The motionless Xia Xiqing reaches his arm out and strokes the back of Zhou Ziheng's head, bringing himself closer.

Once again, the familiar smell of cologne encroaches. Before Zhou Ziheng can formulate a reaction, Xia Xiqing holds out his other hand and grabs Zhou Ziheng's chin.

"You have a very kissable face."

Upon the end of his sentence, Xia Xiqing turns his face and kisses him.

Zhou Ziheng is paralyzed by the kiss. His personal alarm

system is currently experiencing a massive delay in reaction.

Xia Xiqing must be crazy!

He tries to push away, but it's futile; Xia Xiqing's grip only tightens. His tongue invades his mouth. A kiss should be a tender act, but at this moment, it's being used as a weapon.

Xia Xiqing also thinks he's crazy. He's always wanted to do this, and his eagerness and desire grow; compelling his body to do everything it can to satisfy him. Licking, entangling, sucking, the closer he gets, the more he craves. Despite Zhou Ziheng's lack of cooperation, he does not give up.

The kiss between two men is like a tug-of-war that never ends. The temperature rises rapidly between them. Their fragrances mix and the fire burns. Xia Xiqing, being a veteran of love, suddenly panics under Zhou Ziheng's resistance and resumes the kiss anxiously. When he sees Zhou Ziheng's eyes, he can feel his insides begin to burn.

Zhou Ziheng frowns. Xia Xiqing's hands are like a cold snake twining around his body. Zhou Ziheng violently returns to himself and starts to actually struggle, but Xia Xiqing refuses to give up. He even goes to straddle him to keep him in place.

He's gone mad!

Xia Xiqing suddenly notices a sharp taste between their mouths, and his movements slow in reaction to both it and the growing pain at his lip. Zhou Ziheng quickly takes this chance and flips Xia Xiqing onto his back, holding down Xia Xiqing's hands and pressing him against the couch.

He gasps, thick eyelashes covered with misty beads of sweat. Xia Xiqing looks like a different person from this perspective. His pale face is flushed with arousal and his lips are swollen with blood like a blooming flower.

"You're crazy..." Zhou Ziheng's breathing calms slightly.

Xia Xiqing suddenly lets out a short laugh. His white teeth protrude from his red lips. "I am crazy."

His expression looks like a drug addict going through withdrawal.

"You said you weren't afraid."

Zhou Ziheng lets go of Xia Xiqing and steps away. He straightens his own clothes in silence.

"I don't like men," he speaks calmly. "Don't waste your time on me."

Xia Xiqing hasn't moved. He wipes his lips with his wrist and laughs again. "Not the first time I've heard that. They all end up in bed with me."

To Zhou Ziheng, Xia Xiqing is just an unreasonable psychopath. Without even looking at him, Zhou Ziheng turns around and leaves.

Zhou Ziheng finally understands Xia Xiqing's feelings for himself. Like the victim of a serial murderer, he is nothing but a trophy to Xia Xiqing; a selection, and nothing more.

Thinking of this, Zhou Ziheng's chest tightens. When he first met Xia Xiqing, he was just disgusted and annoyed by him. Now, more complicated emotions are mixed into that.

Anger, frustration, unwillingness—much more than what words can describe.

After Zhou Ziheng leaves, Xia Xiqing lays on the couch for quite some time. His mind is chaotic. Images of the kiss constantly replay in his head. He is slightly regretful, but it is not out of guilt. The emotion is more in line with solving a complicated math problem.

Instead of using a more sophisticated algorithm, he chose brute force.

A kiss so sloppy and rough totally ruined the delicate balance the two had since they met. This is not like Xia

Xiqing. His past opponents had not been much easier than Zhou Ziheng, but he'd always been able to plan and execute strategically.

He takes a deep breath and falls off the couch. Feeling slightly dizzy, he turns off the television and wobbles upstairs.

Every light in the house remains on as Xia Xiqing stays up for the rest of the night.

In the morning, Xia Xiqing receives some news from Jiang Yin.

Have you seen the news yet? The ratings for the show exploded. XX Magazine wants you to do photoshoots for their cover. Do you have any time tonight?

Xia Xiqing is about to turn down the offer when his phone rings. He hesitates, but decides to answer.

"What do you think?"

This woman has a very flamboyant personality. Xia Xiqing laughs and responds, "Don't I have time to think about it?"

"This is the only one of the five major magazines Zhou Ziheng hasn't been on. They invited Lin Mo to do the shoot. You know how difficult it is to get him as a photographer?"

Xia Xiqing has heard of him. Lin Mo has quite the reputation in the world of art. Not only is he well-known for his craft, he also has a very interesting and lavish private life.

"So..." Xia Xiqing leans on his bed. "What does that have to do with me?"

Jiang Yin is confused by his attitude. In the past, Xia Xiqing has always been happy to cooperate. "Don't you want a great opportunity?"

"No, I don't," Xia Xiqing replies bluntly. "Not only am I unwilling, your big star is probably even more unwilling."

Zhou Ziheng? Jiang Yin feels a bit strange. "Do you two have any conflicts?"

"Aren't there enough conflicts between us?" Xia Xiqing asks rhetorically while lighting himself a cigarette. "Just send him to the magazine."

"The investor specifically asked for both of you." Jiang Yin sighed. "Your ship is super hot right now. Yesterday's show broke numerous records. People are crazy about you both; gifs of you two are flooding the internet."

Xia Xiqing recalls the scene from last night and responds sarcastically, "Then what? I came to film the show, now I have to be responsible for post-sales and merchandise?"

Jiang Yin is still baffled by Xia Xiqing's response. "I don't know what happened between you two. I gave the news to Zhou Ziheng already, but he hasn't replied; he's probably still sleeping. This is a rare opportunity, so don't let it go to waste."

"If you want me to go with him, then ask him to apologize to me first," Xia Xiqing interrupts.

"Apologize?"

"Yeah, get your big star to apologize."

At this moment, Jiang Yin realizes how difficult it is to be the person in the middle.

For some reason, Xia Xiqing feels better having talked to her; like a child that just told the teacher some other kids were picking on him. He takes a bath and decides to do some painting.

He sits in front of a blank canvas. His lips still hurt.

Xia Xiqing frowns and gives up any thought of the first person that comes to his mind.

Suddenly remembering a painting that he promised

Shang Sirui, Xia Xiqing picks up his brush. Shang Sirui is not present, so he will have to formulate from his memory. His pastel yellow hoodie and his youthful cheer overtake Xia Xiqing's mind.

After signing his name at the corner of the painting, Xia Xiqing takes a photo of it and sends it to Shang Sirui. The message receives an instant reply; odd how this celebrity has so much spare time.

San-San: Ohh! Looks great! Please accept my humble appreciation. [Bow down.jpg]

Xiqing: Where's your office? I can bring it over to you.

San-San: BIG HUG! Sure, I'll send you the address. Cool if I post this on Weibo?

Xiqing: Sure.

In no time at all, Xia Xiqing receives another notification on his phone. Shang Sirui has posted the picture and tagged him in it.

@HighFiveShangSirui:

Love you **@Tsing_Summer** PS: Did you guys watch the show yesterday?

That was quite fast. Xia Xiqing smiles and clicks like. He shares the post with a heart emoji.

His post immediately gathers attention from Shang Sirui's fans. Xia Xiqing's not used to receiving such attention from fans other than Zhou Ziheng's; even though he's heard all kinds of compliments on his fanart before, it just feels different from another group of fangirls.

@33Cutest: Xiqing-taitai! omg two of my favorite guys from the show!

@SiruiSofty: CRYING! Thank you taitai! You guys have such a good friendship! (shipping goggles engaging)

@ILove33: Beautiful style. Taitai was so gentle with 33 on the show too! Thank you taitai!

...

It doesn't take long for them to appear on the trending list. Xia Xiqing knows that it's probably due to Shang Sirui's company buying their way into trending, but he's truly surprised at the heated discussion among fans.

@IAmMarshmallow: Totally blown away by the dynamics of the guys. The ZiXi ship and QingSi ship! Both are interesting. One is like night and day with no sense of trust and full of exploration, while the other is total harmony. I prefer the feel of the latter, just saying.

Fake. That's just called acting. Xia Xiqing swipes down for a few more comments.

@PeterPanAries: Shang Sirui is like Xia Xiqing's little secret lover. What a cute and wonderful pair!

@WonderfulWorld: I support ZiXi more, I guess. Simply electric. I have a good feeling about those two. Their ship name is even a homonym—"Self-Study" has a ring to it.

@ABCDLittleF: I'm all for Self-Study. The atmosphere is too tense between them. Such a fairy tale ship.

@XiyaIsTheBest: Came across this randomly. If this were a novel by Xiya-dada, Self-Study would have already been married. They are a perfect match!

Tens of thousands of comments arguing over their favorite pairing has brought *Survive and Escape* to a whole new level.

@MilkteaIsFuel: How about an OT3? I've even thought of the name: Xia Shang Zhou!

Seeing a potential ship war, Xia Xiqing decides to close Weibo and continue painting.

Suddenly, his WeChat pops up with a notification.

Moral Role Model: Come to the magazine photoshoot with me.

Xia Xiqing is shocked. Is Zhou Ziheng's brain malfunctioning?

Terrorist: Did Jiang Yin not tell you or did you not understand?

There's no reply from Zhou Ziheng for quite some time, and Xia Xiqing's frustration begins to grow. He paces around the apartment, looking at various portraits of Zhou Ziheng. He pulls out a box of cigarettes and attempts to light one.

A few sparks, but no flame. Even the lighter isn't on his side today.

He crumples the cigarette angrily.

Leaning against the side of his balcony, Xia Xiqing stares at his phone screen. Although there are no new messages, he does see a "typing..." bubble near the bottom of the screen.

But a message is yet to be seen.

Terrorist: Are you fucking done typing? We got lives to live...

A few seconds later, a reply finally comes in.

Moral Role Model: I'm sorry.

Xia Xiqing feels almost like bursting into flames.

Moral Role Model: I shouldn't have bitten you. I didn't know what to do. I didn't want to hurt you but you were way over the line. I couldn't think of any other way. I was wrong.

This is not what Xia Xiqing wanted to hear.

Zhou Ziheng has nothing to apologize for, because he did nothing wrong. Xia Xiqing knows that well. He just wanted some reaction from Zhou Ziheng—just some nice old-fashioned groveling to make up for his wounded pride.

But Zhou Ziheng apologized. He really did. As sincerely as a child who just broke a window.

Xia Xiqing suddenly doesn't know what to say.

Lost in thoughts, Xia Xiqing takes a while to reply.

Terrorist: Come pick me up.

Zhou Ziheng has a busy work schedule. He didn't get enough sleep last night and went to a morning advertisement shoot in a state of severe sleep deprivation. Jiang Yin was with him the whole time, trying to convince him to apologize to Xia Xiqing. At first, he felt that he hadn't done anything wrong, but the more he thought about it, the guiltier he felt. So he contacted Xia Xiqing to apologize.

After he saw Xia Xiqing's reply, he felt somewhat relieved. The advertisement shoot was also going smoothly. However, on his way back to the company, Zhou Ziheng came across a new Weibo post from Shang Sirui.

And suddenly, he became upset again.

Turns out his art of other people also looks really good.

Checking the comment section, the posts are mostly from Shang Sirui's fans and shippers of Xia Xiqing and Shang Sirui. For some reason, Zhou Ziheng feels that he's entered enemy territory.

He's even more upset upon seeing that Xia Xiqing has liked the post.

@IAmMarshmallow: Totally blown away by the dynamics of the guys. The ZiXi ship and QingSi ship! Both are interesting. One is like night and day with no sense of trust and full of exploration, while the other is total harmony. I prefer the feel of the latter, just saying.

No sense of trust and full of exploration?

It's true. The commenter wasn't lying. But for some reason, Zhou Ziheng feels uncomfortable reading it.

His apology to Xia Xiqing has brought him some peace and control over his life, but his mood still fluctuates here and there.

"Ziheng, are you heading back to Huasheng now?" asks Zhou Ziheng's PA, Xiao-Luo.

Zhou Ziheng shakes his head. "I'm not going back. Send me to the company and then go pick up Xia Xiqing from Huasheng."

Xiao-Luo nods. He doesn't think anything of it; it's probably just Zhou Ziheng not wanting to get too close to his fans.

Once at the office, Zhou Ziheng doesn't know what to do. He heads directly into Jiang Yin's office and sits on the couch.

@CryingAnotherDayForSomeoneElsesLove: Self-Study for life!

@WhoSaidNo: YES! Their interactions are so intense and emotional. Like, "I didn't ask you to trust me, I asked you to use me" and the scene where Xia Xiqing grabs Zhou Ziheng's hand. Lots of feel. P.S. More fanfics about these two please.

@CindyCandy: In the beginning, handcuffed and blindfolded. I just want to say...insert porno music

@PrettyPlease: To be honest, I don't think Zhou Ziheng likes Xia Xiqing very much. He rarely talks to him. Maybe he just wants to keep a distance from his fans. He also doesn't follow his Weibo like Shang Sirui does. Just a thought... don't hate me.

Seeing this, Zhou Ziheng pauses for a second. He can't refute this, but he wants to.

@BunnyBunnyTasty: Wow, like a love triangle. Self-Study and QingSi. I'd really like to know how Zhou Ziheng feels about the QingSi ship ahaha.

Zhou Ziheng stares at the comment. The more he thinks about it, the more uncomfortable he grows.

Arguing over ships is inherently pointless, and Zhou Ziheng knows that. Any pairing is worth arguing for—there can never be a winner. It's all opinions and imagination.

Nonetheless, Zhou Ziheng feels somehow defeated. His ship with Xia Xiqing undoubtedly wins elsewhere online, but posts of QingSi still bother him.

Especially those last two comments.

To cope with this, Zhou Ziheng signs into his alternate account and leaves a train of likes on anything Self-Study related. Suddenly, his WeChat interrupts with multiple notifications.

Terrorist: Your apology sounded sincere, but now your PA's excuse for your standing me up doesn't even sound like it's been rehearsed. Did you leave him to come up with it on his own?

Terrorist: Should I do the same to you tonight?

Terrorist: I'm curious, superstar, what are you so busy with?

Why can't Xiao-Luo accomplish such a simple task? Zhou Ziheng is about to send him a text message when Jiang Yin enters the room.

"What are you doing in my office? Is everything okay?" Jiang Yin puts down her stuff.

"Nothing." Zhou Ziheng is thinking that he should go check on the situation. "Yin-jie, can I borrow your car? I need to go home."

Jiang Yin pulls out a chair for Zhou Ziheng directly across from her desk. "Hey, wait. I need to tell you something."

"Huh?"

"Do you have something urgent to deal with?"

"Not really..."

"Then sit down. This is a big deal to me." She sits down across from him and pulls out a few file folders, placing them in front of Zhou Ziheng. Reluctantly, he gives up trying to go home and after sending Xiao-Luo a text message about picking up Xia Xiqing, he proceeds to sit down in the chair that was offered to him.

"These are some of the film proposals sent to me recently. I skimmed through them, and you should have a look as well." She walks over in her high heels to pour herself a glass of water. "The impact of that reality show has been shocking. A lot of people have approached me about it after the first episode. I totally didn't expect..."

"You did expect. It's why you forced me to go," Zhou Ziheng interrupts impolitely.

She puts down her glass. "I forced you? Aren't you happy right now?"

"Who's happy?" Zhou Ziheng looks down at the script, wanting to ignore her teasing.

"I had a quick glance at it; the directors are all good. Like this one—Director Li has a comedy coming out on Christmas that stars two Oscar-winning actors. I think it's worth a shot. Even if you're not the main character, it's something new you can try. Also, there's Director Zhang with his award-winning modern horror work; you could be hired as one of the two male leads. The other lead might be Cheng Songming, from what I've heard."

Cheng Songming is an acquaintance of Zhou Ziheng's. As a kid, Zhou Ziheng played the younger brother of Songming's character. He suddenly is struck by the urge to ask, "Hey, did Songming win an award for his last movie, *Lost*?"

"He was nominated for best lead actor, but he didn't win," she replies. "The script won, though. Clearly, he's aiming for the prize this time, which is why I would suggest you turn down this one even though the script, cast, and crew are both top tier. Songming's role is a blind murderer, and yours is a policeman. There isn't much space for your character to develop, while his role has plenty. He would probably make a breakthrough in his career, but you wouldn't."

Zhou Ziheng nods. "My fans want me to play a policeman, though."

Jiang Yin laughs. "Because they like uniforms, and you look good in one."

"There's also doctors, pilots, soldiers..." Zhou Ziheng indulges in a wide smile. "They post me in uniforms on Weibo every day..."

"Up to you," Jiang Yin teases. "Spoiling your fans is easy. We didn't choose that kind of persona for you because it's not unique enough. But then again, if you really want a uniform, go home and borrow your father's."

Zhou Ziheng's expression becomes serious. "I can't wear that casually..."

Jiang Yin laughs. "Okay, fine, let's get back on topic. How about this one? This director, Kun Cheng, is very talented and likes to make independent arthouse films. I think you'll like the topic."

Zhou Ziheng looks at the script, which is titled *Stalking*. The male protagonist, Gao Kun, was born in the mountains of southwest China. He was scammed out of his money when he began working at the age of sixteen. Desperate, he began to sell his blood and contracted HIV in the process. Angry and vengeful, he wants to destroy the cruel world by killing as many people as he can. But when he meets the female heroine, Lin Siya, she convinces him to end his cruelty.

Lin Siya is an autistic girl who is also hard of hearing. The two of them become each other's only friends. The story is about two people saving each other, and it touches on relevant topics like disease, autism, disability, and similar minority group topics.

"Have they chosen the actress for Siya yet?"

Hearing this question, Jiang Yin knows Zhou Ziheng is interested. "No, they haven't. See, the problem is that we need a young actress, but young actresses are often too inexperienced. Older actresses aren't suitable for that kind of role, and most of them wouldn't even want it.

"They're scouting in art and film schools now, and the director is also changing up the script a bit. Hopefully something will come up soon."

Zhou Ziheng nods. "Are these scheduled for filming simultaneously?"

"Only this one and the horror film. If you ask me, I think this one suits you better. It's also award-winning material, if done properly." She walks over and pats Zhou Ziheng on the shoulder. "Who knows, maybe you'll be competing with Songming for Best Lead Actor next year."

She has a good point; one is never too young to receive an award for their accomplishments. Zhou Ziheng looks at the script again and feels something familiar.

"Who's the screenwriter?"

But before Jiang Yin can answer, her phone rings. She takes a look at the screen and immediately answers in a professional tone. "Hello, yes, Ziheng is on his way." After some more polite nothings, she hangs up and starts ushering Zhou Ziheng out of the room. "I almost forgot about the magazine thing. Go downstairs and I'll have a car ready for you."

Zhou Ziheng suddenly remembers that he hasn't replied to Xia Xiqing yet.

Forget it, he'll just play dead.

On the way there, Zhou Ziheng texts Xiao-Luo to ask if Xia Xiqing had been picked up yet, but receives no response. He gives up. If Xia Xiqing doesn't go, someone will surely notify Jiang Yin.

After half an hour in traffic, Zhou Ziheng finally arrives. He sees Xiao-Luo and other staff members as soon as he gets to the elevator.

"Ziheng, you're finally here."

"Why haven't you replied to my messages?"

"Ah? Oh, I gave my phone to Xia Xiqing. He said his was dead. He was bored with makeup and wanted to play games."

Hearing this, Zhou Ziheng almost trips. "You gave him your phone? Did I ask you to give him your phone?!"

Xiao-Luo rarely sees Zhou Ziheng get this upset, and is shocked.

"Well?"

"Uh, yeah. Xia Xiqing has been waiting for quite a while, and he was bored. And so I gave him my phone."

Zhou Ziheng now knows that Xia Xiqing must have seen the messages he sent. Can't play dead anymore.

"Zhou Ziheng, in here."

The staff lead him into the makeup room, and a very beautiful makeup artist named Shania emerges from inside. She has a lip ring on her lower lip which sparkles under the light. This isn't the first time that Shania has done Zhou Ziheng's makeup, so they don't feel the need to greet each other with superficial politeness.

"Hey, Zhou Ziheng, let me tell you more about today's shoot."

Zhou Ziheng nods and follows her into the makeup room. There, he sees Xia Xiqing sitting in front of a mirror. He's wearing a black silk shirt, which makes his skin appear even paler. His makeup artist is adjusting his face while a stylist is working on his hair.

Unlike his usual style, Xia Xiqing's neck-length hair is in

loose waves that lazily cover a portion of his delicate face. His makeup makes him appear equally languid and lazy.

As Zhou Ziheng is looking at him, Xia Xiqing suddenly turns around. He blinks slowly and grins, head slightly tilted.

At that moment, Zhou Ziheng's heart skips a beat, and his brain slows for a bit before resuming normal function. He doesn't know how to respond to Xia Xiqing's smile. After all, they aren't friends, and the relationship between them is more than awkward. This is beyond the capabilities of his people skills.

Shania takes out a few design drafts and presents them to Zhou Ziheng. "Lin Mo gave me this, so we'll try to do something similar. Have you seen *Hannibal*?"

Zhou Ziheng nods. "Are we doing a horror special?"

"Nah." Shania laughs. "But the concept is similar; you're a bloodthirsty murderer. We'll try to give you a more ascetic style. This is the usual you, though."

"Murderer and victim...?"

The reality is completely reversed, ironically.

"Umm, not quite, but close enough," Shania responds.

The styling assistant pushes over a mobile hanger. Shania walks over and takes a white turtleneck, a pair of gold-rimmed glasses, and a pair of surgical gloves. Zhou Ziheng changes into the clothes and sits down in front of Shania. He hears the artists next to him trying to pry spoilers out of Xia Xiqing regarding *Survive and Escape*.

"Hey, hey, c'mon, Xia Xiqing. I promise I won't tell anyone."

Xia Xiqing smiles and looks up at the makeup artist. "Well, if I tell you, you won't watch the next episode."

"I will! I'll watch it with my whole family."

Zhou Ziheng is not happy seeing the fake smile on Xia Xiqing's face. He pulls up his turtleneck and stares into the mirror.

"Hey, what's wrong with your lips? I just noticed," the artist asks, noticing a deep wound on his lip while applying lipstick.

The perpetrator can only glimpse through the mirror silently.

Xia Xiqing smiles and replies, "Bitten by a dog."

No, you're the dog. I was the one who got kissed by a dog, Zhou Ziheng mentally retorts.

"Really? No way, you're kidding."

"Yeah, I lied." Xia Xiqing's eyes drop. "I bit myself accidentally."

The artist gives up on the investigation and focuses on the task at hand. "Hey Shania, there's a scab here, I can't get the color on. You have any ideas?"

Shania, who was discussing hairstyles with Zhou Ziheng's stylist, walks over to check on Xia Xiqing's scab. It seems serious. "I'll find Lin Mo; he's quite the perfectionist about these things. We should let him know."

After the head makeup artist has had her say, nobody else in the room offers any more suggestions, which temporarily frees Xia Xiqing up. He turns his face to prevent his hair from getting into his unset makeup. He also has two small silver clips in his hair, which make look particularly cute.

His face, which everyone unanimously evaluates to be angelic, looks in Zhou Ziheng's direction through the reflection of the mirror. Upon confirming eye contact, Xia Xiqing opens his mouth slightly and raises his upper teeth. He gently bites down on his lower lip.

Once again, Zhou Ziheng feels paralyzed. He quickly

looks in another direction.

Such an action, like a code, is only known between predator and prey. To be precise, the prey takes advantage of the predator's high sense of morality and uses it as a bargaining chip.

Shania walks in not long after, followed by Lin Mo, the big shot photographer. This isn't the first time Xia Xiqing has met him—they once met at a party when he was studying abroad. Not many words were exchanged and it was quite some time ago, so all he remembers is that Lin Mo is as much of a playboy as Xia Xiqing.

Lin Mo's appearance has changed since they last saw each other; he's wearing a leather jacket and has a buzz cut. His neck is marked with tattoos.

He smiles at Xia Xiqing as soon as he walks into the room. Xia Xiqing has no feelings toward him, but he still stays in character and returns a warm smile.

"I heard you hurt your lip." Lin Mo walks over to Xia Xiqing and reaches for his chin. "Is it serious?"

Xia Xiqing quickly evades the touch, sticking his lip out to show the injury more clearly.

"It's pretty obvious."

Shania begins to suggest, "We can take care of it in photo editing."

"Take care of what?" Lin Mo smiles. "Haven't you ever heard the saying, 'A wound on a beautiful person is also a work of art'?"

Hearing this on the sideline, Zhou Ziheng opens his eyes. He gives a slight frown.

"Well, let's shift the concept a little. I heard you have a special effect makeup artist. Call him over and draw a wound on him." Lin Mo carefully examines Xia Xiqing's face.

"On the right cheekbone."

Shania nods and leaves the room to do as she was told. The now-useless makeup artist follows her out.

Lin Mo approaches the prop cabinet and grabs a pair of scissors. He walks two laps around Xia Xiqing with them in hand.

Xia Xiqing has a good idea of what's about to happen.

The sound of the blow dryer stops. Zhou Ziheng is told to wait while his hairstylist leaves the room to get another bottle of hair spray from storage. He looks over at Xia Xiqing and the man next to him. Subconsciously, Zhou Ziheng grits his teeth.

Lin Mo reaches out and grabs onto Xia Xiqing's silk shirt. He takes the scissors and cuts a small slit into the fabric. Placing his finger into the cut, he forcibly tears the shirt apart. The sound of fabric ripping resonates through the room.

"After so long, I didn't expect to reunite with you back in China."

The word "reunite" has subtle implications to it—almost making it sound like they'd once had an affair.

"How serendipitous."

Lin Mo rests his hand on Xia Xiqing's shoulder. His eyes look into the mirror and his hands gently rub the bare skin under the ripped shirt.

Xia Xiqing's face quickly turns cold. Disgusting. How dare he flirt with him? He's running out of patience.

Just as Xia Xiqing is about to get angry, something unexpected happens. A hand comes out of nowhere and grabs Lin Mo's wrist, removing his arm from Xia Xiqing's body.

Zhou Ziheng's height and aura makes him naturally intimidating. Even when silent, his eyes are full of warning.

Lin Mo is surprised. He really didn't expect Zhou Ziheng to interfere. He can't help but laugh. "Ziheng, what are you—"

"You and I both know what the entertainment industry is like, what things happen in this circle." Zhou Ziheng raises his chin slightly. His cold eyes look down at Lin Mo. "But my fans are innocent. I find myself feeling protective."

With that, Zhou Ziheng loosens his grip and puts his hands back into his pockets.

Lin Mo has never interacted with Zhou Ziheng before. However, intuition tells him that there must be something going on between Zhou Ziheng and Xia Xiqing. He smiles and rubs his wrist before he glances at Xia Xiqing and nods meaningfully.

"Yes, innocent..."

Xia Xiqing looks into the mirror and raises an eyebrow. Suddenly bored of this, Lin Mo walks out and closes the door behind him, leaving Zhou Ziheng and Xia Xiqing in the room.

For reasons unknown to Zhou Ziheng, his aura of aggression deflates like a balloon and suddenly disappears. He feels that it was none of his business to intervene; maybe Xia Xiqing was looking forward to this reunion.

The more he thinks, the more bitter he feels. Snapping out of his thoughts, Zhou Ziheng looks down at Xia Xiqing who, unable to hold back his laughter, is now shaking silently, head tilted down in a poor attempt to hide it.

"What are you laughing at?" Zhou Ziheng is getting annoyed. He did that to help Xia Xiqing, but instead of gratitude, he's only receiving mockery.

Xia Xiqing is starting to tear up from laughing too hard. He calmly looks up at Zhou Ziheng. "Innocent?"

He smirks with his chin propped on his hand and his elbow on the armrest, his eyes half-closed in mirth.

Disregarding everything else about you, "innocent" is the perfect description for that face of yours, Zhou Ziheng thinks to himself.

Xia Xiqing's eyes are bright and starry. His fingers tap his cheek as he recites what Zhou Ziheng said to Lin Mo. "You and I both know what the entertainment industry is like, what things happen in this circle." His voice slows down. "What things that happen in this circle..."

He stretches out his hand and touches the soft fabric of Zhou Ziheng's sweater. The slender index finger traces the pattern like a paintbrush. His innocent smile morphs into a smirk.

Suddenly, his finger glides over the belt buckle and curls down around it. Raising his eyes, he looks up at Zhou Ziheng.

"What things?"

Zhou Ziheng's brows furrow slightly. This is one of his sexiest expressions.

This guy is just...

"I was just making an excuse." Zhou Ziheng pulls his hands out of his pockets and tries to remove Xia Xiqing's finger from his belt buckle. Suddenly, he feels Xia Xiqing's finger catching his own and before he can react, Xia Xiqing intertwines their fingers and locks them tightly.

"Why did you help me?"

Intertwined fingers should feel sweet and tender. Yet to Zhou Ziheng, it feels more like Xia Xiqing is a thug holding a knife to his neck.

The hand-holding sets off a burning illusion, and Zhou Ziheng's mental alarm rings. He tries to break free from Xia

Xiqing's grasp and inadvertently glances at his injured lip. Not wanting to hurt him again, he gives up on the struggle.

"I didn't do it for you," Zhou Ziheng replies. "There are a lot of people here. I don't want rumors of a photographer assaulting a fan while a well-known actor turns a blind eye."

Interesting. It's genuinely interesting to see Zhou Ziheng look for excuses. Xia Xiqing raises an eyebrow and further presses down on Zhou Ziheng's fingers.

"So you don't mind offending the photographer right before a shoot?"

"What's to be afraid of? For me, a photo is a photo. Doesn't matter who takes it; a professional photographer or a random person on the street."

Zhou Ziheng's tone becomes calmer and calmer. Xia Xiqing's eyes scan his whole body from top to bottom.

He's not wrong.

"Lin Mo is a perfectionist. His work won't be affected by such an incident." Upon finishing that sentence, Zhou Ziheng feels Xia Xiqing's hand relax slightly. He takes this opportunity to loosen his grip.

Not fully relieved, Zhou Ziheng stretches his sore fingers and tucks them into his pockets.

Xia Xiqing feels that his prey just got away. He stands from the makeup chair and helps Zhou Ziheng straighten out his turtleneck. His fingers are red from squeezing. After fixing the collar, he raises his eyes and looks directly at Zhou Ziheng.

"I like how you look down at me from this angle." Xia Xiqing's voice is soft. His hands slip down from the collar to Zhou Ziheng's shoulders. "Makes me want to kiss you."

Zhou Ziheng reaches out to resist Xia Xiqing's advancements without needing to do it forcibly. "Someone is always watching."

Xia Xiqing can't resist laughing. So ambiguous. Makes it sound like something's going to happen between them.

Xia Xiqing tilts his head with a hint of cunning. "So what you mean is...if we go somewhere more private, I can kiss you?"

Deliberately misunderstanding someone's words is a horrifying skill. Zhou Ziheng is agitated and doesn't know why. Xia Xiqing is so skillful with his words that he always needs a moment to come up with a response. He knows that he isn't the first one that Xia Xiqing has used these tricks on.

When he thinks about how Xia Xiqing regularly practices these routines on people, he begins to feel uncomfortable. Zhou Ziheng breathes and says harshly, "Did I not bite you hard enough last time?"

As soon as Zhou Ziheng is done speaking, Xia Xiqing sticks out his tongue and licks the scab as if it were a sweet. "You sure did."

He then moves his hands up to Zhou Ziheng's neck and puckers his lips as if to kiss.

"Next time, bite a less noticeable area."

Zhou Ziheng shakes off Xia Xiqing's hand and takes a step back. "Don't try anything on me."

"Try what?" Xia Xiqing sits back in his chair and picks up his phone. "Did you think I wanted to come? Who's the one who sent his assistant to pick me up? Who promised to pick me up, then regretted it and sent someone else instead?"

Every question is a jab at Zhou Ziheng's weakness. He is unable to come up with a response to Xia Xiqing's questions.

Xia Xiqing asks again, "Why did you change your mind halfway?"

Zhou Ziheng does not want to tell the truth. He does not

want to mention what he saw on Weibo.

"I don't have much to say."

Zhou Ziheng doesn't want to lie, but he also didn't want to speak in the first place.

Before Xia Xiqing can ask more questions, Shania walks in with a special effect artist. She makes a few complaints regarding Lin Mo being difficult as soon as she enters the room. Xia Xiqing and Zhou Ziheng pretend nothing just happened and go to sit in their respective seats quietly. Zhou Ziheng's hairstylist also returns.

"Zhou Ziheng, I just had a discussion with the crew; we think wet hair will make you sexier." The stylist grabs Zhou Ziheng's hair. "But not too wet, just a little spray over the forehead."

The stylist grabs some hair and mists some water into it. A few drops run down Zhou Ziheng's forehead.

The effects artist draws a long scar over Xia Xiqing's face. He glances at it and decides that it isn't good enough.

"You can do it with an open flesh effect." Xia Xiqing looks at the artist with a smile. "It'll have a greater impact."

Xia Xiqing looks over at Zhou Ziheng. He's wearing gold wire glasses and a turtleneck, and gives off an incredible sense of abstinence. Looking at himself in the mirror, Xia Xiqing sees his torn black shirt, his scab, the blood stains, and a big scary wound on his face. A real victim.

The studio is arranged around a large black backdrop. In the center, there's a light brown walnut chair.

"Xia Xiqing, have a seat in the chair first. I'll take a couple of shots to test the lighting."

"Legs slightly apart, back to the chair, head up," Lin Mo directs Xia Xiqing as he rapidly presses the shutter, capturing every one of his expressions.

Checking the few photos he took, Lin Mo is quite satisfied. "Alright Zhou Ziheng, you go too."

Xia Xiqing turns his head and sees Zhou Ziheng approaching. His long legs are wrapped in dress pants, and there's a dark jacket over his white sweater. He lowers his head and puts on a pair of surgical gloves. The moment he looks up, his glasses sparkle under the stage lighting.

If a perverted murderer had a face like that, surely victims would be lining up to meet their demise.

It's hard to be creative on a double-figure magazine cover. Most magazines opt for conservative positions, but Lin Mo is not one that plays by the rules.

Zhou Ziheng walks around the chair where Xia Xiqing is sitting and stands behind him. Lin Mo issues a reminder, "From this point on, you must remain in character. A perverted murderer and an innocent victim. Feel free to play around with these characteristics."

Zhou Ziheng stands behind Xia Xiqing and tries out a few poses, but none of them seem good. His brain is empty. He hasn't yet entered a good state of mind for this photoshoot.

Lin Mo takes a few more shots and the stylist does a quick fix on Zhou Ziheng's hair.

"This is a difficult concept to shoot," the makeup artist comments.

Lin Mo turns to the effects artist. "I don't think the makeup look is quite enough. We need to be bloodier and more explicit."

The effects artist feels slightly concerned. "If it's too explicit, we'll run into regulation problems; it may never even make it onto the cover."

"Then make it subtle enough so it can pass." Lin Mo shows a hint of impatience. "If you can't do it, ask someone else to do it."

He walks to the side and lights himself a cigarette, leaving the artist looking awkward. Xia Xiqing looks at Zhou Ziheng standing behind him. Indeed, it might be better if there's a little more blood.

"Is there any paint left?" Xia Xiqing walks to the effects artist. "You can use some red paint—the same kind you used to paint the wound."

Zhou Ziheng closes his eyes while getting re-sprayed. Suddenly, the sound of spraying stops.

"Zhou Ziheng."

Hearing Xia Xiqing's voice, Zhou Ziheng opens his eyes. Liquid splashes onto his face, almost hitting him in the eye. He quickly closes his eyes and frowns.

"What are you doing?"

"Is that okay?"

Red paint has been thrown into Zhou Ziheng's face, looking almost like blood. The splash coats his well-defined face from forehead to eye socket and all the way down to his cheekbones and lips.

Xia Xiqing returns the paint bottle to the makeup assistant, then grabs the gold glasses and puts them gently on Zhou Ziheng.

Now he looks like a real murderer.

Lin Mo walks over and looks at the scene. Unable to hide his sense of satisfaction, he says, "Okay, very good, that's a good feeling. Let's give this a try."

Having solved the problem, Xia Xiqing returns to his chair. Zhou Ziheng's eyes follow his figure; he seems tired. He sits with a slouch and cups his chin like he's about to take a nap.

His shirt's wide neckline is open. From Zhou Ziheng's

view, he can clearly see the outline of his collarbone and part of his ribs, and the lines of muscle winding down his chest.

Suddenly, he remembers his first encounter with him in the escape room—Xia Xiqing, sitting in the chair, arms and legs tied. Blindfold covering his eyes. Bowing in a submissive gesture.

"Do we have handcuffs here?"

Hearing this, Xia Xiqing looks up at Zhou Ziheng, and Zhou Ziheng stares back. For some reason, he likes the surprised look on Xia Xiqing's face.

"Yes!" Shania looks over at them. "Xia Xiqing, will you wear them?"

Xia Xiqing laughs. "No problem."

Shania immediately orders her assistant to fetch the handcuffs.

"Just like the scene in the beginning of the escape room!" The assistant brings over some cuffs and hands them to Xia Xiqing.

"Give them to Zhou Ziheng," Lin Mo interrupts. "Let him cuff Xia Xiqing. Everyone else out of the scene, we'll begin shooting."

Zhou Ziheng takes the cuffs from the assistant and walks over to Xia Xiqing. He kneels in front of him and begins to unclip the cuff. Xia Xiqing leans back in his chair and extends his arms. The silver cuffs click.

This feeling is familiar. The sound of the shutter rings through his ears. Xia Xiqing follows Zhou Ziheng with his eyes as he gets up and walks behind the chair.

"Zhou Ziheng, bend down and lean over Xia Xiqing's ear. Yes, hold his chin. Very good, hold steady." Lin Mo captures the scene from various angles with excitement. "Zhou Ziheng, grip his chin tighter."

The first session takes almost an hour. The effects are amazing and the staff are astounded.

"Their expressiveness together is simply excellent."

"I can't believe he's an amateur."

"Don't be a fangirl, get back to work."

When choosing a photo for the magazine cover, Lin Mo and the director quickly come to a unanimous decision. In the photo, Xia Xiqing sits in an exquisite burgundy chair. His hands are cuffed. Zhou Ziheng, with blood on his face, stands behind him with a surgical glove over Xia Xiqing's chin.

The other glove is hanging from his teeth, creating the implication that it has just been removed. His gloveless hand secures Xia Xiqing's head by the cheekbone.

They both look directly at the camera. The eyes behind the gold-rimmed glasses are cold and cruel, mixed with a certain sense of thrilling desire. Xia Xiqing's head is raised and his eyelids are lowered. He is seemingly crying for help toward the camera, but there is also a hint of enjoyment in his expression.

It's wonderful.

The next scenes they have to shoot are individual portraits. Zhou Ziheng is to stand in front of a mirror embedded in a wardrobe. The styling assistant takes the gold glasses away from him.

"Imagine you've just killed him. You're back in your room to change out of your blood-stained clothes." Lin Mo adjusts his camera and points it at Zhou Ziheng. "Yes, look at yourself in the mirror."

Zhou Ziheng adjusts his sweater hem and tucks his hand under it, exposing a bit of skin. Xia Xiqing watches from afar with a drink in his hand, joyfully admiring Zhou Ziheng's abs and his powerful figure. Cold liquid travels up the straw and into his mouth, but his throat still feels dry.

"Hold your sweater with both hands at the waist, look directly into the mirror." Lin Mo changes angles a few times and walks closer. "Take it off, and wipe the blood stain with your fingers. Lift up your chin, very nice."

Xia Xiqing's eyes are still fixed on Zhou Ziheng. His back is now completely exposed. Muscles pull along his spine down to his thin, narrow waist.

His teeth involuntarily begin to bite the straw.

The annoying feeling of being able to see, but not able to touch.

Xia Xiqing's individual shoot takes place inside a bathroom where there is a bathtub filled with hot water. While Lin Mo and Xia Xiqing discuss the scene, Zhou Ziheng changes into another set of clothes and takes a rest to look at his photos.

Xia Xiqing lays down in the bathtub, submerging his body in the warm water. His silk shirt sticks to his bare skin. He leans his head on the end of the tub and rests his arms along the side. Lin Mo likes this pose, so he takes a few shots before he calls the stylist to bring a white lace ribbon to Xia Xiqing.

"Try this on your eyes."

Following Lin Mo's instructions, the stylist gently blindfolds Xia Xiqing with the ribbon.

"Have the lighting technician cast some yellow light overhead," Lin Mo orders.

Zhou Ziheng sits on the side, looking at Xia Xiqing in the bathtub. With his eyes covered in a long lace band, it creates a gloomy sense of beauty. Many men in this business have extremely delicate faces; some more so than girls. Packaged people can only be considered "pretty" to Zhou Ziheng; he believes true beauty must be natural.

After looking at some of the photos that were just taken, Lin Mo is not satisfied. "This is not good enough. Shania, make the water in the tub red."

"No," the director objects. "The blood on Zhou Ziheng's face is already bad enough. That'll never pass regulations."

Shania shrugs. "I told you."

Zhou Ziheng hears every word from the side, and turns to wave at Xiao-Luo.

"We were almost there..." Lin Mo feels very disappointed— his perfectionism does not allow him to compromise. He calls the chief editor to negotiate, but with no luck. Several people are now arguing in the studio. The discussion goes on for over ten minutes, and the water in the tub gradually cools.

Xia Xiqing begins to feel tired. From an artistic point of view, he totally understands Lin Mo. However, legalities are a different matter. He takes off the lace and turns toward Zhou Ziheng.

Zhou Ziheng, sitting in the distance, meets his eyes briefly. He then gets up and walks into the quarrel.

"I have an idea," he says.

The people that were arguing quiet down and Xia Xiqing sits up slowly in the tub.

"What is it?" Lin Mo asks, still with a look of dissatisfaction on his face. He doesn't feel that an actor is qualified to make artistic recommendations regarding his photography.

Xiao-Luo suddenly walks in with a bouquet of roses in each hand. A florist follows him with three more. Each bouquet is stunning, and large enough to obscure a person's entire upper body.

"Ziheng, the flowers are here."

Zhou Ziheng takes one bouquet and grabs a handful of delicate fresh petals. He sprinkles them into the bathtub over Xia Xiqing.

"This is my design."

The petals fall into the water gracefully. Staring at the scene, Xia Xiqing's eyes reveal a sudden surprise. Zhou Ziheng smiles, turns, and hands the rest of the bouquet to the stylist.

Lin Mo freezes for a moment, then bursts out laughing. He seems extremely surprised.

A bathtub full of red—exactly what he wanted.

"There are five bouquets, each with exactly ninety-nine roses. Should be enough to cover anything we need."

Seeing Lin Mo conquered by this idea, the stylist quickly begins to scatter rose petals into the tub. Zhou Ziheng has nothing else to do, so he also helps out. He's always been a good character, without a big ego, and is often found quietly helping out on set.

A petal drops from his hand and wanders onto Xia Xiqing's chest. It melts onto the soaking black shirt intimately.

"How did you come up with this idea?" Xia Xiqing raises his resting head and asks softly. The stylist comes over and blindfolds Xia Xiqing with the white lace again.

Zhou Ziheng does not respond; he just brushes some more petals into the water. It was when he was sitting in his chair staring at Xia Xiqing—the scene suddenly manifested in his mind. No need for any artistic knowledge.

He plucks a petal and places it on Xia Xiqing's lips.

Only roses match you.

That's what came into his mind, but he does not want to

tell Xia Xiqing.

At least not now.

The cover page and individual shots take the team over four hours. Despite the hurdles, everyone is very satisfied with the results.

"This issue will be sold out in no time." The director sits next to Zhou Ziheng. "Might even be selected for cover of the year."

Zhou Ziheng lets out a humble smile.

"I see that you two don't talk much," the director points out. "I guess the rumors on the internet are all fake."

Zhou Ziheng glances at Xia Xiqing, who fell asleep on the couch. "We actually only met during the escape room. We're not that familiar with each other."

Zhou Ziheng feels that his words are all lies; they've even kissed. But he's unable to find a good description of their relationship. Strange.

"I heard Xia Xiqing is a big fan of yours, he even paints portraits of you," the director says while scrolling through Weibo's trending list. "I saw this one yesterday..."

"Wait, that's Shang Sirui. Ah, my bad." The director notices as he clicks on the image. Feeling embarrassed, he puts his phone away into his pocket.

"It's okay," Zhou Ziheng responds, despite feeling quite discomfited. "You can go to his Weibo and find all kinds of paintings of me."

As soon as these words leave Zhou Ziheng's mouth, he instantly regrets it. He feels like he's trying to assert unnecessary dominance.

If he goes to Xia Xiqing's Weibo, he will see Xia Xiqing's like on the QingSi post.

Thinking about it only makes him uncomfortable.

"He's a really good painter, I heard. He graduated from the Accademia di Belle Arti di Firenze." The director nods appreciatively. "That's definitely something."

The venue for the magazine interview is ready. Xiao-Luo comes over to Zhou Ziheng and asks, "Almost time for the interview, do you want to freshen up your makeup?"

"Nah, it's fine." Zhou Ziheng turns and sees Xia Xiqing still asleep on the couch. He's scrunched up like a ball, his hair covering his face. He hesitates a moment and asks Xiao-Luo softly, "Go wake him up."

Xiao-Luo nods and walks over to Xia Xiqing to gently shake his shoulder. The sleepy Xia Xiqing frowns and wakes up in a serious mood. He turns and buries his face into the cushion. A moment later, he looks back at Xiao-Luo, not wanting to wake up at all.

"Xia Xiqing?"

Xia Xiqing hasn't slept for two nights. The magazine shoot has completely drained his energy. After falling asleep on the sofa during break, his eyes are too tired and brain too dizzy to wake up.

"Zhou Ziheng." Xiao-Luo turns to Zhou Ziheng for help. "Doesn't seem like he wants to wake up."

Glancing at Xia Xiqing on the couch, Zhou Ziheng sighs. "Why don't you go get the makeup artist first to freshen me up?"

Just as Xiao-Luo is about to leave, Zhou Ziheng stops him. "Oh, and get me a glass of water, thanks."

Seeing Xiao-Luo walk away, Zhou Ziheng sits on the couch where Xia Xiqing is sleeping. "Hey, get up."

Xia Xiqing buries his face further into the cushion and groans uncooperatively. With no other choice, Zhou Ziheng grabs one of Xia Xiqing's arms and drags him up from the couch.

"Go away!" Xia Xiqing yells, still half asleep. He flails his arms, trying to push Zhou Ziheng away. Being only half awake, his struggle proves futile.

"I don't care, you need to get up." Zhou Ziheng continues to pull him up.

Xia Xiqing's hair dangles over his face, which is twisted in an annoyed scowl. His elbow rests on a cushion while his palm supports his groggy head. Zhou Ziheng wonders if Xia Xiqing is feeling okay.

"Do you have a headache?"

Zhou Ziheng stretches out his hand to move Xia Xiqing's hair out of the way. Xia Xiqing dodges and evades with a frowning face. He looks like a grumpy cat.

Xia Xiqing is completely silent. Too tired to talk, his whole person is in a state of limbo; half-awake and half-dreaming. He's so top-heavy that he might fall over at any moment.

Zhou Ziheng's voice appears further and further, as if it is coming from the sky.

He just wants to sleep.

"How come you—"

Halfway through his sentence, Xia Xiqing, who has just sat up, falls asleep again in Zhou Ziheng's arms.

"—are more tired than me?" Zhou Ziheng finishes the sentence, and catches Xia Xiqing out of reflex.

Xia Xiqing's head rests on Zhou Ziheng's chest. His slightly curly hair is soft to the touch.

In the studio, everyone is anxious and in a hurry. All kinds of voices fill their ears. But mysteriously, Zhou Ziheng is still able to hear Xia Xiqing's breathing and his beating heart.

What is happening?

"Zhou Ziheng."

His imagination is interrupted. Zhou Ziheng quickly helps Xia Xiqing up, and the latter opens his eyes with discontent.

Zhou Ziheng coughs unnaturally and stands up. He says to the makeup artist standing behind Xiao-Luo, "He fell asleep, he probably needs more makeup."

Xiao-Luo is holding a cup of coffee in one hand and protecting it with the other. "Zhou Ziheng, here..."

Zhou Ziheng smells the aroma of the coffee and frowns with dissatisfaction. "Did I ask for coffee?"

"You said water, but I saw they had a nice coffee machine so I made some for you. It's still hot, drink it now," Xiao-Luo explains with a clever look on his face, seeking acknowledgment.

Zhou Ziheng takes a deep breath and takes the coffee. His intention had been to give Xia Xiqing some water after he woke up. Instead, he now has a cup of coffee for himself.

Glancing at his watch, it's almost ten o'clock. Will he still be able to sleep tonight after the coffee?

"Are you going to drink it?"

Looking at Xiao-Luo's puzzled face, Zhou Ziheng begins to drink the coffee. "It's a little bitter, can you also get me a glass of water? Just plain water."

"Sure." Xiao-Luo walks away, still looking confused.

Zhou Ziheng looks over at Xia Xiqing, who has his head leaned back on the couch. The makeup artist is working away at refreshing his makeup.

"Xiqing, you have really good skin. How can you still have good skin while getting no sleep?"

Xia Xiqing smiles with closed eyes. "Really? I never noticed."

"Ziheng's skin is also good." The artist looks back at Zhou

Ziheng. "You've had good skin since you were a child. Some even said you would grow up ugly. They were wrong."

Xia Xiqing finally opens his eyes and looks at Zhou Ziheng, standing not far from him. Thinking that this was the guy who interrupted his beauty sleep, he grabs a small cushion and throws it at him.

So childish.

Zhou Ziheng catches the cushion with quick reflexes. He turns to Xia Xiqing and gives him a look to question his behavior. Xia Xiqing raises his eyebrow like a thug and shifts his view aside.

"So, you guys are cool right?" The makeup artist smiles. "I heard Xia Xiqing is a big fan of Zhou Ziheng. Did you start liking him when he was a child star?"

"Nope." Xia Xiqing laughs happily. "I haven't seen the roles he played when he was a kid. I'm not sure what he looked like back then."

"Ah?" The artist puts away her toolbox and stands up. "So it's true—you're a fake fan?"

She's right. Xia Xiqing can't help but smirk in agreement.

Suddenly, the cushion he threw comes flying back at him. Xia Xiqing catches it and holds it in front of his chest. Zhou Ziheng's eyes glance away, seemingly unhappy. Putting his hands into his pants pockets, Zhou Ziheng turns and walks away.

He really was aiming for the face... How mean. Xia Xiqing sets the cushion to the side, pats it, and stands up to stretch.

Before the interview, the chief editor calls to notify them of a temporary arrangement to make another set of covers and publish them as an alternate issue. Thus, they need to quickly do another modeling set.

"Is this your first time working under such a tight schedule?" Shania asks Xia Xiqing as she tears the fake wound off his face.

"I used to stay up really late to do my homework," Xia Xiqing replies as Xiao-Luo approaches him with a glass of water. "Thank you! You're so sweet. I happen to be quite thirsty."

Xiao-Luo smiles with a sense of embarrassment. He wants to say that it was per Zhou Ziheng's instruction, but when he sees Zhou Ziheng glaring at him, he decides to keep quiet.

The gothic theme continues into the new concept. Xia Xiqing is given a palace-style silk shirt with a lace bow tie. His hair is done up into a half-bun with a single lock drooping down his forehead.

The wound on his face has been removed and replaced with a more delicate and cleaner layer of foundation. The previous eye makeup has been discarded by the makeup artist, and instead, the artist applied heavy dark liner to both the upper and lower lids and some dark brown shadow to get a smoky look.

"Heavens, Xiqing, you're very suitable for heavy makeup." The artist finally sorts out the makeup. Gently supporting his chin, she does a final check in the mirror. "Really beautiful. Xiqing, when you become a star, hire me as your makeup artist."

Xia Xiqing smiles into the mirror. To be honest, he's not used to this evil-looking appearance. He turns to see Zhou Ziheng changing into a new style—he's replaced his old sweater and is now wearing a black hooded jacket with a white low-neck shirt underneath. His bangs are divided in half and split down his forehead. There's some light makeup on his face, and a hat on his head. He looks like a mysterious teenager.

This is a completely different style compared to the previous murderer. His new look resembles a cute stray dog.

Shania calls the makeup artists over. "Lin Mo wants to discuss the second round styling and props." She greets Xia Xiqing and Zhou Ziheng. "Sit tight and we'll begin shooting soon."

Xia Xiqing turns and smiles at Shania. The moment she leaves the room, Xia Xiqing converges his smile and stands. He takes a drink prepared by the staff and walks over to Zhou Ziheng, who is playing with his phone.

Zhou Ziheng is bored, so he's opened Weibo to see what's new. As soon as he opened the app, it automatically signed into his private account. Already startled, he suddenly feels a pinch on his cheek that almost causes him to drop his phone.

"What are you doing?"

Xia Xiqing's index finger and thumb are still tugging on Zhou Ziheng's cheek while his other hand is holding a drink. He bites on his straw and answers vaguely, "Nothing, was just curious. You look so fierce, I wanted to know if your face was also tough. Turns out it's softer than I expected."

Zhou Ziheng attempts to swat the hand away that was tugging on his cheek. To his surprise, Xia Xiqing grabs his other hand that's holding the phone.

"Why were you so nervous? Someone step on your tail?" Xia Xiqing looks down at Zhou Ziheng's phone. "Were you looking at something inappropriate?"

The guilty Zhou Ziheng escapes from Xia Xiqing's grip and puts the phone back into his pocket. He says a few words, pretending to be cold. "Why does it matter to you?"

"Oh yeah..." Xia Xiqing dragging out his last syllable. He walks over and leans on the dressing table, placing his drink on top of it. "I almost forgot. The famous Zhou Ziheng knows everything about the entertainment business."

Can this thing pass already? Zhou Ziheng deeply regrets ever helping out this dickhead. He adjusts his hat anxiously, pretending that Xia Xiqing doesn't exist.

Xia Xiqing looks around at the cosmetics on the table with an indifferent expression. "Hey, I wanted to ask you a question."

Zhou Ziheng closes his eyes and replies impatiently, "What?"

Xia Xiqing puts his feet up onto the support beam of Zhou Ziheng's chair. He holds a black box of foundation and places it in front of Zhou Ziheng's face. "Mr. Celebrity, you're in the makeup room often enough—do you know what this color is called?"

Zhou Ziheng glances at the product and sees various colors, like a palette. The one Xia Xiqing is pointing to is a pale pink. He replies quietly, "How would I know?"

"You don't. I'll tell you." Xia Xiqing stretches out his finger and wipes a bit of the foundation. He brushes away Zhou Ziheng's hair and hood and rubs a tiny amount on his earlobe.

The other hand grabs Zhou Ziheng by the belt and pulls him close.

"*Deep throat*," he whispers in English.

Zhou Ziheng's heart stops for a moment. When he realizes what's happening, he feels hot-headed and immediately pushes Xia Xiqing away.

The pervert is happy and leans on the table indulging in a deep laugh. Looking at Zhou Ziheng, who is going crazy, Xia Xiqing takes a drink and bites his straw. "That's for waking me up."

"You're a very unreasonable person." Zhou Ziheng steps

away from the dressing table anxiously.

Xia Xiqing raises his eyebrow. "I'm totally reasonable!"

He steps closer, but Zhou Ziheng immediately jumps back.

"Why so afraid?" Xia Xiqing smiles. "Don't you want to know more about cosmetics?"

Zhou Ziheng covers his ears, gets up from his chair, and walks away. Staring at his back, Xia Xiqing can't help but laugh.

What?

This is too adorable.

The second shooting session finally begins. All the staff are ready. Xia Xiqing, who just completed styling and costuming, walks into the studio. The layout of the studio remains unchanged, with a black background and a chair at the center.

"We have a different method of thinking for this second edition. Xia Xiqing, you'll still sit in the chair, but this time just sit and look cool instead of being a victim," Lin Mo says softly as he arranges him to sit in the center chair. "Be more aggressive."

Xia Xiqing looks at Lin Mo contemptuously with his legs crossed. He's getting impatient.

Zhou Ziheng's hairstylist is working on his hat. He cannot see Xia Xiqing's expressions, but he can see Lin Mo bending over close to Xia Xiqing's face.

"Zhou Ziheng, why the frown? Did I pull your hair?"

He snaps back into reality. "Oh, no, nothing. Don't worry."

Another makeup artist comes over. "Zhou Ziheng, Lin Mo said you need a small wound at the corner of your lip."

The shoot begins. Unlike the previous edition, Xia Xiqing sits in the chair with his legs crossed. His elbow rests on the armrest and his hand supports his chin like a thinker. His posture and eyes are lazy.

Zhou Ziheng sat on the floor behind Xia Xiqing. His back is against the chair and his right leg is stretched out. His head is slightly raised and his lips are curved in a smirk.

The biggest difference from the last version is that Zhou Ziheng's slender neck is now collared with a black leash. The other end of the leash is in Xia Xiqing's hand.

Murderer and victim versus prisoner and jailer.

Black and white in reverse.

The director is standing on the side looking at the two people in the scene. "They got into it so much more quickly in the second shoot. I'm amazed."

This is the true state between the two of them. Lin Mo looks at the images silently with a smile. He looks up at Xia Xiqing, admiring the graceful lines of his neck. Moving his eyes down, he's met with Zhou Ziheng's glare.

This hostility in this kid is too obvious.

Lin Mo shrugs at Zhou Ziheng from a distance.

"All good!"

A person from the lighting team comes up to the director. "Director Zhang, there's something wrong with the lights; the voltage isn't right. We need to deal with it."

The director tells Lin Mo and he nods. "That's fine, it's almost done. They can go for the interview."

The two have no time to rest, and commence the interview while still wearing makeup. Their hostess has been waiting for them and the interview begins immediately after they sit down.

In the beginning, they're asked simple questions. Xia Xiqing is not afraid of speaking in front of a camera, and is very good at disguising his true self while handling incoming questions. On the contrary, Zhou Ziheng has very few words and says no more than three per question.

"After the first episode of *Survive and Escape* aired, the show has immediately become an absolute phenomenon. The audience ratings are through the roof and it got a lot of attention online. Did you expect these results?"

Zhou Ziheng thinks for a moment and replies, "Well, no. There was no extra energy to think about this while filming. All I had in mind was how to escape...literally."

The hostess is amused by such a serious answer. She turns to Xia Xiqing. "What about you? As a fan, this was your first time on television and it happens to be with your idol. Must be exciting, right?"

He was not excited, Zhou Ziheng thinks.

"Yeah." Xia Xiqing smiles. "I tried to remain calm, but on the inside, I was extremely excited. I've liked Ziheng for a very long time and it was a great opportunity to be able to collaborate with him."

He's good with words. The fake act he's putting on is quite impeccable.

"As we all know, Xiqing, you became famous overnight after the *Seagull* press conference. Can you share with us your mood at that time?"

Xia Xiqing blinks slowly. "Well, it was quite a coincidence. That was my first time going to a live event of my idol." He laughs. "So, I didn't expect to get caught on camera. I went to bed as soon as I got home that day, and didn't find out until the next morning that I got on the trending list."

Zhou Ziheng recalls the first time he saw Xia Xiqing. He was standing in the corridor of the hotel, and his phone had been knocked out of his hand by a bodyguard. Feeling sorry for him, Zhou Ziheng picked it up and gave it back.

The moment he looked up at Xia Xiqing, he'd been really shocked and impressed by his clean and beautiful face.

The hostess laughs. "To be honest, when I saw the video at the time, I was like everyone else. I was so impressed. Xiqing, do you have any thoughts about entering the entertainment industry in the future?"

This question is not easy to answer. Zhou Ziheng, sitting on the sidelines, reacts quickly; after all, he's been in this business for quite some time. He knows that if you answer negatively and yet continue to appear in shows, you'll be a laughingstock. If you answer positively, you'll be regarded as too ambitious.

Xia Xiqing tilts his head. "How to say this... I studied art. In fact, in my eyes, art is art—whether it's music, painting, or performance. As long as there's something that interests me, the form is not important. Since they're all art, why should they be divided?"

Words are truly powerful.

"That makes sense." The hostess turns to Zhou Ziheng. "Ziheng, although you're young, you're already senior in terms of the industry to many of the rest of us. What are your plans for the rest of this year? Many fans are curious as to whether you'll perform in a romantic movie. After all, we have yet to see a kissing scene from you."

Hearing this question, Zhou Ziheng freezes. "Well...about drama..." His words become slightly incoherent. "I don't actually have any romantic films lined up for this year. I still would like to focus on some more realistic subjects. This will bring more influence and attention to the widespread problems in our society."

Zhou Ziheng suddenly has more to say than before. However, it is all in effort to change the subject.

No kissing scene, Xia Xiqing thinks for a moment. Surprisingly, that's true. It was impossible when he was a child, of course, but even after he became an adult, there's been no romantic scenes with any of the actresses he's worked with.

"Isn't Zhou Ziheng twenty this year?" The hostess is unwilling to let this topic go. "Has your family talked to you about your love life? Everyone's curious about your personal relationships, since you grew up under the watchful eyes of your audience."

Xia Xiqing looks at Zhou Ziheng. The expression on his face is calm, but his lips are pursed. He only does that when he's nervous.

"I have a very busy schedule; there's little time for me to visit home. I'll have to leave romance to fate." Zhou Ziheng smiles at the camera.

Fate? That's a very ambiguous answer. Does that mean he has no emotional experience? Xia Xiqing can't help but lean over to look at him. Zhou Ziheng's first reaction is to avoid eye contact.

"Oh, is that so?" the hostess asks with a smile. "Then I'll need to ask the question that concerns our audience most—what's your type?"

Zhou Ziheng raises his hand and touches his neck. His eyes are empty, and he seems to remember something. "Well, kind...kind and gentle. You know, someone who has an aura of warmth and healing."

Not one thing about Xia Xiqing meets these criteria. Xia Xiqing smirks bitterly. Something tells him that Zhou Ziheng's standards are all in reference to someone in specific.

Maybe there's someone he has a crush on. He's twenty years old—it would be difficult to pass two decades without having liked anyone.

"Oh, so Zhou Ziheng likes the little angel type. There must be a story behind that," the hostess jokes.

Zhou Ziheng quickly refutes the idea. "No, no." He wants to say more, but decides not to.

"What about you, Xia Xiqing? Your ideal type is..."

Before she can finish the question, all the lights go out and the studio is left in pitch-blackness.

"What's going on? An outage?" The hostess is startled.

It's like suddenly being choked. Breathing becomes more difficult for Xia Xiqing. His fingers clench the leather surface of the sofa like a drowning person reaching for something buoyant.

His heart beats faster and faster.

Extreme discomfort.

Suddenly, a warm, dry palm covers his hand, like a current rushing through the darkness. The hand hesitates slightly and lifts from his fingers, then comes back and grasps his wrist.

For some reason, his breathing rhythm normalizes slightly. Xia Xiqing endures the discomfort and attempts to divert his attention. People's voices begin to appear around him. The video team shouting to the lighting engineers, who constantly apologize, the interview team rushing to establish communication.

The only voice absent from the mess is Zhou Ziheng's.

He is totally silent.

The hand that is around Xia Xiqing's wrist provides constant warmth to calm his pulse.

Xia Xiqing, still slightly gasping, leans his head toward the direction of his wrist. The darkness engulfs everything in his sight, apart from a person's silhouette. The outline seems to glow with glittering light, like stars leading him forward.

He becomes more at ease.

"Okay, lights are back up!"

Instantly, the room full of darkness is replaced by bright light. The hand quickly withdraws.

Light fixtures come on one after another, restoring the room to its original state. Everything that happened just now in the dark has become nothing but a secret fairy tale. When midnight came and the clock struck twelve, the magic disappeared.

Xia Xiqing stares blankly at his empty wrist. After a while, he looks at Zhou Ziheng. His face is neutral. One hand is holding his mic, just like before, while the other is in his pocket.

"Camera's ready. This section will be cut. Let's start over."

Zhou Ziheng nods and adjusts his sitting position toward the camera. Just as no one knows the hand-holding fairy tale, no one knows that he is hiding his right palm, which is covered in sweat.

When the darkness hit, Zhou Ziheng's immediate response had been to protect Xia Xiqing. Even now, with the lights restored, his heart still beats rapidly.

"Back to the question just now," the hostess asks with a smile. "What is your ideal type, Xia Xiqing?"

Xia Xiqing has already adjusted himself back into interview mode, and smiles as he looks up at the camera. "Actually, just before the lights went out, I had already thought of an answer—that is, my ideal type is someone who is as fascinating as a work of art." He gently touches his mic with a finger. His wrist feels warm. "But I have a different idea now."

Zhou Ziheng purses his lips. His right hand clenches into a fist in his pocket.

"Want to change your answer now? Let's hear it."

"Now..." Xia Xiqing speaks softly, "it's someone luminous."

Compared to the boundless night sky, the light of one star is very faint. But as long as the star continues to shine, it is not pure darkness.

"No disappointment from the art student here; I feel this description is very abstract. But sunny personalities are always very energizing and empowering for those around them. I think you two have very similar ideals."

The hostess looks at her notes. "Now, let's get into some questions from our fans. We asked the internet before this interview, and selected a few with the highest number of votes. The first one is: after airing the first episode of your show, your ship is now called ZiXi. Are you aware of this?"

Zhou Ziheng nods. "Yes."

"I also know they call themselves ZiXi girls. Self-Study, hahaha," Xia Xiqing laughs. "It's got to be the nerdiest ship name I've heard."

"So if these Self-Study girls want to do a meet-up, they'll need to rent out a library?" Zhou Ziheng's humor has always been dry.

Xia Xiqing plays along. "Well, we all have the same nine years of compulsory education. Are our Self-Study girls the most outstanding students of us all?"

"Haha, you two are very funny." The hostess laughs. "The second question is for Xia Xiqing: why did you Like the post about you and Sirui? Are you guys close?"

Upon hearing this question, Zhou Ziheng wants to frown, but he manages to maintain his composure. The online shipping war is at its height right now, so questions about it are inevitable.

Xia Xiqing did not expect this question, and is stunned. "Who liked what? Me?"

"Huh? Isn't it..." The hostess is shocked by his reaction. She pulls out her phone and opens Xia Xiqing's Weibo page. "See, that right there."

Xia Xiqing looks at the mobile phone. Did he really like that post? It's been there for quite a few days now. This is all a huge misunderstanding.

"Umm... That was an accident." Xia Xiqing returns the phone and ridicules himself. "My finger must have slipped. Have to be careful with that when surfing social media."

"So your hand slipped?" The hostess laughs. "That will make some fans quite sad."

For some reason, hearing this answer brings Zhou Ziheng relief. More than relief, it's refreshing.

"No, no," Xia Xiqing explains quickly. "I have a very good relationship with Sirui. He's like a younger brother to me. He's very cute and we chat a lot in private."

Zhou Ziheng's relief is once again shattered. Like a roller coaster.

"Yes. Before that, Shang Sirui posted a painting that you did for him. You two are really good friends," the hostess adds.

Xia Xiqing nods.

The interview proceeds with a few questions toward Zhou Ziheng. He's feeling a bit up and down, and isn't in a good state. All his answers are vague and completely by the book. Nonetheless, this is normal for Zhou Ziheng's interviews, so no one is able to notice that anything is wrong.

"The last question we have is for Xia Xiqing from one of our netizens: why did you choose such a long hairstyle? Normally, boys choose shorter styles. Long hair looks good on you, but it's not very manly. Wouldn't it be less girly if you cut your hair short?"

This is quite an awkward question. Even the hostess feels strange as she reads it.

"I guess this netizen is really into the masculine type, haha."

Why does it matter to you what hairstyle I choose...? That's Xia Xiqing's first reaction. Although he's not very happy, he's always been good at pretending. He smiles gently and explains, "I'm actually just lazy. I was busy with an arts exhibition and didn't have time to get a haircut. When I studied abroad, I saw lots of boys with long hair. I think aesthetics are inherently personal; if they become normalized, the world will be less interesting."

The hostess feels that Xia Xiqing is very cultured and polite, so she quickly adds, "Yes, diversity is what we need. Short hair, long hair. Normality—I remember reading something that told me the concept of 'normal people' is constantly expanding."

Zhou Ziheng cuts in with a calm voice. "Normal people. Who defines what normal is?"

His tone has no emotion. It is a simple question, but extremely intimidating. The hostess sitting on the opposite side is unable to respond.

Zhou Ziheng looks directly at the camera. "If this judgment system is determined by us, can I redefine a new set of standards? For example, it's okay for men to have long hair, and wear skirts, and be protected instead of being the protector. Women can emerge from their continued burden of historical prejudice and do whatever they want."

No one expected this speech from Zhou Ziheng. The professional quality of the hostess' on-the-spot response is completely disturbed under his influence. Even Xia Xiqing is shocked.

Before this moment, Xia Xiqing was quite confident about his understanding of Zhou Ziheng—in his mind, he's a figure of natural power with a soft and childish heart. But now, he's been proven wrong. He can see the powerful and righteous core of his personality.

Zhou Ziheng leans back on the sofa, calmly ignoring the camera. Following his previous statements, he continues to speak, "Like the classic color blindness paradox, how can we know we are normal without knowing the rules?"

The studio is completely silent. The topic suddenly becomes deep and sensitive.

Xia Xiqing smiles.

"Yes, indeed," he says with a breezy tone. "We were born to be ourselves. Not to be a 'normal person.'"

C.06

Trading at a Loss

At the end of the interview, Zhou Ziheng stands and bows to the interview crew.

"Thank you for your time."

"Thank you, Ziheng and Xiqing. You guys must be exhausted by now." The hostess also stands up.

Zhou Ziheng shakes his head slightly. "And by the way, the last question can be cut if necessary."

The hostess smiles. "No need. That's what makes you so adored by the audience."

After all the day's work is complete, Xia Xiqing and Zhou Ziheng take off their makeup and change into their casual clothing. Xiao-Luo is waiting outside for them.

"Zhou Ziheng, let me drive you both home. After all, it's on the—"

Before Xiao-Luo can utter the last syllable, Zhou Ziheng covers his mouth and gives him a fierce look while checking his surroundings.

On the way? I'll be damned if anyone finds out we're neighbors.

Xia Xiqing stands by, looking at the childish Zhou Ziheng. He chuckles. Is this the same Zhou Ziheng as the one who just got interviewed?

"Xiao-Luo, you can go back first. I'll call you a cab." Zhou Ziheng takes out his phone.

Xiao-Luo glances at Xia Xiqing, then at Zhou Ziheng. He hands the car keys to Zhou Ziheng and says, "Don't worry, I can get a cab myself. Are you okay to drive home?"

"Nothing scheduled for tomorrow, right?" Zhou Ziheng twirls the keys between his fingers. "Don't schedule anything for the rest of this week. I have classes and midterms."

Midterms? Xia Xiqing doesn't hold in his laugh. Zhou Ziheng turns and glares at him. He puts the keys into his pocket and accompanies Xiao-Luo out of the building and sees him into a cab. He then turns and heads toward the underground parking garage, only to find Xia Xiqing has been following him this whole time.

"Why are you following me?" With a baseball cap on and a mask on the lower half of his face, Zhou Ziheng's voice comes out muffled. His hands are in his pockets.

It's an early morning in April, and the temperature is cool. Stuck between two seasons, just like their ambiguously friendly, ambiguously romantic relationship.

Xia Xiqing imitates Zhou Ziheng and puts his hands into his pockets. He stands beside him, shoulder to shoulder, with a smile on his face. "Hey handsome, can I catch a ride? I hear I'm on your way."

He deliberately stresses the phrase "on your way" just to catch Zhou Ziheng's cutely flustered expression.

Zhou Ziheng retreats toward the car. His voice becomes even quieter. "What ride? You can call a cab."

Seeing Zhou Ziheng open the car door for himself with no intention of letting him in, Xia Xiqing shivers slightly in the cold. "But it's so late now..."

"Are you afraid?" Zhou Ziheng opens the door wider. "You're the most dangerous person around here."

Xia Xiqing, unaware that Zhou Ziheng has labeled him a terrorist, grabs the car door before it closes. "It's hard to find a cab around here."

"You'll find one eventually," Zhou Ziheng responds from inside the car.

"But you picked me up—well, sort of. Shouldn't you send me back as well?"

"No."

Seeing Zhou Ziheng is unmoved by his words, Xia Xiqing sighs. "Okay, I'll go alone then."

He turns around and takes a few steps away with his arms folded in front of his chest. He looks around the parking garage pitifully, then says, "Oh, it's so dark in here..."

Three.

Two.

One.

Headlights suddenly brighten behind him. The beam passes over Xia Xiqing's shoulders and illuminates the darkness in front of him. His shadow stretches on the ground. Xia Xiqing smiles.

"Get in the car." Zhou Ziheng pulls up next to him. "You're going to annoy me to death."

Xia Xiqing knew all along that his moral role model would not leave him stranded. He gets into the passenger seat and closes the door.

Holding the steering wheel with one hand, Zhou Ziheng uses his other hand to remove his hat and puts it on Xia

Xiqing's head before pulling up his own hood. Turning sideways, Xia Xiqing looks at Zhou Ziheng in a daze.

"What? Don't just look at me, buckle your seatbelt."

Xia Xiqing suddenly remembers the last time he was in this car; he was pretending to be drunk and took advantage of the situation with Zhou Ziheng.

"Why does this car feel familiar?" Xia Xiqing tugs on the seatbelt. "It feels like I've been here before in a dream or something. Must just be déjà vu."

He looks at Zhou Ziheng, who gulps nervously.

Very funny.

"Yeah, probably just déjà vu." Zhou Ziheng turns the steering wheel with one hand.

Xia Xiqing presses the brim of his hat and asks, "You gave me this out of fear of being photographed by paparazzi? I see you don't want people to know that we live together."

"Who lives with you?!" Zhou Ziheng is about to explode.

"Right, sorry, phrasing. I just live next door." Xia Xiqing looks at himself in the mirror and pulls his hair back into a small braid. "There. Now if we get photographed, they'll think it's some random girl instead of me. I would hate to ruin your reputation."

The last sentence is obviously said in mockery; by no means to compliment his clean reputation, but instead to mock him for having always been terminally single.

Zhou Ziheng suddenly feels that his self-esteem is being attacked. "A girl? A six-foot-tall girl? Who are you kidding?"

"What's wrong with being six feet tall? You straight guys only care about faces anyways." Xia Xiqing turns and smirks at him. "At least my face isn't too unappetizing, no?"

He leans closer. Zhou Ziheng suddenly feels embarrassed. Deliberately ignoring Xia Xiqing, he says in an awkward tone, "Don't disturb me while I'm driving."

Xia Xiqing raises his hands in surrender. He leans back on the seat and looks out the window. The streets are empty in the early morning, and there's nothing out there but rows of street lights.

The car suddenly becomes quiet. Zhou Ziheng can't help but recall the scene when he sent Xia Xiqing back to the hotel that night; he'd been hugged tightly by Xia Xiqing and his neck had been rubbed by his soft lips.

Unable to tell what's wrong with himself, Zhou Ziheng raises his hand and rubs at the back of his neck.

The sense of that touch remains with him like PTSD.

"Hey."

Xia Xiqing's voice resonates beside Zhou Ziheng. Zhou Ziheng trembles in fear. His hair stands up from his guilty conscience.

"What are you doing?"

He doesn't know what to say. He doesn't even know what he is guilty of. Every time he's alone with Xia Xiqing, he always feels like something is off about himself.

"Why did you hold my hand?" Xia Xiqing is leaning against the car window. The hat casts a shadow onto his open eyes, making it difficult to see his expression. "You know, when the lights went out."

Holding the steering wheel tightly, Zhou Ziheng gives an answer after crossing an intersection. "Because you told me you were afraid of the dark. If someone is willing to reveal their fears and weaknesses to me, I am willing to help protect them. I'd want protection too, if it were my weakness being revealed."

A true role model.

Under the brim of the hat, Xia Xiqing sneers.

"So, your question at the end of the interview earlier. Did that come from this same logic?"

Zhou Ziheng pauses. "Yeah."

It's true; if anyone else had gotten questioned so disrespectfully, Zhou Ziheng would have defended that person as well. But what he just said was a lie.

The hand that reached out to Xia Xiqing was not offered out of some moral principle, but rather something much more inexplicable. None of his actions around Xia Xiqing are logical like that. He can't just explain why his instincts tell him to do these things for this terrible man, so he gave a false excuse.

The atmosphere suddenly becomes more serious. Xia Xiqing is now silent, which brings Zhou Ziheng's mood down. In fact, he has many questions he wants to ask Xia Xiqing. Why did he agree to come to the photoshoot? Why isn't he asking any more questions about Zhou Ziheng changing his mind about personally picking him up?

And why is he afraid of the dark?

But he does not want to ask.

This moment is like two people in a childish staring contest. He who blinks first loses.

After meeting Xia Xiqing, Zhou Ziheng has become extremely competitive. He definitely does not want to be the one who blinks first.

The rest of the trip to the apartment is spent in silence. The two get out of the elevator and walk toward their respective suites. Xia Xiqing stretches and begins to unlock his door.

"Hey." Zhou Ziheng's voice comes from the other end of the hall. "Give me my hat."

Xia Xiqing turns around and leans on the door with a

smirk.

"No."

Speechless, Zhou Ziheng frowns. "Why are you such an asshole?"

"It's not the first time you've talked to me." Xia Xiqing walks toward him. His voice lightens up a lot. "How come you're finding that out just now?"

Xia Xiqing is almost in front of Zhou Ziheng, and he looks up at him with lifted eyes. Zhou Ziheng is wearing a mask and rolls his eyes impatiently as he reaches out for the hat, but Xia Xiqing grabs his wrist.

"Do you want it?" Xia Xiqing smiles. "I can give it to you, but I want to trade."

Zhou Ziheng tosses his hand off. His eyes are cold. "That's my stuff."

"Doesn't matter; if I want something, it becomes mine." Xia Xiqing smiles and strokes Zhou Ziheng's shoulder. "Now, about our trade..."

Leaving the sentence unfinished, he pulls down on Zhou Ziheng's collar and kisses him through the mask.

Xia Xiqing, with his eyes half closed, looks up at Zhou Ziheng with a breathtaking smile. Their eyes meet during the tender kiss. Their soft lips are pressed tightly together through the thin cloth of the mask.

Right before Zhou Ziheng regains his senses, Xia Xiqing opens his mouth and bites Zhou Ziheng on the lips through his mask.

Everything happens within ten seconds, but to Zhou Ziheng it seems like eternity. Xia Xiqing's pure face, long eyelashes, and the mole on the tip of his nose are all that can be remembered.

With a crooked smile, Xia Xiqing takes off the hat and

places it on Zhou Ziheng's head.

"Deal."

Turning around, Xia Xiqing walks to his apartment without another word.

It's the end of the game they've been playing. He just can't hold it anymore. Zhou Ziheng clenches his fist and smashes the door behind him fiercely. Irritated, he takes off the hat and returns home. He's annoyed that Xia Xiqing can always overcome his defenses no matter how much effort he puts in. He hates to admit this.

He blinked first.

Xia Xiqing doesn't see Zhou Ziheng for days after the magazine shoot, nor does he take the initiative in contacting him. In order to not get him caught in a scandal, he specifically asks Xia Zhixu to hack into the security cameras on their floor and turn them off. In exchange, he gives up some old high school photos of Xu Qichen.

The cover of the magazine is released before the magazine itself, and the official blog is bombarded with various comments. The posted covers of both editions prompt readers with a question: **Two models require two covers, which would you choose? A or B?**

@SelfStudyMakeMeHappy: Whoever can answer this question should be able to meet the entrance requirements for Tsinghua U or Peking U.

@ILoveSelfStudy: Ahhhhh!

@BestHeng: The first edition!!

@XiqingsLady: OMG. BDSM. Loving both editions! Life is meaningless if I can't hook up with Xia Xiqing

@StrawberryGummy: Both are good! Another masterpiece from Lin Mo! And adults shouldn't need to choose—I want them all! By the way, I love the chemistry between Self-Study!

@AlphaHeng: Same here. Not feeling much about Xia Xiqing, but I have to admit, the chemistry...

@SweetWish: Didn't understand why this ship went viral until now.

@LittleAngel: For all those BL novels I read, I can see faces now...

@AFriend: The blood on Zhou Ziheng and scar on Xia Xiqing. I just imagined a dark romance in my head. And I love the second edition too! No nudity but I can feel the hormones and desires of these two gorgeous men. Loving this ship now!

@DuckDuckInTheButt: First one: "If he's dead then he can't leave me." The second one: "You're nothing but my bitch." #WhatADreamyShipLooksLike

@NoDefeatForSelfStudyGirls: Did anyone see the handcuffs and setting in the first one? Very similar to their escape room. It's like they know how to fill our imagination. I am totally satisfied with the effects. Black, white, red, and the gothic aesthetic. I just love it.

@LovingSelfStudy: Seeing these covers, my first thought was, they look so REAL. Oh, please let my ship come true for once. They look so good together.

...

Let your ship come true? Xia Xiqing chuckles.

Maybe.

Xia Xiqing receives a WeChat message from Jiang Yin.

Jiang Yin: Xia Xiqing, the magazine asked you to help promote the covers and share the official blog's post.

Xia Xiqing doesn't want to help, but when he returns to the Weibo page, he finds that Zhou Ziheng has already shared it.

@ZhouZiheng: A.

Fans are also sharing the post like crazy.

@MyOnlyHeng: Ahh my baby appeared!

@AKris: Is this a pun? Hahaha. I chose A because I am A.

Xia Xiqing, who was unwilling to help promote before, immediately shares the post.

@Tsing_Summer: I choose B.

Seeing that both stars have appeared, their shippers drop comments at an unimaginable speed.

@SelfStudyNo1: Lol, catch my Self-Study baby! Their choices are predictable and unsurprising.

@IWantToStudyByMyself: I get you! Like two alphas fighting for the top spot.

@WhoSaidNo: HAHAHAHHA! And once you accept this setting...

@MarshmallowCloud: They shared the post at around the same time, as if they had already discussed it. Are they physically together right now? Just guessing.

@AFishInPekingUniversity: Sorry to disappoint but Zhou Ziheng is studying in our school library right now. I am two rows behind him. Looks like he is struggling for midterms just like me.

@NoDefeatForSelfStudyGirls: Hahahahahahaha Zhou Ziheng is now studying by himself.

@PerhapsYouLikeToSelfStudy: He's self-studying.

@MyShipLockedTogetherAndIThrewAwayTheKey: Guys, he's teaching us how to ship properly.

...

These silly girls...

WeChat chirps again, it's Xia Xiuze.

Xiao-Ze: Brother!!!! I don't have classes today. Can I come over to your place afterward?

Xiao-Ze: [why doesn't brother answer my message.jpg]

Xiao-Ze: [look of expectation.jpg]
Xiao-Ze: [on the edge of my seat.jpg]

How does this guy have so many neurotic memes? Xia Xiqing is about to ruthlessly reject him when a call comes in. Without looking at the call display, Xia Xiqing answers it.

"I don't have the spare time to..."

"Hello, Xiqing?"

Huh? It's not Xia Xiuze? Xia Xiqing takes the phone away from his ear and looks at the screen. It's an associate professor that he used to work under. He coughs and says, much more politely, "Hello professor, did you need something?"

"Oh, I heard from Smith that you've returned to China. I'll cut the small talk—could you come help me out? The sculpture exhibition I have on hand is due soon and apparently some of my students are not capable of handling the pressure. Kids these days, so unreliable. Anyways, if you're free, your help would be much appreciated."

Xia Xiqing frowns; he hates acting as the last-minute relief force, yet for some reason the task seems to always fall to him. "Professor, I've actually been quite..."

But the professor isn't done talking, continuing with, "Peking U, Department of Fine Arts. It's really quite urgent, so please hurry!"

Wait a minute. Peking University?

"Sure," Xia Xiqing agrees swiftly. "I'll contact you once I get there."

It's not until he turns on the GPS that he realizes that Peking University is rather close to where he lives—less than ten minutes by car. No wonder Zhou Ziheng bought a place here.

Upon arriving, Xia Xiqing puts on a mask and enters the campus. He has the feeling that someone is watching him.

After walking for a while, he discovers that his feelings were correct. There's a row of girls holding their phones up and recording him.

He was not aware that he's this popular.

"Xiqing?" A girl walks up to him. "You're Xia Xiqing, right?"

Since he's been recognized, Xia Xiqing has no need to pretend anymore. He smiles softly through the mask he's wearing and walks off.

"Oh my god! It's really Xia Xiqing! The real person!"

"So attractive! So gentle!"

Zhou Ziheng is in the study room of the library revising for midterms, and suddenly feels commotion around him. He pulls out an earbud and turns his head to see some girls in the back row holding up their phones. Frowning, he presses the brim of his hat down, then replaces his earbud and continues to study.

What the hell.

His best friend, Zhao Ke, is sitting beside him and bumps his shoulder. "Hey, Zhou Ziheng."

"What's the matter?" Zhou Ziheng removes his earbud again and looks at Zhao Ke innocently.

Zhao Ke places his phone in front of Zhou Ziheng and says with a teasing tone, "Look, the other half of your pairing is here."

Zhou Ziheng rolls his eyes. "Fuck off. Your pairing..." The hand holding the earbud suddenly freezes. "What did you say?!"

"Isn't this your guy?" Zhao Ke jokes, approaching to show him the photos and videos on social media. "Hey, I gotta say, he looks better than most of the girls in our class."

"There are a total of six girls in our entire class." Zhou Zi-heng sneers and continues to focus on his textbook without putting his earbud back.

"Ha, what I mean is that he's better looking than most girls in our school. Fair skin, pretty face. I thought you guys were just pretending to get publicity; I didn't know you were actually friends. He's even here to visit you." Zhao Ke's imagination is running wild. "I wonder if he brought any food. Maybe some homemade lunch."

Zhou Ziheng twirls his pen and puts it down loudly. He looks up at Zhao Ke with a terrific glare. Zhao Ke immediately shuts up and says, "Study, study, exams soon."

Homemade lunch?

As far as his cooking level is concerned, not dying from food poisoning would be quite a bit to ask.

The strange thing is, now Zhou Ziheng is actually imagining Xia Xiqing showing up with a cutesy pink lunchbox and handing it to him while he's studying. When opened, there's some unidentifiable black matter inside.

I must be going crazy. Zhou Ziheng holds his forehead with his left palm, absentmindedly drawing on some scrap paper.

Why would Xia Xiqing come here all of a sudden? *He could have told me before coming.*

Only a minute ago, he was still on Weibo sharing that post about the magazine.

Could it be true that he came to see me?

No, no, he's definitely up to something.

"Hey, Zhou Ziheng."

The mess of thoughts is interrupted by Zhao Ke's voice. Zhou Ziheng, recovering from his delusions, finds that he's been writing Xia Xiqing's name over and over again on his paper. Frightened, he quickly turns the paper over and covers it. "What? What's wrong?"

Zhao Ke points to his paper with a pen. "Can you prove Bloch's Theorem for me? I don't think I did it correctly."

Zhou Ziheng breathes out in relief. He takes the paper from Zhao Ke and turns his cap around so as to not block his friend's vision.

"To put it bluntly, the hardest part is the eigenvalue of the Hamiltonian. The calculation is huge if we want to solve it by brute force, so here we introduce a linear mapping, because these two functions have the same eigenvalue and it's easier to calculate the eigenvalue." He lowers his head and carefully writes the formula and the derivation process on the paper. "This is equivalent to the formal function. And after making the assumption here, and proving that it's periodic, the proof is mostly done."

"Oh, I think I get it." Zhao Ke takes the paper from Zhou Ziheng and stares at it. "Tell me, do you secretly get tutored while filming?"

Zhou Ziheng murmurs, "If I did, would I still be here studying by myself?"

Self-study...

It feels weird to say that now. Zhou Ziheng takes the piece of paper with Xia Xiqing's name on it and quietly hides it under the table. He wants to crumple it, but instead, he folds it up and stuffs it into his pocket.

Xia Xiqing, who was almost crumpled into a ball, finally arrives at the Department of Fine Arts with the help of many excited girls. Associate Professor Wang has specifically asked one of his students to pick him up, and said student looks young and full of energy. He greets Xia Xiqing enthusiastically upon first sight.

"Xiqing-*shixiong*,"[11] I can't believe it's really you! I've heard a lot about you from Professor Wang. He said you're a very prominent alumnus of the Accademia." He looks totally amazed. "I've seen some of your work on the prof's computer and I absolutely love it, especially your *Girl in the Boboli Garden*. It's so..." He can't seem to find the right adjective to show his excitement.

Xia Xiqing finds this *shidi*[12] of his quite amusing. He pats him on the shoulder. "Thank you."

The student's face turns red and he hurries to follow Xia Xiqing. "And I watched your show. You were great in the escape room. I'd only seen your work before, I didn't know you were also...so good-looking." The last words are spoken much more quietly.

He seems afraid that he chose the wrong words. After all, to most men, it might not be pleasant to be complimented on their physical appearance by another man.

"Then I'm honored that you find me pleasing to the eye." Xia Xiqing turns with a gentle smile.

After this, Xia Xiqing's innocent little shidi is completely enamored with him. He excitedly leads Xia Xiqing to the sculpture exhibition.

On his way to the university, Xia Xiqing already saw an email from Professor Wang with the materials and design drafts of this exhibition. When he arrives at the scene, he finds that the professor was not exaggerating. Only two days

11 In some Chinese industries, terms related to the more traditional models of apprenticeship are still used. In this context, "shixiong" is an honorific title or suffix for any male student who's ever studied under the same master or teacher as the speaker, but only those who started studying before the speaker.

12 This is the converse of "shixiong"; "shidi" is also an honorific suffix or title for any male student who's ever studied under the same master or teacher as the speaker, but is used for those who started studying after the speaker.

left, and there are still a lot of things left unfinished.

"We originally had enough time, but the group in charge of the main exhibit really dropped the ball. The professor is especially dissatisfied with the final product. So we asked you to come help with the sculpture."

The exhibit in question is actually a surrealist sculpture standing at 3.2 meters tall. In the original design draft, a very realistic man's head was prepared using resin and fiberglass. What Xia Xiqing sees is instead a defective lower half head that completely ruins the proportions.

"We were going to dismantle it, but the professor wanted you to take a look first."

Xia Xiqing touches his chin, silent. He picks up a pencil from the floor and walks around the sculpture. Occasionally, he stops and makes some notes on the design plan.

Twenty minutes later, the young student sitting on the floor is just about to fall asleep when a piece of paper lands in front of him. On that paper is a drawing, something completely different from the design draft.

The original style is overthrown. The unbalanced portrait is retained, and the top part of the head is removed to form a hollow skull. Erupting from the skull is an explosion of various materials—wood chips, acrylic, metal, and colored resin. On the outermost layer, black cotton thread winds around the whole thing, tying it all together.

The left side of the face is shattered into countless cracks. Tears made from resin run down from the left eye, filling the skin cracks.

On the lower right corner of the draft, he's written the theme—Imprisonment.

Imprisonment of thoughts.

This concept is brilliant. The young student takes the

design and stares speechlessly. He looks up at Xia Xiqing, who is squatting beside him.

"This... this..."

Xia Xiqing smirks. He points his thumb backward, toward the sculpture behind him. "Time to get to work."

He stands up and straightens his clothes, then notices that he's wearing a knitted sweater in a creamy white. "Uh, shidi, do you have any work-wear I could borrow?"

In the library, Zhou Ziheng remains in the same seat studying for his exam. The commotion behind him grows louder and louder. There are a bunch of girls sitting in a group, whispering to each other.

"Hey, it's been so long. Xia Xiqing hasn't come to the library yet. Is he lost?"

"We have multiple libraries, maybe he's lost."

"Don't spread rumors, maybe he isn't here for Zhou Ziheng. My friend is majoring in fine arts and she said he went toward their department. He didn't ask for physics."

"No way...really? No wonder Ziheng is so quiet."

...

Though Zhou Ziheng has his earbuds in, no music is playing. And they're in a study room at the library, so all discussions remain quite audible regardless of how quiet they are. Zhou Ziheng doesn't respond, but Zhao Ke turns around and glares at the girls in the back.

Zhou Ziheng takes off his black-rimmed glasses and rubs the bridge of his nose. Looking at the scrap paper on the table, he can't help but fetch his phone out of his pocket and unlock the screen.

There are no unread messages.

He opens WeChat. Multiple messages come up, but none

from the terrorist. He scrolls down to find his last conversation with Xia Xiqing, which hasn't been updated recently.

What is that guy doing? He just comes to the university without saying hi, and now everyone is gathered around here like Zhou Ziheng is the last person to know about it.

Forget it.

Doesn't matter what he's here for. He's not here for me.

Zhou Ziheng is not someone who takes other's affection for granted. As an actor growing up under the eyes of his audience, he does not have the narcissistic self-confidence like many others in his line of work. He feels that acting is no different from any other profession, and that he should be grateful to have such a steady career at so young an age.

He never thought that someone would come to the university just for him. But then everyone started telling him that Xia Xiqing was here for him, that he came to see him. All these hints made him believe that Xia Xiqing really would rush to find him.

What's going on? Is it a new play? What sort of strategy is this?

Unable to understand what's wrong, Zhou Ziheng collapses his head onto the table. His phone still in his hand, he buries his head into his arms.

"Hey, big star, big handsome guy, what's wrong with you?" Zhao Ke lowers his voice. "Pay attention to your image, your fans are everywhere. I spent an hour getting ready today just to study with you."

"I'm tired. I need a break." Zhou Ziheng's voice is dull. "My fans won't come close."

Likely due to his young age when he first entered the entertainment industry and how hard it is to juggle a career and an education, Zhou Ziheng's fans are very considerate;

they don't usually disturb him at school.

"Okay, but the other half of your pairing is here. Don't you want to go find him?" Zhao Ke pokes his elbow with a pen, grinning. "What if he finds you later?"

Zhou Ziheng, with his head still on the table, says in an upset and impatient tone, "Shut up, I have nothing to do with him."

As soon as his voice falls, the mobile phone in his hand begins to vibrate. Zhou Ziheng guessed that it must be someone else trying to feed him news. He turns the phone over and decides to ignore it. But then, not long after, the phone starts ringing as a call comes in, making quite the ruckus in quiet study room. He quickly looks at the screen:

Terrorist

Zhou Ziheng immediately sits up straight.

"Who is it?" Zhao Ke glances over at him. "Shit, are you gonna be working on a new anti-terrorism movie? That's so cool, man!"

"Anti your mom." Zhou Ziheng looks at the ringing phone, hesitates, then rejects it.

If he wanted to call, he would have called already. At this point, he's almost certain that this guy is going to ask him for a favor.

"Why aren't you picking up?" Zhao Ke asks, not even hiding the fact that he's fishing for gossip.

Zhou Ziheng glares at him. "Why do you care?"

The phone shakes a few more times, WeChat messages.

Terrorist: Ah, I forgot you're in self-study right now. You can't answer the phone.

Terrorist: I'm at your school's fine arts department, but you probably already knew that.

Zhou Ziheng scoffs. He picks up the phone and begins

to type. Zhao Ke is next to him, observing his best friend's gossip. Something is definitely up. Zhou Ziheng is usually a mild guy, he's not easily provoked.

Moral Role Model: Does it matter whether I know or not?

Terrorist: Of course it matters. I'm hungry, haven't eaten since the morning and I'm about to faint. Oh handsome kind-hearted Zhou Ziheng, can you bring some food for me?

Terrorist: [location pin]

Of course he wants a favor. Zhou Ziheng feels anger rising inside him. *Am I not a famous actor? Do I look like his servant? Isn't it his problem that he didn't eat lunch?*

Zhao Ke watches Zhou Ziheng's face change again and again. He looks like he's about to break down. What if he has a public meltdown and causes a scandal? He prepares to grab Zhou Ziheng and hide him away if anything weird is about to happen.

Suddenly, Zhou Ziheng stands and starts packing his school bag, getting ready to leave. Zhao Ke grabs him and asks in a low voice, "Hey, what's wrong? Where you going?"

Zhou Ziheng hesitates, avoiding the question. "Going out, something came up."

Seeing him leave in a hurry, Zhao Ke shakes his head, face full of complete understanding. He shares his news in a group chat called "Zhou Ziheng Gossip Squad."

Captain Zhao: Report! Heng-Heng left! Attention, team members of the fine arts department, target coming in hot.

Zhou Ziheng doesn't know what's going on with himself. He curses Xia Xiqing as he runs over to Changchun Garden and buys a meal to bring to the Department of Fine Arts.

Following the location shared by Xia Xiqing, Zhou Ziheng

walks through a teaching area and arrives at a semi-indoor hall with a garden in the back. Inside, there are various sculptures of various sizes, many of them covered with cloth. Unlike the sculptures of Zhou Ziheng's imagination, much of the work here is very modern and abstract.

As he walks among the forest of exhibits, he faintly hears Xia Xiqing's voice.

Zhou Ziheng tilts his head and looks at the giant innermost sculpture. A steel frame similar to a scaffold has been built around it. There are two people standing on it, and under them is a protective mat seemingly borrowed from the taekwondo gym. There are a few students busy making hanging pieces.

As Zhou Ziheng approaches, he looks at the man in loose black jeans on the scaffolding. His hair is half-tied; he stands on the shelf at the left end. Facing the sculpture, he fills the cracks with black resin.

This is the first time Zhou Ziheng has seen Xia Xiqing doing serious work.

Next to him stands another young boy. The two are talking and laughing while finishing the creation of this huge exhibit. Everyone concentrates on the progress and no one notices Zhou Ziheng's presence.

Standing on the scaffold, Xia Xiqing turns his head and says to the younger student, "Xiao-Qi, can you pass me that pick?"

Xiao-Qi nods, then squats and takes a pick from the toolbox. He stands up quickly to hand the tool to Xia Xiqing. The scaffolding shakes underneath him and Xia Xiqing quickly grabs the unbalanced student. However, he's unable to stabilize himself and slips out of the safe zone.

Seeing Xia Xiqing lose his footing, Zhou Ziheng's heart

suddenly speeds up. He drops what was in his hand and rushes over immediately. Without any rational consideration, he extends his arms in an attempt to catch the falling man.

The moment of impact brings pain to Zhou Ziheng's arms, making him grit his teeth as he looks worriedly at the person in his arms.

He sees the surprise in Xia Xiqing's eyes.

Despite being tall and strong, the kinetic energy delivered by a falling person is overwhelming. Zhou Ziheng gives into the impact; his knees bend and they both fall to the mat.

Before he completely understands what's happening, Xia Xiqing is already lying on Zhou Ziheng's chest, held firmly in his arms. The body beneath has successfully broken his fall.

But the shock in Xia Xiqing's heart cannot be calmed.

He gets up, with his hair dangling in front of his face. He moves to pull Zhou Ziheng upright and asks in a faint voice, "Hey, are you okay?"

Zhou Ziheng moans and pulls his arm back. "Wait..."

Xia Xiqing grabs his collar and, with an abnormal amount of emotion showing, he yells, "Is your brain fucking hollow? I can't die from such a tiny fucking fall. Why did you try to catch me? Do you really think you the main character in some superhero film?" Breathing heavily, his hands gradually loosen. His emotions are cooling down. Cursing in a low voice, "Fucking insane."

The scolding does not upset Zhou Ziheng at all. He raises his eyes to look at Xia Xiqing, the corner of his lips slightly crooked. He sits up straight by supporting himself with his uninjured arm.

His hat falls off his head, and the hair beneath is slightly messy. The smile on his face is deadly attractive, and his eyes are full of stars.

He pulls on Xia Xiqing's shirt and says in a low voice, "Hey, this is an ugly coat."

He picks up his fallen hat and reaches out to Xia Xiqing, who is still slightly shaken, and puts the hat on his head.

"You might as well wear the one you took from me."

What?

Xia Xiqing raises his head and moistens his lips.

Did this little virgin just flirt with him? Successfully?

"Shixiong, are you okay?" Xiao-Qi climbs down the scaffold in panic. Several other students follow.

"I'm okay." Xia Xiqing waves at Xiao-Qi with a smile. "Good thing you put the mat here. I'm all good, let's get back to work."

Xiao-Qi is embarrassed hearing this from Xia Xiqing. "If you feel unwell, I can take you to the school hospital."

Zhou Ziheng squints and stares at the helpful little shidi. "Are you from the fine arts department?"

Facing a question from Zhou Ziheng, Xiao-Qi immediately becomes nervous. "Ah, yes, yes. Hello, my name is Qi Kai."

"I'm Zhou Ziheng." He smiles at Qi Kai, but with his stature, even his smile feels pretty intimidating.

Qi Kai doesn't actually need any introduction; everyone knows who he is. Star student of the physics department, child star, one of the most popular celebrities of their generation—you'd have to be living under a rock to not know Zhou Ziheng. It's just that Qi Kai never thought he'd ever get to interact with him.

"You say that like there are people who don't know that your name is Zhou Ziheng," Xia Xiqing jibes. He reaches out to Qi Kai and pats him on the shoulder. "Don't worry, you're good."

"Yeah." Qi Kai's face turns red, which is particularly troubling sight to Zhou Ziheng's eyes.

He likes men?

No, he likes Xia Xiqing.

But they must have only met recently. Is it possible that he's become obsessed with him in such a short time? Zhou Ziheng used to think that type of thing is impossible, but then he met Xia Xiqing.

Nothing is truly impossible.

Xia Xiqing leans back on his hands and stares at Zhou Ziheng's tousled hair and black-rimmed glasses. Without makeup, he gives off a very young and energetic vibe. Xia Xiqing lifts himself up and steps on Zhou Ziheng's shoes in the process.

"You were pretty on cue, you handsome sneak."

Zhou Ziheng gives a crooked smile and steps his on Xia Xiqing's feet right back. "I'm not sneaky, I'm a big-time movie star."

"Okay." Xia Xiqing again steps on his toes. "So, big-time movie star, where's my food?"

"Food..." Zhou Ziheng turns around and points to the mess on the floor. "There. Doesn't look edible anymore."

Xia Xiqing sighs and lays down on the mat. "I'm going to starve to death."

"Shixiong," Qi Kai says, deciding to intervene. "Are you hungry? Do you want me to take you to our cafeteria?"

"Sure." Xia Xiqing smiles warmly. "Let's see what our country's top students eat."

Is a meal plan so special? I have a meal card too, Zhou Ziheng thinks to himself.

Xia Xiqing has already stood and handed his coat to Qi Kai. "Don't put it away just yet, though. I'll wear it again later when I'm back from lunch."

So it was actually that guy's jacket.

The three of them awkwardly walk toward the nearest cafeteria. Xia Xiqing walks in the middle and spends most of the walk discussing the sculpture with Qi Kai. As a model STEM major, Zhou Ziheng knows very little about the topic, so he stays mostly silent. Modernism and abstract art are beyond the scope of his expertise.

The closest cafeteria is across the road. It's lunch hour, so lots of people are coming and going. Xia Xiqing, who has been enjoying his conversation with Qi Kai, almost forgot that a celebrity is with him. He turns and tugs on Zhou Ziheng's sleeve.

"Hey, maybe you want to avoid this place. I can go by myself."

He's trying to be nice, giving Zhou Ziheng a chance to escape all the unnecessary attention. But the ungrateful brat puts up the hood of his hoodie and grumbles, "I'm hungry too."

Zhou Ziheng has been at this university for three years now, but he's only been in the cafeterias a handful of times. He still remembers his conversation with the Dean, who asked him to minimize his "influence" around the campus. Hence, Zhou Ziheng only comes to school for classes most days.

Today, he's in a cafeteria. Despite his low-key outfit, his six-four height alone is enough to make him stand out.

"Oh wow, isn't that Zhou Ziheng?"

"Wow it's true! What a good day! Zhou Ziheng is coming to eat in the cafeteria!"

A sharp-eyed girl immediately recognizes Xia Xiqing beside Zhou Ziheng. "My gosh, isn't that Xia Xiqing?"

"Holy shit! Xia Xiqing and Zhou Ziheng coming to eat together! I need to tell all my friends."

"It's true! Self-Study is here!"

...

More and more people are paying attention to them now. The crowd begins to whip out their phones and snap photos. They almost can't even walk forward. Xia Xiqing hasn't eaten anything all day and now he's surrounded by people; it's beginning to cause him breathing difficulties.

He turns to look for Xiao-Qi, but he's nowhere to be found. Must have gotten lost in the crowd.

Camera flashes begin to appear and Xia Xiqing lowers his head. He's slightly annoyed; he should have separated from Zhou Ziheng before they were noticed.

Suddenly, he feels a palm on his shoulder. Another hand wielding a tray appears in front of his face, covering it.

Zhou Ziheng's voice comes softly from behind. "Sorry, could we please avoid the pictures? We're just here for lunch, thank you. Excuse us, passing through."

This makes many fangirls start squealing. Howevere, the crowd gradually thins at his instructions. Xia Xiqing, guarded by Zhou Ziheng's tray, walks slowly toward the buffet.

None of the lunch ladies in the cafeteria are ignorant of Zhou Ziheng, either. When they see Zhou Ziheng walk in, they all light up—this is the kid they've watched grow up on television. Zhou Ziheng and Xia Xiqing only order some chicken, but somehow they end up with a huge pile of food.

"Oh, that's enough for me, auntie."

"No, no, no! You need to eat! You're still growing!"

"Really, it's enough for me..." Zhou Ziheng takes his mountain of food and smiles helplessly. "Thank you!"

Standing on the side, Xia Xiqing smiles and takes a plate

of food as well. "Not bad, Zhou Ziheng. You've made visiting the cafeteria feel like visiting a brothel."

Zhou Ziheng immediately shushes him. "Don't say stuff like that at school."

Xia Xiqing chuckles. He's happy. This guy is funny.

The two find a table toward one end of the room. Zhou Ziheng puts down his food and goes to fetch some cutlery, leaving Xia Xiqing alone at the table.

Two girls build up the courage to approach Xia Xiqing. "Hi, Xiqing-*gege*! You're really here at our school?"

Charmed, Xia Xiqing smiles at the girls. "Maybe I'm just a hallucination."

"Ahh, it's really him!"

As soon as he finishes teasing the girls, Zhou Ziheng returns and sits across from him, handing him some chopsticks and napkins. The girls don't say anything after seeing Zhou Ziheng, and quietly slip away back to their own table after sneaking a few photos.

"Hey, I think the girls at school are afraid of you." Xia Xiqing takes a bite of his food. "They don't even say hello."

Zhou Ziheng, immersed in his food, raises his eyes. "Evidently, I'm not as popular as you, Xiqing-*gege*."

Xia Xiqing certainly enjoys his new title, especially coming from Zhou Ziheng—probably because Zhou Ziheng is a bit more to his taste than those girls were, so a little effort on his part goes a long way.

"You've finally learned!" Xia Xiqing kicks Zhou Ziheng under the table. "Say that again."

Zhou Ziheng pretends to not hear anything and buries his face in his food. Xia Xiqing will not give up, however, and grabs Zhou Ziheng's chopsticks with his own. "Hey, come on. Call me that again."

Zhou Ziheng, unable to use his chopsticks, looks up at Xia Xiqing. "Call you what?"

"Gege."

"Yes?" Zhou Ziheng says.

It is then that Xia Xiqing realizes he got played by this kid. He wants to kick him, but there are too many people watching; he must maintain his angelic persona. Instead, he takes out his phone and begins to type a message.

A moment later, Zhou Ziheng's phone vibrates.

Terrorist: So you like being called gege? I hope you don't regret this.

Zhou Ziheng does not want to be outdone, so he puts down his chopsticks and picks up his phone.

Moral Role Model: A meal for an honorific—I'm not exactly trading at a loss here.

Xia Xiqing laughs and decides to end the nonsense on WeChat. He focuses on his food instead. It's strange that Xia Xiqing is giving up so easily. He must be really hungry.

"Hey, where's that shidi of yours?"

"I don't know, probably lost amongst your fans."

Zhou Ziheng snorts. "Don't blame them for him being too short."

"Protective of your fans, I see."

Finally finished with their meal, the two escape the crowd and leave the cafeteria.

"Still gonna self-study?" Xia Xiqing asks.

Hearing that phrase from Xia Xiqing's mouth, Zhou Ziheng feels strange. He raises his chin toward the path they came from. "I'll send you back and head to the library."

They walk side by side toward the Department of Fine Arts. Xia Xiqing suddenly remembers Zhou Ziheng catching him when he fell and begins to laugh.

"Why are you laughing?"

Xia Xiqing squeezes Zhou Ziheng's arm. "Laughing at your heroic stunts. Good thing I'm skinny, otherwise I'd have crushed you to death."

When they arrive at the Department of Fine Arts, Xia Xiqing turns and throws Zhou Ziheng his hat. "Okay, go study, I'll head home after I'm done here. Thanks."

Zhou Ziheng looks at the hat and panics a little. He doesn't know what's wrong; it's always two steps forward and one step back. *If I ignore him, he constantly annoys me and takes my stuff. If I approach him, he ignores me.*

He can't figure it out and doesn't want to think about it anymore. As he turns around and prepares to leave for the library, he hears Xia Xiqing's voice from behind.

"Hey, I know you want to be the hero, but be more careful next time. The consequences of something going wrong can be pretty severe, especially for you."

Zhou Ziheng sighs silently. *Do you really think I'm stupid enough to go around trying to catch every falling person?* He almost blurts that out, but he's able to hold it back.

Instead, he just hums in compliance and puts his hat back on, and leaves the Department of Fine Arts without looking back. Back at the library, he spends the rest of the day studying silently.

Zhao Ke, who's next to him, doesn't think anything is wrong. Tired of studying, he takes out his phone and opens Weibo. The app presents many hot posts regarding Zhou Ziheng and Xia Xiqing's ship, and about how they were spotted at school. Given his gossipy nature, he does not hesitate to click on the posts. There are many posts showing them in the cafeteria eating lunch, along with countless comments.

@HengHengTopsTheEntertainmentCircle: I envy those university students. Ziheng's unedited photos are amazing. So tall and handsome. The glasses give him a really studious feel. I like it.

@GoTeamSelfStudy: Heng-Heng would be a very protective boyfriend to Xia Xiqing. I think I just shed a tear. Btw, please don't disturb Heng-Heng when he is studying.

@WhoDoesntWantToSleepWithXiqing: Turns out that both Heng-Heng and Xiqing are tall and handsome compared to ordinary folks. Xiqing's nose is heavenly. Just another day of wanting to sleep with Xiqing.

@MaybeYouShipSelfStudy: Zhou Ziheng's smile was so sweet when they were eating. Xiqing even pretended to kick him. Also I think that hat on Xiqing's head was actually Heng-Heng's. I remember Heng-Heng having that hat.

@GoGoGoStudy: Indeed it is Ziheng's hat! He was wearing it when coming out of the library. Somehow it ended up with Xiqing. Who said they didn't get along.

@LittleCloudInTheWind: So, what exactly was Xia Xiqing doing there at the university? Baiting their pairing?

@GuGuLuLu: What baiting? Stop throwing baseless accusations around. Xia Xiqing was asked by a professor of our fine arts department for come help out. The fact that Zhou Ziheng was there was a coincidence. Some people are full of conspiracies.

@LemonFlavourSoda: My friends are in fine arts, and they said Xia Xiqing is a good artist, and that he's technically their shixiong, that he's got outstanding skills and a gentle personality.

@SelfStudyNo1: Ahh I envy your friends. I really want to know what they did when Heng-Heng went to the Department of Fine Arts to find Xiqing.

...

How did nobody discover the most important pieces? Zhao Ke immediately goes on his gossip-monger side-blog to share what his group chat had reported.

@MelonKe: Xia Xiqing was invited by a professor of the fine arts department to help with the upcoming sculpture exhibit. Zhou Ziheng went to see him. It just so happens that he got there in time to see Xia Xiqing fall from a platform. Zhou Ziheng even tried to catch him (but only partially succeeded). Later, they both headed to the mess hall for lunch together. If you're interested in the exhibit, it begins the day after tomorrow. The centerpiece of the exhibit was redesigned by Xia Xiqing.

After that long paragraph, he uploads a few photos of them falling on the mat. The photos were taken from afar, so the quality isn't the greatest. Nonetheless, the people within are recognizable while the sculpture has been blurred out.

The post quickly goes viral, and in just ten minutes, there are thousands of comments and shares. Zhao Ke marvels at the popularity these two people have and feels that he himself is surrounded by the passion of fangirls.

"Oh dear..."

Hearing Zhao Ke's voice, Zhou Ziheng frowns and looks at him. "What's up?"

"Umm, nothing." Zhao Ke hides his phone in his pocket, looking guilty. He smiles at Zhou Ziheng. "I have to go; I've got another commitment. You should get some rest too." He quickly gets up from his desk. "Don't forget the exam is tomorrow afternoon."

This guy is being weird again...

Having studied all afternoon, Zhou Ziheng is tired as well. He packs up his things and prepares to leave. "Wait for me, let's go together."

Zhao Ke drove to school and he gives Zhou Ziheng a ride
home since he lives close by. Sitting in the passenger seat,
Zhou Ziheng opens Weibo and finds he's in multiple entries
on the trending list. Among them are topics like "Zhou Ziheng's theory on the bounds of normality" and "Zhou Ziheng
being protective."

He browses Weibo the whole ride home. Zhao Ke is afraid
that he'd find out about him leaking gossip, but luckily for
him, he notices nothing.

In the elevator, Zhou Ziheng receives a message from Jiang Yin informing him that recording for *Survive and Escape*
is scheduled for Saturday. He's on his phone typing when a
hand appears between the closing doors.

"Hey, what are the chances?"

It's Xia Xiqing's voice. Zhou Ziheng slowly raises his head,
a bit surprised.

"Can't believe we left campus around the same time."
Xia Xiqing walks in. "Could have called you to come back
together."

Zhou Ziheng puts his phone back into his pocket. Not
knowing what to say, he nods.

Xia Xiqing finds him a bit strange. "What's wrong, big
star? Tired from studying?"

The elevator arrives and they stand side by side. Zhou
Ziheng provides no answer to Xia Xiqing's question.

Upon arrival, Zhou Ziheng quietly whispers a bye and
swipes his key card. He enters the door to his loft and
attempts to close the door with his foot. However, the door
is blocked by Xia Xiqing. He turns and gives Xia Xiqing a
confused look.

"Let's talk?" Xia Xiqing smiles and walks into Zhou
Ziheng's place. "You don't look very happy." He approaches a

little closer. "Is it because of me?"

Zhou Ziheng frowns while setting his backpack on the floor. "You wish."

"Yeah? I thought we're friends now." Xia Xiqing's voice is light, falling on Zhou Ziheng's heart like a feather. "I mean the food, your heroic act, and the conversations. You did pretty good, even if you won't admit it."

The words "heroic act" again remind Zhou Ziheng of the events earlier in the day. He is frustrated at himself, for feeling disappointed at Xia Xiqing for not seeing his intentions.

"Like you said, that's just me. I'm just nice like that, running around and saving everyone," Zhou Ziheng admits defeat and puts his glasses down on a table.

Suddenly, he feels a push as he's turning around. Before he is able to react, he falls to the floor.

"What the hell, man..." Zhou Ziheng puts his hands on the floor and looks up at the perpetrator.

Xia Xiqing squats and they gaze at each other.

"Then don't do it again." The clean and innocent face shows a bewitching smile.

Zhou Ziheng looks confused. "What do you mean?"

Xia Xiqing is silent. He presses down on Zhou Ziheng's chest. His hair scatters across his face and the hallway light reflects off his skin. Zhou Ziheng lays on the floor, staring at the mole on Xia Xiqing's nose.

"Don't risk your life for others from now on."

The smell of Xia Xiqing's cigarettes makes Zhou Ziheng slightly dizzy. Forgetting to resist, he remains pressed against the floor.

"Do it just for me," says Xia Xiqing.

Zhou Ziheng murmurs, fearing that his heartbeat will reveal something, "You're talking nonsense..."

The distance is too close; his favorite body is right in front of him. Xia Xiqing clearly hears his breathing getting heavier and heavier. Their lips come closer and closer together. Zhou Ziheng does not resist.

"You don't hate me that much, do you?" His voice is filled with heat, fluttering on Zhou Ziheng's lips.

Zhou Ziheng tilts his head. "Does it matter?"

"Of course it matters." Xia Xiqing hands wander on his chest. "It matters if we have mutual consent or not."

As expected, his hand is caught by Zhou Ziheng, and Xia Xiqing chuckles. "Relax, I'm not that impatient." He tries to free his hands, but his grasp is stronger than he thought. "I was just thinking about what you said in the cafeteria."

Zhou Ziheng looks at him. Despite being on the floor, he is full of aggression. "What did I say?"

"It's not trading at a loss." The corner of his lips lift in a beautiful signature smile from Xia Xiqing.

Xia Xiqing, unable to free himself, lowers his body and presses against Zhou Ziheng. He breathes softly near his ear, releasing a sweet, charming fragrance.

"I'll trade you the honorific if you let me be on top. Is that a loss for you?"

What...?

Before he can react, Xia Xiqing kisses his earlobe.

"Ziheng-gege."

Xia Xiqing's words breathe in his ear, consuming all his oxygen.

In that instant, he suffers the most non-violent yet terrifying attack in the world. Zhou Ziheng's confusion becomes consent to Xia Xiqing, and he licks and kisses his ear. The desire in his heart is a fire that consumes his reason.

The light fragrance on Zhou Ziheng's neck becomes

heavier as the temperature rises. Xia Xiqing loses himself in the cold citrusy scent, continuing to lick and kiss down his neck.

He shouldn't be so impatient, he knows that. The chance of failure is high at the moment, but he wants to take the risk.

What if he doesn't resist...?

Zhou Ziheng, having regained his senses, pushes Xia Xiqing away. "What are you doing?"

Xia Xiqing had predicted this result. The raging fire failed to triumph. Down to his last nerve, he watches Zhou Ziheng get up. On the inside, he constantly tells himself to take this as a victory.

To settle for what he has...

But he doesn't want to go.

He stands up and presses Zhou Ziheng against a wall and kisses him. He simply doesn't want to stop. Even knowing that there will be consequences, he cannot control it.

Drinking poison is better than being thirsty—at least he has something to quench him.

Zhou Ziheng doesn't understand Xia Xiqing's motives. In his mind, this sort of intimacy should only happen between two people in love. However, Xia Xiqing has overthrown his way of thinking. His motive is greed. At this thought, Zhou Ziheng's heart aches. He grabs Xia Xiqing's hand and pushes him away forcefully.

"If you're horny, go find your one of your lovers. I'm sure they're lining up for you." Zhou Ziheng pretends to be calm.

"Are you afraid?" Xia Xiqing looks directly into his eyes, smiling softly. "If you're afraid, we don't have to go all the way the first time."

Zhou Ziheng's heart feels like it's being squeezed.

He wants it to stop.

He's never been in love before. But even with limited experience, he knows this is not a healthy relationship.

"Sorry. Like I said before, I'm not gay." Zhou Ziheng frowns slightly, his hand still holding onto Xia Xiqing's wrist tightly. "I don't like men."

Xia Xiqing chuckles, pressing his lower body against Zhou Ziheng. "I know."

He turns his face to look at Zhou Ziheng's hand on his wrist—like cold handcuffs locking him out of his next move. Xia Xiqing tilts his head and leans toward the wrist, licking Zhou Ziheng's clenched fingers.

Zhou Ziheng is caught off guard by this action, and lets go of his wrist in panic. Unexpectedly, Xia Xiqing grabs his retreating hand and puts his fingers in his mouth, licking and tangling them with his slippery tongue, hooking him into a darker place.

Tobacco and musk, grapefruit and cold spring; their scents blend rudely together.

Xia Xiqing presses further against Zhou Ziheng. The feeling of Zhou Ziheng's fingers in his mouth makes him uncomfortable, yet at the same time it's comforting. Xia Xiqing's other hand wanders aimlessly along Zhou Ziheng's body.

Zhou Ziheng feels like he's going crazy. He's about to become a madman who only pursues satisfaction.

The balance beam in his head shakes and tilts.

He takes his wet fingers out of Xia Xiqing's mouth. His silky-smooth face glows under the light, produced by the sweat of desire. His fingers remain moist.

"Just a kiss." Xia Xiqing raises his eyes at him, hinting his temptation.

Zhou Ziheng cannot understand the look, but Xia Xiqing doesn't wait for him to understand and kisses him. With the tip of his tongue, his words divided by the kiss.

"It doesn't matter if you don't like men. As long as...you don't hate them."

The crazy idea of wanting to embrace Xia Xiqing invades Zhou Ziheng's brain.

"I know you're not gay..." Xia Xiqing sucks on his lips. He assures him with a soothing yet hypnotic tone, holding Zhou Ziheng's wet hand and guiding him to his waist. "It's okay. It's just...pleasure...you should try it..."

Words of desire, wreathed in hot breath. But something like ice water pours over Zhou Ziheng and drenches him head to toe.

He stretches out his hand and holds Xia Xiqing by the shoulder. He pushes him back with force, without giving him any opportunity to return. Wiping his mouth with the sleeve of his sweater, he walks to the door and opens it.

Xia Xiqing's insides burn. He looks at Zhou Ziheng, confused. "Hey..."

"Go back," Zhou Ziheng lowers his head and says with a clear tone. "Please leave my home. I may not ask nicely the second time."

Xia Xiqing does not know which move he made was the wrong one. He's unable to sort out his thoughts. But no matter how confused he is, he can see that Zhou Ziheng is completely calm. It's impossible now, and he doesn't want to cause a scene. Xia Xiqing grabs his sweater and leaves Zhou Ziheng's place in silence.

Hearing Zhou Ziheng close the door, Xia Xiqing stands still, irritated.

I almost had it.

So what went wrong?

Zhou Ziheng's difficulty level has exceeded his imagination. He likes a challenge, yes, but he also hopes to taste victory. Every time he feels close to success, he realizes he's ended up in a minefield.

What exactly is happening in that field of Zhou Ziheng's?

Xia Xiqing feels like he's going crazy—really crazy.

Staring at the door of his apartment, he is reluctant to approach it. He's been rejected again. He doesn't want to return to an empty home and smoke all night like an addict.

If *he* doesn't want to do it, there are always people that do.

Xia Xiqing wipes his mouth with his thumb and walks toward the elevator.

Standing by the door, Zhou Ziheng pays close attention to footsteps. He knows Xia Xiqing hasn't gone home; he knows he's going somewhere else.

Zhou Ziheng is overwhelmed with fatigue. He doesn't feel like his usual self. His heart beats slowly and weakly, like he is ill. These days his emotions have been a roller-coaster, full of sweetness and bitterness. He's almost forgotten that person's true nature.

He walks to the bathroom and takes a shower, washing away every bit of Xia Xiqing.

It doesn't matter if you're not gay.

It doesn't matter if you don't like men.

It's just pleasure, nothing else.

Throughout the night, Xia Xiqing's words echo in Zhou Ziheng's head. He falls asleep many times, only to be woken up by that voice. In his dreams, it's Xia Xiqing speaking to him in his carefree tone.

"Oh wait, you have feelings for me? I'm really sorry, but your attraction to me ends here."

Opening his eyes suddenly, Zhou Ziheng is covered in cold sweat. He stares dully at the ceiling.

He's already aware of the consequences of having feelings for Xia Xiqing.

He can still get out, if he wants to. It's not too late.

Xia Xiqing wanted to go to the bar. As he's driving, however, he realizes that he's now famous. No longer can he enter and leave bars so casually.

He parks his car at the side of the road and flips through his phone, looking for some company. But he hesitates—he usually doesn't sleep at anyone else's place.

Not knowing where to go, Xia Xiqing messages Xu Qichen.

Xiqing: Are you asleep?

He receives a reply quickly.

Chen-Chen: Not yet, still writing. What's up?

Avoiding the seriousness of the situation, he calls Xu Qichen to ask if he can stay over, who agrees without any questions.

Xu Qichen, wearing dark blue pajamas, smiles as he opens the door. "Come in, you must be cold."

Xia Xiqing hugs Xu Qichen and looks over his shoulder. Xia Zhixu is sitting on the carpet playing video games, wearing an identical set of clothing to Xu Qichen.

Xia Zhixu stares at the screen intensely without looking at Xia Xiqing. His face is handsome and punch-able. "What are you doing here so late? Do you actually enjoy being a third wheel?"

"What? You're not giving our Chen-Chen a night off?" Xia Xiqing replies sharply. Seeing Xu Qichen's ears turn red, he decides to not pursue the topic. Instead, he says, "I'll sleep here tonight and leave in the morning."

Xia Zhixu does not notice Xia Xiqing's unusual tone. "What's wrong with the hotel? Don't you have so much money that you're annoyed by it?"

Xia Xiqing does not want to admit he's looking for a place with people. He does not want to appear weak and vulnerable. Xu Qichen, however, is able to see right through him.

"Don't worry. You can stay for as long as you like. Go take a bath and I'll get everything set up for you."

"You're too good to him," Xia Zhixu complains while throwing the controller on the floor. "I can't play anymore."

Xia Xiqing walks to the bathroom. His limbs are weak as he immerses himself in the hot water. He feels dizzy and confused. Images of Zhou Ziheng appear in his mind, reminding him of that cold ending.

He's never been this obsessed with someone before. Zhou Ziheng is more difficult to seduce than anyone he's ever met, or maybe he just likes the way he looks too much. He doesn't know why it all sums up to an affection far greater than anything he's had in the past.

He also knows very well that wanting is not liking.

It's just a desire to conquer.

When Zhou Ziheng said he didn't like men, Xia Xiqing wasn't sad at all; instead, he attempted to subvert his sexuality, tried to make him believe that love and pleasure are completely separate.

Though he failed, that's normal. After all, Zhou Ziheng isn't a regular person. If he wants to pull that moral role model into the swamp, it will take time and effort.

After his bath, Xia Xiqing comes out of the bathroom and finds Xia Zhixu holding Xu Qichen in his arms as they play video games.

"On your right! You're getting shot!"

"Team wipe! All good!"

"If we lose, you're sleeping on the couch. Hurry up, we're dying!"

"We won't lose, I got this."

This is not the first time Xia Xiqing has seen those two like this, but for some reason, he feels empty inside now.

Those two idiots had stumbled around each other for ten years; Xia Xiqing has always thought of it as a miracle. But knowing their hearts are pure and simple, it's pleasing to see. The most important thing is that they liked each other from the beginning—no matter how much time passes or how far they are apart, their relationship has never diluted.

He walks into the guest room and falls onto the bed, resisting the urge to have a smoke.

Miracles like those will never happen to him. His soul is too tainted.

This idea got planted in his head when he was young, and he only becomes more and more convinced as he grows older.

He tries and tries, but no one really loves him.

Although it was agreed that he'd only stay one night, Xia Xiqing shamelessly stays for four days. If not for Jiang Yin calling him out on Friday, he wouldn't have left. Xu Qichen is a good cook and very easy to live with; he's good company. And although Xia Zhixu can be a bit annoying, he's nice to have around.

Jiang Yin reminds Xia Xiqing that he needs to fly out to Shanghai on Saturday to continue filming the program. Due to the show's popularity and hype, the crew is afraid of mishaps during the trip. As such, they've booked everyone on the same flight and in the same accommodations to ensure the entire squad is together.

Over the last four days, Xia Xiqing and Zhou Ziheng have exchanged no words with each other.

Xia Ziqing was considering rejecting future episodes of the show, but decides not to right before replying to Jiang Yin. Zhou Ziheng isn't backing out, so why should he? He sends a confirmation message to her.

Xia Xiqing: Zhou Ziheng is going too, right? Has he said anything?

After some time, Xia Xiqing receives news from Jiang Yin.

Jiang Yin: Of course he's going. Only Cen-Cen has to skip this round, since she's on tour in Japan. Ziheng will be done with his exams soon so he can focus on filming.

He has indeed said nothing, it seems.

Now Xia Xiqing is confused.

Xia Xiqing leaves Xu Qichen's place in the afternoon and goes directly to the airport wearing the same clothes, but now with the lemon scent of Xu Qichen's detergent. The sharp lemony smell irritates his nose, so he has to buy a mask to stop himself from sneezing excessively.

Upon arrival at the airport, Xia Xiqing receives a message from Shang Sirui. Just as he's about to reply, he hears someone call his name. It's Shang Sirui, wearing a red hoodie and a baseball cap.

"Long time no see!" Shang Sirui rushes over excitedly and hugs Xia Xiqing. He buries his head into his neck and begins to complain, "Ah, I've been so tired lately. I've gotten only three hours of sleep a day for the past three days..."

"No wonder your fans call you San-San."

The Sirui fandom's favorite nickname for Shang Sirui means "three-three," and Xia Xiqing uses this chance to make a small pun. But before anyone has a chance to laugh, Xia Xiqing notices Shang Sirui's hair.

"Did you dye your hair?"

Shang Sirui turns his head. "I've been doing some event covers recently; had to get a new look. I tried a few colors and finally decided on this gray one."

Xia Xiqing pats him on the back. Seeing Shang Sirui reminds him of his troublemaker brother. "Being a star ain't easy, I see."

More and more fans begin to surround them. Most of them are here for Shang Sirui, while some are for Xia Xiqing and Zhou Ziheng. One girl leans forward and passes a cupcake to Xia Xiqing.

"This is for you, Xiqing-*gege*."

Xia Xiqing, still held by Shang Sirui, stretches out his hand to receive gifts. Smiling, he says, "Thank you!"

Fans can tell that Xia Xiqing is in a good mood. One asks, "Where is Ziheng?"

A group of girls laugh. Xia Xiqing replies softly, "I'm not sure, he should be here soon."

"Why didn't you arrive with Ziheng?"

"Xiqing, why did you stop going to Peking U?"

"Yeah! We've been going to U of P every day since that day and we never saw you."

"We went to the exhibit as well. It was amazing. We thought you'd go too."

All of these questions are forcing Xia Xiqing out of his good mood. The more he hears, the more it reminds him of being rejected. Shang Sirui feels some discomfort from Xia Xiqing and removes part of his mask to step in.

"Hey, why don't you guys care about me anymore?"

The fans nearby are all amused by Shang Sirui.

"San-San, how do you stay so young?"

"Of course we care about you, our sweet child. We love you."

Shang Sirui smiles and pulls Xia Xiqing in by the waist. "Don't you think we're a good match too? How come there are no shippers for us?"

"Hahaha! Thanks for the recommendation."

"Since you asked... Sure!"

"You're too adorable, San-San! You know that?"

Shang Sirui, feeling satisfied, places his head on Xia Xiqing's shoulder and closes his eyes. "I'm so tired. I could fall asleep standing up."

So childish. Xia Xiqing stretches out his hand and covers Shang Sirui's eyes. "Okay, sleep then."

He gives the silence gesture to nearby fans and pats Shang Sirui on the shoulder. The fans don't dare bother Shang Sirui, and instead silently take some photos and whisper to each other while posting to Weibo.

"Oh wow, I never imagined... But I'll condone this ship now."

"Yeah! Never seen Xia Xiqing and Zhou Ziheng hug. How many times have these two hugged now?"

"Come on, they're just good friends. Plus, two bottoms have no future together."

"Sorry girls, can't betray Ziheng."

And speak of the devil...

In the distance, Zhou Ziheng watches the two from afar— Shang Sirui hugging Xia Xiqing like a koala bear, and Xia Xiqing gently and quietly holding Shang Sirui's shoulders.

Zhou Ziheng is wearing black pants and a leather jacket.

His hair is loose, covering part of his eyes. Sporting a pair of sunglasses, he walks over while chewing gum. His aura is very eye-catching.

"Fuck, Ziheng is here."

"Heavens! What a perfect alpha. The best male model in the entertainment industry."

"Wait, why do I feel like these two have been caught in the act?"

The eyes beneath the sunglasses narrow and look at Xia Xiqing. He's still wearing the same clothes he wore that night. His car hasn't been in the parking garage for four days. He hasn't come home for almost a week. Must've been out fooling around.

Zhou Ziheng sneers inside. He should have come to that realization long ago. He knows exactly what Xia Xiqing is like, yet almost fell into his trap.

"Xiqing, Xiqing. Ziheng is here."

Xia Xiqing, still holding onto Shang Sirui, hears the comments coming from fans. He raises his head and takes off his mask as he looks at Zhou Ziheng through the crowd.

Stomping in Xia Xiqing's direction in his brown military boots, Zhou Ziheng behaves in a leisurely manner. Earlier, Xia Xiqing was uncertain if he wanted to see him again. But right now, all he wants to do is sleep with him while he wears those boots.

When their eyes meet, Xia Xiqing smirks, letting out a beautiful hypocritical smile.

"Long time no see, Ziheng."

Zhou Ziheng blows a bubble with his gum. With a loud snap, the bubble bursts. He also smirks, accepting the challenge.

"Long time no see."

The short intermission has failed to calm them down. Like boxers in their respective corners, the fire reignites as soon as the bell rings.

Neither of them wants to lose.

Ruan Xiao is the last to arrive. She's wearing a classic Burberry coat with her long hair tied into a ponytail. She looks like a competent business woman, but her smile remains very sweet.

"Second episode." Ruan Xiao smiles at Shang Sirui as she walks over. "I even came up with some headlines for you. How does 'Shang Sirui's Astonishing Acting Skills' sound?"

"Or 'Shang Sirui's Skill at Playing Dumb'?" Xia Xiqing joins in on the teasing.

Shang Sirui puffs up and slams into Xia Xiqing. "Who's playing smart then? You? Zhou Ziheng?"

Xia Xiqing looks at Zhou Ziheng, who is focused on his phone. He does not seem like he wants to reply.

Smiling, Xia Xiqing says, "Not me, obviously. I was the first to die."

"Maybe you'll die first again tonight," Shang Sirui jokes.

Ruan Xiao laughs. "Someone's a prophet."

"Zhou Ziheng is so quiet today." Shang Sirui deliberately changes the subject. "Maybe he's guilty of something; maybe he's the Killer tonight."

"When does he ever like to talk?" Ruan Xiao comments halfheartedly.

The teased Zhou Ziheng raises his head and glances sharply at Shang Sirui. "Okay, I'll kill you first tonight."

Shang Sirui immediately smiles and walks over to Zhou Ziheng. "Don't do that to me, handsome. Hey, remember when you said that if you were the Killer, you'd kill Xia Xiqing first? Don't forget your promise."

As soon as he hears him say that name, Zhou Ziheng's mood changes. He pushes Shang Sirui away, pretending to be disgusted. "What promise?"

Having been pushed away, Shang Sirui again entangles Xia Xiqing. "You made a promise, too. If one of you is the Killer, you have to kill each other."

Ruan Xiao crosses her arms. "If it's me, I'll kill you first, Shang Sirui."

Seeing Ruan Xiao speak so solemnly, Shang Sirui immediately asks, "Why? We ain't got no beef!"

"You talk too much."

Everyone is talking and laughing. Xia Xiqing notices Zhou Ziheng has removed his sunglasses. He looks good without makeup. Those dark eye bags look heavy, though.

Maybe he's stressed from his exams.

Several people board the plane together. The seats are arranged such that the crew sit together. Guessing that his seat is beside Zhou Ziheng, Xia Xiqing watches him walk in front of him and sits down beside his assigned seat.

Shang Sirui tugs at Xia Xiqing. "Hey, I'm right behind you."

Shang Sirui walks to his seat and sits next to Ruan Xiao, who has a window seat. "I might just sleep for the whole trip. Wanna trade? Might be easier for you to go in and out."

Ruan Xiao agrees while taking out a warm eye mask. "Here, this might help."

Shang Sirui takes it and sits down, thanking her. Ruan Xiao is kind and also gives an eye mask to Xia Xiqing, who accepts with a smile.

Xia Xiqing stands up and looks at the seated Zhou Ziheng. "Excuse me."

Zhou Ziheng tucks in his long legs and lets Xia Xiqing

squeeze by.

"Thank you."

Xia Xiqing's politeness makes Zhou Ziheng feel uneasy. This person just recently had an "intimate" lunch with him in his school's cafeteria.

"You're welcome." Zhou Ziheng smiles.

As he passes by, Zhou Ziheng smells an unusual scent—a mix of grapefruit and cedar that isn't Xia Xiqing's usual smell; rather, it's like the tastes of other men.

The more he dwells on it, the heavier the scent gets.

Like a detective, he attempts to gather all sorts of evidence against Xia Xiqing to make himself feel better.

With a quick glimpse, he sees Xia Xiqing's slender hand on the armrest—the same hand that once held his chest as his heart pounded. The moment makes him confused again.

It's clear that there's a gap between Xia Xiqing and Zhou Ziheng after the events of the past few days, despite the fact that they weren't even that close before. Xia Xiqing has a lot of pride, and it's been difficult on his self-esteem. Even if he still has the desire to conquer, he will need some time to recover.

Everyone before has fallen for his tricks, but Zhou Ziheng sees right through him, constantly reminding him that no one will ever truly love someone like him.

That's a fact he learned long ago.

Planning on not saying anything, Xia Xiqing looks down at his eye mask and decides to sleep against the window without putting it on.

The eye mask reminds Zhou Ziheng of the blindfold he wore in the escape room. Xia Xiqing is afraid of the dark; wearing that blindfold was probably not easy for him. That's probably why he took a chance using the most direct method to find out if there was another person in the room to help him.

Unable to sleep, Zhou Ziheng takes out a textbook and begins studying quantum mechanics.

The sun shines on the paper. It's 4:30 in the afternoon. The page feels furry, and something is changing inside of him.

In his sleep, Xia Xiqing shifts his head slightly, like a swan dreaming under the sunlight. Zhou Ziheng forces himself to not look at him. He sees the reflection of Xia Xiqing's face in the laptop screen in front of him, making his heart beat uncontrollably.

He enjoys this quiet moment. He knows peeping isn't a decent thing to do, but this is a rare moment when Xia Xiqing isn't trying to seduce him. He stares at this dangerous person sleeping like a dormant volcano; like the beautiful forests and snow on Mount Fuji that rest atop sleeping magma.

Desires are always selfish and complicated.

He feels something missing in his book. Quickly flipping through the pages, nothing odd comes to light; the content is complete. What's missing is a piece of his heart—it's been eaten by a snake from the Garden of Eden.

Unable to stop staring, he notices Xia Xiqing's brow frown slightly. Guessing that it might be too bright, he reaches over to close the visor.

"Don't."

Xia Xiqing's eyes remain closed as he tilts his head toward the window.

"Can't sleep without the light."

Zhou Ziheng pulls back his arm.

Xia Xiqing is not fully asleep. His eyes are closed, but his other senses are alert. He can hear Zhou Ziheng turning pages; the friction of the textbook pages rubbing against each other. Occasionally, he hears Zhou Ziheng breathe something like a long sigh.

Under the sunlight, his eyelids glow orange. As his consciousness gradually sinks, his waves of thoughts sway. Like Monet's Sunset, warm and safe.

Light has no shape.

Closed eyes often have the most accurate perception of light.

The moment Zhou Ziheng reaches out his arm, Xia Xiqing quickly wakes up, desperate to maintain light around him. His emotions, such as fear of being confined in darkness, suddenly pour out.

No one would understand. Xia Xiqing knows this.

Zhou Ziheng makes no further move to disturb Xia Xiqing's sleep. Xia Xiqing can no longer hear any sounds from him.

Usually, Xia Xiqing finds it difficult to fall asleep on planes. He feels like a small boat floating up and down with turbulent waves. This time, the boat is sinking, slowly going down into a deeper dream.

He looks around him. Everyone is very tall. There's blood dripping from his chin to his shirt. The cartoon character print on his chest is drenched in red. People come and go in the hospital, and he is being dragged like a rag doll by some unfamiliar faces into an operation room.

The quarrel in his ears continues. The sensation of a sharp needle piercing his skin makes him shed tears like a child.

A woman cries out sharply.

Why did I give birth to you in the first place?

It'd be better if you never existed.

You are the source of all the misery in my life.

Looking down, he's no longer wearing a bloody shirt. The pain leads him to stretch out his hands, bruises after bruises. Golf clubs and any metal objects worthy of the hand all leave marks on his flesh.

Like an empty canvas, the creator will paint whatever is deemed necessary.

The people who love you the most in the world are your parents. Do you understand?

The whole class of children shouts in unison, *We! Understand!*

He understands. But he also really wants to raise his hand to ask a question.

Teacher, what if my parents don't love me?

Then will there be anyone else in this world who...

The water drowns his breath. The suffocating Xia Xiqing wakes in an instant like a splashing fish, violently gasping for air. He raises his hand in panic and touches the scar on his chin.

When he opens his eyes, it's already dusk. The clouds in the sky are stained with magnificent colors. Through the corner of his eyes, he sees Zhou Ziheng staring directly at him.

Rubbing his eyes, he says with a hoarse voice, "What are you looking at?"

Zhou Ziheng hesitates. His expression seems to have just walked out of a state of distraction. A trace of guilt and confusion lingers.

"How long have you been watching?"

Xia Xiqing wonders how he was behaving during his nightmare. Perhaps he was clutching the seat or the fabric of his clothes; perhaps it was something more embarrassing. He's hoping to get some answers from Zhou Ziheng.

"A while..."

Zhou Ziheng isn't lying; he's stubborn, but not a liar.

"Why? What did you see?"

Zhou Ziheng raises his eyes. The clouds outside the window reflect on his sincere-looking face.

"The Tyndall Effect."

The answer surprises Xia Xiqing.

Zhou Ziheng is again not lying. After Xia Xiqing fell asleep, he felt as if a feather fell on his heart; gently, lightly itching him.

He finally turns his face to look at him.

The sunlight passes through the clouds thousands of meters above ground. Flying through the small window, tiny dust particles float like fog. From the upper corner of the window, a ray of light peaks through, hitting Xia Xiqing directly on the chest in a seemingly solid beam.

"When the Tyndall effect appears, light takes shape." Zhou Ziheng points to Xia Xiqing's chest with a smirk.

Xia Xiqing lowers his head in a daze, looking at his chest. His eyes follow the beam of rose-gold light to the window. Sensitive and worried, sharp and defensive, he is overwhelmed by a small physical phenomenon that turned into a beautiful light piercing through his heart.

Zhou Ziheng suddenly realizes that he just smiled at Xia Xiqing.

After that day, he repeatedly warned himself to not establish a close relationship with him. Yet today, he forgot his principles when he saw him sleeping so heavily with tears in his eyes.

He does not know much about Xia Xiqing. To him, there isn't anything he needs to know. But when he saw the fragile Xia Xiqing wake up, he saw a rose floating in the clouds.

He wants to reach out and hold it, but instead he is pricked by the thorns.

The plane is about to land, the flight attendants walk the isles to ensure everyone is safe. Zhou Ziheng closes the textbook that he hasn't read and sets it aside.

Xia Xiqing finally recovers from his dream. They leave the plane, leaving behind the orange glow of the sunset.

"I'm hungry!" Shang Sirui says, having had some good sleep and a nice discussion with Ruan Xiao regarding dinner.

Xia Xiqing looks up at the clouds, the rose sky, and the formless light.

His phone vibrates, Xia Xiqing takes it out of his pocket.

Moral Role Model: [image attachment]

It's a picture of him sleeping, caught from a side view. The Tyndall effect emerges from the rosy sunset in the window beyond. It's a beam of light so clear that it looks almost tangible, seemingly piercing his chest.

Holding the phone, Xia Xiqing's heart throbs.

With complete disregard for the person beside him, he speaks in a low voice, as if he's asking nature itself, "Why take a photo of me?"

Nature immediately delivers a response in a deep voice.

"I wasn't taking a picture of you; I was capturing the Tyndall effect."

The words are ones of rejection, yet the actions are acts of enticement.

This guy really manages to be both naïve and tricky at the same time.

ROSE AND
RENAISSANCE · VOL.01

Rose and Renaissance

Copyright © ZHI CHU

If you have any questions, please send e-mail to
info@vialactea.ca

Via Lactea

www.ingramcontent.com/pod-product-compliance
Lightning Source LLC
LaVergne TN
LVHW010008130325
805866LV00008B/378